# CLICKERS
## VS ZOMBIES

## J. F. GONZALEZ    BRIAN KEENE

deadite
press

# deadite press

DEADITE PRESS
205 NE BRYANT
PORTLAND, OR 97211
www.DEADITEPRESS.com

AN ERASERHEAD PRESS COMPANY
www.ERASERHEADPRESS.com

ISBN: 1-62105-058-0

Printed in the USA.

# Acknowledgements

*Both authors would like to thank:* Jeff Burk, Rose O'Keefe, Carlton Mellick III, Larry Roberts, Mark Sylva, Tod Clark, Bob Ford, the real Dave Thomas, Michele Mixel, Nikki Graybeal, Geoff Cooper, Mike Hawthorne, and Mike Lombardo.

Special thanks to Mark Williams, who contributed two paragraphs to this novel from beyond the grave.

*J. F. Gonzalez would like to thank:* Cathy and Hannah, my parents, my corporate clients, Guy N. Smith for *Night of the Crabs,* Joe R. Lansdale for *The Drive-In* and *Dead in the West,* Shane Ryan Staley, Paul Goblirsch, Chet Williamson, Bill Furtado, Richard Christian Matheson, Kelli Owen, Mike Lansu, John & Paul Burkholts, Tom Monteleone, James A. Moore, Tim Lebbon, Ray Garton, Deborah Daughetee for her patience when I cease work on the screenplay treatment to work on this, Wrath James White for his patience when I cease work on the novel collaboration to work on this, and the real life Clark Arroyo.

*Brian Keene would like to thank:* my sons, Mary SanGiovanni, Cassandra Burnham, Betty Anne Crawford, Susan Scofield, Nurse Stephanie, Melanie Candra, Michelle Burdette, Kasey Lansdale, Joe Lansdale, Damian Maffei, F. Paul Wilson, Tom Monteleone, Dallas Mayr, Lee Seymour, William Miller, Andrew van den Houten, Greg Wilson, and the Playhouse Posse.

## DEADITE PRESS BOOKS BY J. F. GONZALEZ

Survivor
Hero (with Wrath James White)
Clickers (with Mark Williams)
Clickers II (with Brian Keene)
Clickers III (with Brian Keene – ebook only)
Clickers vs Zombies (with Brian Keene)

## DEADITE PRESS BOOKS BY BRIAN KEENE

Urban Gothic
Jack's Magic Beans
Take The Long Way Home
A Gathering of Crows
Darkness On the Edge of Town
Tequila's Sunrise
Dead Sea
Kill Whitey
Castaways
Ghoul
The Cage
Dark Hollow
Ghost Walk
An Occurrence In Crazy Bear Valley
Entombed
Earthworm Gods
Earthworm Gods II: Deluge
Earthworm Gods: Selected Scenes From the End of the World
Clickers II (with J. F. Gonzalez)
Clickers III (with J. F. Gonzalez – ebook only)
Clickers vs Zombies (with J. F. Gonzalez)

## Author's Note

Although this novel takes place on a global scale, much of the action occurs on the coast of California. We have taken certain fictional liberties with that geography, so if you live there, don't go visiting your favorite pier or beach. If you do, you might end up Clicker food. Or zombie food. Or zombie Clicker food...

It should also be noted that although this novel features characters and situations from both the Clickers series and The Rising series, it does not take place in either of those series' "worlds." As the reader shall see, it takes place in an alternate reality, where characters and situations from those previous novels may have turned out quite differently. This novel also features cameo appearances of characters from a number of J.F. Gonzalez's and Brian Keene's other novels, however, knowledge of those characters or novels is not needed to enjoy this book. Consider the cameos 'Easter eggs' for the hardcore fans who spot them.

*For Kelli Owen,*
*without whom this book wouldn't have been possible...*

*And the sea gave up the dead which were in it; and Death and Hell delivered up the dead which were in them: and all were judged...*

—Book of Revelation 20:13

# PROLOGUE

# JULY 4

*Huntington Beach, California*

It had been warm earlier that day, but it was as cold as a witch's tit by the time Brad Kincaid and Troy Johnson showed up at Steve Baker's Fourth of July party in Huntington Beach that evening.

Steve told Brad that the party was to be held between Lifeguard stations 51 and 52, between Talbert Avenue and Beach Boulevard in Huntington Beach. Brad and Troy surfed this stretch of beach anyway and knew the area well. Troy pulled into the parking slot while Brad reached into the back of the jeep for the beer.

"Let's go!" Troy said.

They trudged through the sand toward the party that was well underway around the bonfire that had been set up about fifty yards from the lot. There was a curfew that was strictly enforced between ten p.m. and five a.m. The Huntington Beach pier, which jutted into the ocean about two thousand feet was about a quarter of a mile north. Across the street from the pier was downtown Huntington Beach, a tourist Mecca filled with surf shops, restaurants, bars, clothing and gift shops, and nightclubs. Between the activity on Main Street and the pier—which boasted a 1950's style hamburger joint called Ruby's—the place was bustling.

The police only allowed gatherings on the beach within a quarter mile radius of the pier after nightfall. Lifeguard presence stopped after six p.m. Alcohol was strictly prohibited. But that never stopped people from bringing it. What were the police going to do? The Huntington Beach Police Department only had two paddy wagons. Troy should know. He'd been hauled off to jail six months ago during a wild party that had gotten a little out of control—in cases like that, the police simply hauled everybody to jail and released them later on their own recognizance. His father, Anthony, had gone through something similar back in the 80's when he was a kid.

As they drew closer to the party and the sound of the music playing on Jim's boom box, Troy's grin faltered. He wasn't into today's music at all. Sure, it was supposed to be

13

his generation's music, but as far as he was concerned the only thing enjoyable his generation had produced was Muse and Lamb of God. Everything else—Black Eyed Peas, Ke$ha, Rhianna, Lady Gaga—they all sucked. Katy Perry was okay. So was that chick Pink. Troy preferred the music from his father's generation, which dad played constantly—The Clash, TSOL, the Adolescents, Circle Jerks, the Buzzcocks. His Dad had been into alternative music when it really *had* been alternative music, and as a result, Troy also had a wide range of other musical interests: David Bowie, T-Rex, Iggy Pop, goth pioneers like the Cure, Bauhaus, new wave synth bands like Duran Duran and Talk Talk, ska bands like Madness and The Specials. Dad even liked classic metal like Metallica.

But this pop shit was just too much. It had to go.

"We ain't gonna stay here long, are we?" Troy asked Brad.

"Forty minutes tops," Brad said.

Some annoying pop tune was playing on the boom box. Steve was sitting between two blonds. He raised a bottle of Bud in their direction, grinning. "Dudes! How goes it?"

"We brought beer," Brad said. Troy set the case down and gave the party a quick survey. No wonder the music was so fucking boring. The half a dozen people that stood around the bonfire nursing beers looked like typical south Orange County yupsters. Steroid-enhanced muscle guys in ratty t-shirts and baggy shorts and buzzed hair standing with their blond perky sperm receptors. Mixed in with them were a dozen or so hipsters. The moment both groups laid eyes on Troy they averted their gaze. Troy got that a lot. Must be the spiked Mohawk and the denim jacket he wore with the various patches adjourned on it.

Steve stood up and addressed his friends. "Hey everybody, this is my friend Brad. We grew up together. And this is his buddy Troy."

Troy already had a beer and he held it up in friendly salute. He smiled. "Cheers."

The hipster couple closest to him offered fake smiles that dwindled as quickly as they were plastered on.

Brad engaged in conversation with Steve. Troy stood

close by, nursing his beer, trying not to look so bored. Why did he bother coming to this thing? This was going to be fucking boring.

"You and Brad been friends a long time?"

Troy turned and saw that one of the yuppie guys had drifted away from his girlfriend. He was nursing a bottle of Bud. The guy seemed cool—Troy was a pretty good judge of character by way of scoping out the way people carried themselves. This guy was short and he was wearing dark baggy shorts, sandals, and a large Hawaiian shirt. His dark hair was shaved close to the skull. His left ear was pierced with some kind of dangling earring and he had a large tribal tattoo that snaked down to his lower right forearm. Troy guessed that he was either of Asian or South Pacific Islander descent.

"Yeah," Troy said, grinning good-naturedly. "Brad and I go back to the sixth grade."

"That's cool, yo." The guy held out his right hand. "I'm Keoni."

"Keoni." Troy shook Keoni's hand. "You work with Steve?"

"Oh yeah. We're in the shipping department." Brad and Steve worked together at Amerimax Building Products. Most of the people at Steve's party were from work or were friends of friends.

"Cool."

"And you've known Brad since sixth grade, you said?"

"Yeah," Troy nodded. "Brad and I go way back. He's my best bud."

"Can't go wrong with that, bro," Keoni said. He took a sip of his beer, his gaze swinging out toward the ocean. "Chilly as shit out here, though."

Troy took a sip of beer. "Yeah, but that's typical. It was seventy-five degrees earlier today."

"You hear about those weird crab things that fisherman found today on the pier?"

"No. What was that about?"

"Guess it happened late in the afternoon. Guy fishing off the pier netted it. It was this hybrid thing. Half scorpion, half lobster or some shit. About this big." Keoni held his hands out about a yard apart. "Connie was working the afternoon shift at Huntington Memorial." He gestured toward the woman on his left who was engaged in conversation with two of the other women. "Connie's my girlfriend. She works at the admission desk in the ER. She was just coming off her shift when they brought the poor sonofabitch in."

"What happened to him?"

"Thing fucked him up good. Tore his arm off."

"It *melted* his arm off," Connie said. She'd heard her boyfriend relating the story and was turned in their direction. She took a drag on the cigarette she was smoking—menthol by the scent of it. She shook her head, her big pouffy hair dazzling in the light of the bonfire. "I saw it as the paramedics wheeled him in. Guy was screaming and they were trying to keep him covered up but you could see it." She held up her right arm. "His arm was just...falling apart." She made a face, indicating disgust. "It was gross!"

"No shit?" Troy asked. He took another quick sip of his beer.

"Yeah," Keoni said. "Crazy shit, huh?"

"They get the thing that did it?"

"Cops shot it," Keoni said.

"They shot it?"

All conversation around the fire pit suddenly ceased and became one. Steve stepped closer to Troy and Keoni, his features troubled. "Yeah, crazy, isn't it? Took a lot of bullets, from what I heard. It's a wonder they haven't closed the beach yet."

"You'd think they would," Keoni said. He took a sip of beer. "I surf this beach every morning and they always close it down whenever there's jellyfish or sharks in the area. Something like this...yeah, they should have closed it."

"So do they know what this thing is that cut his arm off?" Troy asked.

"I don't know," Keoni said. "I don't even think it's hit the news yet." He looked out at the other party-goers. "You haven't seen anything on the news yet, have you?"

Everybody shook their heads. One of the women—she

looked exactly like Keoni's girlfriend; big hair, big tits, long legs, probably had a brain like a toaster oven—tried to offer explanation. "I saw a few people mention it on Twitter and Facebook, but not many. Everyone is talking about the tsunami instead. It's all the news is covering. "

"They'll be talking about that shit for the next two weeks," somebody else said.

That much was true. Last week, an earthquake measuring 9.8 on the Richter scale centered a hundred miles off the northern coast of Australia caused a tsunami of epic proportions. While the earthquake caused no structural damage—geologists were of the opinion that it was centered about fifty miles below the ocean's surface—the resulting tsunami's had caused massive destruction all along the Pacific rim from Australia and New Zealand to much of the neighboring Pacific Islands, Japan, Korea, Vietnam and the eastern seaboard of Russia. Tsunamis were also reported along the US and Canadian coasts as well as Peru, Chili, Argentina, and the Mexican coast.

"So you're saying it was like a sea scorpion?" Troy asked Keoni.

Keoni shrugged. "That's what I heard. Thing was built like a lobster or a crab in the front but had a scorpion tail."

Troy frowned. "That's weird. There's no living sea scorpions left. There was something called the Eurypterid, but it didn't have front claws and it's extinct."

"A Europe-what?" Keoni asked.

Troy pronounced it for him. He suddenly realized everybody was paying attention to him, much like the jocks used to pay attention to him in class when he had spirited philosophical debates with their American Literature teacher over the merits of Saul Bellow versus Charles Bukowski. Troy successfully won that battle by pointing out all the flaws in Bellow's work and demonstrating why Bukowski was more deserving to be remembered in the annals of American Literature. The looks he got from the student body elite clearly said, *wow, man, you're not just a weird punk rocker dude... you're smart too!*

Brad quickly jumped in. "Troy's majoring in archeology at UC Irvine. He's been accepted into their PhD program."

Keoni raised his eyebrows. "No shit! Congratulations, dude."

"Thanks." Troy took another sip of beer.

"So there's no such thing as a sea scorpion?" This came from one of the other women. Unlike the others, this one was short, slightly stocky, and had long dark hair.

"No, there isn't. Like I said, there was the Eurypterid, but they're extinct, and they were quite big. Eight feet long or so."

"Ewww!" Scrunched up faces of disgust. Troy grinned.

"Yeah, they were ugly fuckers. Probably had quite a few battles back in the day with baby Megaladons and T-Rexes."

Conversations started breaking up again, splintering off into individual groups. Keoni and his girlfriend, Connie, talked to Troy about his line of study. They appeared genuinely interested, especially Keoni. Troy indulged them, but not too much. He didn't want to bore them. He was here to unwind and party, not talk about what he had to fill his head with all day during class.

While they talked the fire crackled, warming the air around them. Other groups stood around their own fire pits, some roasting marshmallows, others simply drinking beer and having a good time. A few people wandered past them, heading toward the shoreline. The sun was going down rapidly and the moon was beginning to rise. It would be dark soon. Troy glanced at his watch. It was almost eight-thirty. The beer was almost gone. He was about to nudge Brad and ask him what they were going to do after the beach was shut down for the night when ear-piercing screams rose from the high tide line.

Startled, everybody turned toward the ocean. The screams rose again, male, in pain, terrified. "Ahhhh, get it off me, get it off me!"

Troy acted on instinct. He ran toward the shore, his adrenalin pumping. Half a dozen other guys from various fire pits joined him. Keoni raced along beside him.

When they reached the shoreline, Troy saw what was happening. A man wearing nothing but swim trunks was on

18

the ground screaming. A giant lobster-scorpion thing was eating his left leg. There was blood everywhere. The man's friend, also dressed in swim trunks, was darting around him as if unsure of what to do or how to help him. The second man had a wild, panicked look on his face. "Oh shit, oh shit, oh shit!" the second man chanted.

Everybody that ran to see what was happening stopped short as if they'd hit an invisible wall. Keoni said, "Holy fuck, that's *it!* That's like what they said got that guy earlier today!"

From behind them, back at the fire pit, the women had trotted a few yards from relative safety and stood well back. They called out. "What's happening? What's going on?"

As Troy watched, dumbfounded, not believing what he was seeing, another creature scuttled up from the ocean as if it had surfed in on the tide. It quickly ran up to the man on the ground, who was whipping violently back and forth, trying to shake the first creature off his leg. The second creature darted forward and jabbed the man in the chest with its stinger. The man screamed and arched his back. His friend cried out and jumped back. So did the dozen or so guys who'd run down to the shoreline to offer assistance.

"Fuck this shit!" Keoni said. He was already starting to retreat back.

A guy wearing a sleeveless t-shirt and baggy shorts stepped forward. He was brandishing a large, heavy piece of wood. He took a roundhouse swing at the second creature, as if he were attempting to beat Hank Aaron's home run record. The sound of the wood hitting the creature's back was a sharp *crack*. The man on the ground continued to scream.

More screams of terror arose, fingers pointing toward the ocean by people standing near the high tide line. Troy glanced quickly to his left. Another creature was surfing ashore. It started crawling toward them, it's large pincers clicking together in rapid staccato.

Click-click! Click-click!

"Fuck this," Troy said. He joined Keoni and their loose-knit group from the fire pit and they ran back up the beach.

To Troy's left, somebody shouted. "We gotta get the fuck

out of here!"

The clicking sounds grew louder. To Troy, they sounded like dinner plates being banged together.

CLICK-CLICK! CLICK-CLICK! CLICK-CLICK!

And as everybody abandoned their fire pits and started heading toward the strand and the parking lot beyond, Troy felt a mixture of excitement and terror from the adrenaline rush.

The rest of the evening was utter chaos.

# PART ONE

# JULY 5

# ONE

*San Pedro, California*

As he did most mornings, Jim Thurmond had to remind himself that this was no longer his home. Yes, it was still the place he had lived in for six years of his life. The address was still South Pacific Avenue. If he wanted to, he could still walk the dog, Samhain, from here down to the earthquake shattered remnants of 46th and 47th streets—an area referred to by locals as Sunken City. He still slept on the couch here and ate dinner or breakfast here on rare occasions. But that didn't mean it was still his home. It wasn't, anymore than Samhain was still his dog, or Tammy was still his wife.

While Danny ate his breakfast and watched television, and Samhain sat next to the boy, patiently waiting for any stray cereal that might hit the floor, Jim glanced around the room. The place looked great—much better than it ever had when he was still living here. He didn't like admitting that to himself, and did so begrudgingly, but it was the truth. In the first few months after their divorce, Tammy had thrown herself into a frenzy of remodeling and redecorating. Fresh coats of soft, pastel paints covered every wall. A new plasma screen television was mounted on the living room wall. That wall had once been filled with pictures of their family, and their extended families. Now, it featured a few framed photos of Tammy and Danny, as well as pictures of Tammy's parents. Jim's picture was absent. In his place was a Monet print with a nice frame. Everything was new. New carpet lined the floors, and new tiles had been laid in the kitchen, complimenting the new cabinets that Tammy's new boyfriend had built by hand.

Still smiling, Jim felt acid churn in his stomach.

Silly as it sounded, it was things like the hand-built

23

kitchen cabinets that really hurt. Tammy's new boyfriend, Anthony, excelled at doing things like that. He could build furniture, put a roof or vinyl siding on a house, hang drywall, wire an electrical socket, replace the transmission in a car, and all the other things men were supposed to know how to do— except that Jim had never been good at any of them, which was why Tammy had divorced him. Oh, she hadn't said that was the main reason. Not at first. But she'd admitted almost sheepishly soon after she'd started dating Anthony that it had been a factor.

Tammy and Jim had separated nearly two years ago after sixteen years together—eight years of dating followed by eight years of marriage. The relationship, like any relationship, had its share of the goods and the bads. Eventually, the bads had outweighed the goods. Or so they'd felt at the time. So the two of them had separated one rainy January evening. Ultimately, six months of intense counseling had been unable to save their marriage, and they'd elected to divorce. It was amicable, if any divorce could be considered such. Both of them still cared about each other, but they'd just drifted apart. The one thing they still had in common was Danny, and both doted on him and agreed that he came first and they would work together as co-parents to provide a healthy upbringing for the boy. And they had.

Jim had started dating immediately, determined to lose his sorrows in the arms—and between the legs—of another woman. Tammy had followed suit, admittedly more to spite him than any real desire to begin dating so soon. But why not? They were both in their late-thirties, and had spent the last sixteen years together. Why not try something new?

While Jim had met his partners through the bar scene, Tammy had met Anthony via a dating website, and while Jim's subsequent relationships had crashed and burned pretty quickly, Tammy's had not. Which left Jim in an unenviable position because now, nearly two years after they'd parted ways, he was faced with the certain knowledge in both his head and his heart that he was still in love with his ex-wife, while she was in love with another man. Oh, she still cared about Jim. They'd discussed it at length one night when Jim had poured his heart out to her after Danny had gone to bed. A part of her still loved him. A part of her always would. But she was with Anthony now, and she deserved the chance to see where that would lead. And Jim couldn't fault her for that. He still loved her, but more importantly, he wanted to see her happy. If being with Anthony made her happy, then that was ultimately okay with him. Hard to bare, but okay. A happy Tammy meant a happy Danny, and in the end, that was all that mattered. So Jim smiled a lot, and tried not to let on to the pain he harbored inside.

Or the loneliness.

These were the only moments when he was truly happy— the times spent with his son and his ex-wife. Oh, he had peace. He knew contentment. Jim was lucky enough to be self-employed and still earning money during the last dregs of the Great American Economic Collapse. He made his own hours, and his commute was from his bed to the coffee pot to the computer. As a result, he had joint custody with Tammy. They'd been able to work it out without lawyers. He picked Danny up every morning, spent some time with him at Tammy's house, and then took him to pre-school. In the afternoons, he picked the boy up from pre-school and took him home. After dinner, Tammy picked him up and took him back to her house, except on Wednesdays, when Danny spent the night at Jim's apartment—three blocks away from Tammy's house. They split custody every other weekend. When Jim didn't have Danny, he lost himself in his work, or spent time with his friends, all of whom were also divorced. But although those hours were peaceful after a fashion, it was his time with Danny, and his time here with Tammy, that he'd grown to cherish.

And yes, the house looked great—as long as you ignored the controlled chaos of Danny's toys scattered about.

"What are you thinking about, Daddy?"

"Hmm?" Jim looked over at his son. The five-year old was staring at him, grinning.

"What are you thinking about?" Danny asked again. "You were smiling."

"I was just thinking about you and Mommy, and how lucky I am. And how lucky you are to have a Mommy like her."

"Let's see if Danny feels that way in a moment." Tammy walked back into the living room, carrying a refilled coffee mug for Jim and one for herself. She handed Jim his and sat hers down on a coaster. "Okay, Danny. Time to get ready for pre-school."

Danny stuck out his bottom lip and made no sign of moving. "But I want to stay here and watch TV."

"You can watch TV tonight. Right now, you need to get dressed and brush your teeth."

"Awwww."

"Now, Danny. You're going to be late for pre-school."

Jim picked up the remote control and switched the channel to CNN, hoping to encourage the boy to move along. Instead, Danny pouted more.

"Danny," he said, hating the stern tone of his voice but knowing it was needed. "Listen to your mother."

Danny stood up. "Will you help me, Daddy?"

Jim's heart broke. He wanted to help the boy, but Danny needed to learn to do these things for himself. "You can do it. You're a big boy now."

"Okay." Sulking, Danny trundled off to his bedroom.

Jim stifled another smile, and then saw Tammy doing the same thing.

"What?" he asked.

"I wish he'd listen to me the way he listens to you," she said.

"It's the age," Jim replied. "He's testing his boundaries. Remember, he did this at three, as well."

"I remember. I just thought it was over."

"Oh, it will be. When he's eighteen and moves out of your house."

Jim watched Tammy laugh. He loved the sound, second only to the sound of his son's laughter. He watched her eyes sparkle and noticed how the sunlight streaming through the picture window highlighted her chestnut hair. But he also knew that if he pursued that line of thinking, he'd be depressed for the rest of the day. To distract himself, he turned to the news and changed the subject.

"Look there. Something about an attack in Huntington Beach last night."

"It's the end of the world again," Tammy said. "Every week, it's something different. A hurricane or an earthquake or economic collapse or a terrorist attack or a new virus outbreak. Doomsday cults. That crazy preacher who convinced everybody the Rapture was about to occur. What's next? Last week it was the tsunami."

"Well, maybe one of these time they'll be right."

"Maybe. If they were, then I wouldn't have to pay next month's mortgage payment."

"Do you need more?" Jim asked. "I can start giving you more every month if you—"

"No, no, not at all. What you give me in child support every month is plenty, Jim. I appreciate it. And it's not like I really need pocket money. Anthony usually pays for things when we go out."

"Oh…"

As if sensing she'd said the wrong thing, Tammy switched gears, pointing at the television. "Look there. What in the world is Kiran Chetry wearing this morning?"

"Too many clothes, if you ask me. They ought to just have her read the news in a bikini. I'd tune in every day."

"Pig." Tammy smiled again.

"Hey," Jim said. "I'm single. I'm allowed to drool over newscasters. Hell, maybe I'll follow her on Twitter and ask her out. Why not?"

"You'd better hurry. Remember, the world may be ending soon."

"What would you do?" Jim asked.

"What? You mean if the world was really ending?"

"Yeah. Lets say they came on TV and told us a comet was going to hit the planet in twenty-four hours and there was nothing anybody could do to stop it. What would you do? How would you spend that last day?"

Tammy's eyebrows knitted together as she thought. It was a feature that Jim had always found endearing. She paused for several moments before answering him.

"Well, I'd want to see my parents, I guess. But mostly, I'd just want to spend time with Danny and you."

"What about your friends, and...Anthony?"

"Well, if it's the end of the world, I'm sure they'd have their own people they'd want to say goodbye to. I'd rather spend it with you and Danny."

"Me, too." Jim smiled. "You know, Tammy, I've been thinking. I—"

"I'm ready, Daddy!"

Danny dashed down the hallway and into the living room and jumped into Jim's lap. He'd done a good job brushing his teeth and putting on his pants, but his shoes were on the wrong feet and his shirt was on backwards. Laughing, Jim helped him out. Tammy walked over, sat down on the couch next to them, and assisted. Jim caught a whiff of her shampoo, and Danny's unique little boy smell, and sighed. He closed his eyes, feeling the warmth of them both so close to him. Samhain trotted over, eager for attention as well. Snuffling, he slipped his head under Jim's hand. Jim scratched his ears obligingly.

*If this was how the world ended,* he thought, *that would be just fine. How about it, Lord? Any chance you could end the world today?*

"I know that look," Tammy said.

"What look?"

"The one on your face right now. The one that says you're thinking about something."

Jim smiled. "I was just thinking about prayers."

"Since when did you become religious?"

"It's never too late to change."

"Unless it's the end of the world," Tammy teased.

"There will come a time when you believe everything is finished," Jim said. "That will be the beginning."

"Who wrote that?"

"Louis L'Amour." He turned to Danny. "Come on, kiddo. Let's get going. Don't want to miss anything."

*Mission Viejo, California*

The first thing Rick Sycheck did every morning before he got dressed for work was turn on the morning news.

With the coffee pot burbling in the kitchen and Robin Meade's voice relating the latest disaster in the world, Rick showered and shaved. He noted the gray in his beard stubble and his thinning hair. Noted the paunch of his belly, the flab of his legs. He looked like shit. He felt fine physically most of the time. But when he had to do anything strenuous like climbing a flight of steps or doing any physical activity like yard work or taking out the garbage or walking their German Shepard, Princess, he got short-winded. Chalk that up to being eighty pounds overweight. That's what happens when you spend twenty-five years sitting behind a computer terminal.

Rick was forty-seven years old. He was married to Jeanette and they had two children, Richard Jr. and Melody. Being that it was summer vacation, both kids were out of the house a lot. Richard was going to be a senior in Mission Viejo High School this fall. Melody would be entering the eighth grade. Jeanette worked as a consultant for Deloitte and Touche and was on the road a lot. This week she was headquartered somewhere in central Pennsylvania. Rick didn't remember the name of the city, but he thought it had something to do with the Amish. York? Lancaster? He wasn't sure. His father had family back in Philadelphia and he remembered a family visit out there years ago, when he was a kid. He hadn't been back there in years. Pennsylvania had become Jeanette's second home as of late. Rick hated it when she was gone.

When Rick was finished with shaving, he fed the dog and then got dressed for work, selecting one of two dozen similar pairs of trousers and button-down shirts from the large walk-in closet he shared with Jeanette. He selected a tie. As he stood at the vanity mirror putting the final touch on his corporate attire, he thought about what he was going to do this evening. Jeanette wasn't due back home until Friday. Today was Wednesday. The kids were staying with their friends, Paul and Mary Bryant. The Bryant family used to live a few blocks away but had moved to Palos Verdes, which was about an hour's commute north, during the last week of school. Richard and Melody had spent every weekend with Paul and Mary ever since the move, which Rick could understand. But with his kids gone so much, and his wife on the road so much, the house was lonely, even with Princess's company. He would call the kids at Paul and Mary Bryant's home today and tell them he wanted them home by five p.m. Friday afternoon. They would head out to pick Jeanette up from John Wayne Airport in Irvine and take her out to dinner—Houston's Steak House maybe. Then they would spend the weekend together. Rick loved his family, and spending so much time apart with them was tearing at him. Jeanette wasn't happy about being on the road so much, but what else could they do? This damn economy was in the shitter. Technically it was getting better, but Rick and Jeanette were still trying to dig themselves out of debt from Jeanette's layoff from two years ago. That had really hurt them.

As Rick entered the bedroom something on the news caught his ear. "…three people were killed last night in Huntington Beach, California when large crab creatures attacked several beach goers."

*What?* Rick stopped, turned toward the TV.

One of the local newscasters was reporting from a video-feed through CNN's Atlanta headquarters. Rick recognized him. He sat down on the edge of the unmade bed, stunned.

"Robin, last night this beach community was terrorized by something out of a horror movie," the male newscaster said. He was standing on the strand, the ocean behind him. The sky was blue; perfect Southern California weather. The beach looked deserted. "Shortly before eight-thirty last night, three people lost their lives when a giant crab species currently unknown to modern science washed ashore—and wreaked havoc."

There was a cut to previously taped footage along with a voice over narration from the local newscaster. Rick watched in stunned silence. According to the report, the three people died from blood loss and massive trauma. The Huntington

Beach Police Department had evacuated the beach, the pier, and the three block downtown area. As footage from last night came into view, Rick felt a sense of nostalgia. He recalled moments from his youth in Huntington Beach. He'd moved to the area with his family shortly after high school from Los Angeles. Dad's company had been moved to a larger facility in Costa Mesa and they'd moved to cut down on commuting costs. Rick was working at the company by then too, as a clerk. It wasn't a job he particularly enjoyed, but it paid him money and it made his parents happy. When he wasn't at work, he spent time at the beach. Huntington Beach was his spot.

The news wasn't very forthcoming with information. The names and identities of the victims were being withheld until notification of next of kin. As for the creatures themselves, officials were being very tight-lipped about it. "All I can say is that we're examining the remains now," a middle-aged male marine biologist was saying; he was being recorded live from Long Beach. "The only thing I can confirm is that, yes, they are a completely unknown species."

The local newscaster came back on. "It was also reported that there was an incident earlier that day on the pier when a fisherman caught a similar creature. That man is listed in critical condition at Huntington Memorial hospital. Witnesses to that incident reported that the creature—said to be a cross between a lobster and a scorpion—either stung or severed the man's left arm. Back to you in Atlanta, Robin."

Robin Meade looked grave. "Thank you for that story, Bill." The camera angle changed to a frontal view and when Robin began reporting on President Anthony Genova's new budget, Rick turned the TV off.

He sat on the bed, his mind racing. Princess hopped up on the bed with him, seeking attention. He petted her absentmindedly, his mind still on the news report. Previously unknown species? A cross between a lobster and a scorpion? Something about this story fascinated him and he didn't have the slightest idea why.

Rick got to his feet. He crossed the bedroom, found a pair of slip-on dress shoes and put them on. He exited the bedroom and was just about to head downstairs when he paused at the spare bedroom that had been converted to his study.

He couldn't explain why the news story captivated him so much. It almost sounded like something he'd read—but he was confident he'd never read a novel or a short story with a plot that involved lobster-scorpion hybrids that killed people. He'd read a lot of horror novels; had a good memory for what he'd read. And he was confident such a novel didn't exist.

Rick stepped into the study. The only wall not taken up by bookshelves was the one directly opposite the doorway—a small but comfortable reading chair and end table was positioned by the window.

The other three walls were lined with bookshelves.

Floor to ceiling bookshelves containing a collection of horror, dark fantasy, and science fiction he'd been building since he was sixteen years old. One wall held nothing but rare hardcovers—volumes by Bradbury, Bloch, Lovecraft, Wellman, Long, and Derleth from Arkham House; Etchison, Campbell, Barker, Wagner, Nolan, Matheson (father and son), Shirley, and Blumlein from Scream/Press. Martin, McCammon, Garton, Lansdale, Koontz, and Schow from Dark Harvest Press. And that was just material from classic small press imprints from the so-called horror boom of the 1980's. He also had key volumes from some of the latest small presses, as well as expensive limited signed editions by Barker, King, Grant, Lee, Ketchum, and Laymon in a special case with glass doors. Another wall of bookshelves held nothing but mass-market paperbacks from the 1940's through the latest pulpy mid-list titles. The walk-in closet held even more treasures—white cardboard boxes stacked row upon row consisting of files of hundreds of comic books, pulps, and science fiction magazines.

Rick stood in the room, taking in his collection. In another life he could have been a writer of this kind of material. He'd certainly had dreams of it at one point, at a younger age. He'd doodled on a few stories back then, poor imitations of the great stuff he was reading in the leading anthologies of the day. Rather than follow his heart and his muse, he'd done what was expected of him by his parents and society in general—he'd buckled down and concentrated on his job at the company his father had worked at for over twenty-five years himself—insurance giant Free State Insurance.

He'd left the window in the study open a crack last night to let in the evening breeze. He crossed the room to close it, latching it. He paused, surveying the room again. He'd read every book in this room, some of them twice. Knew every story plot and synopsis. And even though the news story he'd heard had a throb of déjà vu in it, he was absolutely certain it did not resemble any fictionalized story he'd ever read. He took a step toward the paperbacks and ran his finger along the spines, searching among the alphabetized authors last names. He had three of Guy N. Smith's infamous 'Crab' novels—slim novels about giant crabs coming ashore in Wales and chowing down on the human population. Fun escapist reading, but nothing like what the news journalists were reporting.

Rick sighed, cast another look around the room. He glanced at his watch. Time to go. A few minutes later Rick left for work, hoping he'd have enough down time during his work day to do some research on the news story.

*Venice Beach, California*

Sparky was kicking it along the low brick wall that lined the strand when Doc and Joker showed up. He saw them pull the 1957 Chevrolet Impala in the parking lot behind Stan's Surf Shop. Sparky grinned. Joker kept that Impala cherry. It was fire-engine red with real chrome rims, white leather interior and fringe along the interior ceiling. The hydraulic system was powered by eight batteries in the trunk. It was a bad ass ride. Joker had gotten it from his old man, Flaco, who was doing twenty to life in San Quentin on a second-degree murder charge. In Flaco's time he'd cruised the streets blasting the classics—the Platters, Frankie Lymon and the Teenagers, all that good 1950's shit. Weird that guys from Flaco's generation, homies who came up in the late 1970s and early 1980s, had been into music from a past generation. The way Joker told

it, his old man went from the crooners to the hardcore West
Coast rappers like NWA and Ice T without missing a beat.

"How's it going, little dude!" Joker called out. Sparky
raised his right hand and waved as his old friends meandered
slowly to the strand, weaving their way between the other
characters—the rollerskaters, skateboarders, the chicks
strolling along in their low-slung jeans, the gangsta wanna-
be's in their baggy shorts, the jack-offs who thought they were
tough shit walking around with pit bulls on thick stud-and-
chain collars, the hippies scattered here and there doing their
hippie thing, playing guitars, harmonica, painting pictures,
selling t-shirts, discreetly selling grass and mushrooms.
Venice Beach was a colorful place. The most colorful place in
the heart of Dogtown.

Joker held his right hand up for a power shake and Sparky
stood up. The two men clasped hands and embraced, slapping
each other's backs. "Long time, homie, long time," Joker said.
"How you been?"

"I been good," Sparky said.

Doc grinned at him from behind mirrored shades. His
weathered face was framed by a long goatee that was more
gray than the black from when Sparky had known him back
in the day. "How's it going, Doc?" Sparky asked the grizzled
veteran of the streets.

"It's going," Doc said, powershake, embrace, back slap.
"You look good, homes. What they feed you in Arizona State
Penn?"

"The same slop they feed you in Chino and San Quentin,"
Sparky said.

"I wouldn't know that, homes," Doc said. Unlike Joker,
he was dressed down. Joker was dressed out to the max—tan
khaki slacks that were pressed so tight the creases practically
gleamed with their sharpness, white sleeveless t-shirt, red
plaid long-sleeved shirt over it like a billowy jacket, black
dress shoes. Even Joker's walk was low rider all the way.
Doc, on the other hand, was dressed like he just came off
from a construction job site—blue jeans, ratty white t-shirt,
blue work shirt unbuttoned, tan workboots. He wore a blue

bandana over his head, tied in the back. The only thing that told you he was from the bad streets of Dogtown was the way he carried himself; it was in the way he walked with a slinking approach mixed with a cool attitude and a wary size-you-up appraisal. If you were a rival you recognized that look even with the casual dress. If you were a normal citizen, you simply thought Doc was a blue-collar veteran.

Sparky cast a casual glance at the action on the beach, noticed the two beat cops two thousand feet down the strand and turned to his friends. He nodded at Joker. "You clean, homes?"

"Clean as the day I was born, homie!" Joker said, spreading his hands out and grinning.

"We clean," Doc said. He was grinning, his gaze centered on Sparky. "Don't worry about those two cops. This won't take long."

Sparky nodded.

"Tonight, Gardena, Avalon and One Hundred and Sixty Fifth Street. Eighty Seven is the address."

Sparky frowned. "That's Gardena Trese's turf."

"Yeah, and you been a resident of Arizona state for how long now? Twelve years?"

"Don't rub it in," Sparky said. He cast a quick glance down the strand at the cops. They were talking to a couple of girls in skimpy bikinis.

"Yeah, but you hear stuff inside," Doc said. "Or so I heard."

"How does a guy like you never wind up serving time?" Sparky asked Doc. "You must be one lucky sonofabitch!"

Doc grinned. "That's why I'm the Doctor. I know how to play the system, and I know how to play people. I watch. I observe. I form alliances. And I do this for our people. I do this for *you*, my man."

"Why couldn't you pull some strings for me when it went down, then? That was some fucked up shit, homes."

"I'm not here to relive old days, homie," Doc said. "I'm just the messenger today. Eighty Seven, at One-Sixty Fifth Street. Gardena. Eight o'clock."

"You gonna be there?"

"Joker's going with you." Doc said. "He's my *ambassador.*"

Joker grinned. One of his teeth was silver. It gleamed in the sunlight.

Sparky turned to Doc, his voice lower. "So, is that shit true then? Did they...you know...did MM really call for this?"

"That's affirmative."

"And is it true about the clean-up?" Sparky had heard the stories while serving time. Rumor had it that the Mexican Mafia had sent down a directive to all the Latino street gangs in Los Angeles to eliminate the strong-holds the Black gangs had taken in the drug trade. In years past, the Blood and the Crips had controlled areas of their turf and had not crossed borders into the territories of the Latino street gangs. Unlike the Latino street gangs, the Black street gangs were more industrious; they sought wider distribution networks and had grown nationwide in the 1990's. It had caused friction with old time gangsters in other distribution centers in Chicago, along the eastern seaboard, especially with the Italian mob in those areas. While some Latino street gangs had followed suit, most noticeably 18th Street, the Bloods and the Crips had a distinct advantage. They had successfully tapped a market not even the Latino street gangs could capture—they were selling to the average man on the street, the corporate CEOs, the A-list entertainers. The Mexican Mafia saw that as a threat. While in days past, Latino and Black street gangs could pass each other on the street without malice, the situation was different now. The Mexican Mafia's directive had shaken things up. In the past five years, almost a thousand young Black men had been killed in violent street wars all perpetrated by Mexican Mafia soldiers from various Latino street gangs. The bloodshed had claimed the lives of innocent Black men. For the first time ever in the history of Los Angeles, Black men were dying at the hands of not just their own people from rival Crip and Blood factions or racist cops, but Latino gang members who had never posed a threat even in the glory days of the 70's and 80's. Indeed, Sparky remembered hearing stories from his uncles and aunts about parties and picnics in the park, how various Crip factions would attend and kick back with his Venice homies, sharing a brew or a blunt. That sense of camaraderie was gone now.

"It's as true as night and day, my man," Doc said.

Sparky nodded. He'd only been out of prison since April. In that time, he'd laid low at his uncle Ernie's place watching soap operas and visiting his PO. He was prohibited from associating with known felons, and while Ernie was a long-time member of Venice 13, he wasn't a felon; like Doc, Ernie only had minor convictions in the early 1970's and had never spent a day in Federal custody. *That's where guys like me come in*, Sparky thought. The old-timers, the guys with the brains, they get us to do their dirty work for them. And the Mexican Mafia pulls the strings.

"So whatta ya say, homie?" Joker asked. He grinned good-naturedly. "We can meet up at Lucy's for some *carne asada* like old times, then take a ride down to G-town together."

Sparky shrugged his shoulders. He cast another glance down the strand. The two cops—dressed in khaki shorts and white shirts, their badges pinned to their shirt breasts, their belts bearing the requisite stuff like handcuffs, firearm, mace and their shoulder-strapped mikes the only thing that differentiated them from all the other freaks on the strand. Like everybody else out here they were only out to hustle, only they got it both ways—they got paid to hustle the riff raff and they got to hustle for some pussy on the side.

Sparky turned to Joker. "What time shall I meet you?"

Joker grinned. "Six o'clock."

"Six it is." Sparky got up from the low brick wall.

"One thing, homes," Doc said before Sparky could leave. "You and Joker are troop commanders to the Venice boys. You take in everything the MM guys say at the meeting and you follow it to the word. You need support, you come to me."

"*Si*," Sparky said. Power shakes were traded, more half-assed hugs and back slapping, then the three men parted ways. Joker and Doc headed back to their Impala, Sparky headed north along the strand to where he'd left his ride, a 1973 VW

Bug that Ernie let him borrow while he was on probation. And as he got behind the wheel and started the engine, he had the distinct feeling that he was going to play a major part in something very big.

## *Malibu, California*

Augustus Livingston knew there was something wrong. He just didn't know what it was.

His morning meditation had been undertaken with disruption and much tension. As always, when the weather was picture perfect, he'd trudged down the well-worn private path from his cliff-side Malibu beach home and walked fifty paces to the high tide line where he'd sat on the slightly damp sand to commune with nature. The normal beach activity—the cries of the gulls, the sound of the waves breaking, the occasional excited yelps of children playing on the beach, the sight of early morning surfers bobbing in the ocean in their wetsuits to ride the early morning glassy surf seemed broken somehow. Augustus cast his gaze toward the ocean, a frown on his face.

Augustus was seventy years old. Standing at a lean five foot eleven and weighing in at a trim one-eighty, most people would be hard pressed to correctly guess his age. Chalk that up to the clean living. Since the early 1970s, Augustus had been living green both on a business matter and a personal one. Unlike the rest of his contemporaries of the sixties, after turning on, tuning in, and dropping out (and dropping a lot of LSD and mescaline in the process), he had turned off living within the mainstream and had dropped back in to society on his own terms. His first step toward that goal had been to open a commercial art and graphic studio where he'd supplied work for all the major advertising agencies and the occasional film studio. While plying his trade there, he'd tuned in even deeper to the science of natural living, meditation, and past life regression. He'd started conducting seminars and workshops. He authored several books on the subjects. And watched his mini self-help empire grow to a ten million dollar a year company.

Through it all he'd remained with his wife, Marion, for over forty years and fathered four children with her. Their children had produced grandchildren. His oldest son ran his company—*La Raza del Sol*, Spanish for the House of the Sun—with the assistance of eight full-time staff members. Augustus was officially retired, but he was still active in many areas of the business. He still conducted seminars, still guided people into deep meditation states to commune with their past selves, still recorded self-help CD's and Podcasts that were broadcasts to three million people around the world. He loved that part of the job. The business end he was glad to hand over to somebody else.

The crying of the gulls caused him to glance out over the ocean. There was a large flock of seagulls heading inland. Largest Augustus had ever seen. Maybe there was balance after all. He sat back, palms on the sand, and watched them.

Maybe he was just feeling some stress because of what was happening in his daughter's life. Susan had married late in life, and was currently going through a painful divorce with her husband, Carlos. Susan had insinuated infidelity on her husband's part. In observing his daughter's struggle, he had to wonder if much of it had to do with her embracing of those things which society still deemed as more important above all else—material status, social status, socially acceptable career. Susan had rebelled as a teenager by embracing right-wing conservatism. Never one to push his political beliefs on anyone, Augustus and Marion had allowed their children to explore their own paths. And while older son Andy and their youngest children George and Heather had bounced around to various social, political, and religious causes from a wide range of faiths and spectrums, they'd found their niche's and neither was completely in line with their parents. While Andy ran *La Raza del Sol* and could be considered the more liberal of his children, he was a registered Liberatarian (Augustus had not voted in a national election since 1968, after being lied to by both the Democrats and Republicans who'd foisted Lyndon B. Johnson and Richard Nixon on the nation to disastrous results that had only grown worse in recent years).

Heather leaned conservative on fiscal issues, George was a die-hard liberal who made Augustus and Marion seem like communists by comparison. It was probably only natural that Susan had fled in the opposite direction.

Augustus sighed. He couldn't find fault with any of the life paths his children had chosen. It was who they were. It was where their destinies lied. He was only sorry that Susan had not listened to her heart and backed out of her marriage to Carlos. She'd confided to Marion before the wedding that she had doubts about the relationship. They'd been introduced by mutual friends at their company. They shared the same political and spiritual beliefs. They started attending the same church. It was only natural for them to get married, right? After all, they loved each other. There was a physical attraction and they had so much in common!

Sighing again, Augustus closed his eyes, and took several deep breaths. It was time to clear his mind of can't. Time to expel negative thoughts, and focus only on the positive. He turned his attention inward, his mental energy channeling into one perfect pitch melody of meditation and he was almost in the zone when the cries of the gulls grew louder, knocking him out of his reverie.

He opened his eyes slightly, intending to try to get back into his morning meditation, but something made him sit up and take notice.

Off on the horizon, as far as he could see, there was a solid mass of birds heading inland. The group was much larger than the previous flock he'd witnessed. He didn't need a telescope or binoculars to know that that long black smudge that crossed the horizon for...well, it seemed to be all over the place really, but it was broken up here and there...that black smudge could only be one thing.

A gigantic flock of birds. Heading inland.

Augustus felt a pang of fear in his belly. He slowly got to his feet, looking out at the ocean. A slight breeze rippled his long, billowy cotton shirt, his long shorts, his shoulder-length graying hair. Something about all those birds flying en masse inland didn't sit right with him. It felt wrong. Felt...unnatural.

Augustus glanced up the beach. It was relatively empty this morning save for a couple of pre-teen kids chasing each other around. A group of surfers rode waves or waited for the next set. On the other end of the beach heading south was more of the same. This stretch of beach was marked private, about a mile stretch, for the residents who lived along the rocky outcrops that lined the shore. Augustus's home was fifty yards behind him. Marion was probably on the back deck facing the ocean, enjoying a cup of coffee while reading the morning paper.

Now on his feet, Augustus turned around and trudged back up the beach, heading toward the walkway that led to his secured private gate. He couldn't explain the feeling he had, but he'd never been wrong before regarding his instinct. And this morning his instinct was telling him that something bad was heading in from the ocean.

# TWO

*South Pacific Ocean*

They were a hundred miles off the coast of South Africa, on a shoot for *Discovery Channel's* upcoming Shark Week event when Dave Thomas noticed something peculiar going on in the ocean.

He frowned and pointed to an area about twenty yards away, opposite of where Doug Chambers and the camera crew had gone down in the shark cage to capture stock footage. "Check that out," he said to Todd Perry, the ship's first mate.

"What?" Todd was a beanpole thin white South African who owned the fifty-foot yacht they'd commissioned for the shoot. He shielded the glare of the sun from his eyes and looked to where Dave was pointing. "Oh, that? That's your basic flounder and tuna going ape-shit in these waters."

"That's not flounder and tuna," Dave said, trying hard not to sound annoyed. This was his second trip to these waters as Producer of Shark Week. Each time, he'd had the misfortune of being paired up with Todd and his yacht. Dave liked the yacht, but its owner was an arrogant prick. Todd didn't seem to care for Dave either, so Dave made sure he annoyed the man every chance he had when they were on shore. "It isn't their migration season. In fact, whatever's making those splashes is a lot bigger—"

Jack Becker leaned forward, squinting in the water. He was Dave's assistant. "Those are lobsters."

"Lobsters?"

"Yeah." Jack pointed at a spot to Dave's left. "See that claw. Jesus, that's a big one! Those are probably North Atlantic Lobsters."

"What's a North Atlantic Lobster doing in the South

Atlantic ocean off the Cape Horn?" Dave asked.

"Your guess is as good as mine, mate," Todd said. He kept his gaze at the water, trying to follow the splashing sounds. "But they're chasing the fish. Take a look at that!"

Dave saw. Sure enough, he could see fish of all shapes and sizes zooming through the water as if in a blind panic to escape. The giant lobsters, or whatever they were, seemed to be chasing them. "This is weird."

"You said it, mate," Todd said. "Gotta wonder if your crew is getting this action on film down below."

"I hope so," Dave said, watching with amazement. "I can't wait to take a look at this footage later tonight."

As much as Dave loved his job as a Discovery Channel producer—his specialty was producing original programming on sharks, large carnivorous lizards, giant pythons, bats, and giant spiders—he hated this part of the Atlantic. South Africa was fine. He'd once produced a still-unaired documentary about a rumored thirty foot African Rock Python that had killed and eaten seven full-grown human beings. The footage he and his director had shot were still unassembled, and the powers-that-be at Discovery Channel wanted him to complete it by venturing into the South African veldt with a team of poachers to kill the monster serpent. Dave refused. He saw no reason to tamper with mother nature like that. A snake that big deserved to be respected; it was only doing what genetics had programmed it to do, and that was attack, kill, and devour anything warm blooded that it could get. People should realize that and not venture out into the veldt unprepared. If a giant snake ate you, well, you deserved it.

Rather than head inland to the veldt to appease his bosses (and kill an animal that was really doing mankind a favor by eating people too stupid to take precautions), he'd elected to put up with Todd and shoot another shark feature. Dave loved sharks more than any other creature. Great Whites and Tiger sharks were his favorites. He loved them the same way he loved all large carnivorous animals. They commanded respect due to their sheer power. He understood this, and insisted that his cinematographers, scientists, and assistants who went down in the shark cage were always well prepared. He made sure everybody followed all safety precautions. They never took any unnecessary risks while getting shark footage. They'd never had an accident in ten years of work.

Which was why when he saw the explosion of bubbles from below, followed by a frothing mass of blood that billowed to the surface, it felt like his heart stopped. The foamy blood quickly spread outward in concentric circles and Dave gasped. "What the fuck?" He suddenly called out. "Peter!" He turned toward Bob Thurman and Peter Oldsdale, who worked the crane that lowered the shark cage in the water. "Pull him up!"

Peter leaped to duty and activated the crane. The engine whined and the crane started lifting the cage up.

Everybody leaned forward, trying to see into the water. The frantic activity of the fleeing fish continued. Something large moved through the water about twenty yards to the left. Dave gasped—it was a fifteen foot Great White; a beautiful animal. It bobbed up then streaked back downward, followed by scores of smaller fish. "What the hell?" Dave asked.

Suddenly, the top of the shark cage came into view. Doug's fingers were clenched around the top bars. As the crane lifted the cage out, Peter reached out to help Todd, Jack, and Dave bring the cage closer to the boat. Doug was inside the cage, his eyes wide with fright from behind the face mask. He pulled his oxygen tube out of his mouth. "Did you see that?" his voice was high with panic.

"We saw a bunch of blood," Dave said.

At the same time, Peter and Jack said simultaneously, "Oh shit!" and "Oh my God!"

Dave and Doug turned to what they were looking at and Dave gasped again. Amid the widening circle of blood was large chunks of flesh. A fin floated to the surface. It was definitely a shark fin, lying flat against the water. Bits of the shark's back still adhered to the base of the fin. Dave looked at the scene in complete amazement and growing horror. The remains of the shark's rear end floated to the surface— tail fin, rear dorsal. Bits of flesh from that part seemed to be bubbling...dissolving.

"What the hell?" Dave said again.

The cage was now completely out of the water and Doug was rattling the bars, indicating he wanted out. Peter began sliding the cage over to the deck. He fumbled for the door and Doug got out. He threw his face mask off and looked out at the water. He was breathing heavily. His eyes were wide, bulging from their sockets as if he'd just seen something monstrous.

"What happened down there?" Dave asked.

"You saw those lobster things, right?" Doug asked. His eyes were all pupil, large and black in his face.

"Yeah, we did," Dave said.

"A bunch of them started swimming by me as I was shooting footage." For the first time, Dave looked at the bottom of the cage to check on the equipment. Doug's camera was intact, lying on the cage floor. "I didn't think anything of it at first but then it hit me—they're fucking huge and they've got stingers!"

"Stingers?"

"Yeah!" Doug looked at his producer, the fear evident in his eyes, in his face, in his crackling voice as he spoke. "They got tails like a scorpion, with stingers. And they were chasing everything. Look!" He pointed to the water and they all looked. Dave knew what Doug was getting at. The frenzied activity from the fish, their seeming frantic motions to swim as fast as possible was due to the fact that they were being chased by these monstrous lobster things.

"Some of these creatures were snapping their claws at the fish," Doug continued. "And I started shooting this. Then... then a Great White, a twenty footer easily, it was swimming by off to my left. I'd noticed it earlier, just sort of cruising around before all this other shit started happening. As this... this migration started whipping by, the Great White swam closer and just barreled in like they usually do. It grabbed the first thing it could, which happened to be one of the lobster things. Chomped it once, then swallowed it. It started moving in on some other fish. I didn't think anything of it, just kept shooting. The shark swam away, but then started circling back. That's when I noticed that it was swimming kinda funny."

"What do you mean?" Todd asked. The yacht owner looked terrified.

"It was..." Doug seemed to search for the correct words. "It was flopping around, as if it was in pain. It even swam on its side for a minute, like goldfish do when they're about to die. I could see this weird bulge in its middle and then...I swear to God man, I ain't making this up...this *split* appeared in its side, like a fissure, and blood started leaking out. And the more it came apart, the more the water started getting all bubbly and frothy and then the thing just fucking exploded in the water!"

The crew on deck greeted this with stunned silence. Doug was adamant. "I swear to God man, it exploded! The fucking shark *exploded!* I was so stunned I didn't know what to do. I think...I think the camera was still rolling, but then the cage started going up and I knew you'd seen it."

"Why would it explode?" Dave asked. He was dumbfounded. He looked out at the ocean, his eyes telling him that, yes, those were chunks of Great White shark floating in the bloody water. He noted that parts of the flesh were still dissolving, as if from some powerful corrosive chemical. "How is this possible?"

"I don't know," Doug said. "But it is possible, apparently. And get this. As Peter's pulling the cage up I started shooting again and the thing that shark ate—that lobster-scorpion thing—it was *alive!* It was alive and swimming around in the middle of all this blood and shark guts like nothing ever happened to it."

Suddenly, Dave connected the dots. "You said these things have stingers?"

"Yes! Big ones! About this long." Doug put his palms about two feet apart.

Further out in the ocean there was another spreading pool of frothy blood. Pieces of some unidentifiable fish spewed to the surface. The frantic migration continued around them, more frenzied now.

"I think we better get the fuck out of here and back to shore," Dave said. "And the faster the better."

Todd didn't have to be told twice. He swung down into the cabin, put the boat in gear, and a moment later they were speeding back to shore.

*Santa Catalina Island, California*

Cathy Hernandez hated Melissa Reinhardt with a passion.

It was bad enough working for the passive-aggressive bitch. It was even worse to be her direct report. Melissa hadn't wanted to bring the team to Catalina Island for the team building exercise, but it had been Jim Sunn's idea. Cathy thought it was a good idea, to be truthful. They could use some of the techniques the team building consultant was teaching them today for their work on the mainland, which was on the second floor of a non-descript office building in an equally non-descript office park in Fountain Valley, California, a small suburban community in Orange County just south of Los Angeles. Jim Sunn was the owner and Chief Operating Officer of Sunn Advertising, a small ad agency that handled print, web, and all forms of broadcast media advertising. Cathy was employed as a database analyst. Melissa was her boss— exactly what Melissa's title was, Cathy wasn't sure. She was even more unsure of why Melissa was even at the company.

"Okay, we're on the other side of the island now," Melissa said. She was standing on a rocky outcrop and turned to Cathy. Wendy Snow, her co-worker and chief confidant, was standing beside her. Both women had been put on Melissa's team in what was obviously a concerted effort by Jim to foster a stronger team unity among the three women. All the other teams had been broken up with different employees from different departments. *It must be really obvious that we don't work well together*, Cathy thought.

"Yes, we're on the other side of the island," Wendy said. She glanced at Cathy and shrugged.

"So now what?" Melissa asked.

"We join hands and sing kumbaya?" Cathy suggested.

Melissa frowned. Her brown hair blew in her face from the offshore wind. They had hiked down to this section of the island per the consultant's directions and diagram on the chart he'd provided to them. He'd divided all twenty employees of Sunn Advertising into groups and scattered them in all directions on the island with the instructions that once they reached their destination they were to observe their surroundings, take stock of the people they were with, assess the situation and act accordingly. "It doesn't matter what it is," he'd said, strolling before them in the park on Lime Street where they'd started their day. The consultant was a man in his mid-thirties with an open, sunny disposition, brown hair, blue eyes, giving Cathy the impression he was a typical Southern California native. He'd introduced himself as John. "Some of you may end up at the strand. There might be a lot of kids playing, there might be an ice cream stand, a hot dog vendor, people throwing Frisbees with their dogs. What will you do as a group? Have a picnic in the park? Get ice cream? Start your own game of Frisbee? You will need to make this decision as a team. Another group of you may end up outside a shopping mall with a food court. Do you decide to go shopping? Do you get lunch? If there's a jogging path near the mall, do you decide to go jogging? Again, you must make a decision on one activity based on your surroundings and you must come to this decision as a team."

And on and on it had went. John had tossed out half a dozen other possible scenarios based on the environment they might wind up in. As a group, they were supposed to decide what to do and arrive at that conclusion by working together with minimal arguments. He'd held a football in his hands. "After all," John had said, "this exercise is all about how you react naturally to the things around you. This isn't about ladder climbing or jockeying for position to attain another notch in your belt. This is about working together toward a common goal." Then with a smooth, practiced move, he'd tossed the football at one of the half dozen groups he'd paired off. One of the graphic artists, Andy Saunders, caught the ball, but barely.

"Why'd you catch that ball, Andy?" John had asked.

"Because you threw it toward me," Andy responded.

"Is there another reason why you caught it?"

Andy had shrugged. "Well, yeah…if I hadn't caught it, it would've hit me."

"True. It might have bounced off you and hit somebody else in your group, too. Correct?"

There'd been a small chuckle of amusement from Andy's group. Andy grinned sheepishly as he regarded his team mates. "Yeah, I guess so."

"By reacting instinctively to that situation, you not only prevented this football from bouncing off you, you also shielded other members of your team. In other words, your reaction to my action benefited your team." John regarded them. "That's what this is all about folks. Working together toward a common goal. The common goal is the good of Sunn Advertising. Reacting against sudden actions like my tossing the football may seem like an act of self-preservation, and it is. You may perform acts of self-preservation on the job—working to get that website done before the deadline, for instance. You do it because if you don't, you'll get fired, right?"

Jose Garcia, one of Sunn Advertising's web designer's laughed. "You got that right, bro."

John smiled. "So there you go. Go forth and when you get to your destination take in what's around you. Assess it. Consider the team members you are with. Then, act accordingly."

Cathy wasn't sure what to act on in this remote part of the island. John must have picked this spot on purpose just for the three of them. She glanced at Wendy, who shook her head. A silent communication seemed to pass between them. *I bet Jim told that consultant that we're his problem children*, that look seemed to say. *And he stuck us out here to torture us.*

Melissa glanced around at the remote section of beach. "Well, this is just stupid. I don't know what he wants us to do here! It's just the three of us. There's nobody else here!"

"He must have picked this spot for a reason," Wendy said. She nodded out at the ocean. "Take a look, Melissa. Isn't it beautiful?"

Melissa glanced at the ocean and frowned. The sky had

49

been filled with a bunch of birds earlier that day—seagulls, pigeons, crows. It was like that old Hitchcock movie, *The Birds*. Cathy glanced out at the ocean and saw what Wendy was getting at. The view from this end of the island, the peacefulness of this spot, the nature, it was very beautiful.

"All I see is a bunch of sand and rocks and water," Melissa said. She craned her neck around, looking up at the large cliff wall that rose fifty yards and ended in scrub bush above. A second path wound its way steeply up the cliff toward civilization, with residential streets, homes, and apartments. "It's ugly down here. Why didn't he lead us up where there's people?"

"He wanted us to come down here," Cathy said, trying to wrap her mind around this exercise and what the end of this particular path meant. "He had a reason. Let's try to figure that out."

"I think he wanted us to appreciate this," Wendy said. She tilted her head in the direction of the ocean. Wendy was twenty years younger than Cathy, in her early thirties. She was short, slightly chunky in hip and bust, and wore her brown frizzy hair to mid-back. "I think that when you pluck us out of our environment, which is constantly busy, and you come to this…" She looked out at the ocean, shaking her head. "We seem to get so worked up by such trivial things at the office. You know? The kind of things that don't mean anything in the grand scheme of things. Who answers the phone first. Not listening to each other when one of us is trying to make a system work, or ridiculing a new process—"

Melissa sighed. "Jesus Christ, this isn't about the new database, is it?"

Cathy shrugged. "Wendy has a point, Melissa. Jim hired me to create the database and you've been nothing but resistant to the idea. It's made my job kinda difficult."

"How has it made it difficult? You're doing such a fine job on it!"

Cathy looked at Melissa as if she'd lost her mind. Wendy chuckled sarcastically.

"You're looking at me as if *I'm* the problem," Melissa said, her features incredulous.

"You hired me to create and maintain the database, correct?" Cathy asked.

"Of course."

"And I did that. I also sat with you on three one-on-one training sessions to teach you how to query the database and pull the results into an Excel spreadsheet. Right?"

"Umm...yeah?" Melissa was getting that look that said, *oh no, here it comes.*

"What have you been doing since then?"

Silence from Melissa. Wendy answered for her. "She's been going back to doing manual data entry on five different spreadsheets on multiple workbooks and adding things up on a manual calculator."

Melissa turned to Wendy. "And that system *works!* It's what our customers *want!* It's what they expect."

"Our biggest account likes the web portal I created for them based off that database and the Crystal Report Cathy created," Wendy said. "Our sales contact there was really confused when you sent them that last report with all those Excel attachments."

Melissa heaved a big sigh that said, *you idiots!* Cathy and Wendy glanced at each other, then back at their direct report. "Maybe they like your database and your web portal thingy better, but the Excel spreadsheets we have is the way we've been doing things at Sunn for twenty years and—"

"Jim brought the both of us into the company to move us into the twenty-first century," Cathy said. "He likes the work we're doing. Our clients love the new reports. Our sales team will like it too if you'll only let them use it."

"Okay, this is enough!" Melissa put both hands up in exasperation and turned her back on Cathy and Wendy. She was breathing hard and fast. "What, are we supposed to just argue here or something? What kind of a stupid team building exercise is this?"

"We're supposed to work together as a team," Wendy said. "That's the whole nature of this thing. By being thrust in this situation he's created for us, we're supposed to mutually work together for the whole of the group. We've been trying to do this since Jim hired us, but it's become more and more difficult for us when you keep insisting we use your spreadsheets that are a waste of time, a waste of—"

Melissa whirled back around, her eyes smoldering with anger. "They are *not* a waste of time!"

CLICK-CLICK! CLICK-CLICK! CLICK-CLICK!

The sudden loud clicking noise startled all three of them and Cathy jumped in fright when she saw the creature amble forth from behind a rock. It was approaching from Melissa's blind side, and she turned around and screamed at the top of her lungs when she saw it. Another flurry of clicks behind them and Wendy screamed too. When Cathy looked toward her left—the south side of the island—she saw two more of the creatures.

They were like something from outer space. The biggest one was about the size of a small sofa, the other two about the size of large dogs. They looked like a weird mash up between a lobster and a scorpion. Their blood-red claws clacked together furiously, creating a cacophony of noise that sent all three women into shrieks of hysteria. Their segmented tails arched over their backs and Cathy saw that their stingers were long, heavy, and sharp. A yellowish fluid dripped from one of them.

Melissa scampered away from the creature near the water, joining Cathy and Wendy. The three creatures moved in, their claws clicking loudly. From behind them, another creature emerged from the water. She caught a whiff of the briny stench wafting off the monsters' shells. Overhead, a bird squawked in panic as several more of the beasts emerged from the ocean. These were larger than the first—each one the size of an automobile.

Cathy glanced toward the path they'd come down on. It was completely blocked by the creatures.

"There!" Wendy grabbed Cathy and pointed at another path in front of Melissa, who stood rooted to the spot, staring with wide-eyed fear as the creatures advanced. It was the second path that led toward the road above. "We can escape that way!"

Cathy grabbed Melissa's shoulders and tried to shove her

forward. Melissa screamed and tried to fight her. Cathy's fight or flight instinct kicked in and for five seconds there was a flurry of slapping hands and yells, screams of "get your hands off me, bitch!" and "stop struggling, we're trying to help you!" As quick as the brief catfight had erupted, it stopped. Melissa glared at Cathy and Wendy but it wasn't out of anger—it was out of cold fear. "There's no way out," she said.

The creatures let out a warbling sort of hiss and advanced closer, black eyestalks bobbing back and forth. They were only twenty feet away now. Cathy had the feeling they could move incredibly fast if they wanted to. They had only seconds to flee before the creatures charged toward them. If they could only get past Melissa....

"We need to leave now," Cathy said. She grabbed Melissa's shoulders and tried to herd her forward again toward the second path. Wendy tried to help, but this time Melissa protested again. She fought them off, screaming at the top of her lungs. "There's another one in the bushes over there! It's right there, it's coming this way!"

"Oh, fuck this," Wendy said. The younger woman was clearly frightened half to death, but Cathy could read the frustration in the tone of her voice. She gripped Melissa's blouse.

"Then get the hell out of our way then," Cathy said to Melissa. And then, with what seemed to be a synchronized effort, Cathy and Wendy grabbed Melissa and shoved her aside, sending her sprawling into the bushes at the side of the path. They ran toward the path and began climbing it as quickly as possible.

A creature surged forward, looming over Melissa and waving its claws. Then, with one quick movement, it seized her around the hips with its pincers and began to squeeze. The serrated edges sliced into her flesh. Her bones cracked.

Oblivious to her plight, Cathy and Wendy fled. The clicking sounds behind them were followed by screams of pain.

"Oh God," Melissa shrieked, "get them off me, oh God, that hurts! Oh Goooooodddddd!"

"Get me out of here, please get me out of here," Cathy chanted to herself as she clambered up the path, her complete effort on getting the hell away from the beach. Wendy was hot on her heels behind her. They clambered up a good fifty feet before they were able to reach a spot where they could afford to look down.

The four creatures had completely forgotten about Cathy and Wendy. They were swarming over Melissa, eating her from the looks of it. Giant claws plucked chunks of meat from her ravaged body. Cathy was almost frozen to the scene, rapt in its gruesome violence, but Wendy snapped her out of it. "Go!" The younger woman said, slapping her shoulder. Cathy started and resumed her climb, Wendy behind her. And as they made their way back to civilization, Cathy began to laugh maniacally. She really couldn't help it. She'd heard of people losing their sanity when faced with extreme life-threatening situations and had always dismissed them. Obviously it really happened because she was laughing now and she couldn't control herself. She couldn't stop laughing. After all, it was funny when you stopped to think about it.

Their team building session had proven to be completely successful. She and Wendy had worked as a team and saved themselves. In doing so, they'd had to sacrifice the life of Melissa to save the group, but isn't that what the exercise was about?

Wendy must have been on her wavelength because Cathy could hear her laughing too. "We reacted to the environment! We worked together as a group and in doing so, we saved ourselves. And we got rid of some dead weight in the process!"

This made Cathy laugh harder as they continued their climb. By the time they reached the top of the trail, which ended at a two lane highway that wound through the hills that overlooked the ocean, they were laughing so hard they had to stop and rest. And by the time the Santa Catalina Police car pulled up five minutes later, their temporary insanity had completely taken over.

*South Pacific Ocean*

They were seven days out at sea from the pickup in Australia. At the rate they were going, they'd reach home—Newport Beach, California—in about two days. Perfect timing.

Kyle Hodge reclined at the rear prow of the boat and closed his eyes, letting the sea smell wash over him. They'd been cutting a leisurely track through the Pacific for the past two weeks, embarking on a round-about fishing trip that was part leisure, part business. His brother-in-law, Hank, was up above, manning the wheel. His sister Carrie, Hank's wife, was down below in the galley with his girlfriend, Melody, preparing lunch and probably talking about how fucked up things were going to be when they got back. It figures. Women always talked about how fucked up things might get. So long as they didn't do the actual fucking up, things were going to be fine.

Sitting at Kyle's side was a large ice chest with today's catch—a nice sized yellow-fish tuna. He'd caught it earlier that morning. Their previous catches from the past week resided in the large freezer below deck. Once back home they'd arrange to have the fish transported to a place Kyle knew of where he'd have time to properly gut and prepare it, then he'd arranged to have a couple of them stuffed and mounted. He'd already arranged that end of the deal with his contacts back home.

Hank could deal with the delivery of the heroin.

They'd received the heroin in Australia, on the north side of the continent, through Hank's usual contact who was a first tier broker. Upon arriving in Australia, they'd taken quick possession of 100 kilos. The street value was ten million dollars. Once delivered to Hank's contact in Newport Beach, they would receive ten percent. Split four ways, ten percent of ten million bucks was a lot of money.

Kyle took a deep breath, gazing out at the ocean. This was the second such delivery they'd made in the past six months. He was also determined that it would be his last. He wasn't a dope smuggler. This is not what he'd signed up to do. But with a job layoff from two years ago thanks to the shitty economy brought on by shitty business practices and shitty politicians, it had been hard to find a job in his line of work. Kyle was a DBA—Database Administrator. Unless you wanted to move to India, jobs as DBAs were hard to come by in the States. He was overqualified for everything else he applied for, and under-qualified for other things. And he lacked the financial resources to return to school to earn a degree in another discipline. As a result, he'd been forced to work at jobs that paid half of what he used to make. And with this lack of funds, he was now in danger of losing his house, his car, and going to jail for failing to make timely child support payments to his ex-wife. The court system didn't care if you were underemployed. Ex-wives didn't give a shit either. Both wanted their money.

He didn't join this operation to get rich. He just needed enough money to keep the wolves at bay and buy him enough time to tide him over until things got better.

Movement in the water caught his eye and Kyle leaned forward, squinting. Fishing had been great so far. Hank said it was probably on account of that tsunami/earthquake, which had happened two weeks ago and had almost destroyed their plans. They'd been two days out from their journey when it hit. By the time they reached their destination in Australia the worst of it was over. Thankfully, due to the turmoil, they'd been able to make their transfer and pickup that much quicker. Who said natural disasters were a bad thing?

Kyle's pulse quickened as he frowned. He reached down to where he kept his binoculars and brought them up to his face. He adjusted the lenses, trying to get a sense of what was going on.

There was a lot of activity and it was too far away for him to discern what was happening. Kyle put the binoculars down and frowned. Shortly after they'd set forth from Australia and began heading back, Hank mentioned that he thought things were different in the water. "It's probably due to the earthquake," Hank had said. The two of them had been fishing on the starboard side, reels constantly bending with whatever happened to snag onto their baited hooks. "Animals can sense that shit. Remember that tsunami that hit Indonesia and Thailand? Right before the first waves hit, people reported that the birds took off, animals started heading inland, even the fish started acting up. That's what we're seeing here."

"The tsunami hit last week, though," Kyle had said.

"Don't make no difference," Hank had said. He'd been leaning back in his seat, strapped into his harness for the next big catch. "They're probably still freaked out. They're more sensitive to this kind of thing."

If that was the case, they'd been feeling it for the past week now. In addition to the influx of seagulls there was also more dolphins, whales, sharks, marlins, and other fish. They'd observed them swimming past their boat as if on some migratory quest. Melody had commented one night that it almost seemed like they were fleeing from something. "What could they be fleeing from?" Hank had asked. They'd been hanging out on the top deck, lounging in deck chairs drinking beers. Carrie and Hank were smoking some Thai stick which they'd brought along with them from California—a good few ounces. Kyle hadn't smoked pot in years and indulged for once after Carrie told him he was being a wuss. Whatever. She didn't have a lot of shit hanging over her head like he did. "They're swimming like something's chasing them."

"There *is* something chasing them," Melody had said. "The tsunami waves."

"Now I know you're full of shit," Carrie had said.

Melody had turned to her friend. "I'm serious. Think about how it affects the sea life. It's gotta fuck with them in some way, right? Water pressure and all?"

"That only works with us," Hank retorted.

"Yeah, but if the water is thrown off balance like that, it creates waves of increased and decreased pressure as the waves move along the ocean floor. Some fish live way deep in the surface, so deep that if they ascend higher up, they'll die. Other fish can't live that deep because *they'll* die. So when shit is off balance like that, they know it. And that's what we're seeing here—the wildlife fleeing what they sense to be something unnatural to their habitat."

Hank turned to Kyle. "Your woman's full of shit, Kyle."

That had been last night. Now as Kyle scanned the ocean with his binoculars, he saw a very peculiar thing far off in the distance.

He focused in on the object. Way off in the distance there was a white line along the tip of the horizon. The foaming of the sea? The approach of a giant tsunami? Further up and a tad bit ahead of this line was what appeared to be a dark cloud that Kyle immediately recognized as a huge flock of birds.

The birds were heading straight their way.

Kyle lowered the binoculars. "Hank! Carrie and Melody! Come up here! I think you should see this."

Hank climbed down from the upper deck. "What's going on?"

"Take a look at this," Kyle said, raising the binoculars again.

Carrie and Melody were approaching from below deck. Hank called out to them. "Carrie, can you head up deck and get my binoculars, please?"

A few minutes later Hank and Kyle were gazing out at the ocean through their binoculars. The women were staring out at sea, hands held above their eyes to cut out the glare. "Looks like the most gigantic flock of seagulls I've ever seen," Carrie said.

"They're flying so far away!" Melody sang. She laughed, then quickly stopped as she realized the others weren't laughing.

"Fish still zooming by?" Hank asked.

"Yeah, I think so," Kyle answered.

"I think what we have way out there is the biggest goddamn school of dolphins I've ever seen," Hank said. He removed the binoculars from his face to stare out at the sea. "Probably five miles out?"

The first wave of birds was much closer. They could hear their frantic cries. Kyle felt a primal sense of dread settle in his belly. He looked at the others, who seemed more awed by this freak of mother nature than afraid of it. "Um, guys, I don't think this is a good thing. In fact, I'm getting a bad feeling about this."

"You get a bad feeling about everything, Kyle," Melody protested. She snatched the binoculars out of his hands and looked through them. A moment later she gasped in surprise. "Wow! Will you look at that? Jesus!"

Hank still had his binoculars glued to his face. "That's some shit, isn't it?"

"It is," Melody agreed.

"What is it?" Carrie asked. "Let me see!" Melody handed the binoculars over to Carrie, who took a quick look. "Oh wow!" she said. She looked for a moment, then tore her eyes away from the lenses to look out at the ocean again.

"I've never seen dolphins move that fast," Hank said in awe. He was watching the scene through his binoculars very carefully.

"How many of them are there?" Kyle asked.

Hank turned slightly to his left and began a slow scan to the right. He whistled in amazement. "You're not going to believe this," he said, "but that line of...that mass of dolphins...or whatever they are...it spans as far as I can see."

The pit of dread grew heavier in Kyle's belly. "We need to get out of here," he said.

Hank and Carrie weren't paying attention to him. Their gaze was frozen to what was heading their way. "It's *dolphins!*" Carrie said, her voice taking on a tinge of excitement. "I can *see* them! Some of them are actually *leaping* out of the water!"

"Dolphins do that, honey," Melody said, standing between Kyle and Carrie, her gaze directed toward the sky at the approaching line of birds. The wild frantic cries of the gulls was more discernable now.

Kyle looked down at the water in their immediate vicinity. While the yacht was trotting along at a leisurely pace, he could see traces of movement in the ocean as fish of a variety of sizes zipped past. Could fish swim that fast? Kyle wasn't sure, but he was astounded by the activity broiling around them. It seemed that every form of aquatic sea life was in a mad rush to escape whatever was heading their way. He heard a loud braying honk. Turning in the direction of the sound, he sighted a large black hump rising out of the water—a whale. It vanished beneath the surface again, swimming fast.

"I really think we need to get the hell out of here," Kyle said, hating the panic in his voice.

Hank set his binoculars down. His features were grave, his blue eyes showing a hint of fear and worry. "I think you're right, hombre." He handed his binoculars to Melody and dashed toward the ladder that led to the upper deck. "Carrie, I need you and Melody to tighten our belongings below deck! Kyle, get those reels in now!"

Kyle didn't have to be told twice. He reached for the rod—Hank's fiberglass Pinnacle—and began to reel the line in. Melody and Carrie set the binoculars down and scampered back below deck. A moment later Kyle felt the motor of the yacht rev up. The nose tipped back at a slightly higher angle as the thrust of the engines propelled them forward much faster just as the birds began flying over them.

Their frantic cries were deafening, a sea of clamor that mirrored the sea they were flying over. Kyle got the first line up quickly, noting that the bait of shrimp Hank used had gone unmolested. He grabbed his own rod and began to reel that one in.

Kyle didn't know shit about boats. He had a feeling that large ocean cruisers could go at a much faster speed than the yacht Hank was currently piloting. He was pretty sure they could reach speeds of fifty miles an hour or more—or whatever the equivalent was in knots. He had no idea how fast they were traveling now, but they had to go faster. The birds were passing them quickly. Kyle got his line up, then grabbed both fishing poles. He looked out at the ocean and gasped in terror at what he saw.

He didn't need the binoculars to see they were drawing closer. In addition to dolphins, there were other fish big and small as well as whales, porpoises and what looked to be like sailfish and swordfish. And was that a shark? The ocean was now alive with the activity of fish and other aquatic life swimming quickly past them, some completely overtaking the boat. The bigger fish definitely had the advantage of speed. Kyle took a quick look around, his heart hammering, then glanced ahead at what was gaining on them.

The first wave was less than two thousand feet away and rapidly catching up. A whale leaped through the air and splashed back into the water. Great foams of water crashed over the other creatures. A dolphin leaped through the air, flinging itself like a missile. Kyle was transfixed by the scene. Dolphins don't leap out of the water with that much strength! It was almost as if they were in a mad dash to escape from something that was chasing them.

Amid the mad cries of the birds and the sounds of the fish swimming by the boat, there was another sound that Kyle couldn't place at first. The ocean was in turmoil, the foamy sea seeming to boil in a solid mass toward them. Kyle looked around at the ocean and his heart stopped as he saw a foam of red settling in the water. Blood?

"Oh shit!" Kyle breathed. He stared wide-eyed at the back end of a dolphin, its tail floating about fifty yards from the boat. Something had cut it cleanly in two. The engine's rudder? Impossible!

From the upper deck where Hank was at the wheel, he yelled out. "Jesus Christ, what the fuck is going on? These goddamn things are swimming past us!"

The wave of sound that was riding the ocean suddenly became more discernable to Kyle. In a way, it sounded like thousands of castanets clicking together. Just a constant unsynchronized *Click-click, Click-click, Click-click!*

A splash of red caught his eye and Kyle glanced to the left. A fish leaped in the air twenty feet away, half of its body sheared completely off. A giant lobster claw the size of a table crashed into the water amid the blood. From beneath the surface of the ocean, Kyle saw another gigantic claw snap shut over a large yellowfish tuna. Kyle gasped as he took in the size of the creature through the brief glimpse—it had to be the size of a small fishing boat!

It was obvious what everything was fleeing from. There were literally thousands of these things in the ocean!

*CLICK-CLICK, CLICK-CLICK, CLICK-CLICK!*

Kyle could feel the boat going faster, but it wasn't fast enough. He grabbed both pairs of binoculars by their straps with one hand, grabbed the fishing rods with the other and took one last look just as something else leaped out of the ocean in a mad attempt at escape from the frenzied horde below.

Kyle gasped, frozen in terror at what was flying toward him. It was a Great White Shark over twenty feet long and it had launched itself out of the ocean!

"Oh fuck!" Kyle screamed.

Luckily he didn't feel pain as it slammed into him mouth first and plowed into the rear deck of the yacht. Kyle was killed instantly.

His sister Carrie, her boyfriend Hank, and his girlfriend Melody weren't so lucky.

*Southern California Marine Institute, Long Beach, California*

Dr. Alfred Post examined the shattered remains of the creature that had been transported from Huntington Beach earlier in the morning, his features grim.

He was safely ensconced in his lab with the best equipment in his field. To access the lab, one had to have a special security-coded badge. The only people who had access was Dr. Post, his colleague Dr. Pete Brunner, and three lab assistants—Julie Hawthorne, Dan Collins, and Chelsea King. Dr. Brunner was down south along the Baja coast with Dan and another marine biologist from Monterey doing studies on the long-term affects of oil drilling off the California coast. That left Dr. Post alone with Julie and Chelsea. Both women hated each other. Their disdain for each other affected their work so much that Alfred had thought of firing one of them just so he could have some cooperation. Chelsea was a good kid; he could tell she clearly loved the field and wanted only to contribute to it. Julie, on the other hand, was in it for the glory of getting the college credits. Julie was a junior at Long Beach State majoring in marine biology. Alfred had no idea why she'd chosen this field as a major. The girl clearly had no passion for it, much less aptitude.

As a result, Julie thought Chelsea was a kiss-ass and that she was sleeping with Alfred, Pete, and Dan, which was impossible. Pete was gay and was infatuated with Dan, who was clearly straight and was as oblivious to Pete's homosexuality as Chelsea was. While no complete dummy, Pete was clearly as clueless as Chelsea was in a lot of things. They'd make a great couple.

Al pursed his lips in contemplation, looking down at the remains before him.

Dissected on the stainless steel table before him lay the body of the specimen delivered to his lab last night. Al had gotten the call last night at home that it would be transported to him, and rather than have it delivered at his office at Long Beach State, he'd directed the animal control warden to have it delivered to the Institute, which was situated between San Pedro and Long Beach proper, on a man-made island close to the Port of Los Angeles. Chelsea had checked the specimen in and had called him at home last night around ten-thirty. "You gotta see this thing Dr. Post! It's frickin' weird!"

Alfred had been enjoying a glass of wine with his wife, Janice, on the veranda of his friend Manuel Diaz's home in Palos Verdes. Manny owned a communications company that specialized in marketing and corporate communications— direct mail, email lists, the works. Al and Christine loved spending time with Manny, who was twice divorced and currently single, the father of two adult daughters. Manny had a sunny disposition that never failed to brighten Al's day. "The reason I like spending so much time with you is because your happiness rubs off on me," he always told Manny with a laugh.

The specimen on the table resembled a cross between a *Homarus americanus* and a *Hadrurus arizonensis*. It had arrived at his lab with several gunshot wounds to the back of its thorax, which had shattered its hard shell, the bullet fragments completely destroying its heart; the accompanying report stated the creature had taken several rounds from a police standard-issue .45 caliber handgun, which had initially done no harm. It had the round fired from an M16 semi-automatic rifle that had finally killed the thing. Amazing when you stopped to consider it. It's shell had been powerful enough to withstand multiple rounds from a .45 caliber handgun.

Al had performed a necropsy on the animal, first donning the necessary protective gear that was required when dealing with previously unknown or unidentified specimens—latex gloves, rubber vest and apron over the blue knee-length lab coat, surgical mask over his mouth and nose and a large, clear plastic face mask over his face. It was the first time he'd ever taken such extreme measures during a necropsy, but the guidelines at the Southern California Marine Institute were clear—when working with previously unknown species, all personnel who came in contact with the specimen were to use extreme caution at all times and were to wear the necessary protective gear. In hindsight, the guidelines were a good thing—they saved his ass after the specimen was brought in.

The necropsy started out normal. After starting audio and video recording to capture the necropsy, Al started by making a diagonal slit down the soft underbelly of the abdomen, slipping his fingers past the exoskeleton and gently pulling it apart. As he worked, he narrated his findings. Internally, the creature had the same physiological make-up as a common-day scorpion or lobster. As Al removed organs and set them aside for further testing and weighing, he noted several key differences.

For one, the creature possessed both gills and lungs. Second, its claws were considerably stronger and heavier than those of a common North American Lobster of similar size. The serrated pincers were beautiful, in a way—tinted with a delicate crisscross pattern of red and magenta, deepening to a thick, almost obsidian shade of black at the tips. Alfred took density tests of both claws, then amputated the limbs from the thorax, which was harder than he'd originally thought. He wound up having to use a pair of heavy duty shears, like the kind used to cut through rib cages, just to cut through the heavy cartilage and exoskeleton. Once he had the limbs severed he set them aside for later study. He turned his attention to the tail.

When he pinned the tail back and prepared to cut into the lower portion of the thorax to get at the lower digestive tract and the reproductive organs, the body began to move. Al gasped and took an involuntary step back, almost colliding with the table behind him. His heart leaped into his chest as he watched the creature writhe on the table. The rear portion of the creature was moving more rapidly, and as Al watched he realized that what he was seeing was a result of post mortem nerve stimuli, which caused the muscles to spasm. A moment later the writhing movement slowed, then ceased altogether. With a relieved sigh, Dr. Post warily approached the table again and resumed his work.

Holding the tail end of the creature flat to the table, he continued to cut into the lower portion of the creature, revealing the lower intestine and bowel and reproductive area. Surprisingly, Al discovered the creature possessed both sexual organs, which wasn't normal for most lobster species he knew. He set this set of viscera aside for further tests, then turned his attention to what he presumed to be the poison sac, located at the base of the tail.

He removed the poison sac, set it aside, then turned his attention to the tail itself. Smoothing it out lengthwise on the table, he marveled at the size of the stinger—it was a good six inches long and as hard as steel. So far, from what he'd seen, the anatomy of its defense mechanism was very much like a common scorpion. With that in mind, Al set the blade of the scalpel at the base of the tail and began to slice downward toward the stinger.

He was halfway down when a yellowish liquid began to spurt from the tail and pool along the edge of the sheet of plastic the specimen had been laid on. Alfred paid it no mind; that's what the latex gloves were for. He recognized it as the creature's venom, which was unusual. In modern scorpions, the venom sac was located in the telson section of the tail, right at the base of the stinger. He paused for a moment, noting that the stinger on this specimen was positioned much differently than that of a scorpion. While the tail was segmented, the last piece—the telson in a normal scorpion—was not present. This meant the venom sac was located elsewhere, probably at the very base of the tail. He would have to root around in that area when he was finished slicing through the length of the tail and pay greater attention to that. Most likely venom was sent through the poison sac through a tube that ran lengthwise along the tail to the hypodermic-like stinger.

Dr. Post turned his attention to the stinger itself. He sliced carefully at the base of the stinger, sliced through the vein-like tube that delivered venom, then plucked the stinger free. He held it up to the light, noting the hollowed center. *My God, he thought. This thing is capable of delivering a huge dose of venom. Probably a good five ounces or more. I wonder what the toxicity rate is?*

On the heels of that thought, he noticed that his hands were growing warm.

Al frowned and brought his gloved hands up. They were slick with the creature's blood and other abdominal fluids, now bubbling and frothing intensely. With rising alarm, Al detected a faint odor beneath the surgical mask as his palms grew hotter. A second later, he felt the first sting of acid burn—like hot grease landing on your bare skin while standing at a stove. Al yelped and quickly tore both gloves off his hands and let them fall to the floor.

"Ahhh!" Al yelled. He backpedaled, crashed into the table behind him again, noting that the skin along the base of his left thumb was turning fiery red. The pain was a burning sensation but it started to fade immediately once the gloves came off. Likewise, the warmth that he'd felt along both hands—palms and the back of his hands and fingers—was starting to fade as well. He rushed over to the water station and washed his hands. Then he splashed water on his face guard, just as a precaution.

*Jesus Christ, what the hell?*

Al looked at the floor with wide-eyed amazement. The bubbling, frothing of the fluids on the gloves continued, culminating in a cauldron. They were melting.

*It's the venom,* he thought, his breath rising and falling fast. *My God, its venom is so toxic that it's—*

It wasn't impossible to come across a creature so toxic that having its venom touch the skin would cause a reaction. Certain snake venom had that capability. But to completely melt a pair of latex surgical gloves?

Alfred was overwhelmed. He needed assistance and he needed it ASAP. Stepping away from the shattered remains of the creature on the examination table, Al lifted his face mask, pulled down the surgical mask and picked up the phone on the wall near the locked door. He dialed a series of numbers and waited until the line was picked up on the other end. "Dr. Post here," he said. "We have a problem."

*Redondo Beach Pier, California*

Gary Goodman and John Hydo were playing games in Ted's Arcade halfway down the pier when Steve Watanabe peeled in. He was out of breath, eyes wide, tan features deathly pale. "Guys, you hear what's going on at Catalina Island?"

"No, and I don't care," Gary said. He was seated in the Rocket Launch game, intent on blowing the Evil Lord Balazar back to the galaxy he came from. He was only two levels away from reaching the Zenith level, which would blast him into a completely different stratosphere. "Fuck off."

"Those weird lobster things that killed those people in Huntington Beach last night ate some chick on Catalina!" Steve exclaimed.

Gary turned to Steve and he saw that everybody within earshot had also heard the news. Whatever games kids were playing were now abandoned as John leaned forward.

"What happened, where'd you hear this?"

"On the radio!" Steve said. "KROQ broke in to an announcement. They're closing the beaches!"

"Closing the beaches?" Somebody else exclaimed.

The news Steve had delivered echoed around the arcade and within moments the entire place was buzzing with the news and the atmosphere darkened. Gone were the high-pitched catcalls, the excited talk, the jabber of friends. Now the mood had changed. It was not unlike the mood immediately after the terrorist attacks on September 11, 2001. Or so Gary had heard. He'd been only five years old when that happened, but he remembered his mother picking him up from day care early that afternoon. He remembered the look on her face, the mood of the day care aides, the teachers, the other parents.

It was very much like this.

*Something big is happening,* Gary thought. *It's like the end of the world or something.*

He climbed out of the driver's seat of the Rocket Launcher and joined his friends in learning what was happening on Catalina Island. Minutes later, when a swarm of Clickers scrambled over the beach and onto the pier, Gary found out how right he had been.

# THREE

*San Francisco, California*

The oddest thing about the job, Michele McKenzie thought to herself as she walked down the brightly lit corridor, was how normal everything seemed. Anyone wandering in from the street would have encountered just another non-descript office building with an aesthetically pleasing proper lobby and a chipper receptionist. They would have noticed the security cameras on the wall, perhaps, or the curious symbol inlaid on the lobby's tile floor. But what they wouldn't have known is that there were safeguards around the building. Indeed, most would have found themselves unable to enter through the building's sidewalk-level revolving doors—not without saying the proper word or possessing the correct glyph. They would have never guessed that the symbol on the floor was a circle of protection, or that the perky receptionist was a master telepath and fourth level Adept, or that in addition to the security cameras, there were other—invisible—sentries monitoring their every move.

Ninety-nine percent of the world's population would have never known these things.

But ninety-nine percent of the world's population weren't working for Black Lodge—an international organization that worked for no one government or entity, and answered only to a higher power, protecting humanity from supernatural threats. Their origins began during World War One, but there were rumors that the organization had existed in another form much earlier. Indeed, some said that such legendary figures as the Three Wise Men of Biblical lore were early predecessors to Black Lodge. Shortly after the end of the Second World War, the group gained autonomy. Now they answered to no worldly authority. They operated in secret, spoken of only in the dark, conspiracy-ridden corners of the internet, or in the halls of power in various nation's capitals.

And now Michele was one of them. Granted, she was only a first level adept, and she was still in the midst of her ninety-day probationary period, but just to have made it this far was reason enough to be proud—and she was. They'd recruited her two weeks before she'd graduated from college (she'd been majoring in education). Michele learned that they had been aware of her abilities for years, and had been monitoring her. Once they explained everything, she said goodbye to thoughts of a career teaching elementary school and hadn't looked back. Now she worked in the Remote Viewing and Astral Projection Department.

Her shoes echoed on the tile floor. The fluorescent lights buzzed overhead. A dark-skinned man in a crisp black suit passed by her and nodded. Michele returned the greeting. She turned left and entered the break room. She bought a candy bar and a bottle of water from the vending machines, wolfed them down, and then proceeded back down the hall.

She passed by two more people—a man and a women—and overheard a snatch of conversation.

"...Clickers. We intercepted a call from a Doctor Alfred Post to his superiors, and then to the Department of the Interior. More reports are coming in hourly. President Genova has been made aware by now, but on this level, they don't know what they're dealing with."

"Surely the President has dreamed of them, at the very least? He's one of the Seven, across all levels. Many of his other selves would most likely have had experience with them."

"I don't know. We should just be grateful that in this reality, the Dark Ones became extinct thousands of years ago. Otherwise, it would be a lot worse. If they..."

Michele rounded a corner, and the voices faded. She frowned, wondering what they'd been discussing. Clickers? Levels? She hadn't seen anything about them in her employee manual. And what was all that about President Genova?

She'd forgotten about it by the time she reached her destination—a room at the end of the corridor. She knelt by a panel in the door and allowed her retina to be scanned. Then she entered a four-digit number and the door slid open with a hiss. Michele entered a dark, circular room. The only furnishings were seven black chairs, each one thickly upholstered with luxurious leather and facing back-to-back in a circle. Each of the chairs was hooked up to an array of cables which ran to a computer and printer in the corner. Runes and symbols covered the floor. Six of the chairs were occupied by her fellow employees. Each one appeared to be asleep, but Michele knew better. All of them had a number of leads and wires connected to their heads and fingertips.

Her supervisor, Clark Arroyo, stood by the computer, monitoring the data as it streamed across the monitor. With a click of the mouse, he switched to a different stream of data. Then he turned as Michele approached.

"I'm really sorry about being late," she said. "There was—"

"A lot of traffic on the bridge," he said, finishing her sentence.

"It made the news?"

"No." Clark smiled. "It's on the surface of your thoughts. No worries, Michele. I'm just glad you're here. We've got a busy shift ahead of us. Morgan is monitoring some current events occurring deep beneath the surface of Mars. Thompson is spying on the Kwan, and it's taxing his abilities, I'm afraid. James is observing a ritual being conducted in Brazil. Colbert is currently eavesdropping on the White House. Atkins has the same duty, but at the Kremlin. And Abigail is, of course, on guard for breaches to this level."

"Wow. You weren't kidding. We are busy."

Clark nodded. "Luckily, this isn't the organization's only remote viewing site."

Michele slid into her seat and Clark began to attach wires to her.

"So what am I doing tonight, sir?"

"Walden, Virginia. I want you to focus on a guy there

that's been giving us some trouble lately. His name is Dez. I have a photograph you can use to focus. He's—"

And that was when Abigail began to scream. Her eyes snapped open, wide but unseeing anything in the room. Her attention was focused on something far away. Her fingers dug into the plush arms of the chair with such force that her fingernails pierced the leather. Her lips pulled back in a snarl, exposing gums and teeth. Spittle flew from her open mouth and mucous ran from her nose. The woman's body began to jerk and twitch.

"She's having a seizure," Michele cried. "We've got to get her out of that chair."

"Don't touch her!" Clark rushed to Abigail's side and pulled a digital voice recorder from his pocket.

"But, Mr. Arroyo—"

"Stay back, Michele. That's an order. She's still viewing. We pull her out of it now and we could kill her."

*We might kill her anyway,* Michele thought. She stood there, not knowing what to do and feeling helpless and scared. Her fellow remote viewers all remained in their trance-like states, oblivious to what was occurring next to them.

"What do you see, Abigail?" Clark turned on the recorder and held it next to the spasmodic girl's mouth. "What's happening? Remember your training."

"T-they're…c-coming through!"

"Who? Who is coming through?"

"T-the…the…oh my God, they've breached the Void. They're coming through…the Siqqusim…they who…speak from the head…Ob, the Obot…they're here, Mr. Arroyo. The Siqqusim are here!"

Michele had no idea what Abigail was talking about, but it had an obvious effect on her supervisor. Clark's complexion turned gray, and his shoulders slumped. His body sagged for a moment as if he'd had the wind knocked out of him. The digital recorder shook in his trembling hand. When he glanced at Michele, she saw that he was visibly shaken.

"Oh no," he whispered. He grabbed Abigail's shoulders, shaking her hard, despite the convulsions already wracking her body. "Are you sure, Abigail? Are you absolutely certain it's them?"

Instead of answering him, Abigail made a choking cry. Her head slammed against the back of the chair hard enough to rock it, even though it was bolted to the floor. Blood streamed from her eyes, nose, mouth and ears. More of it pooled on the seat beneath her. Her complexion turned red, then purple.

"Get her out of there," Michele screamed. "Please…"

A huge gout of blood flew from Abigail's mouth, splashing Clark in the face. More of it flew across the room to splatter on the wall and computer console. Clark retched. Both Michele and Abigail shrieked. Then Abigail went limp.

Wiping the blood from his eyes, Clark checked the woman's pulse.

Michele gaped. "Is she?"

He nodded. "She is. Find me a weapon."

"W-what?"

"A weapon. A gun. A fire extinguisher. A broom handle. It doesn't matter what. Anything I can use to bash her head in before she comes back."

"I don't understand, sir. She's dead. Why would you want to—"

"Never mind," he snapped. "I'll do it myself. Call security. Right now! Tell them we have a Code Zulu. Do you understand?"

Nodding, Michele hurried across the room and reached for the phone. Behind her, she heard the door hiss open as Clark ran out into the hallway. She quickly consulted a list of extensions hanging on the wall next to the phone and then dialed a number.

"Security." The voice on the other end of the line was crisp and quick.

Michele gave them her location and a summary of the situation. Before she could say more, the line went dead.

"I hope that means they're coming," she muttered.

*"Oh, they are coming."*

Michele jumped, startled. She turned to Abigail, who was sitting up and staring at her. The injured woman grinned.

Blood dribbled down her chin and matted her long blonde hair.

"Abby? Oh my God, are you okay? We thought you were dead!"

*"Abigail is dead, you fool."*

Frowning, Michele slowly hung up the phone. Something was wrong here. First of all, Clark had insisted that Abigail had been dead. Was it possible he'd been wrong? Secondly, there was something wrong with her voice. She sounded like Abigail, and yet, she also sounded like someone—or something—else.

"Abby. Abigail. Listen. You should lie back until help arrives. Mr. Arroyo—"

*"You stupid slab of meat. I told you that Abigail is dead. My name is Ob. Ob, the Obot."*

"I'm sorry…?"

Abigail sighed. *"Why is it that your kind no longer remember us? No matter how many Earths we destroy, it's the same on each one. We are forgotten among your kind. We are nothing more than legends now."*

"Who? Abby, I don't understand what you're talking about. You've been hurt. You're confused. You saw something during your session. I don't know what."

*"We are the Siqqusim. We are the abominations that speak from the head. Your kind used to call us demons and djinn. You thought we were spirits of the dead, but we are not. We are among the oldest things in your universe. We existed long before Michael and Lucifer chose sides with their 'angels.' They were nothing more than inferior versions of us. We were banished long ago, banished to the Void by the one you call God. But we have returned. Now is the time of the Oberim, what you call 'the Rising.' We have laid waste to a dozen versions of your Earth before this. Now it is your Earth's turn. So many of my brethren wait for release. Our number is more than the stars. More than infinity."*

Abigail removed the wires and leads connected to her and slowly rose from the chair. She stretched out her arms and looked at them, as if seeing them for the first time. Then she put her hands on her hips and wriggled back and forth.

*"Yes,"* she said. *"This body will suffice, for now."*

"What are you doing?" Michele backed up against the wall.

*"I told you. My brethren wait at the threshold. I must get about the business of finding them hosts. We are free to walk the levels again, as we did long ago. As your kind dies, we replace you here. When your spirit departs, we enter your bodies. We reside in your brain. We control your flesh. But to do that, you have to die. And so, without further ado…"*

Abigail circled the other remote viewers, studying each of them. She paused in front of Thompson. Then she leaned forward, as if to kiss him.

*"A search of my host's memories tell me that this man is named Thompson. Did you know the one you call Abigail had a crush on him? Probably not, nor does it matter. What does matter is that according to her memories, this Thompson is monitoring a renegade occult group known as the Kwan. I have interest in them, so we'll start with Thompson first."*

Then Abigail leaned even closer, undid the top buttons of Thompson's shirt, opened her mouth, and bit into his throat. Thompson immediately came out of his trance. His eyes snapped open. He tried to scream, tried to sit upright, but when he did, Abigail shook her head like a dog and his throat ripped free. Shreds of flesh hung from Abigail's crimson mouth. Blood jetted from Thompson's throat. He clawed at the wound with his fingers and more blood sprayed between them in geysers, showering both Abigail and himself. Laughing, Abigail raised his arms, turned her face to the flow, and bathed in the gore. Then Thompson slumped over, dead.

Michele screamed, but Abigail ignored her. Michele glanced around for something to defend herself with, saw nothing, and opted to escape instead. She ran for the door as Abigail opened Morgan's throat in a similar manner.

*"Where are you going, Michele? Don't worry. Stick around. I'll be with you in just a moment."*

Still screaming, Michele dived for the controls to the door. Before she could jab the button, the door opened from the outside, and Clark dashed into the room, holding a fire extinguisher over his head. He slid to a halt, gaping at the carnage taking place. As he and Michele watched, Thompson and Morgan's corpses sat up and ripped the wires from their bodies, while Abigail killed Colbert and Atkins.

*"Hail, Lord Ob,"* Thompson croaked, raising his hand in greeting. *"I await your orders."*

*"Engastrimathos,"* Morgan said. *"Du aba paren tares! Hail!"*

*"Welcome brothers,"* Abigail roared. *"We are in the base of operations for a division of Black Lodge. You know what to do."*

"The hell you will," Clark said. He charged at them, extinguisher held high, and tried to bash Abigail in the head. She ducked the blow and stepped to the side. Morgan backhanded Clark, knocking him off his feet, and leaving a bright-red handprint on the supervisor's face. As Clark toppled to the floor, the newly resurrected Colbert climbed out of his seat and picked up the fire extinguisher.

*"Kill that one,"* Abigail told Colbert, pointing at Clark.

*"Lord,"* Thompson said, *"my host body was conducting psychic surveillance on the Kwan. I have their location."*

*"Excellent,"* Abigail replied. *"We will need to target them next, as well as Genova and the rest of the Seven, Levi Stoltzfus, all divisions of Black Lodge, and anyone else who might disrupt our destruction of this level. As always, if we destroy them first, this world will fall just like the others."*

While the others talked, Colbert squeezed the handle on the fire extinguisher and blasted Clark in the face with a stream of foam. Sputtering, Clark crab-walked on his hands, trying to escape. The others surrounded him.

"Leave him alone," Michele shouted from the doorway. She was terrified and felt helpless and confused.

*"I'll see to the girl,"* Abigail said. *"The rest of you finish with this one. I know you are hungry, but remember to leave enough of him intact that the corpse has no mobility difficulties when it reanimates."*

Abigail took a step toward Michele. Michele backed out into the hall. The others began raining kicks and blows on

Clark. Just then, Michele heard booted footsteps thundering down the corridor. She turned to the right and saw a security detail bearing down on her. They were armed with rifles and wore black body armor and helmets.

"Move," they bellowed, shoving Michele aside, and charging into the room. "Down, down, down! Everyone down now."

*"More meat,"* Abigail laughed. *"Brothers, let us feast!"*

"Don't move," one of the security officers shouted.

The emergency response team ventured further into the room, and Michele backed down the hall until she could no longer see inside. A moment later there was gunfire, followed by screaming. The shots echoed loudly, making her ears ring, and the corridor filled up with smoke. More screams, and then Clark crawled out into the hall on his hands and knees. He glanced over his shoulder, back into the room, and his eyes widened.

"They're Siqqusim. You've got to shoot them in the head, god damn it. The head! Center of mass shots won't work."

Another round of staccato gunfire greeted this, followed by more shrieks and then a terrible, cruel laughter.

*"Look,"* Abigail called. *"Don't his intestines make a lovely necklace?"*

"Damn it," Clark yelled. "They are incorporeal spirits and reside in the brain of their host body. The only way to stop them is to destroy the brain. Shoot them in the fucking head!"

There was another short burst of gunfire, but then it was overwhelmed by shrieks and the sounds of tearing flesh.

"Mr. Arroyo," Michele called.

Clark turned to her, then jumped to his feet and rushed to her side.

"Come on." He grabbed her hand and pulled.

"Where are we going? What's happening in there, sir?"

Before he could answer her, one of the security men stumbled out into the hallway. Shrieking, he rolled around on the floor, clawing at his face. Michele noticed that his eyes and nose were missing.

Clark urged her forward, pushing and pulling until they

reached the lobby. He ran over to the receptionist.

"Seal the building. We've got a Class Zulu emergency."

"The entity, sir? Do we have a name?"

"More than one."

The receptionist blinked. "Pardon?"

"Siqqusim. We've got Siqqusim inside the fucking building."

"Oh my God…"

"That's right. Worse, Ob himself is here. Now seal the goddamn thing and alert the other divisions. Tell the council that I'm on my way to try to shut the door."

"Absolutely, Mr. Arroyo. Right away."

The receptionist simultaneously spoke into her headset and pressed some keys on her computer. Michele noticed that the woman's hands were severely trembling. That scared Michele more than anything else she'd witnessed. The receptionist was a fourth level adept. For her and Mr. Arroyo to be so afraid…

"Come on," Clark said, ushering her out onto the sidewalk.

The heat and sunlight felt strange on her face. People bustled by, oblivious to what was going on inside the building. They were clueless. Michele knew how they felt.

"I parked in the garage a block down," Clark said. "We'll have to hurry."

"Where are we going?" Michele asked.

Clark paused, as if thinking about it. "I'm not sure, yet. Mount Shasta or Bodega Bay. Whichever is closer. I'll find out once we reach my car and turn on the GPS. If it's still working."

"Why wouldn't it be working?"

Clark turned to her. His expression was grave.

"Because, Michele, unless somebody acts quickly, civilization will begin to collapse within the next few hours. And that's just the beginning. Within a few short weeks— maybe even sooner if the Siqqusim have improved their methods—we'll be looking at the absolute certain extinction of every life form on Earth."

*The Pacific Basin*

Three hundred miles south of Fiji, the USS Sterling was moving at a north east trajectory heading toward Hawaii. First Lieutenant Dan Pearce noticed the blip on his radar screen and called out to Seaman Lance Fisher. "Got some unusual activity out there!" Meanwhile, a hundred feet above deck, Second Lieutenant Kerry Richards was the first to confirm visually what Lieutenant Pearce had just reported over the system. He couldn't tear his eyes off his binoculars. "What the hell is this shit?" he muttered.

One thousand miles east of Hawaii, Boatswain's Mate First Class Aaron Miller made visual confirmation of the phenomenon after Radioman Byron Mace made the announcement that there was a large mass of sea life barreling toward the ship.

The luxury cruiser Wild Grapes was currently on a tour of the South Pacific Islands and was hours from its first stop in Tahiti. As one of the largest luxury cruises in business, Miller didn't think the large mass of fleeing fish and other wildlife would pose much of a threat, but it was better to be safe than sorry. He put in a quick call to the luxury cruiser's Captain. "At the rate this mass of sea life is approaching, do you think you can veer a hundred nautical miles due south?"

The Captain replied. "Not without going wildly off course. What's the deal?"

"Check out the radar on screen two."

A moment later. "Oh shit."

Scattered around the Pacific were hundreds of buoys. Many were planted in cooperation with the governments of Australia, Japan, China, and the United States to monitor sea levels, help predict tsunamis, gauge ocean temperatures, and record the activity of sea life. Similar buoys were in place in the South Pacific, also planted in cooperation with various world governments. Starting in the north Pacific, the buoys began recording and transmitting activity to various scientific centers around the world. The activity was chaotic, unpredictable. One marine biologist stationed in Guam was convinced she was witnessing a malfunction in the equipment. Another in Hawaii could only sit by his machine in nervous anticipation, wondering what it all meant. Still another in Monterey, California deciphered the activity for what it was— something catastrophic was about to happen.

That scientist, Gerald Dunning, placed a call to his supervisor. "I'm getting increased readings of migration patterns all across the board," he said. "This isn't from the tsunami. Migratory patterns from the tsunami dissipated as expected about a week ago. This activity happened spontaneously and it appeared to start fifty miles from the epicenter of the earthquake from two weeks ago and is spreading outward. I anticipate the first wave to Hawaii in about four hours—"

"First wave?" his supervisor asked. "First wave of what?"

Gerald paused. "Well…I don't know. A mass beaching of fish, of whales possibly?"

"Is there any visual confirmation of any of this?"

"Absolutely. We have reports coming in from all over."

"But what's causing this? What's driving them?"

Gerald ran a hand through his hair. "I don't know, but I think we're about to find out."

*Ivory Coast*

A group of fishermen casting heavily-wound nets from the shore reeled back in horror as dozens of giant lobster-scorpion creatures crawled onto shore. As the creatures clicked their claws in a mad cacophony, the fishermen dropped their nets and ran screaming at the top of their lungs.

One of the fishermen had an infected foot. He'd cut it on a piece of coral only days before. He limped along behind his friends, who, overcome with terror, ignored his pleas for help. Those pleas turned to screams as a Clicker seized him with its claws and squeezed, cutting him in half. His upper torso fell to the sand. The last thing he saw was the monster looming above him, sucking the blood from his own severed legs.

Moments later, while the Clicker was still feeding, the dead fisherman opened his eyes and attacked it. His teeth shattered on the creature's hard shell, but that didn't deter him. Hissing, the Clicker tried to back away, but the dead man worked his fingers into a crack in the creatures shell, heedless of how the sharp edges flayed the skin from its hand. The corpse reached the soft meat beneath and burrowed deep. Then the predator became the prey.

*Cochin, India*

Along the coast, beach goers scrambled in fear up the beach as the Clickers moved inward. A few unlucky ones fell in the sand, barely having time to scream as the horde swept over them. Claws and tails lashed out, severing arms and legs, lopping off heads, and impaling bodies. The air was filled with shrieks and screams and tearing sounds—and the noise of the Clickers' claws clacking together.

One creature jabbed a young boy in the stomach. As the child wailed and screamed in pain, more Clickers scrambled onto shore. They began stuffing bits of boy-meat into their mandibles, ripping flesh off the child's body with their giant serrated claws even as the boy's abdomen began to swell and burst open from the highly venomous sting. The child's mother rushed forward and managed to tear her child free of the creatures and flee up the sand as they turned their carnivorous attentions to other prey. She collapsed behind a dune and clutched her bleeding child tight, moaning and shrieking. When the boy began to twitch and move, she assumed he was still alive.

She was wrong.

Her son sat up and bit into his mother's cheek, ripping the flesh from her face just as the Clickers had done to him only moments before.

*Rota, Spain*

A horde of Clickers emerged from the surf during the busiest part of the day. Hundreds of beach goers fled, creating a mad stampede as the creatures scuttled up the beach. Two teenagers who had been making out on a blanket and at first had been oblivious to everything else around them, broke their embrace in time to find one of the creatures looming over them. The boy had time to yell before the monster's segmented tail lashed forth, stabbing him in the chest with its stinger. The creature's tail pulsed, pumping venom through the appendage. The boy's eyes rolled back into his head, showing white. Both the pain and the pressure were incredible. He screamed as his body began to swell. He jittered on the sand as his skin began to sizzle and slough off him.

His girlfriend reached for him in an attempt to pull her lover away, but a second Clicker grabbed her with its claws, waving her back and forth in the air like a flag, before finally cutting her in half. Her innards and blood spilled and splashed against the creature's shell and then slid off onto the hot sand. The monster dropped her limp form and began to greedily slurp up her sizzling intestines and organs.

Then the girl began to move again. Her upper half crawled across the sand to her boyfriend, who was still alive and shivering from the pain as the venom coursed through his veins. He turned to her and gasped.

"I…love…you…"

"*Aw,*" the dead girl cooed. "*How sweet! I love you, too. Especially your eyes.*"

And then she gouged his eyeballs from his skull with her fingers and popped them into her mouth like oversized grapes.

"*Eww,*" the zombie rasped. "*That venom makes them taste funny.*"

The Clickers continued rushing ashore. Their size belied their speed. Each time the surf crashed into the shore, more of them emerged from the waves, scuttling after their prey. The foaming surf turned red, and the waves receded around dead bodies—that then began to move.

One car-sized Clicker found an elderly couple, who were having a hard time getting up amid the mad rush to flee. Two minutes later, the couple was reduced to bits of scattered flesh and gristle as the giant creature dined on their remains. The old man's severed head, cast aside by a Clicker and resting amidst some trash, opened its eyes and looked around. Frustrated with its lack of mobility, the head silently cursed in an ancient language.

*Cardigan, Wales*

Along the Welsh shore, a middle-aged balding man named Tim stood on the deserted beach. He'd come to the shore today to think, to ponder his latest career move. He had a cottage perched on a cliff high over the shore. However, he liked to sit on a rock twenty feet from the shore and let his mind wander. His career was in a standstill and he was unsure of what to do. He was so into his thoughts that he almost didn't see the Clickers come storming out of the ocean. When they did, they swarmed over the man and reduced him to a pile of bubbling flesh from their highly toxic stings, making it easier for them to scoop their bloody congealed meal into their beaked mandibles.

Tim did not reanimate, for there was nothing left of his body to come back.

The sea churned as yet more of the creatures surfaced. The smallest was the size of a sheep. The biggest was nearly three-stories tall. Seawater streamed off its carapace. It clutched the carcass of a marlin in its pincers. The dead fish flapped and struggled, trying to get away.

*San Francisco, California*

The battle between the living and the dead inside the Black Lodge building raged for just under an hour. Ob and his fellow Siqqusim made quick, violent work of the security detail. Once the initial commandos inside the Remote Viewing room were dead, their bodies were possessed, just as Abigail and the others had been. The difference was that these Siqqusim now had weapons and armor. They poured out into the hallway and cut down a second emergency response team that had just converged on the scene. Adding to their numbers and weaponry, they then made their way through the building, floor by floor, exterminating every living being—from the Black Lodge operatives who fought or fled to the aquarium full of fish they discovered in one office. As each one died, they rose again, a host shell for another Siqqusim.

The slaughter continued. Throats were slashed, cut or torn out. Veins were opened. Limbs were severed, and then used as weapons to beat other humans to death. Using a letter opener, Ob sliced open the belly of a victim and strangled her with her own intestines. Moments later, when the corpse reanimated, it tore the innards free so they wouldn't hamper its mobility. The zombies killed—and fed. It wasn't that they *needed* to eat—at least, not while in their spiritual form. But still, they needed energy, and when they took over these empty corpses, that energy was drawn from food. Eating the living served three purposes. First, it was an affront upon the Creator, who had banished them to the Void eons before. Secondly, it allowed them to convert the flesh to energy while in human form, even if their host body no longer had a digestive system, since their kind processed energy by a different method. Finally, it served as yet another way of killing humans, dispatching their souls so that another Siqqusim could take over the bodies.

The Black Lodge operatives fought back with weapons and more esoteric defenses. But while circles of protection and binding spells slowed the zombies down, and while explosive rounds and grenades destroyed their physical forms, the dead ultimately won the battle due to their sheer numbers. Only the destruction of a corpses' brain would successfully dispatch a Siqqusim, because that was where they resided. Blowing them up didn't work. Even with no legs or arms, they still proved determined and deadly. They moved and operated with a singular purpose—the extermination of every living soul.

And once they had succeeded, they poured out into the streets of the city, and began the slaughter all over again. Their numbers grew.

The scene was repeated slowly around the world. All across the globe, the dead began to rise. Felled by heart attacks or cancer or automobile accidents or murder, death was not the end. One by one, they rose again, and joined in the killing.

# FOUR

*Lancaster, Pennsylvania*

It was easier to call home by stealing some time from the late work day by slipping out of the conference room and making her way to her rental car where she could steal some time in privacy. Jeanette Sycheck cast her gaze out the windshield toward Hempfield Road where she was currently working with a client, listening as Rick's cell phone rang. He picked up on the fourth ring.

"Hey there!" he said.

"Hi!" Her mood instantly brightened. "So, how are things going?"

"Busy, as usual." She heard him set something aside in his office cubicle. Rick's day job office was in a cubicle in a secure room just off the computer room at Free State Insurance. He was one of three mainframe programmers in the Computer Operations department. His direct supervisor, Wally Green, typically worked out of the larger cubicle at the end of the room. Wally was a cool guy, but she knew if she called before lunch, Wally would demand to speak to Jeanette and would waste her time by telling her fart jokes. "How are things going over there?"

"Same old shit," she said. "I swear to God, the Controller of this company is such a raging idiot. Honestly, I don't understand how he got this job. Their programmer calls him a bobble-head. Did I tell you that?"

"Yeah, you did." Rick chuckled on the other end. "A thousand times."

"Sorry. I'm just tired of this assignment because of these people. They're complete idiots. And it's going to be another late night. It's already after five o'clock here, and I'm still stuck at work."

"Well it's only two more days, then you're coming home for a week."

"Yeah, that's true." Jeanette couldn't wait to work out of the house next week. After that it was two more weeks of being on site here in Amish country, then she was home with her family—and then they were going on vacation! They were driving up to Sequoia National Park to a resort for the week. All four of them had been looking forward to the getaway for months. "So how're the kids? And the dog?"

"Doing good. Princess misses you. The kids spent the night at their friends' last night, but I called them this morning from work. I told them I wanted them home by tomorrow night so we can pick you up at the airport. I thought maybe we could go out to dinner."

"That would be great!"

"So, have you heard about what's been going on at our beaches?"

"No, what?"

As Rick told her about the strange lobster-scorpion-crab creatures that attacked the night before in Huntington Beach and how other sightings had been reported from Portland, Oregon to Ensenada, Mexico, Jeanette listened with numbed shock, hardly believing it. *Surely this has to be some weird kind of joke, right? He's teasing me, pulling some kind of practical joke?* But she knew her husband better than that. Rick's demeanor and tone were utterly serious.

"I haven't heard anything about that," Jeanette said. "Though I've got to admit, I didn't watch much TV last night. Watched the news a little bit, then read a book for the rest of the night."

"You didn't take a dip in the pool?"

"No." Jeanette smiled. Rick knew that she loved to swim every night. She hardly dipped her toe in the water when she was traveling, but she made good use of their backyard pool at home every night the weather was good. " And came straight to work this morning. So again, not much time to watch the news."

As they talked, Jeanette opened her laptop, which she'd brought out to the car to kill time with in case Rick hadn't been home. After connecting to the company's wireless network, she double-clicked on her internet browser, and then checked the news.

"Oh my God," she said.

"What?" Rick asked. "Everything okay?"

"Yeah, I just went online to see if I could find the reports."

"And did you?"

"Yeah, I see something here about it, but that's not the top story."

Rick made a clucking noise. "What can possibly top giant lobster-scorpion-crab hybrids?"

"There's a riot going on in San Francisco. Some kind of mass shooting, but with multiple suspects and spread out across the city."

"You mean like when those terrorists shot up Mumbai, India a few years ago?"

"I don't know. The reports are pretty chaotic right now."

"Okay. Listen, I'm going to let you get back to work, and go watch the coverage for myself. Call me tonight before you go to sleep?"

She glanced toward the building and noted the time on the dashboard. "Yeah, I've got to get back. I'll call you from the hotel."

"Sounds good," Rick said. "I'll be here."

"Okay. Love you. Tell the kids I love them."

"I will. Love you, too."

After saying goodbye, Jeanette pressed the disconnect button and glanced back out the windshield. The late afternoon sun had burned hot, and even though it was dark now, the interior of the car was still roasting. She exited the vehicle, relieved to be out, then started to head back inside. She had to finish this database design, then she was knocking off early and heading back to the Holiday Inn. She'd be grateful to be back in the hotel room, where she could kick off her shoes and lay back on the bed. She felt...unsettled. She wasn't sure if it was just that she missed her family, or the stress of traveling for work, or the news reports of strange lobster-scorpion creatures back home and the killings in San Francisco. It was all just too weird.

Jeanette went back inside the building and entered the conference room. She said nothing as she sat back at her spot at the table and began resuming her work. Even though she put on the appearance of being the dutiful working bee, she found it hard to concentrate on her work and found herself opening a web browser and hitting refresh on the search terms on the sea creatures to see if anything new popped up.

Within a half hour, there were so many reports that her browser locked up.

An hour later, the internet went down and the lights flickered.

Outside the building, a distant fire siren began to wail. A few minutes later, three police cars raced by, lights blaring.

Jeanette wondered what was going on.

*Gardena, California*

The house on Avalon and One Hundred and Eighty-first Street was filled to capacity. Joker found a place to park around the corner; he'd switched out his classic ride with something more conspicuous—a late model silver Toyota Tercel, cut normal. He'd also dressed down, like a normal citizen, in blue jeans and a tan polo shirt. Only his decorative tattoos and his look gave him away.

After a quick meal at Lucy's, where Sparky got a taste of that *carne asada* he'd grown to miss while a resident of Arizona, they'd headed down the Harbor Freeway toward Gardena. They'd made small talk. Sparky had been a little surprised to learn that Joker had a cache of weapons in the trunk, everything from fully automatic rifles, clips, and hundreds of rounds of ammunition, to hand grenades. He was carrying a 9 mm handgun—it lay on the console between the front bucket seats. "I got a piece for you too, homie," Joker had said, indicating the glove compartment with a nod. Sparky had checked. Sure enough, a black semi-automatic handgun had lain in the glove compartment. It looked brand new.

Sparky recognized a few familiar faces in the house, all rivals—from Tortilla Flats, Redondo Beach Trese, Lomita Mafia, Los Compadres, Lawndale and Hawthorne Trese, San Pedro Locos, and other South Bay crews. Sparky had asked Joker why Venice was included in this meeting. All the gang bangers assembled here were from the outlying communities of the South Bay and Long Beach. Wouldn't it have made sense to fall in with crews from Santa Monica and the West side? Joker had shrugged. "I don't make the rules, homie, I just follow them."

Sparky and Joker found places to lounge near the front door. The sofas and chairs were all taken. Other homies stood around, huddled in small groups. Most were dressed down, and the average age of everybody assembled was wide ranging, from late teens to late thirties. Sparky glanced at his watch. It was eight-thirty. It would be fully dark in another thirty minutes.

A short, thin man dressed in tan slacks a striped polo shirt with slicked back black hair addressed the crowd. "Okay, listen up."

All conversation stopped. The short thin man nodded once as all attention turned to him. "I won't keep you here long because we don't have much time. You are all here because you've been selected by your leaders as being loyal and trustworthy. This is what we're looking for, and you all know about our current struggle. With your help, we are going to turn things around drastically tonight."

Tonight? Sparky thought.

The thin man continued. "Many of you know me from past meetings, but others of you don't. I am Emilio Hernandez, from the Hernandez family." Sparky nodded in recognition, as did several others. The Hernandez family was one of half a dozen interconnected Los Angeles area families who comprised the Mexican Mafia, an organization that went back to the 1940's. "Other meetings are taking place in four other locations across Southern California. We also have gatherings in San Francisco, Chicago, Dallas and El Paso, Texas, Phoenix, and in various locations on the east coast. I will say that most of the concentration is here, in the southwest. Where our status is under the most threat."

Whispered murmurs erupted. Emilio raised his hands again for silence. "LAPD is strapped thin. You know that from the past five years as your foot soldiers took our first series of orders. Those orders have been carried out perfectly and have played just the way we want. This is why you have been called here tonight, to carry out part two in our mission."

Outside, the sound of a police siren. It rose to a screaming crescendo and was joined by others from other directions. Everybody was silent as the sirens drew closer—to Sparky, it sounded like they were barreling somewhere down Avalon, maybe even down Normandie Avenue—then began to fade as they headed for their destination.

"Okay, real quick then," Emilio said, with a humorous grin, "before the next one comes for our asses."

Scattered laughter at this. It broke the ice.

"Tonight we hit Crip and Blood safe houses," Emilio said. "I'm splitting you up in teams of seven. Blanca has detailed maps and locations for each of you." At the mention of Blanca, a woman Sparky hadn't noticed before stepped up bearing several file folders. She was a looker—shoulder-length dark brown hair, ruby lips, shapely figure, nice cantaloupes. She looked like she'd just gotten off work as a secretary at some office. Despite her dress code, her make-up was a dead-giveaway—she was a veteran of the streets all the way. "Only two of you will be paired up with rival homies and you'll be hitting their turf." Ernie glanced in he and Joker's direction. "Doc has already dispatched four of your homies to another meeting taking place in Santa Monica. We needed the numbers in the South Bay. Dig?"

Joker nodded. "It's cool, homes."

Sparky nodded too, but he couldn't help but feel a little disconcerted at Emilio's gaze, the way he'd casually addressed them. The son of a bitch knew who they were!

"Everybody got the required hardware?"

Assorted nods and acknowledgements. Joker nodded.

That explained all the weapons in the trunk of the Toyota.

"When you leave here, you're to go to the first location on the route Blanca has mapped out. I suggest you familiarize yourself with your routes before you leave. Each group will travel in a minimum of two vehicles. Sparky and Joker from Venice? I'm having Midget from Gardena Trese ride with you to be your navigator. The three of you will be paired up with Josie and El Gato from San Pedro, and Cyclone from T-Flats. El Gordo and Psycho from Harbor City? You guys are being paired up with…"

It didn't take long for Emilio to pair everybody up. Sparky had to hand it to the guy. When the Mexican Mafia gave orders, they got right down to business. As Emilio paired them up, his recitation of groups and territories by memory, Blanca handed out the folders to each group. A short, wiry dude with a shaved head and the slinking approach of an alley cat joined Sparky and Joker—this was obviously Midget— and began consulting the print-outs Blanca had handed them. Four other homies also joined them, all casually dressed. Sparky acknowledged them quickly with nods, then turned his attention to the computer-printout map Midget and Joker were consulting with the others. Blanca had highlighted four locations for their territory, with the first one in Lomita, the second in San Pedro right on the edge of Sunken City. The other two were in north Long Beach, solid Crip territory.

"Damn, so we're like, doing this shit tonight, then?" Sparky whispered, mostly to himself.

Joker, Midget, and the others looked at him. "This is it, man," Joker said. "The beginning of the ride for all of us. This is what you been training for."

Sparky nodded. "I know, man. Just didn't think it would be so soon."

One of the homies in his group, dressed in tan khakis and a tan polo shirt, his head bullet-shaped, nodded. "I hear you homes. These marching orders are quick, but marching orders is marching orders."

"I hear you," Sparky said, nodding. It was best not to discuss this anymore. He didn't want to give his team the false impression that he was against this. He was just surprised it was happening so quickly.

"Okay, listen up, people!" Emilio was calling for attention. He stood in the center of the throng, hands held up for silence. "Everybody has their maps. If you finish, destroy the maps. Dump 'em in the trash, burn 'em, whatever. Report back to your home turf and lay low. Your leaders will report back to me. If any of you are caught by the police, you know the drill. You encounter women and children in these locations and they get hit, not our problem. You recognize any players, they're fair game. Ideally, you should be in and out within one minute. Questions?"

"So if we finish, we just head back to our hoods?" This from a light-skinned man in black jeans and a white shirt standing with a throng of men from the beach communities.

"Si. All told, if the cops don't pick you up, this should only take you two hours tops."

"Cops'll be pissing all over themselves once this shit starts," Joker said. He was grinning. "And with all this shit happening all over the fucking place, at the same time? Shit!"

"You got it, homie," Emilio said. He nodded and winked at Joker and Sparky, then turned to the rest of the assembled group. "That's why we're hitting tonight. First work night after Fourth of July, less police activity, less cops. We're hitting when they least expect it."

Sparky nodded, feeling that old adrenaline rush come back. He grinned. It was time to step up to the plate. Time to fight for his homies, to take back what had been taken from them. To be a part of the big picture, the grand struggle.

A moment later, with addresses committed to memory and their group of seven ready, they filed out of the house with the others and headed out to do their part.

*San Pedro, California*

Jim awoke from his nap with a start, and at first, he wasn't sure where he was. He'd been dreaming that he was in some sort of bomb shelter, and somebody had kidnapped Danny.

He'd been unable to leave the bomb shelter because there were people waiting outside to kill him. The dream faded now, but he frowned, trying to remember if one of the killers had been Tammy.

Yawning, he got up off the couch, checked his email, and then walked down the street to the local coffee shop. He did this every day—a late-afternoon latte to wake him up from his regular power nap. He'd drink it on the way back to the apartment, and then call Tammy's house so he could tell Danny goodnight.

He slowed as he neared the coffee house. Two ambulances and several police cars were parked curbside in front of it. Their revolving dome lights flashed off the sides of the buildings. A crowd of customers, employees, and curious passerby stood outside the store, beyond a line of yellow police crime scene tape. Jim recognized one of the baristas—Kelli, a perky, exuberant Wisconsin native who had moved out here to be in show business and instead had ended up selling coffee. Jim liked the young woman. She always made him laugh. He approached Kelli and tapped her on the shoulder.

"Hey, Mr. Thurmond. What's up?"

"I was about to ask you the same thing."

"Oh, you know how the homeless are always using our restrooms? Well, one of them died inside the men's room. He was sitting on the toilet." Kelli's nose wrinkled in disgust.

"Just like Elvis, huh?"

She smiled at the joke. "I don't know if it was a heart attack or a drug overdose or what. The manager found him. Anyway, here's the kicker. Turns out the guy was dead. I saw it myself. He didn't have a pulse. But when the paramedics got here, one of them tilted his head back to clear his airway, and started to give him mouth to mouth. And all of the sudden, the homeless guy bit him!"

"Bit him?" Jim shuddered. "What was it? Some kind of reflex?"

Kelli shrugged. "Apparently, he just came back to life. Or maybe he was never dead after all. Maybe his pulse was just weak. Anyway, he chewed off half the paramedic's face, and then an off-duty cop shot him, and then we all got herded out here. Pretty weird, huh?"

"Yeah," Jim nodded. "That's pretty damned weird. Whole world is getting weird. Was just talking about that with my ex-wife this morning."

"It's nice that you two get along the way you do."

"Yes," Jim said. "It is. Speaking of which, I'd better give them a call. See you later."

Kelli raised her hand and waved. "Later, Mr. Thurmond."

Jim tried to call Tammy and Danny as he walked home, but his cell phone service was out. He had five bars, indicating a clear signal, but when he tried calling Tammy, the call didn't go through. At first, he thought that maybe it was her phone, so he tried calling his friend, Adam Senft, but the call to Adam's cell also didn't go through.

Scowling, Jim wondered what was going on.

*San Francisco, California*

"There's another one," Michele cried out as they rushed toward the Golden Gate Bridge in Clark's car.

Heeding her warning, Clark jerked the steering wheel, swerving out of the way as a dead homeless man ran out into the street, wielding a brick and trying to smash his way into passing cars. One of his ears dangled from the side of his face by a thin strand of gristle, and there were horrific gashes across his face and chest.

A second zombie charged out into the street several car lengths ahead of them. This one had terrible burns across most of its body. Charred clothing had merged with blackened flesh. The burned skin slipped off it in sheets with each step that the corpse took, but still the creature didn't slow. It clutched a handgun in one burned fist. As they watched, it opened fire on a taxi cab. The cab's passenger window shattered. The second shot caught the driver in the throat. The cab rolled to a halt, crashing into the car ahead of it. The zombie lurched forward and emptied the gun into the chest and abdomen of the passenger in the cab's back seat.

"Oh God," Michele moaned. "Oh my God, what is going on?"

"Just give me a minute," Clark urged. "Calm down. I'll get us out of this, but give me a few minutes to think."

The cab driver stumbled out of the vehicle, dead but moving. Grinning, it lumbered toward them. Without pausing, Clark stomped the accelerator and ran the zombie down. It bounced up over the hood of Clark's vehicle and then back onto the road. The car bumped and screeched as the rear tires ran over the attacker. Michele glanced behind them and saw the dead man stumbling to his feet. The zombie gave them the finger, then lurched off in search of easier prey.

The city's streets echoed with a cacophony of screams, gunshots, shattering glass, wailing alarms, and blaring car horns. The only silence was inside their car. Clark drove without speaking, focused on the task of weaving them in and out of traffic. They drove past a burning police car that had crashed through an intersection, plowing into a minivan. The van was on its side, and a horde of zombies had surrounded it and were menacing a family trapped inside. Tears welled up in Michele's eyes when she saw the panicked, horrified expressions on the faces of the four children and their parents.

"We should stop...do something..."

Clark stared straight ahead and gave the car more gas. They raced past the accident just as a few of the zombies turned toward them. Michele's gaze locked with the mother trapped in the minivan.

"We have to help them," she pleaded. "We can't just keep going."

Clark shook his head. His eyes didn't leave the road.

Michele fumed. "Doesn't it bother you?"

He opened his mouth to respond, but all that came out was a low, wounded moan. It was then that Michele noticed the tears on his cheeks.

"Of course it does." His voice broke—a hoarse, mournful whisper. "But we can save them, or we can save everyone. If we had stopped back there, we'd be dead. Now let me focus."

"I'm sorry..." She turned away and stared out the window,

wanting to close her eyes to the horrors around them, but afraid to do so.

They drove through Hell.

The traffic lights were blinking. Buildings burned. Broken fire hydrants spewed geysers of water and severed body parts littered the streets. Michele's gorge rose at the steaming piles of viscera and haphazardly strewn limbs. A man running from a zombie slipped in a pile of intestines, and plowed into the sidewalk. Stunned, he barely managed to regain his feet before the zombie reached him. He fled again, dragging one foot behind him. Both the man and the zombie left red footprints in their wake.

A man dressed in some sort of martial arts uniform and armed with a sword fought off three human zombies before a dozen undead rats swarmed him, climbing up his legs. He screamed, dropping the sword and beating at them with his hands. Sharp little teeth bit and chewed, gnawing his fingers to the bones. The man fled, but the rats held their grip. He sagged to the pavement and they went for his eyes and mouth, shredding his lips, eyelids, and nose. The head of one of the zombies he'd decapitated was still alert. It stared into Michele's eyes as they drove past.

The city echoed with chaos. Dead humans and animals ran riot, killing everything in their path. The living fought them—and each other. Clark slowed as they approached another intersection. A trolley car and a bus had collided. Black smoke belched from them both, and the air smelled of burned meat, even with the car windows closed. Clark blew the horn at the stopped cars in front of him.

"Shit. Come on, people. We can't just sit here."

"Mr. Arroyo?" Michele's eyes widened as she pointed out her window. "We need to go."

He turned to her and saw what she was pointing at. "Oh shit…"

A group of zombies converged on the intersection. A three-legged pit bull hobbled towards them, followed by nine human corpses, a dead cat, and another swarm of rats. Several of the zombies wielded weapons—lengths of pipe, butcher knives, a golf club, and a shovel. Behind them, several humans had been tied spread-eagled to a fruit-vendor's stand. The zombies had apparently been torturing them before Clark and Michele's arrival.

"Hang on," Clark said.

Michele gripped the door handle as he threw the car into reverse and stomped on the accelerator. Their rear bumper smashed into a mailbox on the curb. Then Clark dropped the transmission in drive again and floored it. The tires screeched as the car raced directly toward the horde. He smashed into the zombies, sending them careening into the building behind them. He made a hard left turn and swerved onto the sidewalk, then sped down the pavement. Michele's passenger door scraped against the side of the brick building next to them. Her side mirror snapped off. The car shuddered and bucked as they mowed down the dead. Then, once they were clear of the wreckage in the intersection, Clark whipped the car back into the street.

Michele didn't realize she'd been holding her breath until they reached the Golden Gate bridge. She exhaled, gasping. Ahead of them, traffic had once again slowed to a crawl. She glanced in the rearview mirror, but saw no sign of the zombies.

"Look down there." Clark pointed at the water far below. Dozens of large shapes could be glimpsed near the surface, swimming toward the shore. They were big enough to be easily visible despite the distance from the bridge.

"What are they?" Michele asked. "They don't look like whales."

"They're not. They're Clickers. More properly known as *Homarus Tyrannous*. They're sort of a cross between the *Megarachne Servinei* and the *Woodwardopterus*. They were supposed to have been extinct for the last two-hundred million years. There's been fossil evidence of them discovered in Greenland, Nova Scotia, and Scotland."

"Two-hundred million years? So they're dinosaurs?"

"No. Dinosaurs we could deal with. These are something else. I don't know much about them. I was briefed on them earlier today, but another division is handling the problem.

Apparently, wherever they've been hiding, that tsunami last week has stirred them up. But like I said, they're for somebody else to deal with. We've got more important problems."

"The zombies."

"Correct. The Siqqusim."

"But they're just here in the city, right?"

"No. What we just went through—what we just escaped from? It's spreading everywhere. The entire world will be like that by tomorrow morning."

"What do we do? How do we stop it?"

"Open the glove compartment."

Michele did as he asked while Clark alternated his attention between the traffic ahead of them and the ominous shapes in the water far below. She pulled out a small hardcover book, bound in black leather with gold foil embossing.

"That's one of your field manuals," Clark said. "It documents everything we know about the Thirteen. I'm supposed to wait until your probationary period is up before I give it to you, but…fuck it. Let's just say you've fast-tracked. Welcome to the team."

Michele was stunned. "Thank you, sir."

"Please, call me Clark. Michele, you've been doing great, but I'm really going to need your help in the task ahead. We've got a big job ahead of us. First thing I need to do is focus my energies for a while."

"You can meditate and drive at the same time?"

"Sure. Later—if there is a later—I can teach you how. It will be dark soon. In a little while, I'll answer all your questions about where we are going and what's happening. But first I need to focus for a bit. Turn my attention inward. So what I want you to do, in the meantime, is read the first few entries in that book. That will provide answers to some of your questions. Okay?"

She nodded, unable to disguise her eagerness to open the book.

Clark grinned. "Okay."

He fell silent, staring straight ahead. His eyes remained open and focused on the road, but his breathing slowed.

Once Michele was certain that he wouldn't drive them off the bridge, she turned her attention to the field manual and opened to the first page.

She began to read.

**TOP SECRET**
**EYES ONLY**

**G42-667-666-777-MU**

The following information is for Black Lodge operatives with a security classification of Adept or higher, to assist them in the field. Please note that sigils, binding rituals and banishing techniques are not included in this pamphlet. Only operatives with a security classification of Magus or higher shall have access to that information. The material contained herein is not to be disseminated with any other parties or persons, be they living or otherwise, under penalty of our laws, by order of Kaine.

**I.**
**WHO ARE THE THIRTEEN?**

In the beginning, the entity we know as God, Yahweh, Allah, and more (herein referred to as the Creator), whose true name is known only to a handful of people, created the heavens and the Earth. In order to create this new universe, He needed a lot of energy. So the Creator destroyed the universe that existed before ours, down to the very last atom, and utilized the harvested energies as building blocks. The old universe ceased to exist.

However, in addition to the Creator, there were thirteen other denizens of that previous universe who somehow escaped the destruction. These entities are collectively known to us as the Thirteen.

They are not gods or demons, though mankind and other races have often mistaken them for such. Indeed, they are often mistaken for the Devil, or are worshipped by servants who do not understand that the Thirteen will not hear their entreaties unless it somehow benefits their plans. They are not susceptible to all of the same magicks and supernatural laws that govern, banish or bind demons, angels, and other supernatural entities. Very specific magicks and rules must be used when confronting them. Most of these have been verified by a number of different sources, including copies of the *Daemonolateria* from both this level and others.

While it is folly to apply human logic and emotion to their motivations, the Thirteen seem to have one single-minded goal. They seek the total obliteration of everything the Creator has made. Perhaps it is revenge for His destruction of their old universe. Perhaps they seek to build a universe of their own— one in which they are in charge.

They will not stop until all of creation is destroyed.

That includes all of the Earths.

The universe is composed of different 'levels'. Some call these levels alternate realities. While string theory has scratched the surface of this, mankind, for the most part, remains woefully ignorant as to the vast extent of these levels. Just as there are different planets in the sky, there are also different versions of those planets, existing simultaneously on a different level of the universe. Beings, including some humans, can traverse this multiverse by means of something called The Labyrinth.

The Labyrinth is a dimensional shortcut through time and space. It is not actually a labyrinth, but that is how mankind perceives it, thus the name. Only a handful of humans know of its existence—madmen, magi, a few in the highest levels of government, and of course, operatives of Black Lodge. But the Thirteen know it well, and they use it to traverse the various levels of reality, and lay waste to creation.

Their methods are many—global floods, plaques, fires, the resurrection of the dead, planetary darkness, and a host of other means. Sometimes, they work together. Sometimes, they act alone. Once a planet is utterly destroyed, they move on to the next.

We do not know why the Creator has not taken steps to stop them. All we know is that their war rages unchecked. It is whispered that throughout the multiverse, there are seven individuals who can stand against them. Herein, they are collectively referred to as The Seven.

## II.
## OB

NAME: Ob
OTHER NAMES: Mictla-techuhtli. The Obot (see below)
TITLE: Lord of the Siqqusim
FIELD REPORT: Ob is the brother of Ab and Api. Most of Ob's other names are unknown. There is a possibility that the Obot serves as another name for this entity, but there has not been a definitive consensus on this.

Ob is the leader of an incorporeal race of beings known as the Siqqusim. We do not know if Ob created this race or if they were created by another, but he does command them. The Siqqusim have the ability to possess the dead bodies of major warm and cold-blooded life forms after the soul has departed, in effect, turning them into zombies.

Ob is mentioned seventeen times in the Old Testament (although one of these references, Job 32:19, is rather dubious). Ob is also mentioned in other texts of that era, and while the word Ob is a Hebrew term, it also shows up in Sumerian, Ugartitian,

Mesopotamian, Assyrian, Martian, and Reptilian texts as well.

Most scholars agree that the worship of Ob involved the act of necromancy, and the conjuration, consultation, and control of the dead. He is often mentioned in conjunction with engastrimythos, meaning "one who speaks from the head." It is said that Ob possessed King Niqmaddu III upon his death, and "spoke from his head."

One early Mesopotamian cult falsely believed that Ob referred to a group of spirits of the dead, rather than a singular entity. They used a series of spells, called gidim-hul, as necromantic rituals that could, in turn, conjure or expel the spirits of the dead. In this context, Ob was worshipped alongside Baal in Moab. Other cultures believed incorrectly that Ob was not an entity or group of entities at all, but rather, a location—the point of contact between our world and the realm of the dead. We know this to be false.

Eventually, singular worship of Ob changed into worship of the Siqqusim as a whole. Cults sprang up in Assyrian, Sumero-Akkadian, Mesopotamian, and the Ugaritic cultures. The entities were consulted by necromancers and soothsayers. It was at this point that the Creator banished the Siqqusim and their leader to a place called the Void, along with Ab and his Elilum, and Api and his Teraphim.

At some point, Ob gained temporary release from the Void and possessed the body of Lazarus, a close companion of Jesus Christ of Nazareth. Ob taunted Jesus, telling him that the Creator had released him from the Void in order to teach Jesus a lesson. However, there is some speculation that Ob may have been lying to the Nazarene. We do not yet know the reason for such a lie. Eventually, Ob was banished again to the Void. Secret worship of the Siqqusim continued into the Middle Ages.

Early in the Twenty-First century, on another

level other than our own reality, mankind managed to breach the Void by ripping open the walls of the Labyrinth with the use of an ion collider (we do not know if this was by accident or if there were more sinister forces at work). Ob and the Siqqusim, Ab and the Elilum, and Api and the Teraphim were released. They quickly ravaged the Earth of that level and have since moved on to other levels and other worlds. On one such Earth, Ob's plans were at least temporarily thwarted by two organized crime figures named Anthony Genova and Vincent Napoli. That Genova is the other universe's version of our Anthony Genova, the current President of the United States of America. Genova and Napoli's counterparts on other levels have encountered supernatural creatures, as well. We know that on all levels, Genova is one of The Seven. He is unaware of this, and is also unaware that we are monitoring him and the other six.

The field manual went on to talk about other beings— Ob's brothers, Ab and Api, a creature known as Leviathan, and many others. When she was finished reading, Michele closed the book on her lap and glanced over at Clark. He still seemed to be in a trance. She noticed that they had left the bridge and were now on the highway. The GPS was silent. She considered turning on the radio, but was afraid to disturb her superior. Instead, she sat patiently, terrified of what might happen next.

"I should have stayed in college," she mumbled, staring out the window as the landscape rushed by. "Elementary school teachers don't have to deal with things like this."

# FIVE

*Washington D.C.*

At the White House, President Anthony Genova was getting briefed by his Secretary of Defense Melissa Peterson. Until today, President Genova—Tony to his friends—had been filled with a sense of pride at his administration. Not only was he the first Italian-American President, but Melissa was the first female Secretary of Defense. Both had worked hard to get where they were. His entire campaign had been bedeviled with stereotypes from his opponent's supporters; that he had ties to organized crime being the most persistent (and totally unfounded) rumor. Still, they had prevailed.

Until today.

He listened with a growing sense of dread. There was a global zombie outbreak taking place, and it had apparently manifested in several U.S. cities—with San Francisco being the heaviest hit. Worse, an invasive and hostile species that the media had termed Clickers was emerging from the waters of the Pacific, and now there were reports of the creatures appearing in the Atlantic and Mediterranean oceans, as well.

"The beaching," Melissa said, "occurred so quickly that scientists weren't sure what to make of it. An underwater disturbance such as a severe change in temperature or an earthquake can cause it. Changes in underwater pressure will sometimes damage the eardrums of mammals such as whales and dolphins, causing them to become disoriented. But since this wasn't just the ocean's mammals stranding themselves on the beaches, scientists assumed it must be due to last week's tsunami. Now, of course, we know better."

Tony grimaced. "No shit."

He noticed the look of disapproval on Cabinet Secretary

105

Vincent Napoli's face.

"Don't start in with your 'the President shouldn't curse' bullshit, Vince. Not now."

"Well, I'm sorry, Mr. President, but it's true. You know the media has a field day every time you drop an F-bomb on a live microphone."

"I don't see the media in here right now, you fat fuck."

Vince's face turned beet red.

Ignoring him, Tony turned to Melissa. "Go ahead. What about San Francisco?"

"The Governor mobilized the National Guard. With your approval, we'll put troops on the ground there, as well."

Tony noticed that Vince was flexing the fingers of his left hand. The overweight man's forehead was slick with sweat.

"We've already mobilized the Marines and Navy personnel in San Diego," Melissa said. "They're engaging both the Clickers and the, um…zombies already."

"Congress will just love that," Tony groaned, "seeing as how we did it without notifying them."

"The base was under attack, Mr. President. Our forces were merely defending themselves. Lieutenant Colonel Jack Ripley says that—"

"Wait a minute, Colonel Ripley? Colonel *Jack* Ripley?"

"Yes sir."

"I thought Colonel Ripley was retired. Was going to open up a rare comic book store in the remote woods of Maine or some fucking place."

"No sir, not anymore. He's requested another year, sir."

Tony sighed and rubbed his face. He was about to tell Melissa to continue when Vince grabbed his chest, moaned, and then fell over. His face made a loud, wet smacking sound as it struck the table.

"Jesus Christ on a pogo stick!" Tony leaped to his feet and turned to one of the Secret Service agents. "Get some help in here!"

Cabinet members, Secret Service agents, and civilian personnel all hovered around. Some tried to help, while others just got in the way. Tony was about to order them to clear the room when Vince began to stir.

"Is he okay?" Melissa asked, shoving forward.

Vince sat up slowly and grinned. A line of drool ran down his double chins.

*"I'm fine,"* he said. *"But very, very hungry."*

Then, with a speed that belied his prodigious bulk, he jumped out of his chair, rushed forward, and clamped his teeth around Tony's nose. The pain was excruciating. Tony beat at him with his fists as he felt the man's teeth grind together. Vince pulled back a few inches, and spat Tony's severed nose in his face. Then his head darted forward for another bite.

The room erupted into chaos. The Secret Service agents flung themselves at the two men, reluctant to open fire lest they hit the President by mistake. Vince tossed them aside like they were rag dolls, and chewed off Tony's face. The President's lips stretched like taffy, and his eyeballs dribbled down his cheeks as Vince's fat fingers gouged into his sockets. One of the agents shot the attacker, firing three shots into his chest. Laughing, Vince ignored the gunfire and moved toward Melissa. The President collapsed to the floor, jittering, and then lay still. His bladder and bowels vented.

A moment later, the President sat up, grinning blindly.

*"Let's get this fucking party started,"* the Siqqusim inside President Genova said.

*Palos Verdes, California*

Dr. Post sat on his back deck, nervous anticipation settling over his lanky frame. Fishermen had hauled three more of the strange hybrid creatures in from various beaches today and had taken no chances. Being smaller specimens, they'd crushed them with heavy blows with various steel tools, then contacted animal control officers who had in turn contacted the Marine Institute. Dr. Post had confirmed the remains of these new specimens were identical to the one killed last night to the Department of Agriculture official he'd talked to last night on the phone. "But they're juveniles," he'd told them. "All three of these are. In fact, these two," he'd said, pointing to the two latest ones from this afternoon, "are just babies."

"Babies?" The Department of Agriculture official had said, the color draining from his face. He'd flown in to California from Washington just this morning to view the remains. Dr. Post had turned to him, trying to convey how serious this was.

"Yes," Dr. Post had said as gently and as convincingly as he could. "These are babies. The one from last night was a juvenile. If it were a canine, it would be the equivalent of a five month old puppy."

"Are there more of these, Doc?" the Department of Agriculture guy had asked. The grim look on Alfred's face told the government official all he needed to know. Where there were babies, there were parents.

He'd sat out here all evening, mulling the facts over in his mind. He preferred to think in silence and had neglected to turn on the television or radio. As a result, he'd been unaware that his theory had already been proven correct as the adult Clickers came ashore, streaming from the ocean on their segmented legs, frenzied and hungry, to terrorize numerous cities and communities all along the coast.

Alfred half-dozed, lulled by the sound of the waves. He wondered if perhaps they should move further inland, if only for a few days. Maybe rent a hotel room somewhere? As the sun bobbed on the horizon, preparing to sink for the evening, he heard fire sirens wailing in the distance and wondered what was happening.

An anguished cry from his next-door neighbor's house pulled his attention from the sirens. Disturbed and concerned, Alfred got out of his chair and moved to the railing. His neighbor, George, ran out into the yard.

"Doctor Post," George shouted. "Oh, thank God you're there. I think Ginny may have just had a heart attack. I can't get her to respond to CPR and she doesn't have a pulse. My daughter tried calling an ambulance, but our phone is out. Will you please call 911?"

"Oh my Lord. Absolutely, George."

The frantic neighbor ran back inside his house. Al reached for his cell phone, which was sitting on a spare deck chair.

He'd muted it while he was thinking. He un-muted it and saw that there were no service bars. Cursing, he tried dialing for help anyway, only to receive a recording telling him to try his call again later.

George ran back outside again, looking excited.

"Doctor Post," he cried, "it's okay! She's alive. It was the most amazing thing. She wasn't breathing. Didn't have a pulse. And then all of a sudden, she sat back up again. My daughter is in with her right now."

Before Al could respond, screams erupted from George's house. The startled neighbor hurried back inside, yelling his daughter's name. A moment later, his own screams joined hers.

Then, both their shrieks were drowned out by a sound coming from the beach below. Al gripped the rail and stared out into the surf as the noise drew closer.

CLICK-CLICK! CLICK-CLICK! CLICK-CLICK!

*Malibu, California*

Thirty miles up the coast, Augustus and Marion, sat down to a late dinner of spinach salad with balsamic vinaigrette dressing with grilled mahi tuna overlaid on it with his wife, Marion. For the first time in years, they had the news turned on. Augustus was distressed by what he was hearing from the talking heads. It wasn't so much on what they were reporting, it was from what they *weren't* saying. Their coverage of the strange deaths of beach goers along the west coast by the strange lobster-creatures was subdued, as was the coverage of the riot in San Francisco. He got the keen sense that there was a wealth of information behind both but that the media were forbidden to elaborate on it. This was unusual for the news media, especially mainstream news media journalists, who tended to dwell on the same subject for hours at a time whenever there was a hot topic. But with no celebrity poop to gossip over—they'd grown tired of Charlie Sheen preaching evangelical Christianity on *Praise the Lord* and the reports of industrial black metal singer Justin Bieber's live performances on his most recent world tour that was out-shocking Marilyn Manson—they weren't fixating on anything. Surely the deaths of innocent civilians by strange creatures coming out of the ocean were more newsworthy, right? Even stranger, he had gone online earlier, hoping the social media networks would offer a clue as to what was really going on. To his dismay, he'd found that most of them were offline.

"Maybe we should charter a flight to our cabin in Vail tonight," Augustus said to Marion. "I'm getting a very ominous impression about the west coast."

"You mean other than what the news is showing?" Marion asked. Her expression was fearful.

Augustus nodded. "Much worse. I don't want to call it a vision yet, but—"

Marion laid her hand on his, stopping him. "Let's just do it. Now. We can leave tonight."

Augustus saw the urgency in her eyes. He nodded. "You're right. Call the kids. Get everybody rounded up. I'll call the private jet company and arrange to leave out of Thousand Oaks in an hour."

Dinner was finished quickly as they made their plans. And as Augustus confirmed that a private plane and pilot would be waiting for them within an hour, he felt a strange sense of urgency. He couldn't help but feel that he was experiencing his last moments in this house, that he and his wife would never see this beautiful place again.

*Aliso Viejo, California*

Rick was glued to the news on TV and the Internet. He sat on the living room sofa, laptop in hand, trying frantically to keep up with the news reports regarding the creatures. Before, there had only been a brief news story regarding an incident on Catalina island from earlier in the day, and various theories on conspiracy-theory websites and various message boards. Now, the reports were everywhere, and on every channel. Worse, something new had been added to the chaos—a so-called zombie outbreak.

He picked up the phone to call Jeanette, but the service was out. Then the lights flickered and his internet connection went down. The lights blinked again, and then the power died. Princess looked up in concern.

"Shit." Rick patted the dog, reassuring both her and himself.

The house seemed more silent than usual.

"Jeanette," he whispered, "please be okay."

Then, with his pulse quickening, he scrolled through his contacts list and tried to call his son.

"Pick up, Richard. Pick up…"

*San Pedro, California*

Richard didn't really want to go to Sunken City, but he was outvoted.

They'd just slipped through the wrought-iron gate at the end of Paseo Del Mar, a coastal road that wound around the southern edge of San Pedro. They'd parked across the street and up a ways, near Point Fermin Park. It had been Paul's idea to go to Sunken City. Ever since Paul and his sister, Mary, had moved to Palos Verdes, he'd been wanting to venture into Sunken City and hang out. The way he and Mary described it to Richard and Melody, Sunken City was the place to go to if you wanted to party. That didn't make sense to Richard. "I just thought it was an old part of San Pedro that's condemned due to the fact that it's sliding down the cliffs into the ocean."

"It is," Paul had said. "But it's more than that, too. It's said to be a magical place. That's why it's a cool place to go to if you want to get high."

Richard could think of better places to get high. A few weeks ago, he'd casually asked his father if he'd ever heard of Sunken City. His Dad used to live in the South Bay area of Los Angeles, and had told him that when he was in high school, Sunken City was the place where underage stoners went to get high. Richard didn't pursue the matter with his father any further, and he wondered why Paul would want to even chance a visit, especially at night. Paul and Mary just weren't the stoner types. They came from upper middle-class families like his. In fact, when their father got promoted to Senior VP at his company, the promotion necessitated a change in corporate buildings. This required a move north, to be within closer commuting distance to Torrance, where Paul's dad now worked. They'd exchanged their well-to-do home in Mission Viejo for a similar well-to-do home in the foothills of Palos Verdes, a rural community south of Torrance and west of San Pedro.

So now they were at Sunken City, trudging down the steep, broken-concrete sidewalk that lined what was left of a street that had all but started sliding down the rocky cliffs into the ocean.

Street lights from the road above cast sufficient light. Richard cursed himself for allowing Paul to talk he and Melody into coming down here. Paul was leading the way. Mary and Melody were in front of him, whispering and giggling to each other. Paul's friend Max was slightly ahead of Paul, leading the way. Max was a tall, total blond hair blue-eyed surfer boy. It had been his idea to head to Sunken City tonight.

"What are we going to do when we get to the bottom?" Richard asked.

"I got some weed," Max said.

"Hear that? Max has some weed!" Paul turned around and grinned at Richard.

"We could've smoked weed in your car!"

"What fun is that? Besides, we're in a magical place. Sunken City!"

"Yay for magic!" Richard's tone was slightly sarcastic. Weed, he could handle. He just didn't understand the attraction of going to what was essentially ruins. Didn't Morlock's lurk in such places? Judging from the neighborhood they'd driven through to get here, that was highly likely.

"Don't be grumpy," Paul said. They were nearing a somewhat level section of Sunken City. "Cops don't come down here at night anyway. Right Max?"

"Cops have more important things to do, Ritchie," Max said. "There's donuts to eat, niggers and spics to harass, and old people to help cross the street."

Richard frowned. If Max ever found himself stranded in the eight block stretch they'd driven through to get to Sunken City, he might not be so quick to use those kind of racial epithets so freely.

"Besides, we're just going to hang for a little bit." Paul eased over to the side of an old dilapidated building. The doors and windows were shuttered over. Graffiti dotted the walls, criss-crossing over each other with arcane symbols and barely illegible writing. "I mean, just look at this place! Isn't it cool?"

Richard admitted it was cool, in a way. They were standing on what remained of what had probably been a beachside street before shifting tectonic plates had caused this section of San Pedro to become unstable, forcing city officials to declare the area as unlivable. As the years passed and mother nature did her work on the area, the street, sidewalk, and various buildings had begun a slow slide down the cliffs and into the ocean. Richard figured the place had been condemned for over thirty years, if not more, especially when you considered his dad had been there when he was a kid.

In the distance, they heard a police siren. It grew louder as it neared them, but then faded again. Richard shivered.

"What about all that stuff on the news?"

"You see any Clickers here?" Paul scoffed. "I heard that was just on Catalina Island. And that zombie stuff is bullshit. You watch. Twenty bucks says it's a hoax. Some kind of viral marketing campaign for a movie or something."

Richard shrugged. A fire siren wailed in the distance.

Melody turned to her brother. She was younger than Richard by about a year and a half, and was more daring. She cocked an inquisitive eye at him. "Bet you anything, Dad got stoned here when he was a kid."

"He probably did," Richard admitted.

"So why not continue in the family tradition?" Max grinned. He pulled a clay pipe and a baggie with a sizable chunk of weed from the pockets of his baggy shorts. He began to fill the bowl. "This a nice spot, too. You can see Catalina Island from here."

Paul, Mary, Melody, and Richard turned toward the ocean. Sure enough, Santa Catalina island was awash in twinkling lights about a mile out to sea. As Max finished tapping the weed down into the bowl and getting the pipe lit up, Mary said, "You hear any more about that shit that went down over there earlier?"

"You mean those creatures?" Paul asked. "Like I said before, just what was on the news." The sweet smell of marijuana drifted in the air. "You'd think they'd evacuate the island, or something."

"Especially if somebody was killed," Melody said. Max passed the pipe to her and she took a drag. Richard felt a sudden well of guardianship for his little sister. Max had been making moves toward her all day, and Mary and Paul weren't really doing much of anything to discourage it. Max seemed like an okay enough guy to hang out with, but he was clearly not in Melody's league for boyfriend material.

Melody passed the pipe to Mary, then down to Paul, who passed it to Richard. As it was passed around, the Catalina incident was discussed more in depth. "I heard they were able to kill some of those things," Paul said, taking a hit. "Apparently they're being studied."

"Wonder what they are?" Richard wondered aloud.

"Alien hybrids?" Max said.

Richard took a hit. He frowned. Skunk weed. He hated skunk weed. He passed the pipe back to Max. "Where'd they come from?"

Max shrugged. "The ocean?"

"No shit, they came from the ocean, dumb ass!" Melody said. Richard grinned. Maybe Melody wasn't warming up to Max after all.

"No, I mean, maybe they came from some hidden cave or something." Max took a deep hit, held it in for a moment and exhaled pot smoke. "I heard about this shit today on the internet. Lots of weird shit is happening in the ocean, ever since that earthquake in the South Pacific. Maybe it opened some secret cavern or something and spilled all these things out."

Richard frowned. "Where'd you hear this from?"

Max passed the pipe to Melody, who took a second hit. "I don't remember. Some website or message board. It was some crazy shit. Just like those zombie reports."

"I'm telling you," Paul said, "that's bullshit. There's no such thing as zombies, outside of Hollywood."

As Melody passed the pipe to Mary, Max looked down the street toward another section of Sunken City and frowned. "Well, that's weird."

"What's weird?" Melody asked.

"How come we're the only ones here?"

Paul shrugged. "Who knows?"

"Hey! Hey, you over there!"

They turned toward the voice. Richard tried to see where the voice was coming from, but it was hard to make out in the dark. He felt Melody tense up beside him.

About thirty feet down the road, a shape moved in the dark recess of an old, abandoned building. "Are they gone?"

Max stuck the clay pipe back in the baggie. All five of them subconsciously drew closer together, as if seeking protection from each other.

The shape became more distinct. It was a head, with long, stringy hair. Just a head, with the body beneath it concealed in the shadows. From where Richard stood, the head appeared to be looking down the road, toward the rocky shore far below.

"They're gone," the figure said. "They're gone. We've got to get out now, while we still can."

The teens glanced at one another and then back to the head.

The shape materialized out of the abandoned building and they saw it for what it was: a man, dressed in threadbare jeans, a ratty-looking button-down long-sleeve shirt and tan oxfords. His jeans were short—they came up to his shins. As the man drew closer to them, it became clear to Richard what they were dealing with. The man's threadbare clothing, his long, gray, matted hair, his thick beard, the smell of body odor and alcohol; it was a tramp, a hobo.

"They're gone," the bum muttered. "We gotta get out of here!"

115

As the man drew up to them, they shrank back involuntarily.

"Who are you?" Mary asked. "Why do we have to get out of here?"

The man's eyes were wide, red-rimmed, crazy. When he spoke, Richard could see the rotting remains of his teeth.

"It's okay," he said, holding his hands up. "I'm not going to hurt you. My name's Roy…Roy Conklin. And we have to get out of here."

"Why do we gotta get out of here, old man?" Max said. What brief fear Max had was gone now. He was no longer trying to hide his clay pipe. He'd taken it out of the baggie after deciding the old hobo wasn't a threat.

"There's things coming out of the ocean!" Roy said. He pointed a jagged finger toward the ocean. "I seen 'em. A few hours ago, there was a few dozen people. Kids like you, taking pictures and hiking over the rocks and drinking beer. And then the monsters came out of the ocean and ate 'em!"

Paul and Max were chuckling. Mary was regarding Roy Conklin with a look that said you're off your rocker, old timer. Only Melody and Richard seemed to be taking the hobo seriously. Richard turned to Paul. "Maybe we should take his advice and leave."

Max dismissed it. "Fuck him. He's just an old wino who's had too much firewater. Isn't that right, old timer."

"I'm telling you, I saw it!" Roy said. The tone of his voice, his expression, all conveyed alarm. "They swarmed over the beach and just started tearing into people. Tearing them apart with their claws, stinging 'em. But that ain't the worst part. Some of the folks that got killed—the ones that didn't get dissolved—they didn't stay dead for long. Some of 'em started coming back, but that didn't stop the monsters. They just kept cuttin' em up with those big lobster claws of theirs and—"

"Lobster claws?" Paul asked. "Did they look like those things everybody's talking about on the news?"

"They ate everybody, even when they started coming back from the dead!" Roy cried out. "Don't you get it, kid! They ate everything! Just look at it." And with a sweep of his arm, he indicated the vast expanse of broken cobblestone and sidewalks that comprised Sunken City. And for the first time since arriving here, Richard noticed something about the cracked cement sidewalk they were standing on.

It was sticky. And large portions of it were stained a dark maroon color. There was also dark, glistening globs of what looked like decaying flesh scattered here and there. Then he noticed something else—a round shape, about the size of a football, half-hidden beneath the graffiti-covered rubble. Squinting, he stared harder and realized that it was a decapitated head. Richard blinked.

The severed head returned the gesture.

"What the fuck?" Melody said. She clutched Richard's arm. She'd seen what he was seeing.

The head smiled, flashing bloodstained teeth. It moved its mouth, forming words even though it lacked vocal chords or lungs with which to speak.

Melody grabbed her brother's arm and squeezed. "What is it?"

Before Richard could answer, gunshots erupted from nearby. Judging by the sound, they were only a few blocks away.

"Lets get out of here," Mary whimpered.

A low moan answered her. Richard turned to see a woman crawling toward them. She emerged from beneath a jumble of boulders about twenty feet away and pulled herself toward them with one arm. Richard was amazed that she could move—amazed that she was alive at all. Her left arm had been severed halfway between the wrist and elbow, and a splintered bone jutted from the ragged tatters of flesh. Both of her legs were missing, too. One had been cut off mid-thigh. The other below the knee. The rest of her body was mangled, as well. Through what little scraps remained of her clothes, he saw horrific gashes and lacerations.

"Guys?"

They turned to look at Richard and he pointed.

*"Help me,"* the injured woman groaned. *"Please help me…"*

"Holy shit," Max exclaimed, rushing toward her.

Richard grabbed him and pulled him back.

"Don't," he warned. "Something's not right."

Max shoved him away. "She's hurt, you asshole. We've got to do something."

*"That's right,"* the woman called, her voice loud and strong despite her condition. *"Come help me. Come closer."*

Richard's cell phone buzzed. He glanced at the display, and saw that it was his father calling.

"Who is it?" Melody asked, still clinging to him.

"It's Dad. Should I answer?"

"Call 911," Max told him, and then started toward the injured woman.

More gunfire and screams echoed from the streets behind them. A car horn blared. A dog barked, then began to howl. Richard's cell phone continued to buzz.

Max knelt before the injured woman. "You're gonna be okay. Just stay still and try not to move. My friend is calling for an ambulance."

The woman grabbed his pants leg and laughed.

"Hey!" Max tried to get to his feet, but his attacker tugged at his leg, tripping him. He fell hard, sprawling on the broken pavement.

*"You're a cute one,"* the woman cackled. *"And I bet you taste good, too!"*

Baring her teeth, the woman darted her head forward and tried to bite Max's ankle. The youth kicked her in the face with his other foot. Her nose crunched beneath the blow. That only made her laugh harder. Max kicked her again, freeing himself, and then scampered backward until he was out of reach. Regaining his feet, he rushed back to the others.

"Jesus," he panted. "Jesus fucking Christ…"

From the rocky shore below, came another sound: CLICK-CLICK! CLICK-CLICK! CLICK-CLICK!

"See?" Roy Conklin shouted. "They come back! I told you kids they would."

"What the hell is that?" Mary said, eyes wide with fright. She clung to her older brother Paul much in the same way

Melody was clinging to Richard.

"Oh fuck," Max said.

Far below, where the ruined streets and sidewalks collapsed onto the rocky, debris-littered shore, dozens of Clickers were crawling from the surf and making their way up the cliff. They moved cumbersomely, legs gripping boulders, roots and exposed pipes and cables. They clicked their claws together in frustration, tails raised over their backs. The biggest creature was as large as a mid-size car. The smallest was about the size of a dog.

"See?" Roy squealed. "They're back! We've got to go!"

"Oh my God!" Melody said. She pulled at Richard, stepping back toward the gated fence. As she did, her cell phone began to ring.

"Is it Dad?" Richard asked her. "Answer it! Tell him we're in trouble."

"It went dead," Melody cried. "There's no signal now."

Cackling, the half-woman began pulling herself toward them again. Far behind her, the Clickers clambered closer to the top of the cliff.

"We've got to run!" Roy threw up his hands and barreled past them, heading toward the gate. And as the first Clicker ambled over the debris, and a fury of clicking claws erupted from further down the slope, Richard, Melody, Mary, Paul, and Max turned tail and ran after Roy. They ran for the gated fence, their terror driving them out, and as they reached it Paul heard the wailing of more police sirens in the distance, a bunch of them, coming from all directions. Roy was sliding through the gap in the fence and everybody was fighting to get through first and then there was what sounded like a staccato of gunfire coming from a few blocks over and then hell came to San Pedro.

*San Francisco, California*

Ob—still wearing Abigail's body—and his undead minions were massacring every living being on curvy, crooked Lombard Avenue when a squad of National Guard troops

119

arrived to confront them.

All of the zombies were armed, carrying everything from automatic weapons to pipes and clubs. Methodically, they proceeded down the street, entering office buildings and stores, apartment complexes and places of worship, and slaughtering everyone inside. They pulled people from their cars, knocked them off their bikes, and gunned pedestrians down in the street. They shot them, stabbed them, ran them over, beat them, choked them, and bit them, always being careful to leave the brain intact so that another Siqqusim could inhabit the corpse once the soul had departed.

By the time the National Guard troops arrived on the scene, the zombies outnumbered them ten to one. The soldiers found themselves battling undead Black Lodge operatives, police officers and other emergency responders, gang-bangers, civilians, and an assortment of zombie animals, as well—pigeons, rats, dogs, cats, and other inner city wildlife. The slaughter was quick and merciless, and when it was over, the dead army's ranks swelled even more, as zombie National Guardsmen joined the fight against the living.

From their vantage point atop a bank building, Privates First Class Wagaman and Messinger watched the chaos unfold, choking down bile as their fellow soldiers were killed. The two men had darted into the bank, seeking cover during a running gun battle with three zombies. When the horde charged them, they had retreated to the bank's roof, barricading it.

"We're safe up here," Wagaman repeated, crouched at the roof's edge and staring at the carnage below. Fires dotted the city landscape, and black clouds of smoke curled into the gloom. It would be nightfall soon, and he wondered what would happen then.

"Yeah, but the others," Messinger cried. "Clark and Sylva. Planters. The Sarge. Jesus, dude, our whole squad is down there."

"Nothing we can do for them now. Keep your shit together. We're gonna sit tight, and when things clear out, we'll make our way back down and try to hook up with another squad. Maybe we can radio somebody."

"How? The fucking zombies drove off in our vehicles! Look. There goes one right now, driving over pedestrians. It's fucking Scofield driving that thing."

"Not anymore," Wagaman reminded his distraught friend. "Scofield's dead. I saw her get killed. That's a zombie."

Messinger checked their barricade for the tenth time, assuring himself that they were secure. While he did, Wagaman raised his weapon and peered through the scope, surveying the situation. Messinger had been right. It was Scofield driving the urban assault vehicle down the sidewalk—or at least, it was what was left of Scofield that was driving. Somehow, Wagaman didn't think the Scofield they had served with would have grinned with such maniacal glee as she drove through storefronts and mowed down fleeing civilians. Wagaman watched a mother and her toddler disappear beneath the vehicle's front grill. The oversized tires bounced up and over the two thrashing forms. Blood squirted across the pavement like a juice box that had been stomped on. Then the mother and her child lay still.

"Fuck this."

Wagaman took a breath, held it, exhaled, and then took his shot. The first round took out the windshield. The second exploded Scofield's head. The vehicle swerved, striking a fire hydrant. A stream of gushing water exploded into the air.

"This can't be happening," Messinger moaned. "This wasn't what I signed up to do."

Ignoring him, Wagaman stared through the scope, lining up another shot. He squeezed the trigger and another zombie dropped. The machete the creature had been carrying clattered to the sidewalk. Wagaman picked through them, destroying zombie after zombie, all with shots to the head. It wasn't until he realized that he was needed to reload that he noticed the new arrivals coming down the street.

Clickers. He knew what they were because he and the others had been briefed on them. But pictures in a briefing room or television news footage paled in comparison to the real things. They marched down the street, their great claws clacking together as they fanned out.

121

CLICK-CLICK, CLICK-CLICK, CLICK-CLICK.

The zombies paused in mid-massacre to note the new arrivals. The Clickers rushed forward, seeing only prey. The few remaining humans who were unfortunate enough to still be alive now found themselves trapped between the two opposing forces.

"Messinger," Wagaman called, reloading. "Come have a look at this. Fucking Clickers! There must be close to fifty of them."

The frightened solider didn't move from the barricade. "Get down," he pleaded, shaking his head. "You're gonna let them know we're up here."

"So? Those monsters can't climb, and the zombies are about to have their hands full. We're okay."

When Messinger still refused to move, Wagaman returned his attention to his rifle scope and the stand-off below. As he watched, the Clickers stormed forward, attacking human and zombie alike. In response, a female zombie with long, blonde hair began shouting orders to the rest of the dead. Wagaman focused on her. Obviously, this zombie was some sort of leader. He knew from his briefing that the Clickers were pretty much bulletproof. Only a lucky shot or a heavy round could penetrate their shells. But the zombies were a different story. He decided to concentrate on them—in particular, the apparent leader. He steadied the rifle, aiming the crosshairs at the corpse's head.

Down in the street, Ob rallied his troops against their unexpected new foe. The frenzied Clickers ran amok, stabbing anything that moved, regardless if it was alive or dead.

*"Oh,"* he whispered. *"We need some of those on our side."*

He saw a flash above him and to his right, and heard the gunshot a second after the bullet sheared away his ear. The zombie lord darted to the left and ducked flat behind the smoking ruins of a city bus.

*"We've got a sniper on the roof,"* Ob shouted, pointing. *"Take them out!"*

From his safe vantage point, Ob watched as the Clickers

mowed through the few remaining humans and then started in on his brethren. The dead met them head-on, shooting and stabbing, trying to crack through their hard shells to the soft flesh beneath. Their methods had little impact. The Clickers battered them aside, stabbed them with their stingers, or severed and crushed them with their massive claws. Then Ob noticed one creature that stood out from the others. It's shell was black, and its tail was longer than those of the other Clickers. A mutant, perhaps? He'd encountered the beasts before, on many different worlds and in many different times, but this was the first time he'd seen a black one. Ob watched with interest as the beast charged a group of zombies. The corpses, all armed with high-caliber assault rifles, prepared to open fire, but before they could defend themselves, a stream of venom erupted from the obsidian Clicker's bulbous tail, immediately dissolving its foes. The flesh sloughed from their bodies, bubbling and sizzling. Their skeletons smoked and fizzled, as did the concrete and asphalt beneath them. Cackling with glee, Ob clapped his hands.

*"Amazing,"* he said. *"The black ones can spray their venom like a fire hose, rather than merely pumping it into their victims."*

He watched as the black Clicker unleashed a stream of corrosive fluid at a nearby building. The venom splattered against the steel and glass, pocking them, and then began to smoke.

*"That one,"* he ordered. *"Concentrate your attack on the black one first. Try for its underside. The belly. Cut its legs off if you have to. But don't damage it too badly. I want it mobile when one of our brothers inhabits the shell!"*

The zombies did as ordered. Ob poked his head up from behind the bus, glanced up at the roof and winked, just in case the sniper was watching.

Atop the bank, Wagaman cursed. The fucking bitch had winked at him. Winked! Enraged, he brought the rifle up again and waited, trying to be patient. When the zombie stuck its head out again, Wagaman pulled the trigger.

This time, his shot was true.

Ob cursed as his incorporeal form was dispatched from Abigail's body. With her brain destroyed, there was nowhere for him to reside. He wondered what his next host vessel would be.

On the rooftop, Wagaman cheered as the female zombie's head ruptured like a ripe cantaloupe and collapsed to the pavement, bleeding out all over the curb. He sighted another shambling corpse, preparing to blow its head off, when the sky grew dark above him. Wagaman glanced up…

…and screamed.

A massive flock of zombie birds—pigeons, crows, sparrows, seagulls, robins, and more—hovered above him, black against the slowly deepening twilight. Feathers floated down to him as their dead wings beat the air. Their terrible squawks drowned out the sounds of battle from below.

"Fuck!"

Wagaman raised his weapon and fired, knowing that it was a useless gesture. He needed a shotgun—something with a wide spray pattern—to make an impact on the birds. His reaction was solely out of instinct and desperation. The birds dove, swarming toward him as one. They slammed into Wagaman, forcing him backward through their sheer numbers. The rifle slipped from his grasp and fell over the side. Wagaman tried to stand but was driven back down. He crawled away from the edge of the roof, and heard Messinger screaming, but couldn't see through the fluttering corpses. He collapsed, falling onto his stomach in the middle of the roof, and felt several birds crushed beneath him. The creatures landed on his back, pecking and slashing at him with their beaks and claws, tearing through his uniform and slashing at the skin beneath. Shrieking, he curled into a ball and rolled around, trying to crush more of them, but his foes took advantage of the movement and lashed out at his exposed flesh. He ended up flat again, this time on his back, and the flock fell on him en masse. When he tried to rise, he found that he couldn't. The birds weighed him down. He could only wiggle and scream as they tore him to ribbons. And when a large, black crow pulled out most of his tongue, he couldn't even scream anymore.

Messinger gaped at the red, quivering mass his friend had become, and then ran for the barricade. He fumbled with the boards, trying to pry them loose from the door before the birds reached him, but to no avail. Half the flock launched themselves from their meal and bore down on him. He tried running away, but the zombies were so numerous that it felt like he was racing through wet cement. Claws raked his cheeks and the back of his neck. Another bird seized his hair and began pecking his head. He slapped at them, trying to chase them away, but they only nipped at his palms. A seagull darted at his face, and plucked at his left eye with its sharp, pointed beak, plucking it from the socket. In anguish, Messinger opened his mouth to scream, but the pain was so great that no sound came out. Seconds later, another bird took his other eye. Blind, he ran with his hands stretched out in front of him, and toppled over the side of the roof, exploding like a wet sack of grain on the sidewalk below.

A Clicker scuttled forward and began sucking up the ruptured innards that had spurted out of his broken body. A moment later, when a Siqqusim took residence in his undamaged brain, and Messinger's corpse began to squirm, the Clicker, assuming its meal was still alive, speared him through his splintered chest with its scorpion-like tail. The segmented appendage buried itself between the corpse's broken and exposed ribs, and began pumping poison into the zombie victim. The zombie struggled feebly to free itself, but Messinger's body was too badly damaged from the fall. It could only lay there as its host body bubbled and steamed. Huge blisters appeared all over its skin. Then they burst and the zombie's skin melted away in a noxious, glistening mess. When Messinger's brain liquefied, the Siqqusim departed to wait for another host body.

Night fell. All throughout the city, the battle raged on.

# SIX

*Lomita, California*

"First house on the right."

Joker pulled the Toyota to the curb. Behind them, the four other vatos in their group pulled up in a white Honda. Sparky was sitting in the backseat, cradling an AR-15. He saw the house Midget had just referred to. It was a little cracker-box with peeling yellow paint and a threadbare lawn. A brand new Mercedes sat in the driveway, sleek and sinister.

Five of them got out, leaving one driver for each idling vehicle. As Sparky ran up the lawn toward the house in loose formation with his homies, he felt his heart pound, the adrenaline race through his body. Cyclone was in the lead with an AR-15 of his own. He didn't even knock on the front door—he pointed the barrel at the lock on the front door and let loose with a barrage of gunfire.

Sparky and Midget ran around the side of the house to the back according to the instructions they were given at the meeting. As they crouched beneath the windows and paused at the tiny concrete back porch, excited shouts and voices rose from inside the house. A moment later there was a crash, then the sound of running footsteps followed by a sudden barrage of bullets flying.

There were few screams, if any.

But there was one straggler.

That's why Midget and Sparky were assigned back door duty. Five seconds into the slaughter, the back door burst open and a wiry black kid leaped out, eyes wide with fright. He didn't even see Midget and Sparky as they stood in his blind spot at the side of the house.

The kid rounded the corner and stopped suddenly, as if

he'd hit a brick wall. Sparky and Midget pulled the triggers of their weapons simultaneously, knocking the kid back. He was dead before he hit the ground.

Midget stepped onto the porch. "Yo!"

"Clear out here," called a voice.

"Coming in!" Midget called out again. Sparky and Midget mounted the back porch steps and entered the house through the kitchen.

By the time they reached the living room, El Gato and Josie had already made a quick search of the bedrooms and bathrooms. Cyclone was waiting for them in the living room, his body tense.

"Let's get the fuck out of here," Midget said.

They filed out of the house and piled back into the waiting vehicles, speeding away. The entire operation took less than two minutes.

Neither of them saw the bodies of the three Crip members who'd been slain in the house, and the young gang banger who was shot outside, rise from the dead, pick up their weapons, and begin making their way to the neighboring houses.

*Mission Viejo, California*

When he couldn't get through to Jeanette, Rick Sychek tried getting in touch with his kids again. He'd tried them earlier, but had no luck. He dialed Richard's number, then Melody's. Each time he called, it rang five times before going into voice mail. Rick had already left messages. The fact that they didn't pick up on subsequent calls bothered him.

Frowning, Rick scrolled through his numbers until he found Paul and Mary Bryant's home number. He hit the connect button and he listened as the phone rang. Surely Mr. Bryant would have some idea of where the kids had gone.

The phone was picked up on the third ring. "Hello?" It was Stacy Bryant. She sounded hesitant.

"Stacy? It's Rick. Rich and Melody's dad."

"Oh, Rick, how are you?" Stacy's voice became light, slightly bouncy. When the Bryant's used to live in Mission

Viejo, Stacy used to flirt with him like crazy, always making sure Jeanette wasn't around, of course. Once she'd made a bold pass at him when he'd arrived at their house to pick up Melody. As his daughter was upstairs getting her things, Stacy had told him, in a low voice, that if he ever wanted a blow job, just come to the house any time before the kids came home from school. After all, she was home all day. What else did naughty housewives like her have to do all day? Rick had been taken aback by the bold sexual proposition, had stammered sure, maybe he'll take her up on it, and then the girls were galloping down the stairs like fumbling colts. Stacy's voice and facial expression changed in an instant from sultry and seductive and slutty, to All-American Mom.

Rick got straight to the point. "Are Melody and Richard around?"

"They went out," Stacy said. There was some background noise, as if Stacy was talking to somebody. "Doug and I are chilling out on the back deck with a few drinks. It's noisy out here tonight, though. Sounds like a fourth of July party is still going on in places. We were wondering if you and Jeanette want to come by some night. We could chill on the deck, have some beers, maybe a little something extra."

"Sure," Rick said. "About my kids, though…"

"They're out with Max Wellington. Paul met him at Palos Verdes High. A nice kid. You'd like him."

"Did they take their phones? Can you give me Paul's cell number, or even Mary's?"

"But of course."

It took awhile for Stacy to get the numbers to him. First, she had to retrieve them from Doug's cell phone. As he waited, Rick heard sirens in the distance. He looked out the window, not knowing why he felt uneasy about all those sirens. He could hear them in the distance forty miles north, too, from over the connection with the Bryant residence. "Is everything okay over there?" he asked Stacy when she came back on the line. "I hear a lot of police sirens."

"That's been going on all evening. Like I said before, probably due to all those fireworks."

Still, it didn't sit well with Rick. "Can I have those numbers?"

Stacy rattled the numbers off to Rick, who jotted them down on a scrap of paper from the pad Jeanette kept mounted on the refrigerator by a magnet. "Thanks," he said. He hung up just as Stacy said she was looking forward to seeing him again, then he began dialing Paul's number. As the phone rang on the other end, Rick had a fleeting thought that at another time, Stacy might have been a hell of a lot of fun back in the day. She'd probably been the kind of girl he would have loved to get stoned with and fuck all night. She exuded that vibe.

Paul's phone rang an even dozen times but it never went into voice mail.

He tried Mary's number. Same thing.

Rick stood at the kitchen counter, looking out the window at the dark night beyond. There were more police sirens.

*This isn't right*, he thought.

He dialed the Bryant house again.

This time, Doug Bryant answered. "Did you get a hold of them this time?"

"No. Paul and Mary aren't answering their phones, either. How do I get in touch with this Max kid?"

"Let me get his number." Paul sounded worried too. "Jesus, that wasn't a firework!"

"Excuse me?"

"Oh, sorry, Rick. I was talking to Stacy. Sounds like there's gunshots in our neighborhood."

Rick started to respond, but just then, somebody screamed outside his home. And for the first time that night, a real spike of fear stabbed into his gut and Rick felt very, very afraid.

*San Pedro, California*

They hadn't gotten very far from Sunken City when they heard the fireworks.

They were running down a dark street toward Max's car, which was parked in a lower middle-class neighborhood. Roy Conklin, the homeless guy who had initially warned them, was

129

behind them, shouting at the top of his lungs. "They're coming to get us! They're going to eat all of us! And when they do, the Great Iguana King will eat *them!* We'll have a great big barbecue! Bwwhahahahaha!" Richard wished the weird fuck would shut the goddamn hell up and stop following them!

As they ran past a small cracker-box house with several jacked-up cars in the driveway, the sound of the fireworks went off like gunshots. Just then, two dark clad figures stepped out of a classic Lincoln Continental that had just pulled in to park across the street. As Richard, Melody, Paul, Mary, and Max drew abreast to the house, several figures ran out the front door, as if they were fleeing a crime scene, and Richard saw they were all brandishing what looked to be assault rifles. The two dark clad figures who'd got out of the Lincoln suddenly drew handguns. One of them shouted out, "Eight Trey Crips, muthafucka!" and started shooting.

"Oh shit!" Richard said. He stopped running and the others stopped too, Melody almost crashing into him from behind. For a brief moment it was like an old cartoon, where the characters crash into each other only to abruptly run in another direction. That didn't happen. What happened next occurred so fast that Richard was left breathless by its sudden intensity of violence.

Several of the men that had come out of the house were hit by the gunfire, but some started to shoot back at what Richard assumed were members of the notorious Crips street gang. The burst of gunfire that came from the assault rifles was deafening. They cut the two Crip members down and then there were only two men left from the group that had left the house. They started heading toward a Toyota and a Datsun that were idling at the curb. "Let's go, let's go!" One of them shouted.

A short man with a rifle shouted to one of the cars. "Cyclone and El Gato were hit. Go!"

The Datsun tore away from the curb and sped off into the night.

The small man dove for the Toyota. His partner was on his heels when he noticed Richard and Melody and their friends.

He started toward them, turning the barrel of the rifle toward them.

"Fuck those *putos!*" Yelled the small man from the Toyota to the man approaching them. "Let's go!"

The two dead Crips who'd been gunned down in the street suddenly got up. Richard gasped. He could see them clearly from the glow of the streetlight. They were clearly gang members—both men were black, wore baggy jeans and white shirts and had large gold chains around their necks. One of them had a huge hole in his chest. His partner had his left arm blown off by the gunfire. Both started across the street toward the man that was brandishing the rifle.

The group of men that had been gunned down on the front lawn of the house—Richard could clearly see they were of Hispanic descent, some heavily tattooed—also got up. All of them bore multiple gunshot wounds, all of them fatal. As this group got up, the first of the dead men from inside the house shambled outside. More black gang members.

"Oh shit," Max said. The five friends had remained frozen, crouched near a parked SUV.

"They're here! Behold, they're here!" Roy Conklin had finally reached them. He was twenty feet behind them on the sidewalk. He was barely panting.

The two black gang members lunged for the Toyota. One grabbed the driver, the other leaped over the car and went for the small man sitting in the front passenger seat. The driver tried to drive away but immediately crashed into the SUV Richard and his friends were hiding behind.

The men on the lawn and the gang-bangers who'd just come out of the house headed toward them. The man standing on the sidewalk with the rifle was quick thinking and moved fast. "You're supposed to be dead," he said to the advancing corpses. He opened fire on them. Bullets riddled the men but they had no effect. The burst of gunfire was quick, only a few seconds worth, but enough to convince the man that this wasn't normal. "Shit!" he cursed. He turned and started running toward Richard and his friends.

That single act, from seemingly different random events,

was like flipping a switch. Richard, Melody, Paul, Mary, and Max also turned and ran back down the street in the direction they'd come. The six of them ran past Roy Conklin and somebody collided with him, knocking the hobo to the ground. Whoever it was that ran into him kept going—Richard wasn't sure if it was Max or Paul. He was thinking of only one thing—getting as far away from this weird, fucked up shit as quickly as possible.

Behind them, the dead Crips and the dead Hispanic men, who Richard had pegged as gang members also, gave chase. A moment later, Roy Conklin started screaming.

As they ran down the street back toward Sunken City, people came out of their homes, attracted by the commotion going on outside. "What's all the racket about?" A middle-aged black lady dressed in a long robe said. Richard didn't have to see what happened to know the outcome. Judging by her screams, one of the dead men—zombies, Richard thought—had gotten her.

Thanks to the looky-loos who ventured out of their homes, Richard, his sister Melody, their friends, and the Hispanic gang member they were running with made a clean getaway. They ran past some of these pour souls as they stood on the sidewalk, obviously slow in realizing what exactly was going on. They became quick lunch for the reanimated dead.

Before they knew it, they were back in Sunken City, slipping through the chain-link fence. Richard didn't know if they were being pursued. He only knew that they had to get away from the zombies.

"Hold up, hold up!" Paul said. He stopped running, grabbed Max and pointed down the cracked street that led down the rocky cliff. "Don't you remember those things?"

Richard remembered. "Those crab things...shit!"

"What crab things?" The Hispanic man with the assault rifle had stopped with them. He no longer looked like he wanted to kill them for being witnesses to a mass murder.

Richard ignored him, his mind racing as he quickly surveyed his surroundings. What looked to be an old apartment building loomed in front of them. The first floor windows and doorway were boarded up, graffiti dotting the face of the building. Richard pointed to it. "There! Quickly!"

They moved toward the building and Max tried to pry the wood off that had been nailed over the front door. "It won't budge!"

"Around the back," the Hispanic man said. He darted down the side of the building, still cradling the rifle. Max and Paul followed him.

Richard started to follow but was grabbed by his sister. "Are you crazy? That guy was going to kill us!"

"And those zombie things are trying to kill all of us," Richard said. "We have no choice. Come on!" He returned Melody's grip and pulled her along. Mary stayed close by her friend's side.

They ran down the side of the apartment building and rounded the corner. The Hispanic man was crouching down to access a window set along at ground level. He pulled at a board that had been set across the window, grunting. "There," he said. He gestured for them to crawl in. "This building has a basement. Get in, quickly."

Max and Paul slipped through the window. Richard ushered Melody and Mary in ahead of him. Melody cast him a look. Are you sure? Richard nodded. Melody darted down and squeezed through the window. Mary followed.

Richard paused at the window. "How are we going to get this thing back over the window?" he asked, motioning toward the sheet of plywood the Hispanic man had pried off.

"Don't worry about that. I'll pull it back into place. Just go."

The sounds of screaming people, of police and fire sirens, decided it for him. Things were disintegrating very rapidly. Richard slipped through the window. He hoisted himself down into the darkness, sensing Melody and Paul there to guide him down. He dropped lightly to the floor, surprised that this building had a basement. A moment later, the Hispanic man was slipping through the window. He dropped down, his chest and abdomen hugging the basement wall as he pulled the sheet of plywood down over the window. "Hold me up," he urged. Paul and Max darted forward and boosted him up, each grabbing him at either side. With sufficient support, the Hispanic man was able to pull the sheet of plywood back into place. "Okay," he said, and Max and Paul helped ease him to the ground. "That's not gonna hold them if they find out we're in here. But from the outside it'll look like it's firmly in place."

"How'd you know it would be loose?" Max asked.

The Hispanic man nodded at the basement. "Hold your cell phones out to light the place up and I'll show you."

Paul and Max did that. The light from their phones gave them enough illumination to see that they were in an empty cement basement. The floor and the walls were stained with a dark maroon substance. There was trash in the corners, empty beer cans, and what looked to be empty shell casings. "What the hell is this?"

"Old buildings like this are common meeting places for underground fight clubs or dog fighting rings," the Hispanic man said. "I had a hunch this place had been used for something like this. I'm glad I was right."

"Yeah," Max said. He looked absolutely spellbound by the remains of old violence that had been spilled in this basement.

"I don't want to be stuck down here, though," Richard said. "This is like being trapped."

"We should head upstairs," Paul suggested.

"What if there's somebody here?" Melody asked. She hadn't left Richard's side since they'd entered the basement.

"Then I'll take care of 'em," the Hispanic man said. He brandished the rifle.

"Yeah, and then what?" Paul said. "You saw what was going down out there! You kill anybody, they come back."

"Maybe if you shoot them in the head they stay down." Richard shrugged and caught Paul's eye in the feeble light from their cell phones. "You know, like Dawn of the Dead."

From outside, they heard a sound, muffled from being in the basement. CLICK-CLICK! CLICK-CLICK!

The cell phones were flipped shut, turned off. They stood there in absolute silence.

CLICK-CLICK! CLICK-CLICK! CLICK-CLICK!

The sounds moved up the street toward the outskirts of Sunken City. Beyond Sunken City, in San Pedro and probably beyond, was the sound of civilization falling apart: hoarse screams of pain, of panic; warbling police sirens; cars crashing into each other, people running and shouting at each other ending in frenzied screams; the sounds of explosions.

Through it all, they huddled together in the dark in absolute silence.

"I want to call Dad," Melody said. Richard drew her close, hugging her. He could tell she'd been crying silently. She reached into the pocket of her jeans and fished her cell phone out, flipped it open. Four bars. They had a strong signal in here.

Melody's fingers stabbed at the keypad. She put the phone to her ear. Richard glanced at the Hispanic man; he still didn't know the man's name, but as threatening and dangerous as he appeared to be, things had changed. What had once been an immediate threat had now become an ally.

"Dad? It's Melody."

Richard could hear his father's voice as he spoke to Melody. "Dad, I don't know what's happening…we're in Sunken City, in this basement and—"

"Let me talk to him," Richard said. Melody was quickly loosing control of her emotions. He took the phone from Melody and put it to his ear. "Dad, we're in San Pedro."

"What the hell are you doing in Sunken City?" Dad sounded surprised and panicked. "I've been trying to reach both of you for the past two hours! Why haven't you been paying attention to your phones?"

"I'm sorry, Dad, but—"

"Where are you again? Exactly?"

"San Pedro. In the basement of this old apartment building in Sunken City."

"Are Paul and Mary with you?"

"Yes. Dad, what's happening? It sounds like…"

There was no sound from the other end of the line. Richard looked at the display on the phone. The connection had been broken. There was no signal anymore.

135

"Damn it!" He folded the phone, flipped it back open, hoping to jar the signal back into existence again. That didn't work. The signal was completely gone.

"Let me see if I can get a signal," Paul said. He pulled his cell phone out. Richard handed the phone back to Melody and dug for his own. The rest of them dug for their phones as well, all except the Hispanic man who stood close by, holding the rifle. Five different cell phones, each display showing no cellular signal.

The five friends looked at each other, then turned to the Hispanic man. The light from all five phones showed his face more clearly. He looked to be in his late thirties, of medium build with a shaved head. His forearms were heavily tattooed and the left side of his neck bore a tattoo. He looked hard. But he was on their side now. "Signal's lost," Richard said.

The Hispanic man took this news with stride. He showed no emotion. Outside, the muffled sounds of a dying city continued. "My name's Carlos Garcia, but my homies call me Sparky. We should head upstairs. We'll be able to see shit better." He turned and headed for the stairway that led up to the first floor.

The five friends regarded each other silently amid the glow of their cell phones, then followed Sparky upstairs to the ground floor of the condemned apartment building.

*Thousand Oaks, California*

Augustus and his wife, Marion, were sitting in the rear of the limousine, heading to the airport, when the shit really hit the fan.

Their driver navigated through the snarl of traffic on Foothill Drive, muttering under his breath. The man was in his early sixties with a walrus mustache and longish graying hair. He even dressed the part, with a blue cap and a dark suit. His hands were large and knobby on the steering wheel.

Augustus held Marion's hand, caressing it. She was worried sick about the kids. They couldn't get in touch with George and his wife, but their other three kids were meeting them. Andy was bringing his wife and the new baby; Susan was on her way to the airport from Woodland Hills, and Heather and her husband Mike were taking a later flight. It bothered him that they couldn't reach George and his wife, Kelly.

"Do you think they're all right?" Marion asked Augustus for the umpteenth time.

"They're fine," Augustus said. "They have busy schedules. George was in that meeting today with Simon and Schuster's media people and Kelly had a meeting with some sound engineers from the Record Plant for the next audio book recording. I'm sure they—"

"Why haven't they been in touch?" Marion looked worried sick.

"I'm sure there's a reason," Augustus said. His voice and his persona exuded calm strength in the mount of rising terror. Deep down, he was starting to be afraid too, but he couldn't let Marion see it. He had to be strong, for both of them. "I've left messages with their assistants and on their voice mail. They have explicit instructions on what's happening. I'm sure they're already following things to the letter and are on their way to the airport."

Marion had no response. She looked out the tinted window as the limo drove down Foothill Boulevard.

"Shit," the driver whispered from the front. Then he glanced in the rearview mirror. "Sorry, sir."

"That's perfectly alright," Augustus said, forcing himself to smile. "Is everything okay?"

His eyes met Augustus's in the rearview mirror. "Yes, sir. We just lost our GPS, is all. The unit itself is functioning properly, but we've lost communication with the satellite. The network must be on the fritz. But don't worry. I can get us to the airport without it."

"Very good."

Augustus looked out the left passenger window. He was already getting an impression that there was a disturbance in the atmosphere. It was the same disturbance he'd felt earlier this morning when he'd seen that immense flock of birds heading inland, only this time it was a thousand times bigger.

As the day went on, he'd gotten several ominous impressions but was unable to pinpoint details. What he was certain of was one thing: something horrible was about to happen. Something global, something that would change the face of the world and the way human beings lived forever.

He hadn't told Marion this. He'd given her very little in the way of information, preferring to leave her in the dark as much as possible. All he wanted her to know was that he had a bad feeling about remaining in California, that they would be safer in their cabin in Vail. Off season they would have very little in the way of neighbors, and the cabin was well-stocked with a month's worth of dried and canned goods. They would have water. They would have contact with the outside world via satellite radio and internet. And there were weapons at the cabin. Augustus didn't believe in guns, but his son George was an avid hunter and his daughter, Susan, was a member of the NRA. The guns belonged to them. But if Augustus had to learn to use them, he would.

He hadn't told Marion about what he'd heard on various news and internet reports either. Stories about mutant crab-lobster-scorpion hybrids the news journalists were calling Clickers swarming the beaches on the US west coast, Australia, Japan, India, and South Africa, attacking and eating people. Stories about the dead rising to attack and eat the living. He'd kept watch at the home office as he went about his routine, monitoring the day's operations from afar while at the same time paying attention to what was going on in the local community. He'd only had to venture into Malibu proper once today, to pick up some flax seed and ginkgo biloba at Helen's Health Food store in the mall. Helen Ocasek, the proprietor, had asked him to stop by to autograph copies of his first book, *You Have Been Alive Forever*, which she had on constant reorder. This was a common business arrangement between them, and when Augustus had taken the afternoon walk for this errand, everything had seemed normal in Malibu—people were on the beach enjoying themselves, kids were playing in the sand, people were window shopping along mall storefronts. There was a hell of a lot of birds flying inland—

that phenomenon hadn't let up. But if it wasn't for Augustus's second sense about what he was feeling, he wouldn't have insisted they leave for Colorado immediately.

The limo slowed down as traffic became more congested. Marion sat on the far side of the rear seat, a look of extreme worry in her features. "George knows to meet us at the cabin, right?"

"Yes, he does. I left explicit instructions. He, Kelly, and the grandkids will meet us in Vail. I already arranged with a limo company in Boulder to have a car on standby at the airport."

The driver cut in. "Excuse me, Mr. Livingston, but we have a situation."

Augustus sat up, trying to see what was going on from his vantage point. "What's happening? The GPS again?" All he could see was massive congestion.

"No. I don't know. Some kind of riot or something."

Marion gasped and gripped his hand. The limousine stopped. He could hear people shouting and screaming outside. There was what sounded like gunfire up ahead. "My God, what's happening Augie!" Marion cried.

"I don't know, honey," Augustus said. He pulled his hand away and darted toward the partition that separated them from the driver. He tapped on the partition and it slid open. A quick look through the front drive windshield told him everything. They were in a standstill and there was some kind of civil disturbance up ahead. "Oh shit," Augustus said.

"Oh shit is right," the limousine driver said. "Hold on, Mr. Livingston. I'm gonna see if I can get us the hell away from this mess."

Augustus didn't see how he was going to do this. They were boxed in from all sides.

The limousine driver put the vehicle in reverse and backed up quickly. They banged into the car behind them. Augustus wasn't prepared for the impact and almost tumbled off the seat. Marion was thrown back slightly. She held her right hand over her chest, her eyes wide. Augustus turned to her. "Get your seat belt on!"

Marion snapped her seat belt on and Augustus planted himself on the side seat and did the same. The limousine moved forward and bumped into the car in front of them, then backed up and hit the car behind them again. The driver's of both vehicles started laying on their horns, but he was paying them no mind. *Do what you have to do to get us out of here*, Augustus silently urged the limo driver. As if he'd heard this subliminal command, the driver continued bashing the limo back and forth, turning the limo around with each backward momentum. Within moments, he was bashing the vehicles on either side of him. Angry honks arose from those drivers, too.

"Hey, what the fuck are you doing, asshole?"

The limo driver paid the protests no mind. He plowed forward and hit the car on their left again with a resounding crash. Even though he was bracing himself for each impact, Augustus was jostled around pretty good. There was a slamming of a car door and an angry male voice. "Get the fuck out of the car, you old, fat, piece of shit!"

Backwards—*smash!* The squeal of tires on asphalt and forward—*smash!*

There were more car horns honking now and this time Augustus felt that their driver had broken through. The limo continued forward and there was thump of tires, as if the vehicle had just driven up the curb, and then they were moving forward, probably at about ten miles an hour. There was a sound of running feet behind them and the angry male voice shouted, "Get back here, you fucking asshole, I'm gonna kick your ass!"

*Go, keep going*, Augustus thought.

"What the fuck?" the driver said. The limo started to slow down.

"Keep going, just keep going!" Augustus shouted. The dark impressions he was getting had just spiked in their intensity. They were overpowering.

"Ah, fuck!" The limousine skidded to a stop. Marion and Augustus were thrown violently against their seat belts. Up ahead there was the unmistakable sound of two vehicles colliding in a sickening crunch of metal. There were screams of pain, of anguish.

And above it all, the voice of something else. Something overpowering that rode over all.

Augustus looked out the front windshield and what he saw punched a hole through his soul.

Foothill Boulevard resembled the worst NASCAR wreck ever in the history of stock car racing. Several vehicles were on fire. Cars and SUVs were scattered haphazardly along the road in various stages of demolishment. Those people who weren't running from the scene screaming in terror were being attacked by other people. The ones doing the attacking were biting their victims with a savagery Augustus never in a million years would have expected, or using anything as a weapon—sticks, knives, still-operable vehicles, guns, and other items. For a brief moment he thought this was a dream—he was in a dream state, trapped in a nightmare that was so vivid, so real, that he could hear the screams of victims, smell the smoke from fires, and taste the fear in the air. But then the driver's side door to the limo opened and their driver spilled out. His hands slapped the roof of the limo on Augustus's side. "Get out, get out! We gotta get out of here, Mr. Livingston! Now!"

Augustus fumbled for his seat belt, got it unlatched and dove for the door. He opened it and half-stepped out. The limo driver was already on that side of the limo to help. "What's going on?"

A man wearing green knee-length shorts and a gray tank top appeared. An axe blade was buried in his chest. The front of his shirt was stained with blood. By all rights, he shouldn't have been alive, but he grinned at them with a sense of malevolence Augustus found utterly terrifying. He took an involuntary step backward as the man advanced on them quickly and grabbed the limo driver. *"Another tasty vessel!"* he said. His voice sounded like a thousand voices speaking together in unison, as if there were a chorus of demons inside him. The limo driver yelped and tried to squirm out of the thing's grasp, but it was no use. The thing's grip was too tight, and it bent its head down and took a deep bite out of the limo driver's neck.

"Yaaaahhh!" The limo driver screeched. Blood spurted, gurgled out like a fountain. Augustus felt his stomach drop. He was dimly aware of Marion in the limousine screaming, telling him to get back inside but he was frozen, shell-shocked by what he was seeing, and then a gaggle of them were suddenly there—a teenage girl with braces, a fat Asian kid with a Mohawk, a tall brown haired surfer-looking dude wearing shorts. All of them had suffered grave wounds to their necks, to other areas of their bodies, as if chunks had been torn out of them. But they walked. And something lived within them. Augustus could see it in their eyes. He couldn't identify it, but somehow, through some psychic communication, he just knew. He dove back into the limousine and slammed the door shut, locking it. A moment later, their limo driver sat up again, occupied by an entity.

Augustus frantically grabbed his cell phone and tried to place a call. As he did, the driver pulled out his keys, thumbed a button on the remote, and the doors unlocked. Before Augustus could react, the driver yanked open the door of the limousine and, with a grin, seized Marion.

"Augustus," she shrieked, wide-eyed, her lips pulled back to expose her gums. "Help me!"

He reached for her, but the zombie yanked Marion out of the car and dragged her toward a grove of palm trees along the side of the highway. When she struggled, the corpse slapped her twice, hard. Marion went limp.

*"Going to have some fun with this one,"* the zombie crowed.

"You bastard!" Augustus scrambled over the seat. "Leave her alone…"

Ignoring his cries, the zombie dropped Marion on the ground, seized her by the ankles, and continued to drag her toward the trees. Augustus started to give chase, but a dead woman darted toward him, her chin and mouth stained with someone else's blood. She clutched a ball-peen hammer in one hand, the head of which was also bloody and matted with hair.

She snarled at him. *"Give us a kiss, meat."*

Speechless, Augustus glanced around for a weapon. The only thing within reach was an acoustic guitar. He didn't have time to wonder how it had gotten there—probably spilled from a car wreck or discarded by a fleeing pedestrian. He grabbed the instrument and swung frantically, smacking the zombie in the face. The creature uttered a squawk, and stumbled backward, dropping her hammer. Augustus swung again, breaking the guitar over her head. Then, without pause, he jammed the broken guitar neck into the zombie's stomach. The corpse fell to the ground.

Sickened by what he'd done, Augustus turned his attention back to Marion. To his dismay, he saw that the zombie had reached the side of the road, and was disappearing into the trees with her. Other shadowed forms moved and thrashed among the palm trunks. Augustus squinted, and then his eyes went wide when he realized what was happening. It was some type of orgy.

No, not an orgy.

The dead were raping the living, savagely abusing them while simultaneously feasting on them. As he watched, three zombies held a helpless man down. One arched its hips and thrust inside the man, while the other two took bites out of his chest and neck. The depravity was repeated throughout the grove of trees.

"Marion!"

Augustus started forward, pulse pounding, unable to catch his breath, when something thudded against his toe, sending pain rocketing through his body. Screaming, he glanced down and saw the zombie he'd just speared with the guitar neck. She'd regained her hammer. The creature cocked her arm back to deliver another blow to his foot, but Augustus was quicker. He kicked her in the chin, knocking her backward, and then proceeded to stomp on her head again and again. He heard her skull crack and felt her blood soak through his socks and shoes. He didn't stop until she ceased to move. Then, panting, he turned back to Marion.

"I'm coming, Marion! Just hold on."

He shuffled forward. Each step brought a fresh jolt of pain

to his toe. He'd taken four steps when he heard a new sound, echoing above the screams of the living and the joyous cries of the dead.

CLICK-CLICK. CLICK-CLICK. CLICK-CLICK.

Augustus gaped as a new terror strode onto the highway from the other side. It looked like one of the crab-monsters he'd heard about, but the creature's coloration was different. He'd been told the Clickers were red, but this one was completely black. The beast towered over the cars, taller than even the tractor trailers. Black, beady eyes the size of basketballs goggled at the scene, suspended on stalk-like appendages. The monster paused in front of the line of palm trees. Then, spying the figures inside the grove, it reared back and began to spray venom from its tail. The noxious liquid splattered across the trees—and the figures beneath them, both living and dead. The foliage began to smoke and hiss, and the tree trunks splintered and cracked. On the ground, both the zombies and their victims congealing together into a massive pool of rapidly liquefying flesh. The melting tree trunks fell, splashing the gore out onto the road. Hissing, the black Clicker rushed forward and began shoveling the sizzling, soupy mess into its beak-like mouth.

"Marion…" Augustus was frantic. Marion was in there, being violated by one of those things and now…now they were screaming in agony.

The monster ignored him, busying itself with devouring the remains. Augustus cast a look back at the grove where he last saw Marion and, unable to make out what was going on, he stumbled back to the limo and collapsed into the seat, barely shutting the door and locking it before he passed out.

*San Pedro, California*

Jim had started drinking to stop stalking Tammy.

When she'd first begun dating Anthony, Tammy had been very careful not to expose Danny to the new boyfriend. She'd insisted that Anthony spend the night only once or twice a week, arriving after the boy had gone to sleep and leaving in the morning before Danny woke up. Jim had appreciated that thoughtfulness, and it had assuaged some of his concerns for Danny, but it had done nothing to calm his emotions over the fact that another man was sleeping with his wife. Granted, they were separated at the time, and soon to be divorced, but that didn't make his jealousy and torment any less palpable.

One night, he'd found himself parked outside the house, staring at Anthony's car, which was parked in Jim's old spot. He watched as the lights went out one by one inside the house until only the bedroom light was left. Then, it blinked out as well. Jim had gotten out of the car and slowly crept to the window. Part of him had wanted to flee, but another part felt pulled, as if the window was a magnet and he were steel. He'd gotten within a few feet. The window was slightly open to allow the breeze to blow through the screen. The curtains fluttered as he drew nearer. At first, Jim had thought it was his breath that made them move, but then he realized, feeling foolish, that it had been the wind.

And then he heard them. Two slight sounds. A masculine whisper. And Tammy's soft moan. That was all, but it was enough. His brain filled in the rest, overwhelming him with vividly imagined details. He'd fled back to his car, and when he arrived home, he'd cried himself to sleep.

The next night, when the compulsion to go over to Tammy's house had struck him again, Jim had polished off a quarter of a bottle of bourbon. His reasoning had been simple. If he was too drunk to drive, then he'd be too drunk to stand outside her house like a raving lunatic, torturing himself with the sounds of their lovemaking.

It was a philosophy that had served him well those first few months. He didn't drink at all on nights he had Danny, but otherwise, he self-medicated at sundown, drifting off around eleven each night in an alcohol-induced sleep. After a while, after he'd grown used to the idea of Tammy and Anthony and had gotten laid a few times himself, the urges to go to her home passed, and now Jim only had a single drink—two fingers of bourbon before bed, sipped while watching a DVD, followed by falling into a dreamless sleep on the couch, his face lit by the television's glow.

He followed the same routine the night of July 5th, falling asleep while ruminating over the events at the coffee shop, and the conversation he and Tammy had earlier that day, and his silent, half-humorous prayer for the end of the world. As a result, he slept through it when all of the cable stations interrupted their regularly scheduled programming to broadcast the news reports of two seemingly unconnected occurrences—reports of the dead coming back to life and mass riots all across the globe, and hordes of bizarre sea creatures emerging onto the world's shorelines and attacking everything that moved.

He awoke to a different world than the one he'd fallen asleep in, and found that his prayer had been answered.

# PART TWO

# JULY 6

# SEVEN

*Mission Viejo, California*

Dawn.

Rick roused from a fitful sleep, coming to sudden wakefulness in the upstairs hallway.

He looked around bleary-eyed, then realized where he was. He'd fallen asleep on the hallway floor between Richard and Melody's bedrooms.

He lay back on the floor, feeling a wave of desperation wash over him. The realization of what had happened last night was forefront on his mind. The noise from outside told him last evening had not been a dream.

Off in the distance was the sound of hundreds of car alarms. The house smelled of smoke from a fire burning in the hills of the Saddleback Mountain region. Rick had retreated upstairs after raging through the living room last night shortly after receiving that phone call from Melody and Richard. After the connection had been broken and he'd been unable to reach them again, he'd tore through the house, yelling in rage and frustration. Princess had cowered in the downstairs bathroom. After experiencing the terror of not being able to get in touch with his kids, Jeanette had called him from Lancaster. She'd been frantic. There were National Guardsmen all over and the Governor of Pennsylvania had declared martial law. "It's happening all over," she'd told him. "Zombies. I know it sounds hard to believe, but I'm seeing it on the news and—"

Rick believed her. He'd had the TV turned to the news all afternoon and early evening as he tried to track Richard and Melody down. And at some point during their conversation, the connection had been broken. He hadn't been able to get back in contact with her. Even worse, he hadn't been able to get in contact with her team leader at the corporate office in Irvine, nor the hotel front desk where she was staying, nor the corporate headquarters for the company her firm was consulting for. The line for the Pennsylvania State Police was busy. Then, Melody had called.

He'd been relieved to speak to Melody and Richard, but that relief had quickly jumped to anger and frustration when the call was disconnected. Unable to reconnect, he'd expended his anger on the living room furniture. He'd been on the verge of grabbing his keys and wallet and heading to his car in the garage to make the sixty-mile drive north to San Pedro when common sense prevailed. *If you head out there now you might never see them again. There is shit happening and if those things get you, Richard and Melody don't have a chance.* The temptation to dismiss that voice and forge ahead had been strong, and he'd almost ignored it and ventured out, but he decided to heed the warning and stay inside. It sounded like World War III outside anyway. And it was only getting worse.

So he'd gone back into the house and made sure all the doors and windows were locked. He drew all the drapes over the windows. Then he'd called Princess in and when the dog came to him, slinking toward him in that fearful way dogs get when they think they've done something wrong, he'd swept her into his arms, buried his face in her fur, and wept.

Once he got control of himself, he'd gone through the house and turned off all the lights. He'd stolen upstairs, Princess following, and made his way to Richard's bedroom, which looked out over Pablo Lane. He'd peeked out between the drapes and looked out at the chaotic scene below.

Their neighborhood was descending into an apocalyptic war zone. Off in the distance he could see the glow of distant fires. There was the sound of gunshots. A man wearing no shirt, his guts spilling out of his belly, walked down the street. The neighbor girl two doors down, Brooke Rey, darted out of the house screaming. The man with his guts hanging out zoomed after her and took her down, tearing into the flesh of her neck and face with a resounding crunch. Rick had watched, spellbound, barely able to breathe. The thing that had killed Brooke was still feeding on her, eating her face, when Brooke's eyes opened. She rose to her feet and the other zombie—that was the only description Rick had for them— stopped feeding. Together, Brooke and the zombie headed down the street.

Rick had retreated from the window, his heart racing. *Oh God, please watch over my kids, pleasegodohjesuschristplease!*

He hoped Jeanette was safe, too. But try as he might, his thoughts centered entirely on Richard and Melody. At least they were safe. They'd had the resourcefulness to act quickly and sequester themselves indoors. It was probably best they were seeking shelter inside an abandoned building in Sunken City rather than somewhere else, where there were more people. There would be less people in Sunken City, if any.

He'd tried calling the kids again. And he'd tried calling Jeanette again, too. And at some point he'd crept downstairs in the dark. Princess followed him, keeping a discreet distance behind him. She could tell something was wrong, and it was a wonder she wasn't barking at the disturbances outside. Maybe she sensed that the chaos outside wasn't normal. He'd gone to the kitchen and found lunch meat for a sandwich. He fed Princess, then quickly made a ham and cheese sandwich for himself, which he'd wolfed down with some bottled water. Then he'd gone back upstairs, went into the master bedroom and turned on the TV. Princess hopped up on the bed with him and he'd watched the news until the station suddenly got jolted off the air.

The two hours he was able to see was enough.

In short, it was global chaos. The dead were returning to not only eat the living, but to kill every living thing, which in turn, joined the ranks of the dead. These weren't the shambling corpses of the Romero films. These were cunning, fast, creatures. Reports were coming in from traumatized witnesses claiming these zombies could run, drive, shoot guns, and even talk. Furthermore, when they spoke it was as if they were being powered by something that was controlling them.

Simultaneously, there were reports of strange sea creatures invading beaches all over the world. These creatures were being described as monstrous scorpion-lobster hybrids. They were highly venomous. One sting resulted in painful death by massive corrosion of the flesh. Their claws were as strong as steel, and the creatures themselves ranged in size from as small as a housecat to as big as a tank. Some wag in the media had named them Clickers because of the sound their claws made, and the moniker had stuck.

When the TV went out, Rick tried calling the kids and Jeanette again. Then he'd wandered around upstairs, moving between Melody and Richard's bedrooms to the master bedroom, as if searching for them. Finally, he'd settled down on the floor in the hallway, where he'd fallen asleep.

Rick sat back against the wall and stretched. Princess had stretched out beside him last night. She looked at him with sad eyes that seemed to ask, *is everything going to be okay?* Rick looked at her, then patted her head, caressing her muzzle. "Just me and you for now, puppy. Okay?"

Princess wagged her tail at the sound of his voice.

"Come on. Let's go downstairs and get some breakfast."

Once downstairs, Rick went to the kitchen. He fed Princess, made sure she had fresh water, then prepared a bowl of cereal for himself. As he sat at the kitchen table eating, he thought about what to do. He hadn't looked out the window yet, but it was much quieter now than it had been last night. In fact, he didn't hear a thing from outside. He could smell the smoke from the fire—that might be a concern if it spread and started coming down the hills into Mission Viejo. There was a very good chance that could happen. If so, he had to get out of here.

But not without making a plan of action.

Rick pulled the cell phone out of his pocket. He'd charged it the night before, and it still had a full charge. He tried Richard and Melody again. Once again, there was no signal.

That left only one option.

He had to venture out and head to San Pedro. To Sunken City. To find his kids.

## *Lancaster, Pennsylvania*

Jeanette cowered inside a milking stall in a barn, trying not to scream. The previous night, shortly after speaking with Rick, the local fire company had come to her hotel, announcing an evacuation. It wasn't mandatory, but with martial law in effect, her choices were simple—remain inside the hotel and hope that things got better, or go with the volunteer fireman to a safe location. That location, as it turned out, was a National Guard Armory in Wrightsville. The firemen had loaded Jeanette and the rest of the evacuees into a commandeered school bus. An armed civilian volunteer sat up front next to the driver. Another one guarded the back. They'd used back roads mostly, avoiding the highways due to massive congestion, and when they began to cross the Susquehanna River via a bridge in a town called Columbia, the driver had announced that they were only ten minutes from their destination.

Jeanette had breathed a sigh of relief—and then the guard up front shouted.

"Look out!"

Jeanette and the other passengers had leaned forward and crowded into the aisles, trying to see what was happening. The guard in the rear cautioned them to sit down, but everyone ignored him. Through the windshield, Jeanette saw a man with arrows sticking out of his chest and his bottom jaw sheared away barreling towards them on a motorcycle. He raced across the bridge, weaving in and out of stalled and wrecked cars.

"Move," the guard shouted at the driver. "Get out of the way!"

"I can't," the driver yelled. "The bridge ain't wide enough for us to turn around. We're—"

The rest of his sentence was cut off as the dead man on the motorcycle rammed into them head-on, crumpling the hood and driving part of the motorcycle into the engine block. Steam erupted from the radiator and the bus shook as if struck by lightning. The zombie flew up and over the hood and smashed through the windshield, exploding in a shower of gore. A piece of shrapnel sheared off the top of the driver's

153

head, killing him where he sat. The passengers were silent for a moment, and then everybody screamed at once.

"Quiet," the guard at the front ordered. "Everybody quiet down! We've got to get our shit together."

The guard at the rear of the bus collapsed into the seat beside him and began to weep. "It's fucking hopeless, man. We're screwed."

"We're not screwed," his associate said. "We're only a few miles from the armory. They knew to expect us. We'll just have to go the rest of the way on foot. Once we cross the bridge, we're in Wrightsville. We can follow the river the rest of the way. Keep off the roads, and we should be okay."

"Better shoot him," an old man said, nodding towards the bus driver. "If what they've been saying on the news is true, he's liable to come back any minute and start trying to eat your face off."

"His brain is damaged. I can…I can see it from here. That metal shard gouged a furrow in it. I don't think he'll be coming back. Now, everybody off the bus. Single file. Bring only what you need. Leave your belongings and stuff here. We've got a long way to walk, and we don't need to be weighed down."

There were thirty-six of them when they left the bus. An aerial attack from a flock of zombie birds subtracted two from their number when the unfortunate victims jumped over the side of the bridge to avoid being pecked to death and were killed in the fall. By the time they reached the far side of the bridge, they'd lost another—the old man who had suggested shooting the driver suffered what appeared to be a heart attack. The guard shot him in the head before he could get back up again. The gunshot attracted unwanted attention, and zombies began converging on them from all directions, including the corpses of the two evacuees who had jumped from the bridge and now waded out of the river, water streaming from their bodies, and their expressions alight with malignant pleasure.

At that point the group broke up because everyone ran in different directions. Jeanette dodged two waterlogged zombies and fled down the riverbank, not knowing or caring where she was going. Indeed, she cared for nothing as she ran, save her own survival. She remembered crossing the bridge again back into Columbia. From there, she'd headed into the country, figuring the less people, the less chance she would have in running across any of the living dead. When she stumbled upon the dairy farm at the top of a hill overlooking the river, she'd run inside, not bothering to seek help at the farmhouse. For all she knew, the inhabitants could be dead—or the living dead.

The barn was empty. All of the dairy cows were out in the pasture. She'd seen them off in the distance as she approached the building. She wondered if they were alive or dead. She'd watched them for a moment from the safety of the barn, then slunk back inside. She started walking down the barn, trying to figure out where the animals were kept. Toward the end of the barn was a single stall with a name plate etched in a gold lettering affixed to the door—Imogene. Engraved next to the name was the figure of a cow.

*Who the hell names their cow?* Jeanette thought. Regardless, she headed back down the barn, looking for a more suitable spot to hide. Then, hunkering down inside an empty stall in the middle of the barn, she'd wept silently until exhaustion and fear overwhelmed her. At last she'd fallen into a deep and dreamless sleep.

And now here she was, awake only a few minutes, and all of the fear and panic from the night before fresh in her mind again. Although she'd left her suitcase on the bus, Jeanette still had her purse with her. She rummaged around inside of it, found her cell phone and checked it, only to find that she had no service. When she tried to call Rick anyway, she received a message that simply said 'Network Error'. She tried calling the kids, but the message was the same. When she tried checking the internet, it didn't connect.

She leaned back against the wall, and watched a spider skitter past. Jeanette wondered if the spider was alive. Obviously, animals could become zombies, too. She'd seen it herself first hand when the birds attacked. But how far did it extend? What about the cows outside? What about this spider? Could insects become zombies? Fish? Reptiles? Amoeba?

Jeanette closed her eyes and ran her hands through her hair. Her thoughts strayed, returning once again to Rick and the kids. She prayed they were okay. She was just about to try the phone again when she heard footsteps outside. It sounded like people running. She froze, her heart hammering. The footsteps were joined by more. Some of them sounded like galloping. She wondered if it was the cows returning to the barn.

Then somebody shouted. It was a man. She could tell that much. But his words were garbled and slurred, and it sounded as if he was in great pain. A cow mooed, drowning him out. The sound was malicious and baleful. Then another man spoke.

*"What's wrong, Levi? Can't cast your spells with your tongue bitten off and your hands broken? Too bad for you!"*

The injured man tried speaking again. Jeanette cringed, hearing the anguish in his voice. And yes, it occurred to her that he did indeed sound like someone trying to speak without a tongue.

*"Take him,"* his tormentor said. *"Let's finish this. Ob will be pleased."*

There was the sound of a struggle, followed by a gruesome, decidedly wet noise. Then laughter. Pulse racing, Jeanette peered over the top of the stall. She saw a group of dead humans and cows standing over a headless body dressed in blood-splattered Amish clothes. One of the zombies clutched the severed head in its hand. The victim had a long, curling beard and beautiful, soulful eyes that seemed to be looking directly at her.

*"Here, Levi,"* croaked the zombie. *"Look at your body before you leave."*

It turned the head toward the lifeless form lying on the ground. Jeanette shuddered.

*"And now he has departed,"* the zombie said to the others. *"The great magus Levi Stoltzfus is no more. A pity our brethren will find this head useless."*

The creature tossed the head into the open barn door. It smashed against a wooden support beam and then rolled across the floor, coming to a stop only inches from Jeanette's stall. She bit her hand to keep from screaming, but her efforts failed her when the severed head opened its eyes again, stared at her, and grinned. Jeanette shrieked, stumbling backward. The dead, alerted by her outcry, stormed into the barn and dragged her outside, where they gleefully fell upon her.

By the time they were finished, there was barely enough left of Jeanette's corpse to rise again.

*Palos Verdes, California*

Like most of those across the planet who survived the first night, Dr. Alfred Post and his wife, Janice, stayed barricaded in their home, turned off the lights, shut the drapes, and retreated to the rear bedroom. They monitored the situation on the TV for as long as the networks were on the air. One by one, the networks went off the air beginning with the local affiliates. Then, at one a.m., the power went out.

They'd stayed in the back bedroom, which used to be their son Ben's room. Ben had just graduated from Harvard Law School and had accepted a position with a Washington DC firm just six months ago and relocated. Al and Janice hadn't even had the chance to fly back to visit.

"What are we going to do?" Janice asked. Her voice cracked.

"What else can we do?" Alfred asked. "We stay put."

That seemed to be the general consensus of their immediate neighbors. Palos Verdes was an upper middle-income area. There were a number of cul-de-sacs that were nestled within the winding hills of Palos Verdes that could be considered wealthy—mansions behind gated fences, patrolled by private security. Al and Janice didn't have nearly the income to live in one of those neighborhoods, but their spread was certainly better than most citizens. Their neighbors were physicians, lawyers, high-level executives, entertainment professionals. There was even a professional surfer that lived in the next neighborhood.

When things started escalating in the city below last night,

Alfred had stepped outside briefly. His next door neighbor on their left, Carlton Burke, had also stepped out. Alfred had ventured out clutching the 9mm handgun he'd bought ten years ago and only used at an indoor firing range he went to in Torrance. After thinking about George's wife and what had happened with her, he was pretty certain she'd died, and that when George had come back to tell him she wasn't alive, she was really deceased. The brief screams coming from George's house he could have sworn he'd heard had been on his mind ever since, and he'd retrieved the pistol from it's storage space in his office, making sure it was loaded and he had spare clips. If George and his wife had risen from the dead, Al wasn't sure why they hadn't shambled over to try to get them. He'd peeked through the blinds at their house, which sat in the lot below them in the hilly neighborhood, and it was quiet. Had they moved downhill into the streets below? Perhaps. But he was taking no chances. The 9mm was staying with him at all times.

Carlton was a retired physicist who used to work at JPL in Pasadena. He'd worked on the first Apollo moon landing in 1969 and had assisted in several other missions for NASA. He'd done other government work as well. When Dr. Post saw Dr. Burke, the older man had nodded at him from his back deck. "This is really happening, Al."

"Yes, it is," Al had answered.

"And your ticket for surviving the next forty-eight hours is staying put inside your house. You have enough food?"

Al assured Dr. Burke that he did.

"CNN says to shoot them in the head," Dr. Burke said. "That stops them cold. But they're cunning. And fast. If we hunker down and hide, any that might happen to come up here won't bother trying to hunt after us. They seem to hone in on people who are out on the street. They're easy prey. Do you understand?"

Al said he understood Dr. Burke completely.

"There's those other things, too. Fox News is calling them Clickers."

Al said he knew what Dr. Burke was talking about. He'd performed a necropsy on one of them yesterday.

158

Dr. Burke had raised his bushy eyebrows. "Really? And did you notice anything unusual about them?"

"Aside from the fact that they're completely different than any other species I've ever seen?"

"So they're not of this world?"

Al had shrugged. "I've examined thousands of specimens in my line of work and I have never seen anything like this."

Dr. Burke had nodded. "I've hypothesized about this. That earthquake in the Pacific two weeks ago? It's location and size on the Richter scale was large enough to disrupt the dimensions. Those Clickers that are invading everywhere? They're a result of the shifting dimensions—they got let in. So have the things that are invading and reanimating the dead."

Al had blinked. Dr. Burke was one of those guys that held three PhDs—Physics, Mathematics, and Archeology. He spoke twelve different languages. His IQ was probably on the very high end of the chart. He was so smart he made guys like Al seem like Snooki. "Are you certain of this, Dr. Burke?"

Dr. Burke had regarded Al over the fence of their property. Each man was standing fifty feet apart, but Al could see the look in Dr. Burke's eyes. He was dead serious. "I haven't been more certain of this than I was about my work with NASA during the Apollo missions," he answered. "If there's a God, he really fucked this one up."

Al had taken Dr. Burke's advice. He'd hunkered down in the house with Janice.

And now this morning, things were strangely quiet.

Al approached the window and peeked out. The window in Ben's old bedroom looked out on the back deck. From this vantage point, on a clear day or evening, you could see the entire city of Los Angeles spread out like a great vast plain of twinkling lights. Al had once been to the home of a film producer in the Hollywood Hills, and the view from the back deck of that house had afforded a similar view, albeit from the opposite side of the Los Angeles basin. Now, when he looked out at the Los Angeles cityscape, he wasn't too surprised to see a thick layer of smoke covering the city like a blanket. He could make out several fires in the streets below. Dimly, from several miles north, he could hear the bray of car alarms.

What he didn't hear, however, were people.

They'd heard plenty last night. Screaming. Begging for mercy. Then, several times, cruel laughter followed by bloodcurdling screams, then silence.

Janice approached him from behind. She laid a hand on his bare shoulder. Last night, Janice had driven herself sick with worry over Ben. She'd tried calling him over a dozen times but couldn't reach him. Halfway through the night, they lost LAN line and cellular communication. Janice had wound up crying herself to sleep.

Al had dozed.

"What are we going to do?" Janice asked. Her voice was soft. Tinged with fear.

"I don't know," Alfred said, at a complete loss for words. "I just don't know."

*Los Angeles, California*

As he always did upon taking possession of a new host body, Ob paused to assimilate himself with his new form. He searched through the host's memory, and to his surprise, found himself inside a Clicker. The creature's rudimentary memories were like a writhing nest of vipers. It had been consumed only with eating. Of its death, from what he could discern from its memories, it had been gassed by soldiers. Ob took over the beast's motor controls, and then looked through its eyes to determine where he was.

He found himself in a river winding through a city. He assumed it was in America, given the writing on the billboards around him. Probably California or Florida, if the foliage was any indication. The river was bordered by graffiti-covered concrete abutments. Trash clung to the overgrown vegetation that drooped over the banks. He searched his memory—or rather, the memories of the various host bodies he'd possessed over the years. When he surveyed his surroundings again, he recognized several landmarks and realized that he was in Los Angeles.

The sun glinted off a mirrored skyscraper, and Ob turned the creature's eyestalks in that direction. Then he cackled with surprised glee. He wasn't just inside any Clicker. Instead, he had taken possession of a two-story tall behemoth.

*"Well, I think I'll have to take this thing for a little test drive!"*

Although he spoke aloud, the Clicker's vocal chords, which weren't designed for speech, merely chirped and hissed in a crude pantomime of language. He directed the monstrosity over to the bank, and then clambered from the foul water. All around him, hundreds of Clickers waded ashore on their insect-like legs, including several as large as the corpse he inhabited. The monsters trampled everything in their path, leaving destruction and death in their wake. Their claws clacked together, the noise audible over the shrieks of those fleeing in terror. Then the Clickers began to feed. Ob watched as they speared their prey, injecting the victims with poison and reducing them to biological slag.

*"That's no good. How are my brethren supposed to inhabit the dead if you don't leave behind anything for them to take possession of?"*

Ob thundered onto the choked freeway, battering cars and buses aside with his massive tail and snapping trees and electrical poles in half with his serrated claws. The hot asphalt cracked and split where he trod. Sewer and water mains erupted, and a ruptured fire hydrant spewed a geyser into the air, adding to the choking smoke from the nearby burning buildings. Experimenting with his stinger, Ob stabbed a few of the other Clickers with his tail and pumped venom into them. The results were unremarkable. While the appendage itself was indeed strong enough to penetrate the tough, resilient shells, the poison seemed to have no effect. Hearing a series of popping sounds, he looked down to find several humans shooting at him. Laughing, Ob scooped the entire group of humans up in one monstrous claw and sliced them all in half. They spilled onto the pavement below, squirming and screaming in their death throes. Moments later, more of his kind inhabited their soulless, mangled forms.

*"Sorry, my brothers,"* Ob chirped at his fellow zombies. *"I didn't mean to leave you such useless shells. I'm still learning this host form's strength."*

The city streets were filled with a cacophony of sounds—car alarms, screams, breaking glass, gunshots, the laughter of the dead, and the trilling cries of the Clickers. Smoke filled the sky as cars and buildings burned unchecked.

Moving toward the mirrored skyscraper, Ob raised his claws and smashed through the glass, shattering windows and slicing through steel support beams. Then, rising up on his hind legs, he began to do the same to the people inside. He pulled screaming humans from the upper levels and dropped them to the ground below. Something exploded inside the structure, making it vibrate from the concussion. Ob pressed his weight against it. The building groaned and tilted, spilling more hapless victims into the air, along with office furniture and other debris. Black smoke billowed from the upper levels. A horde of smaller Clickers converged on the scene, intent upon consuming the plummeting victims, but before they could begin, they were attacked by a group of zombie Clickers. Ob paused, watching the battle play out below him. The living Clickers were no match for their dead brethren, and once they were defeated, their corpses reanimated with more Siqqusim inside them.

Turning his attention back to the leaning skyscraper, Ob backed up and then pivoted, lashing his tail through the air. It struck the building's lower wall, pulverizing concrete and buckling steel. The skyscraper trembled, and then collapsed, blowing out the windows of the nearby buildings. A tremendous cloud of dust and smoke billowed from the wreckage, spreading out across the highway and engulfing everything in its path. Flames shot upward and the sidewalks shook as gas mains exploded. A news helicopter hovered over the scene, capturing the horrific aftermath as Ob emerged from the destruction, unharmed, and trudged downtown.

*"City of Angels,"* he rumbled. *"Not anymore."*

## San Pedro, California

Jim awoke to the sound of sirens. What sounded like a fleet of police cars raced by his apartment. Seconds later he heard a volley of gunshots, followed by a scream. This was followed by a bizarre sound he couldn't fathom.

CLICK-CLICK...CLICK-CLICK...CLICK-CLICK...

Still groggy, he leaped to his feet and ran to the window. Parting the blinds, he peeked outside and recoiled in horror. Although he had fallen asleep on the couch, he'd apparently awoken in Hell.

In the yard of his apartment complex, one of Jim's neighbors was firing a handgun at a horse-sized monster that looked like a cross between a crab, a scorpion, and a lobster. The neighbor—Jim didn't know his name, and indeed, had never spoken to him before—stood calmly, aiming carefully, but his bullets had no effect. The creature scuttled forward, its eyestalks waving like wheat in a field. It seized his left arm and squeezed, severing the appendage just above the elbow. Blood welled out around the pincers, and when the beast opened its claw again, a scarlet fountain sprayed from the wound. Shrieking and in shock, the unfortunate victim tried to run, but his attacker was quicker. The crab-thing raised its segmented tail high in the air and then lashed out with the stinger, jabbing the man in the abdomen. His flesh bubbled and hissed as if he were being cooked from the inside. His arm stump still sprayed blood, but now the liquid steamed and smoked. Blisters formed on his body. Jim watched in horror as they swelled and then burst. The man melted into a puddle, his skin and bones breaking down and disintegrating in a matter of minutes, which the monster began to devour.

Jim's attention was momentarily distracted by a motorcycle racing by on the sidewalk. In the distance, more sirens wailed. It was then that he became fully aware of what was happening outside. Each scene was more horrific than the last.

Several more of the crab-monsters roamed the streets and sidewalks, attacking anything that moved. But worse, Jim saw people attacking each other. A young man raced by on a bicycle, hunched over the handlebars and pedaling as fast as he could. A half-dozen people charged out of a doorway and fell upon him, knocking his bike to the ground. The young man struggled, flailing as they stabbed him with knives, clubbed him with rocks and pipes, and clawed his skin with their bare hands. Only then did Jim notice that the attackers didn't appear to be ordinary people. Some of them sported horrific injuries—bites and gunshots and deep lacerations. A broken bone jutted from one of the women's arms, but she didn't seem to care. Indeed, she raised her arm and used the splintered end of the bone to stab the victim in the throat.

Stunned and in shock, Jim let his gaze wander the street. A burning car belched smoke on the curb two buildings away. It looked like there were people inside of the vehicle, but they weren't moving. Body parts littered the street. Dozens of people thrashed in yards and on the sidewalks, the obvious victims of the crab-monsters. Their arms and legs were severed, and some of their bodies were cut in half, but despite this, they moved. They crawled and rolled after other victims. Other injured people roamed the street, feasting on their fellow neighbors or battling the crab creatures. A flock of birds dive-bombed a speeding car, shattering the windshield. The car swerved, smashing into a telephone pole. Before the driver could escape, a horde of rats spilled out of an alleyway and swarmed into the car. The driver stumbled from the vehicle, trying to flee as the small, brown creatures raced up his legs. They bit and clawed at his groin, abdomen, and face. The man collapsed, screaming.

"Danny," Jim moaned, letting the blinds go shut. "Tammy!"

He glanced at the television. As usual, he'd left it on the night before, watching Cartoon Network's Adult Swim until he fell asleep. But this morning, the network wasn't showing cartoons. It wasn't showing anything. The screen was blank.

Jim rushed to the coffee table and grabbed his cell phone. When he tried to call Tammy, the phone beeped at him, flashing a message that said 'No Service'. Cursing, he tried again, silently willing the call to go through. When it didn't, he quickly typed her a text message and tried sending that instead.

While he waited to see if the text would go through, Jim picked up the television remote and scrolled through the channels. Many of them were off the air. A few were showing news coverage rather than their normal programming. He jumped to the cable news outlets. FOX was off the air. MSNBC's had video but no sound. CNN was still broadcasting, but their coverage was chaotic and disjointed. Jim stood there, gaping at footage of a two-story tall crab-monster plowing through buildings in downtown Los Angeles. A graphic beneath it read 'CLICKERS IN LOS ANGELES RIVER'. He turned up the sound.

"—numerous casualties, Ali. Officials tell us there may be as many as five-thousand people dead in Los Angeles alone, and that figure is expected to rise. In addition to the Clickers and the zombie outbreak, we're also seeing widespread looting and other crimes. Just a few moments ago, we saw—"

"I'm going to stop you right there, Candy," the anchorman reported, "because we've got an update from Kiran. She's joining us via satellite phone. Kiran, what can you tell us?"

A woman's garbled voice sputtered static. Then the signal strengthened.

"...and none of the news is good...with each passing moment...highways are clogged with traffic as people rush to escape...bumper to bumper..."

"We're losing her," the anchorman said. "Kiran, are you there?"

If she heard him, Kiran gave no indication, continuing with her report. "...martial law has been declared...the traffic jams...heading further inland...dead...Clickers reanimating, as well...and with the outbreak showing no signs of... experts...destroy the brain...incapacitate..."

"We'll come back to Kiran," the anchorman said, his expression shocked and his pallor pale, "because we're just getting word the White House has confirmed that President Genova was among the victims in Washington D.C. Again, if you're just joining us, the world is in chaos this morning as..."

Jim's door shook as someone pounded on it. He jumped,

startled, and the remote control slipped from his hand. He glanced down at his cell phone, and saw that the text hadn't gone through.

"Damn it!"

The pounding at the door continued.

*"I know you're in there,"* a female voice crowed. *"I can hear your TV!"*

Jim frowned. "What the hell?"

More blows hammered the door, rattling it in its frame. The wood splintered and the hinges squealed. Jim glanced around, searching for a weapon, and then the door crashed inward. The woman from out in the street, the one with the shard of bone sticking through her skin, shuffled into the living room, dragging her broken leg behind her. She wagged a finger at him, and Jim noticed that her fingernail was missing.

*"Shame on you,"* the woman rasped. *"Didn't you hear me knocking?"*

"Get out of here," he warned, inching toward the kitchen. "I have a gun."

*"Oh, I bet you do, cutie. Why don't you pull out your gun and let me see it?"*

Grinning, the zombie loped closer. Jim recoiled from her stench. As hard as it was to believe, the evidence was right there in front of him. This woman was dead—a zombie. Dried blood had stained her clothing brown. Fresher blood shined on the sharp edges of the broken bone sticking out of her arm. Her pale skin had blotches of black and purple on it, and her hair was matted with leaves and twigs. But the worst thing was the flies. They swarmed about her, lighting on her head and shoulders, and busying themselves with her wounds. Jim cringed in disgust as several flies crawled out of her open mouth and took flight.

*"Give me a kiss,"* the zombie said.

Jim turned and ran. Laughing, the zombie lumbered after him. He raced through the kitchen and into the bedroom. He slammed the door shut behind him and shoved hard on the dresser, pushing it against the door. Then he flung open the closet door and stood on his tiptoes. On the shelf at the top sat a pistol box. He'd bought it when Danny was born, wanting to safeguard his firearm and not let it fall into his son's hands. Jim pressed the buttons, entering the four-digit numerical code, and the lock clicked. He opened the box and pulled out a .45 handgun. His fingers shook as he loaded it.

"Fuck," he whispered. "Fuck, fuck, fuck..."

Outside, the zombie pounded on the bedroom door. Taking a deep breath, he stood in front of the door, waiting. The next barrage knocked the dresser to the floor. The door cracked. When the woman burst through, he fired. The first shot hit her in the shoulder, driving her back against the wall. She left a bloody smear on the plaster as she slid across it. Then, regaining her feet, she reached for him again. Jim's next shot hit her in the forehead. The back of her head exploded, driving skull fragments into the wall. Jim fired another round into her face, just to be sure. Then he checked the living room. The busted door hung open, and there was no way to close it, but the doorway stood empty. Apparently, the other creatures were too busy to notice what had occurred. He reloaded the .45 and stuffed his pockets with extra ammunition. As he was doing so, the power went out. With the television suddenly silenced, the noises from outside grew louder.

"Not good," he muttered. "Not good at all."

It wouldn't be long before others noticed that the front door to his apartment had been battered open. He had to escape now. Making sure the apartment was still deserted, he retreated to the bathroom, locked the door, and opened the window. It faced out into the backyard, which was fenced-in and deserted. The window was small, barely wide enough for him to fit through, and Jim had a moment of panic when he thought he'd become stuck, but then his shoulders slipped free and he dropped softly to the ground.

Jim crouched in the backyard, listening to the sounds of death and violence all around him. He'd never been more afraid than he was at that moment. Then he thought of Tammy and Danny.

"I'm coming guys," he whispered. "Just hang on. Daddy's coming."

# EIGHT

*Mendocino National Forest, California*

Clark and Michele had encountered a National Guard roadblock while they were still ten miles from Bodega Bay. Clark had displayed his identification to the young Guardsman who approached the car, but the kid merely glanced at it and blinked.

"Can't go that way, sir. The highway is overrun with Clickers."

"How far?"

"Pardon?"

"How far up the highway?"

The young man blinked again. "All of it, sir. The entire West Coast, from San Diego all the way up to Seattle. Those things are crawling out of the ocean."

"We need to get to Bodega Bay," Clark said. "Official business."

"I'm sorry, sir. It's not there anymore."

"What do you mean?"

"Artillery shelled it a few hours ago, trying to wipe those things out. First it was the Clickers. Then the zombies. The two groups started fighting each other. Commander called in an artillery strike. Killed two birds with one stone."

Cursing, Clark had driven away.

"Where to now?" Michele asked.

"Mount Shasta. It's the next closest power point. We can close the doorway there. All we have to do is reach it in time."

"That easy, huh?"

He turned at her and smiled. "You're doing fine, Michele. Just hang in there."

They'd said very little to each other since then. Both

168

were stunned by the magnitude of what was happening. They listened to the radio, desperate for news. A few of the stations went off the air as they listened. They avoided the highways, which were hopelessly jammed with cars, and opted instead for rural back roads.

And as a result, they were now lost in the middle of the National forest. Michele stared at the towering Redwood trees as the car bumped up and down over the ruts in the dirt road.

"So beautiful," she murmured.

"What's that?" Clark yawned, rubbing his face. His fingernails made scratchy-noises against his fresh stubble.

"The trees," Michele said. "They're just…I don't even have the words to describe them. And not just the trees. This whole area. It feels so…old? Powerful?"

"This is Bigfoot country."

"Is there really a Bigfoot? That's always one of those things I wanted to know—I assumed I'd find out sooner or later, working for Black Lodge."

Clark nodded. "Yep, they're real. I've never seen one, but I've read field reports. Nothing really supernatural about them though, so they're not our responsibility. As I understand it, they're nothing more than an as-yet unclassified species of gorilla. Some experts believe they're on the verge of extinction."

"Maybe we'll see one," Michele said.

"If we do, knowing our luck, it'll be a zombie."

Michele laughed. "A zombie Bigfoot? That's the stupidest thing I've ever heard of."

"Oh, come on." Clark grinned. "Are you telling me an army of zombie Bigfoots warring against humanity doesn't strike your fancy?"

"No. It's the dumbest thing ever. And it's Bigfeet, isn't it?"

"What?"

"You said Bigfoots. I think the plural is Bigfeet."

Clark shrugged, stifling another yawn. "Maybe…"

"Do you want me to drive for a while?" Michele asked.

"Not yet. I'm okay. Let me get us un-lost again, and then we'll see how I feel."

"Okay." Michele glanced out the window again, watching the forest pass by. "It would be a shame if they were extinct."

"What—the Bigfoots?"

"Bigfeet."

"You say tomato. But yes, it would. Although if we don't shut that doorway, they won't be the only thing that's extinct. Everything—including that forest out there—will cease to exist. The Siqqusim are only the first wave. After them come the—FUCK!"

He slammed his foot against the brake pedal and spun the steering wheel, sending the car into a slide. Screaming, Michele thrust out one hand against the dashboard for support, and turned her attention to the road in front of them. A deer stood there, mere feet away from the car, staring at them balefully. The animal didn't move, even as the back end of the car whipped around and headed right for it. And then Michele saw why. The deer's soft, white stomach had been ripped open. It's fur was stained red, and its organs hung from the ragged wound, dangling to the ground.

The back bumper slammed into the deer, sending it flying through the air even as the car shuddered to a stop. The engine died. In the silence, Michele heard Clark breathing heavily.

"Are you okay?" he asked.

Swallowing, she nodded. Behind them, a huge cloud of dust drifted in their wake, obscuring the road and the forest. Michele glanced around, frantically looking for the deer, while Clark turned the key, re-starting the car.

"It was already dead," she said. "I saw, right before we hit it. It wasn't a deer anymore. It was a zombie."

"Let's go, before it comes back."

Clark backed up and then drove forward again, heading down the dirt road. Michele watched for any sign of the deer, but it had vanished. They rounded a bend, and the hard-packed dirt gave way to gravel.

"Well," Clark muttered, "at least it wasn't a Bigfoot."

*Mission Viejo, California*

Rick sat behind the wheel of his car as it idled in the garage. He stared at the closed garage door and tried to stop hyperventilating. Princess sat on the seat next to him, panting. She whined, low and mournful. "It'll be okay, girl." He patted her head, trying to soothe her, and noticed that his hand was shaking. "It's only forty miles from here to San Pedro. We can do this."

Princess looked at him as if to say, *are you sure?* Rick offered her a weak smile. Then, making sure he had everything he'd packed—cell phone, first aid kit, his Ruger .22 rifle, which was the only firearm he owned and was a gift from his father-in-law, along with several boxes of ammunition and half a dozen clips that held thirty rounds each—he started the vehicle, opened the garage door with the remote clipped on the visor, and slowly crept forward.

The vehicle moved down the driveway. Rick closed the garage door. Then, looking carefully up and down the deserted street, he drove out of his neighborhood and meandered toward Interstate 5, which would take him north.

*San Pedro, California*

For the most part they'd stayed awake out of sheer terror throughout the night.

Richard was sitting on the basement floor of the abandoned building, his back against the wall. Melody was sitting next to him on his right. The rest of the group was huddled close together. Sparky had taken up residence against the wall on the opposite side of the room.

Richard fumbled for his cell phone. He pressed the button to activate it. It didn't return a time. Melody stirred beside him out of a light doze. "What's happening?" she asked.

"Just checking the time," he said. "Go back to sleep."

"It's ten a.m.," Sparky said.

Richard looked across the room. In the meager light from the cell phone, he could make out Sparky. The gang banger was resting with his back against the wall, legs splayed out in front of him, right leg bent at the knee casually. He was glancing at the shuttered basement-level window they'd entered, as if sizing it up. "I just checked my watch."

Richard didn't say anything. He could hear and sense movement from his friends. Like him, they hadn't gotten much sleep either. They'd spent most of the night hiding in the basement.

Last night after heading upstairs, Sparky had led them through all the rooms in the building. He'd led the way with his rifle, moving as if he was a well-trained Special Ops sniper. It was a four-story building, and as they moved up to the upper floors it became quickly apparent that they weren't going to find anything. Every apartment they entered (all of them unlocked, some with the doors already broken down or entirely removed from their hinges) was bare of furniture with the exception of one that contained a threadbare table, a rotting sofa in the living room, and a stained mattress on the floor of the bedroom and what looked to be an old fashioned crib. Some units bore the tell-tale signs of squatters. One of the back rooms in an apartment on the second floor was littered with old used condoms, dirty spoons and filthy hypodermic needles. That room had stunk of stale urine and old feces. Melody had gagged and almost thrown up. For some reason, the most tidy apartment was on the third floor. It was free of all signs of break-ins from the homeless. The only thing that had marred its walls and floors was the dust of time and the old shells of spiders and the remnants of their webs.

They'd all had a peak outside from one of the big windows that overlooked the street below. While it was dark, they could see the zombies moving about. The Clickers roamed forth, at one point pouring from the rocky beach a block and a half down as if the ocean was vomiting them from its depths. They'd watched spellbound as the creatures clogged the street, their claws clicking together like mad castanets. From this vantage point they saw several giant specimens lumber forth from a distance. Some looked big enough to knock the apartment building down, and for a moment Richard was struck with a momentary flare of panic. He was pretty sure one of the creatures would veer in the general direction they were hiding and blunder into the apartment building, knocking it down. Instead, the creatures moved on, and forty minutes later they were gone.

But outside, beyond their vantage point in Sunken City, out in San Pedro and Lomita and probably the neighboring cities of Torrance and Harbor City and Gardena and into Los Angeles proper, was madness and chaos.

As the screams of the dying and tormented echoed outside amid the sound of scattered gunfire and destruction, Richard had turned to Paul and Max. "I don't know if it's entirely safe up here. I mean, we can see everything, but—"

Sparky had nodded. "I get you. If one of those big ones knocks the building apart, we're fucked."

"So what are we going to do?" Melody had asked. Her eyes had been wide. She and Mary clutched each other like frightened little girls.

"We should hide back down in the basement," Sparky said. "That basement level window is secure enough that nobody will think of checking it out. And we can lock the door to the basement from the inside."

"Yeah, but if the zombies get in the building and somehow find out we're down there, we're fucked," Paul said.

"If they come in, they'll be doing it through the front entrance," Sparky said. "The building doesn't have a back door."

"You sure?" Max asked.

"It doesn't," Richard said, nodding. "Only door that leads anywhere else but an apartment or out the front is the one to the basement."

Paul looked nervous. He'd shaken his head, clearly not liking the idea of holing up in the basement. "I don't know, man. Seems to me like we're sitting ducks down there."

"If we keep quiet, nothing will hear us," Sparky had said. Richard had grown to admire the gang member in the brief time they'd spent with him. He was fast thinking. Everything he was saying made sense. "I have several weapons. If the zombies *do* find out where we are and break down the door, I can hold them off while you guys slip out through the window."

Richard had nodded, running potential evacuation scenarios in his head. "He's right," he'd said. "If we stay up here and the zombies manage to find out we're here, there's no way out. We can't exactly jump out the window."

They'd retreated back to the basement. Using the light from their cell phones, they managed to get the door locked from the inside, then made themselves comfortable for the long night ahead.

They'd spent most of last night talking in low, whispered tones. Max had asked Sparky point blank if he had really intended to shoot them back in that neighborhood. "If none of this fucked up zombie shit hadn't happened, yes, I was. No offense, *ese*, but you *cabrones* were in my way."

"How were we in your way?" Max asked. "We were trying to get the fuck out of there!"

For a moment, that hardness crept back into Sparky's demeanor. It was in his eyes, which narrowed slightly. "You want to start something about it?"

"Good Christ, no, he doesn't want to start anything about it," Richard barked. He turned to Max, angry. "You need to shut the fuck up."

Max had responded in kind. He'd almost leaped over to Richard. "Oh yeah? Well fuck you!"

"Will you both shut your traps?" Paul had said. "Jesus fucking Christ on a moped, if anything hears us in here, we're dead meat."

"You better listen to your homeboy, *ese*," Sparky said. He leaned against the wall casually, a slight grin on his face. He was cradling that black assault rifle as if it were something sexual. "Whatever the fuck those things are—zombies, monsters, whatever—they got ears. They'll hear us and try to break in here."

Melody had clutched at Richard's arm. She'd been clearly afraid, on the verge of tears. Richard had tried to assuage her fears. Sparky had noticed the exchange. "She your little sister?"

Richard had nodded. "Yeah."

"And what about you two?" Sparky had motioned to Paul and Mary.

"We're siblings," Paul admitted.

"Which just leaves dick head over here without a family," Sparky said, acknowledging Max with a slight smile.

Max muttered something under his breath. If it was meant to taunt Sparky, the gang banger either didn't hear it, or he didn't care.

"Whatever," Sparky said. "Listen, I don't want to fuck with you kids tonight, you know what I'm sayin'? Whatever the fuck is happening outside, it's some serious shit. You want to hang out with me down here and hide from those fucked up things, that's cool. But you can't be fightin' with each other and shit. And you can't be sayin' shit to me, you understand?"

"We've got to be cool," Richard said, directing this to his sister and his friends, his mind racing, already figuring the gang banger out.

"You're right, homie," Sparky said. "We all gots to be cool. Can we do that?"

Richard nodded. He sensed Melody and his friends nodding and murmuring in agreement in the darkness of the basement. Across from them, Sparky had sighed and shifted position. "Cell phones aren't working for shit now, but if anybody gets a signal, let me know. In the meantime, I think we should just hunker down and wait for this shit to pass."

And that's what they'd done. Aside from some discussion among themselves about what to do, within full earshot of Sparky and not really caring that he could hear them, Richard and Paul had taken over the discussion and talked Melody, Mary, and Max into sitting it out in the basement for now. The battle that was being raged outside—they could hear gunfire, explosions, screams, and other sounds from blocks, even miles away—continued to filter into them. That was enough to keep them down here for the night. The other concern was the lack of cell phone coverage. "If Dad heard us say we were in Sunken City, he'll come up here," Richard had said.

"What if those things got him?" Melody had asked.

"We can't consider that right now," Richard had answered.

As they'd talked, Sparky said nothing. He'd hung back on his side of the basement, observing, listening. Finally, when the discussion was over, they'd settled into waiting it out.

At some point during the night they'd taken turns dozing. Richard told Melody she could sleep if she wanted to and for a while she did, her head resting against his right shoulder. When she woke up she whispered to Mary. The two girls cried at one point, their sobs muffled as they comforted each other. Paul had moved over to be near Richard and told him if he wanted to doze a little bit he could—Paul could keep watch. Richard took him up on it and managed to sleep lightly for a few hours. When he woke up, there were explosions in the distance.

Everybody had gotten up at the concussive reports of the explosions. "What the hell is that?" Max had asked, his voice trembling.

"The oil refineries in Long Beach maybe?" Paul said. Melody and Mary had turned their cell phones on, and in their glowing light Richard could see their frightened expressions. Even Sparky looked a little freaked out by it.

"Maybe." They'd listened to the sounds for a while as smaller explosions erupted in the distance. *It has to be the refineries*, Richard had thought. *What else could it be?*

Now it was ten a.m. The air was heavy with the smell of smoke. Wherever it was coming from, it was strong enough to seep into the basement.

"If shit's on fire, it might spread this way," Max said, his voice low, humbled. Last night's verbal dress down had taken him down a peg or two.

"Maybe we should head upstairs and see where it's coming from," Richard suggested.

Sparky was standing at attention cradling his rifle, looking up at the ceiling as if trying to see through it to the deserted street outside. "Yeah, that sounds like a plan. Let's go."

They headed up the stairs with Sparky in the lead. After getting the door open, they moved slowly down the first floor hall to the staircase that led upstairs. It wasn't as dark up here as it was in the basement, and the windows that looked out to the street were still boarded up. They headed up to the third floor quietly and once in the clean apartment they moved to the windows that overlooked the street below.

"Well, something's on fire, that's for sure," Sparky said.

Amid the typical blue sky Southern California was known for, there were big splotches of dark smoke that were drifting from the east. It was hard to tell where the fire originated from unless they looked out a window on the other end of the building. Paul exited the apartment and headed to the apartment opposite this one, which was sparsely furnished with rotting furniture and bore the evidence that squatters had taken temporary residency. "Wow! You guys should see this!"

The others left the apartment and entered the unit Paul had drifted into. Paul was standing in what had presumably been the bedroom, looking out the large window that looked out over San Pedro to the north and Lomita and Long Beach to the south. About ten miles to the distant south, in what Richard was positive was Harbor City and North Long Beach, the oil refinery that was located just south of the 405 freeway was on fire.

"Holy fuck, will you look at that," Richard breathed.

"If Dad can drive up here to get us, how's he going to get past *that?*" Melody asked. She looked transfixed by the fire. From this distance it appeared something had bashed into one of the large oil tankers—that giant Clicker, perhaps? Flames shot hundreds of feet into the air, billowing thick clouds of black smoke. The smoke was so great in size and density that it practically covered the entire South Bay and South Central Los Angeles area. It was now starting to drift southward toward the beach, which was evident by the tendrils of smoke that was beginning to seep over Sunken City.

"He'll get here," Richard said, trying to soothe his sister's fears.

"I hope so," Melody said.

From behind them, Sparky was messing with his cell phone. "Still no service," he said. He looked up from his phone, his features solemn. "I hope your old man can get up here."

Richard was thinking about this when something fell to the floor in the room behind them.

Everybody froze. Richard's heart was lodged in his throat. His belly felt like lead. "What was that?" he whispered.

"I don't know," Sparky said. He was instantly alert. He cradled his assault rifle, his finger brushing the trigger guard.

Melody grabbed Richard's arm again, melting against him. With the four friends huddled in close formation, Sparky stepped out of the room to see what had made that sound.

## Foothill Boulevard, California

When Augustus finally regained consciousness, the first thing he noticed was the sunlight on his face. It had been night when he blacked out.

He sprang up quickly, expecting something to come at him. Then he realized where he was and what had happened. His breath was held in his lungs and he released it in a long sigh as he sagged in the plush leather seat of the limousine.

*God, I've been conked out all night*, he thought. He looked out the tinted windows of the vehicle, noting that the street was completely deserted now. The chaos that had erupted yesterday was no more. The zombies, the crab-monsters, all were gone. He wondered why the limo driver hadn't come back for him. The zombie had unlocked the doors from outside when it took Marion. Why not come back for him and do the same?

Marion…

Augustus whined, low and mournful. His body trembled as he thought of her. His ears began to ring and his face felt flushed. He put his head between his legs and breathed deeply until the spell had passed.

"Oh, Marion," he sobbed. "I am so sorry…"

Augustus inspected his surroundings more closely. His senses were garbled, not on track. They felt sluggish. The last thing he remembered was Marion being dragged off into a grove of trees by one of those zombies. Augustus had rushed to her rescue but had been driven off by another zombie. He'd seen what they were doing to people in that grove of trees. They'd been torturing those poor people...raping them.

Augustus shook his head in disgust. How could the dead rape the living? It didn't make sense. What was powering these creatures? In all his studies on past life regressions and the afterlife, the one thing he learned was that the soul always yearned for peace. It didn't seek death and destruction, the pain and suffering and degradation of other living things. So what was going on here? He remembered his intuition from the night before, that another entity was inside the corpses. What could it have been? The only thing that came to mind was an explanation his daughter, Susan, would have been quick to supply. Demons.

As Augustus looked out the window trying to gauge his surroundings, he tried to put everything in perspective. He didn't subscribe to a Judeo-Christian worldview like his daughter, but he did believe in negative supernatural forces. People like Susan would call those forces demons, but Augustus and people who practiced New Age spirituality preferred to think of them as negative energy forces. The amount of psychic energy a human being expels and holds is greatly influenced by that individual's personality and mood, by the acts they commit, the way they carry their lives. People prone to committing horrible acts or dwelling on the negative often exude bad energy. People who worked at positive things often exuded positive energy. Augustus had always lectured that it was important to live clean, and to always portray a positive energy. When a person died, that positive energy— the spirit—could go forth and work its magic or it could be reborn in another human being. However, if a person with negative energy died, the life force lived on as a malignant force. Augustus had been called in as a consultant on so-called haunted house cases. Most of those cases had to do with the negative energy—the spiritual residue of a person who had lived an unhappy or negative life—remaining in the house.

Truly evil people, however, sometimes left a psychic energy that was very malignant. This energy could wreak havoc on the living in a way that led most people to believe that demons were present.

Whatever had happened here, it wasn't just a huge giant case of bad psychic energy. This was something far worse.

Augustus reached into his pocket for his cell phone. He pulled it out and saw that it was still turned on. There was no cellular signal. Cursing, he put it back in his pocket and moved toward the front of the vehicle. The partition that separated the driver from the passenger was still open and the front seat was empty, the doors shut and presumably locked. Augustus looked out the front windshield at the empty street in front of him. His first thought was for his children. Were they okay? Were they able to get out of California? Was this mass chaos and destruction limited to California or was it global? Augustus was pretty sure it was global; he was beginning to remember the news reports yesterday afternoon as they were speeding down Foothill Boulevard toward the airport. Whatever had happened, it had happened fast. And those things…

Clickers. That's what the media had called them. Thinking about the path of destruction they'd carved, August was lucky to be alive.

Augustus cast another look around and gripped the handle of the door. *Marion,* he thought. *I've got to find Marion.*

He opened the door to the limousine and stepped outside cautiously. The first thing that hit him was the smell. It was the stench of smoke from a dozen fires underlined with a chemical scent and something else…

Death.

Augustus turned to the grove of trees where those things had taken Marion. That area seemed deserted now. He stood there for a moment, trying to let his senses guide him. Right now he could feel nothing. He detected no vibration, no negative energy. All he felt was a vast emptiness, yet at the same time he sensed something was out there, something old, so old it defied human perceptions of time; it was older than anything in the universe, and it was powerful and it knew all worlds, had amassed an army of similar beings under its power, and it was here on this world to overtake it, to overrun it, to destroy it, and when it was finished it was going to move on to the next world, no, the next *version* of this world, and it had to be stopped, it had to be taken down, had to be—

Augustus began heading toward the grove of trees. The heat from the fires made the temperatures even hotter in this mid-July morning. Supposed to be one hundred and one today, Augustus thought, but it feels even hotter. He looked south toward Los Angeles, which was covered in a thick cloud of smoke.

"First things first," he muttered. "Look for Marion in that grove of trees. You have to brace yourself for the fact that she might be dead, or she might be one of those things now. If so, you have to get back to the house. Get behind the wheel of that limo and head back to Malibu. Hole up there."

Surely there had to be some form of government still around. Didn't he read somewhere that in the event of some catastrophic event key government officials could retreat to hidden warrens and tunnels beneath Washington DC? Somebody had to be down there now, maybe some skeleton government. Surely plans were already being made to stop this carnage. In fact, the military was probably already engaging in battle with them now and…Augustus shook his head.

"Engaging in battle?" He was aware that he was speaking out loud again, but he didn't care. "Where did that phrase come from? You're starting to lose it, old man. You've never had the slightest interest in the military and now you're tossing around military terms in your conscious mind as if you're a four-star Colonel."

At that thought, Augustus grinned. Maybe at some point he was a four-star Colonel. After all, he could have been one in another life, right?

He continued on toward the grove of trees. He ignored the smears of blood on the grass, the scraps of bloody clothing that littered the bushes, the trees. He noted that there were no dead bodies lying around. Either they'd been consumed by the Clickers or wandered on as zombies in search of other prey. Or maybe both. Many of the trees were withered and blackened. Several had fallen to the ground, or leaned with splintered, blackened trunks. A few were nothing more than charred stumps. He remembered the black Clicker from the night before. It had been spraying the trees with some sort of venom that had acted as a defoliant. Some of the zombies had been sprayed with the venom and had melted, which the Clicker had eaten. He was mindful not to touch any of the vegetation, and watched where he stepped.

As Augustus moved deeper into the ruined undergrowth he couldn't help but think about Marion. He felt himself getting emotional; she was most likely dead, melted from the corrosive venom of that black Clicker and devoured like soup, or her body was a shell, being used by one of those creatures. The thought of this overwhelmed him, stabbed him with grief. Augustus paused in his trek and leaned against a tree for support. *What if I can't find her?* He thought. *What if she's really gone?*

He couldn't imagine life without Marion. They'd been together for fifty years. A lifetime. Memories of their youth flashed in his memories. The early years of their marriage. Their first born child and how happy they'd been. Sure, they'd had some stressful times in their marriage—what relationship didn't? But despite the bad times, they found strength in each other. They'd always had each other to lean on for support. And as the years had passed and the kids had grown from toddlers to elementary school aged, to being in high school, his career had taken off, and then Marion had joined him in the business and life had opened up far and wide for them. Their relationship had blossomed on so many levels. And through it all, they still managed to find time for each other. They had still gone on dates—the movies, dinner at their favorite restaurants, or just a quiet walk on the beach at sunset. Augustus still bought Marion a bouquet of flowers every Friday afternoon and presented them to her as if he were still courting her. And when they made love on those rare nights when nobody was pressuring them for something, whether it was for business or family, it was very much like making love to the eighteen-year old girl he'd fallen in love with he'd met in college. Slipping her clothes off to touch her bare skin, feeling her body pressed against his, the way it made him stiffen in arousal, it was still very much like being a young man again, touching her for the first time. Marion had made him feel young again every time they came together in love.

Thinking about this made him think of a song his older son used to listen to. "Feels Like the First Time," by a band called Foreigner. That was a lifetime ago, when George was in Junior High school and he would spend hours in his bedroom listening to albums by the likes of Styx and REO Speedwagon and Ted Nugent. Those albums, and the Foreigner record that was now playing in his head, had been on constant replay in their home back in the late seventies. Augustus hadn't cared much for George's choice in music, but he hadn't discouraged it, either. Still, that song had spoken to him, and it spoke to him now as he stepped through the vegetation into a small clearing and stopped.

Marion stood there, silhouetted in the morning sun that cast iridescent beams through the trees behind her. "*Hello, Augie,*" she said with a smile.

Augustus felt the blood rush from his face. "Marion…"

"*I've been waiting for you.*"

"Is that…is that really you?" Heart pounding, still aroused from the erotic day dreams he'd just entertained in his mind, he stepped forward.

"*Of course it's me,*" Marion said, her grin revealing bloody, broken teeth that Augustus failed to notice, he was so enraptured by the thought of seeing her. The thing that was Marion held her arms open. "*Come, my darling. Fill me up. I'm yours.*"

"Oh Marion," Augustus said. He was weeping. Tears blurred his vision as he stumbled to Marion, the love of his life, the center of his universe. Just a few moments ago he'd been torn at the prospect of living the rest of his life without her and now he didn't have to face that moment. She was here and they could escape together, head back to the house in Malibu near the ocean, with its peaceful beachfronts and clean, brisk sea air, and they could hide out together until this negative energy spent itself.

Augustus took her into his arms, embracing her, not even

aware that pieces of her were missing, that his right hand was resting on the back of her bare rib cage which had been stripped of flesh. He wept and held his Marion close to him and he felt her fingers touch his belly as she loosened his trousers. He felt cool air on his buttocks as his trousers fell down to his knees and then she was grasping his hardness, and even then, Augustus did not notice when the flesh of his penis scraped against the bones of her bare fingers.

"*Let me have you,*" Marion whispered in his ear.

"Yes." Augustus closed his eyes.

And then they fell together and when Marion guided him into her and he began to love her, he didn't even feel it as her teeth clamped down on his neck and bit down, tearing into his flesh. She coaxed him along, thrusting with her hips, and the last thing Augustus felt was that it felt so good, so *wonderful*, to be back in the arms of his lover, partner, and soul mate.

Then his soul departed, and something else slid into his body. Slowly, the two corpses rose from their coupling and went in search of prey.

*Palos Verdes, California*

Dr. Alfred Post decided to try raising somebody on the Ham radio. Al had been involved in amateur radio since he was twelve years old. His call letters were K87R-RT3, and he'd been licensed since he was twelve years old. He was past president of the Los Angeles Ham Radio Operators club, and had been involved in all aspects of the hobby including radio teletype, Dxing, APRS, satellites, and everything in between. He also made an annual pilgrimage to Dayton, Ohio every May for Hamfest, a convention that drew radio enthusiasts from all over the world. It was at Hamfest where Al would talk to vendors and manufacturers, buy new equipment, get tips on upgrades, and learn about emerging technologies in the hobby.

The power was out, but Al had spent the morning quietly getting his emergency generator running. It was humming along now, generating power to the radio equipment in the spare bedroom on the ground floor of the house. Janice had sat in the corner chair, afraid to leave his side as Al had worked at hooking things up. "Don't know why I didn't hook this stuff up sooner," he said as he sat at his desk and began powering his system up. "I should have had this on yesterday but I was so caught up in things."

"Don't blame yourself," Janice said. She had gotten over her shock somewhat. Her brown, wavy hair hung limply about her face.

"There" Al said. He dialed the tuner knob across the band, trying to pick up something. All he heard was dead silence across all channels.

"Maybe you should give out your call signal," Janice said. "Maybe we just aren't receiving."

"Good point." Al flicked another switch, then picked up the microphone. "This is K87R-RT3 broadcasting from Palos Verdes, California. Repeat, this is K87R-RT3 broadcasting from Palos Verdes, California."

Al repeated this for a few minutes. He moved the dial slowly across the band, hoping to pick up something, but all he received was silence.

"Damn!" He leaned back, dejected.

"Keep trying," Janice said. "Just keep giving out our call signal. Somebody is bound to respond. I can't imagine you're the only Ham operator in the country left."

Al tried again. He continued broadcasting his call letters across an open network, hoping for a response.

An hour later he gave up. He sat behind his desk, head cradled in his hands. Behind him, Janice had buried her face in her hands and was sobbing quietly. Last night, they had been able to hear explosions and chaos from outside. Today, it was quiet. Deadly quiet.

After a few moments, Al stepped back from the equipment. He walked over to Janice and laid his hand on her shoulder. "Come on honey," he said. "Let's head upstairs. We can try again tomorrow.

Janice wiped her eyes with her fingers and nodded. "Okay," she said. He helped her to her feet and they turned to head out the door when an electronic squelching sound emitted from the Ham radio equipment speakers.

They turned around quickly. The squelch sounded again. It was the unmistakable sound of communication. Al froze, trying not to get his hopes up. Surely it was just dead air.

But it wasn't. There was another squelch, a burst of feedback.

And then a voice spoke to them from the Ham radio equipment speakers in response to Al's broadcast.

# NINE

Ob rampaged down Hollywood Boulevard, leaving a devastating path of destruction in his wake. It was a beautiful, sunny California day and he was in a great mood. His monstrous host body had performed wonderfully so far, and he was delighted with its capabilities. Even better, he had received word from his forces that all of this planet's protectors were now dead. Each of the Seven had been killed, the heads of the world's governments were slaughtered, and the Black Lodge organization was utterly decimated—its fearful remnants scattered and hiding. No one remained on this Earth to stymie their conquest or send them back in the Void. He mulled this over while snatching a fleeing human from the street and slowly pulling the hapless victim's arms and legs off one by one.

All around his behemoth host body, battles raged between his fellow Siqqusim, the Clickers, and the humans trapped between the two forces. The Clickers' motivations remained the same as ever—food and self-defense—but the zombies had a much bigger motive. Upon seeing how well their leader had benefited upon taking possession of a dead Clicker, they were now focused on killing the crab-things first, to better utilize the monstrous forms in then killing the city's remaining humans. It was glorious sport, and Ob was enjoying the grisly spectacle until he reached Hollywood and Vine.

A rag-tag band of policemen, gang members, private citizens, and the remnants of a National Guard unit had blockaded the intersection with an array of vehicles, and were hunkered down behind them, gunning down both zombies and Clickers with equal furor. As Ob lumbered toward them, a few humans broke from the group, fleeing down the boulevard, but the of them majority remained. Immediately, they concentrated all of their firepower on him. Most of the bullets were ineffective, ricocheting off his behemoth host body's thick carapace and striking surrounding buildings instead. Then one of the humans scrambled atop a military Humvee with a fifty-caliber machine gun mounted on its top, and opened fire, aiming for Ob's underside. He felt the heavy rounds puncture his abdomen and tunnel through the soft meat. Roaring, he charged the blockade, slamming his claws together and lashing his massive tail back and forth. The barrage continued, severing two of Ob's legs. His heavy bulk crashed to the pavement, cracking a bronze star for an Oscar-winning screenwriter named David J. Schow. Ob seized an awning from a nearby restaurant and flung it at his opponents. Then, taking advantage of the momentary distraction, he struggled to his feet and tried to run, but it was impossible to do with two missing legs. He jabbed at the blockade with his stinger, but the humans were too far away to reach. Frustrated, he snapped a nearby tree off at the base, intending to use it as a club. Before he could lift it, however, several small, oval-shaped metal objects rolled toward him from behind one of the wrecked cars. He had time enough to realize that they were grenades, and heard the human who had thrown them holler at his companions to duck, and then his host body was blown apart. Pinkish-white Clicker meat and fragments of shell rained down on the Walk of Fame, but Ob wasn't there to see it. His incorporeal form was already back in the Void, waiting to take possession of his next vessel.

It didn't take very long, and once he was inside the new body, and had searched his host's memories, Ob laughed for a very long time—for there, among the faces of the people his host new, was someone that Ob recognized. Someone he'd encountered before. Someone who had previously bested him.

*"Jim Thurmond,"* Ob said, still laughing. *"Well, aren't you going to be surprised!"*

Humming a happy tune, Ob took his new body for a walk, deciding to kill as many people as he could until Jim showed up.

## San Pedro, California

Jim crouched down behind a row of bushes, watching Tammy's house and trying not to vomit. Less than five feet away from him, just on the other side of the hedgerow, two dog-sized Clickers were slurping up the liquefied, still-bubbling remains of a man that Rick had watched them kill just moments before. It wasn't the sight that horrified him the most. It was the smell of the venom, the stench of dissolved tissue and bone, and worst of all, the sounds the creatures made as they devoured the slop.

He knew that the Clickers were virtually bulletproof. He'd seen it for himself during his perilous journey here. He'd watched as a man emptied an entire magazine at one of the creatures. The Clicker hadn't even slowed down. Instead, it had ignored the bullets and severed the man's legs just above the kneecaps. That had been mild compared to some of the other horrors Jim had witnessed. Upon escaping his apartment, the first thing he'd been overwhelmed with was the sounds. A soundtrack to the apocalypse. Cars crashing. Horns blaring. Breaking glass—and breaking bones. Wailing alarms. Volleys of gunfire. The guttural laughter and cruel taunts of the dead. The living—men and woman, adults and children—screaming out in agony or terror or quite often both. Then he'd heard a different sound.

CLICK-CLICK…CLICK-CLICK…CLICK-CLICK…

Moments later, a horde of Clickers had rushed down the street, scattering both the living and the dead in their path. The living fled. The zombies tried to fight back, but were vastly outnumbered by the sea creatures. They attacked with weapons—everything from guns to clubs—and those who weren't armed simply flung themselves at the crab-things, breaking their teeth on the hard shells or trying to immobilize them through sheer numbers and weight. Jim had cowered beneath a mini-van, lying in a half-congealed pool of blood and transmission fluid. His eyes flicked upward, verifying that the van did indeed have a bad transmission. Then he'd turned his gaze to the right, following the blood trail to where a pile of intestines lay cooling in the street. There was no sign of their owner.

A garbled cry caught his attention. Lying still, Jim watched as a zombie without a lower jaw ran toward the Clickers, swinging a golf club in an attempt to smash through their shells. Seconds later, two of the creatures seized the corpse in their claws and pulled it apart like taffy. Another zombie ran out into the street with a can of gasoline, and dumped the fuel over one of the smaller Clickers. Then the zombie lit a match, seemingly uncaring that he too was covered in gas. Both monsters were engulfed in the blaze. Jim felt the heat from his hiding place. He cringed, squinting his eyes, but there was nowhere for him to retreat.

As he watched, another zombie charged into the fray, swinging a rusty axe. The corpse managed to crack open a few shells before a massive Clicker reared up on its back legs and squealed with rage. As they turned toward it, the creature's segmented tail whipped forward, jabbing the zombie in the chest. The axe slipped from its grasp, landing on the road with a loud clank. Even as the zombie struggled to free itself, the Clicker raised its tail, lifting the zombie off the ground. The dead man hung suspended in the air, thrashing and kicking as the monster pumped venom into his body. The zombie opened its mouth to laugh and blood welled out, splattering the Clicker and the pavement below. Blisters formed all over its body. The corpse continued to laugh even as its flesh began to bubble and hiss, sloughing off the bones and splattering onto the road. To Jim, it appeared as if the zombie was being cooked from the inside out. The zombie didn't stop laughing or jittering until its liquefied brains oozed out of its ears. Finally, the Clicker tugged its tail free and the skeleton fell to the pavement, exploding into jelly. Gore and poison dripped from the stinger. Jim was close enough that he could smell them both.

Eventually, the zombies began to gain the upper hand through their sheer numbers and the ferocity of their attacks. Jim grimaced as a dead woman lifted the fallen axe and finally managed to crack through a shell. The zombies swarmed, shoving their hands through the crack in the carapace, and pulling out fistfuls of meat. The Clicker shrieked, and then died. Seconds later, it rose again and began to attack the other Clickers. After a few more of the crab-things had joined the ranks of the undead, the battle turned in the zombies' favor. Through it all, Jim lay there beneath the mini-van, shivering and waiting.

When it was over, and the street was deserted once more, he slowly crawled out from beneath the vehicle and cautiously checked his surroundings. Satisfied that the coast was at least temporarily clear, Jim stretched, working out the kinks and aches in his muscles. He found himself standing alone in the midst of the carnage. Slowly, he'd made his way to Tammy's, careful to take a path that provided lots of cover to hide behind.

And now here he was, concealed behind some shrubbery, while two Clickers feasted just a few feet away from him. He held his breath, trying not to move. His senses reeled at the briny stench wafting off the creatures. Their black, stalked eyes waved to and fro, reminding Jim of ball bearings affixed to sunflower stalks. Then movement caught his eye, and a second later, he forgot all about the Clickers.

A man wearing a hardhat and dirty overalls darted across a neighbor's yard and crept up to Tammy's front door. It took Jim a moment to realize that the stranger was dead. He had no obvious injuries or signs of trauma. It wasn't until he spoke that the truth revealed itself. There was no disguising the maniacal cruelty and otherworldliness in his voice.

*"Hello in there?"* The zombie knocked on the door with one meaty fist. *"I need help. Please let me in. I'm not one of them. I was working down the street, putting in the new sewer line."*

Jim's breath caught in his throat, and his heart throbbed in his chest.

*"Hello,"* the zombie called. *"Please? I know you're in there. Please, you've got to hurry! They're coming."*

"No," Jim whispered. "Don't open the door."

The Clickers paused in their feast, eyestalks swiveling, seeking the source of the sound. One skittered toward the zombie. The other turned in Jim's direction.

The zombie's pounding grew louder. *"Open the door, bitch!"*

The Clicker hurried toward it, even as the other raised its claw and parted the shrubs. The zombie turned toward them. Jim's grip tightened on his pistol.

A dog barked further down the street. Something rustled through the hedges, zipping right between Jim and the Clicker. Seconds later, a gunshot echoed. Jim, the Clickers, and the zombie all turned as one, to see a teenage boy and a dog standing a hundred yards away. The boy gaped, holding a still smoking pistol in his trembling hands. His eyes were wide and panicked. He shouted something, but Jim couldn't understand him. The dog stood at his side, shaking, head lowered, ears flat. He fired again, and the pistol jumped in his hands.

Hissing, the Clickers ran after the duo, speeding forward on their segmented legs. The boy fired again, and then fled. The dog issued a low growl and then took off after him.

Seeing his chance, Jim sprang out from behind the hedgerow and charged toward the house. The zombie, hearing his footfalls, turned in surprise.

*"Hey, buddy. Where'd you come from?"*

"Drop the bullshit," Jim said, sliding to a halt. He stood with his feet apart and raised the .45, aiming for the creature's head. "I know you're one of them."

The dead man held up his hands in protest and did a remarkable pantomime of appearing confused. *"No, I'm not. What's your problem, friend?"*

Jim squeezed the trigger, splattering the zombie's head all over Tammy's eggshell white vinyl siding. The corpse slumped into the yard and lay still.

"You're between me and my son. That's my problem."

Jim kept the weapon trained on it for a moment longer, making sure it was really dead. Then he glanced back down the street, verifying that the Clickers were still pursuing their other prey. Satisfied, he raced to the door and knocked.

"Tammy? It's me! Open up."

There was no response, so he knocked again, louder this time.

"Tammy? It's Jim. Open the door!"

He paused, listening. After a moment, he tilted his head and put his ear to the door. He heard a soft thump from inside the house.

"Guys, come on. It's me. Everything's okay. I got rid of him. Hurry up now."

Then he heard Tammy cry out, "Danny, no!"

"But Mommy, it's Daddy."

"Danny, get away from the door. It's not your Daddy anymore."

Frowning, Jim knocked again. "Tammy, Danny—it's me. It's really me. Are you guys okay?"

"You're not Jim," Tammy screamed. "You're not Jim just like Anthony wasn't Anthony. It's a trick."

"Tammy, what are you—"

"Leave us alone!" she sobbed through the door.

"Tammy, god damn it, let me—"

CLICK-CLICK…CLICK-CLICK…CLICK-CLICK…

Jim paused. "Oh no…"

He turned to see the two Clickers returning down the street. One of them dragged the upper half of the dog's corpse in its left pincer, leaving a crimson trail of meat and fur on the asphalt. More and more of the fraying corpse scraped onto the rough surface with each step. Jim gasped when he realized that the dead dog was moving. The front paws kicked, scratching ineffectively at the Clickers' shell. From its mouth came something that sounded like speech, but the words were nothing Jim recognized. Of course, a dog's vocal chords weren't designed for speech, but that didn't stop the zombie from trying.

He turned back to the door. "Tammy. Tammy, for God's sake, those things are coming back. I promise you, I'm still your ex-husband. I'm Danny's father. Please open the door."

Her only response was a muffled, frightened sob.

"Okay," Jim sighed. "We met at Mike and Melissa's New Year's Eve party. You remember? It was the year 2000, and everybody was worried about Y2K. I'd just broken up with Carrie, and you had just broken up with Rick."

CLICK-CLICK...CLICK-CLICK...CLICK-CLICK...

"For our first date, we went to that little coffee shop across from the Chinese Buffet. We sat there all night, and I stole two coffee mugs as souvenirs. You invited me back to your place, and we stayed awake all night, just talking. The next day, I left my Danzig and Soundgarden CDs there, so I'd have an excuse to come back again. Do you remember?"

Jim risked a glance to the street. The Clickers were only two houses away now. They hurried toward him, squealing and hissing. The zombie dog slipped free of the claw and splattered onto the pavement. The remainder of its organs spilled out in a steaming flood, but still it moved, trying to crawl after them with its two front paws. Jim put the gun to his head and continued.

"When we found out you were pregnant, and that it was a boy, I wanted to name him Timmy and you wanted to name him Benjy. We settled instead on Danny. His...his first word was Daddy. His first curse word was son of a bitch. He learned it from you." Jim smiled at the memory. "Somebody cut you off in traffic and he said it from his car seat."

The Clickers closed in, scuttling across the next door neighbor's yard. Behind them, the dead dog inched along, determined to join the fray. It bared its teeth at Jim, and he was certain that it was grinning. He pressed the gun tighter against his head. His finger was sweaty on the trigger.

"Tammy...Tammy, you've got to listen to me. I'm Jim. I'm the guy you married. I'm the father of your child, and I'm so sorry that it didn't work out between us. You don't know how sorry I am. All I want is for you to be happy. If you're happy, then Danny is happy, and at the end of the day, that's all that matters to me. But it's the end of the world, Tammy. Remember yesterday? You said if it was the end of the world, you'd want to spend time with Danny and me. Well, here we are. Here we are and—"

He heard the chain rattle and the bolt being thrown. Tammy peeked out at him, her face shining with tears. Jim lowered the gun and forced the door open. Shoving past her, he slammed it closed and locked it again.

194

"You're you," she gasped. "Not like Anthony. You're really you."

Frowning, Jim nodded in confusion.

"Daddy!"

Danny raced to him, grabbing his leg and hanging on tight. Jim reached down, picked up the trembling boy, and looked him in the eye.

"Listen to me, Squirt. It's going to be okay. I promise it's going to all be okay. But right now, we've got to do some things. Help me out, okay? I need you to be brave. Can you do that for me?"

Danny nodded. "Okay, Daddy. I'm so glad you're here."

"Me, too, buddy." Jim sat him down. "Me, too."

The Clickers hit the closed door with their claws. Their enraged cries sounded like fingernails on a chalkboard. The door buckled in its frame. The hinges squealed.

"What do we do?" Tammy shrieked.

"You still have those Tiki torches out on the back patio?"

"Y-yes…"

"You have the extra fuel for them?"

She nodded.

"Get them. Meet me upstairs. Danny, come on."

Tammy rushed to the kitchen as Jim started up the stairs. Danny followed at his heels. Jim was halfway up when he stopped.

"Danny, where's Samhain?"

The boy's face clouded. His lower lip protruded. Then he began to weep. Long lines of snot dripped from his nose.

"He…he…Mommy let him out in the backyard and… there were birds. There were dead birds…"

Jim's knees went weak. "What?"

"They started eating him, Daddy. The birds were eating at him. Then Anthony…"

"This is all I have," Tammy said, coming up the stairs. She held up a plastic gallon jug of tiki torch fuel. When she saw that Danny was crying, she stopped.

"Here," Jim said, reaching for the jug. "Take him."

Tammy picked up Danny and held him to her, while Jim

walked into the master bedroom. He tried to ignore the fact that it was different than he remembered. Why wouldn't it be? Like everything else in the house, Tammy had replaced their old bedroom suite with new furniture. He glanced sidelong at the bed, grimacing at the rumpled red sheets and the pillows, each of which had a head impression on them.

Anthony was here, he thought.

Jim went to the window, which directly overlooked the front door. He slid it open and looked down. The Clickers had been momentarily distracted by the zombie dog, but now it was a sizzling pool of red goop, and their attention had returned to the door.

"You have matches?" Jim asked.

"On the nightstand," Tammy said. "Next to the candle."

He picked up the matchbook, trying to ignore the images in his head of Anthony making love to his ex-wife by flickering candlelight, and instead focused on the threat below. Returning to the window, he waited until the Clickers renewed their assault on the front door. Without a word, Jim unscrewed the cap and upended the jug, dumping flammable liquid on the creatures. Then he struck a match and let it fall. The fuel caught fire instantly, and the flames raced along the Clickers' shells. Squealing in pain, both creatures fled into the road, flaming and smoking. They ran down the street blindly, claws waving in the air like torches. Jim watched them go, gripping the windowsill tightly. Then he took a deep breath and turned around to face his family.

"What happened?" Tammy asked.

He shrugged, and then smiled. "Like I said. It's the end of the world."

The three of them embraced, and for a brief moment, everything was okay.

*Downey, California*

It had taken Rick five hours to drive over thirty miles north. He had made the trip in a white-knuckle heat, slaloming around stalled cars on the highway and the various side streets. At times he'd been forced to stop and head back the way he'd come, detouring around major road blocks, mostly consisting of multi-vehicle crashes that had long since burned out. Occasionally he'd hear high pitched squeals accompanied by clicking noises, which he took to be the Clickers snapping their gigantic claws together. Sometimes, amid the high pitched squealing, he'd hear what sounded like voices, but the tone of the voices was non-human, as if uttered from a throat not of this world. These sounds always came from far away, for which Rick was thankful. Once he'd encountered a human road block—a pair of military vehicles had blocked the road and a dozen soldiers stood guarding the street. This had been on Beach Boulevard and Talbert Avenue just south of the 405, which he'd been forced to exit due to a huge pile-up just past the Harbor Boulevard exit. He couldn't tell if the soldiers were real or if they were undead. He'd seen a few undead roaming about and luckily he'd been able to outrun them with the SUV.

He was taking no chances, though. He skirted the side street he was on, winding through the cul-de-sac to find another route that headed north. He found it a few blocks up, on Warner Avenue. He hung a left and found Warner to be completely deserted.

Princess sat in the front passenger seat looking out the window. She'd been silent most of the time. A few times after they'd been forced off the freeway, she'd let out a low growl deep in her chest, her hackles rising. Rick would slow down. "What's going on?" he'd said, looking out at his surroundings. Then he would feel it. Something was out there. He had the unmistakable feeling that something was lying in wait for him around the corner, on the next block, so he would turn around and head back in the direction he came. Only then would Princess relax.

He saw his first Clicker in Huntington Beach as well. Driving down Talbert Avenue just past Magnolia he came across a small horde of them. The ones he saw were small—nowhere near the behemoth's he'd heard described on the news. Instead, the ones he encountered ranged from the size of a small dog to the largest being the size of a sofa. A few times he'd come across them feeding on a recently dead human, one so ripped up that it could barely move. The quick glimpse he got of this involved an undead zombie trying to pull itself forward on one arm, its body eaten below the chest in a stringy mass of congealed flesh that was being quickly devoured by the Clickers. As Rick drove by he saw the zombie raise its head up and for a moment their eyes locked…

…and then a dog-sized Clicker darted forward and with a quick snap of its claw, it sliced into the zombie's face and Rick turned away from the scene, concentrating on what lay ahead of him.

And now he was in Downey, a small city in the central Los Angeles area commonly known as a suburb. The only thing Rick knew about Downey was that the original version of Metallica was formed there. Aside from that, Downey had no other claim to fame that he knew of. It was the kind of place you drove through to get to somewhere else.

Rick approached an intersection that appeared deserted. He looked up both streets, noting the crashed vehicles and the utter absence of any living thing. He swore he'd heard people yelling for him to stop during the five-hour drive up here, but he'd paid them no heed. Normally, Rick would have felt guilty for not stopping to help others in need, but he had to tend to his own first. He had to save his kids. Fuck everybody else.

Rick pulled his cell phone out of his breast pocket and turned it on. As it powered up, he patted Princess. "We'll find them," he told her. "Don't worry." Princess's tail wagged a few times in response to his voice. That made Rick feel a little better, but not much. He was still very worried.

As the phone powered up he saw the following message: NETWORK NOT FOUND. Below that was the following: JOIN NETWORK? A YES and NO followed. Rick selected YES.

CHOOSE YOUR NETWORK: AT&T, SPRINT, VERIZON, T-MOBILE.

Rick scrolled to his network, which was T-Mobile. The progress bar began to react as the phone tried to find the system. As Rick waited, he looked around again to make sure nothing was trying to sneak up on him. It would be his luck that their network was down. Maybe if they'd stayed with Verizon this wouldn't be happening and he could connect to his kids.

The phone returned a message: NETWORK NOT FOUND.

"Shit!" Frustrated, Rick looked around again. Nobody alive in sight. Now what?

Curious, Rick powered his phone down. He waited ten seconds, then powered it back on again, all the while keeping a wary eye on his surroundings. At the first sign of movement he had to bug out of here.

Once again, the system could not find his network and he was invited once again to join a network. This time, Rick chose Verizon. He waited.

A moment later: NETWORK CONNECTION ESTABLISHED. WELCOME TO VERIZON!

"Yes!" Rick cried, not caring how this was possible since he didn't know jack shit about cell phone networks. The end goal had been achieved. He quickly brought up Richard's number and hit speed dial again, praying that he would get a connection. It rang once, twice, three times…

"Dad?" Richard sounded panicked but relieved.

"I'm here, Richard. Where are you?"

There was noise in the background. It sounded like the other kids, Mary and Paul and Max yelling. They sounded terrified. "We're still in San Pedro," Richard said. "Still hiding in that building."

"What's happening over there?" Rick said, feeling his own fear start to rise. "Are you okay?"

"I'm fine, but one of us—" A scream cut him off and then Richard started yelling at somebody. "Just lean against the door! Lean against the damn door, he won't be able to get out if we keep the door closed!"

"Richard!" Rick yelled. "Talk to me! What's happening?"

Richard was back, his voice coming fast and clipped. "One of us turned into a zombie, dad! We've got it shut down in the basement and it's pissed."

Rick felt himself go ashen. It felt as if somebody had scooped out his insides and replaced it with ice. He almost dropped the cell phone, his hand was shaking so badly. "Is Melody all right? Is she…"

"She's fine Dad," Richard answered, "she's just…yeah, yeah, like that, put your shoulders into it. If you all just lean against it like that, he won't be able to get the door open."

At the mention of Melody being fine, Rick felt the tension rush out of him, like air escaping from a punctured tire. He was still a nervous wreck, but he realized they still had a chance. If he could just get there. "Tell me where you are," Rick said.

"We're in an abandoned apartment building in Sunken City," Richard said. "It's like, the third building past the chain-link fence on Paseo del Mar. You know where that is?"

"Yes." Rick hadn't been to Sunken City in thirty years, but he remembered how to get there. If he could find Crenshaw Boulevard he'd have a straight shot. He didn't think he'd be able to get there from Long Beach. From where he was sitting it looked like Long Beach was on fire. Thick plumes of black smoke were coming from that general direction and the wind was carrying it east. If Rick continued west he'd soon be driving into it. "I know how to get there. I don't know how long it'll take me to get to Sunken City, but I'm almost there. I need you to hang on and—"

But he was talking to nothing. The connection had been broken.

"Goddamn it!" Rick cried. He jabbed at the buttons on the cell phone again, trying desperately to reconnect with Richard again. This time he had a NO CONNECTION message on the phone's LED screen. He tried Melody's number, cursing under his breath as the screen indicated the number was dialing but there was no sound coming from the ear piece. There was no indication that a connection to the other number was being made at all. There was just dead silence.

Through it all, Princess sat calmly in the front passenger bucket seat, her dark soulful eyes conveying hope that her master would get himself together. When Rick gave up on trying to get a hold of his daughter he cast an anguished face toward her and she looked up at him in that same look she'd given him the night before—*did I do anything wrong? If I did, I'm sorry!* Her tail thumped on the seat. Rick hitched in a breath, fighting back tears as he ruffled her fur. "We'll be fine, girl. We're gonna get Richard and Melody. You ready to head into Sunken City and kick some zombie ass? Huh girl?"

At the mention of Richard and Melody's names, Princess's tail thumped harder against the seat. She whined softly, leaned forward and licked Rick's face.

"We're going to get them, Princess. Don't worry."

Suddenly, Princess's posture changed. She leaned across Rick's end of the SUV, a low growl emanating from deep within her chest. Rick turned left and saw what Princess had already seen. Zombies. A dozen of them. Heading their way.

Rick checked behind them, as well as the street to the right. The coast was clear in those directions. They just had the zombies on their left to contend with. They were heading west, away from the zombies, skirting the cities of Compton and heading into Gardena toward Crenshaw Boulevard where he would hang a left, which would take him through Torrance and into the heart of San Pedro and right into Sunken City. On a good day through surface streets this would be a thirty minute drive. Maybe forty minutes with traffic. But now?

"Don't think about it," he told himself as he put the vehicle in gear and started heading west. "Let's just do it."

And they did. In no time, Rick had the vehicle on a good straightaway going about fifty miles an hour. Princess sat up in the front bucket seat, her dark eyes focused on the road ahead as if she were scoping their path out. Rick kept one hand on the steering wheel and the other on the Ruger .22 rifle that he'd placed between the seats. He'd placed it there so he'd have easy access to the weapon when needed. They passed very few Clickers. And what few zombies they passed, they quickly outdistanced them.

Rick drove with a grim sense of determination, weaving his way down side streets whenever he saw a traffic jam or zombies. A few times, the undead came dangerously close. One time, while maneuvering through the city of Compton after having been diverted by a massive pile up on Artesia Boulevard, a large throng of zombies that were gathered in a park gave chase. Several of them had guns and they started shooting at them. Rick had yelled and ducked, instinctively pushing Princess down into the seat. He sped away in a blind heat and almost clipped a Lincoln Continental that was moving slowly on Grape Street. The Lincoln was being piloted by a young black kid wearing a dark jacket and a white tee-shirt. The kid's throat was torn out. When Rick drove by the kid—zombie—it hissed at him and tried to give chase, but something must've been wrong with his vehicle because all it did was hitch back and forth and belch smoke.

"We're gonna get there, Princess," Rick said as they sped down Grape Street. "We're gonna get there."

Part of him was beginning to have doubts about that, though.

*San Pedro, California*

The moment he was off the phone, Richard immediately dived toward his friends, who were leaning against the basement door, trying to keep Sparky imprisoned down there.

"Jesus, he's strong," Richard grunted. He shouldered his way between Max and Paul and moved his shoulder into the door, using his legs to lean into it and give more pressure. The girls were positioned in the center of the door, lending their entire weight to it. The thing that had once been Sparky roared and shoved at the door from within the basement. The door budged open half an inch and then was slammed shut by the combined effort of Richard, Melody, Paul, Mary, and Max. Mary was crying in panic; of the five of them, she was lending the least effort in keeping the basement door shut.

"What the hell are we going to do?" Paul asked. He was looking at Richard as if Richard had all the answers.

Richard had no answers.

The speed at which everything had disintegrated in the last thirty minutes as they'd ventured out of that third floor apartment to investigate that falling sound coming from across the hall seemed like a bad nightmare now. The girls hadn't wanted them to investigate what the sound was. Melody had clutched Richard's arm and said, "Don't go, Rich, please!" But Max and Sparky were already moving into the room, the older gang banger brandishing his weapon, ready to shoot anything that moved. Richard had urged the girls to stay behind in the back bedroom of the empty apartment—they were just going to check it out. They'd entered the darkened room, trying to make out the rotted furniture that had been left behind. Richard remembered their earlier trip up there yesterday; they'd done a quick sweep then, and Richard noticed this room must have been a nursery. The walls had the remnants of pink and green wallpaper with baby elephants on it. There had been a large oak dresser near the corner and an old-fashioned looking crib against another wall. The position of the sun and the drawn, heavy curtains gave the room a dark, gloomy appearance.

They'd entered the room and stood there, looking around, trying to see what had fallen. Paul had motioned to the open closet door. "It's an old building," he'd whispered. "Maybe it's just the place settling."

That's when something had darted out from beneath the crib and launched itself at Sparky's ankle.

Sparky had bellowed in rage and pain, flaying back, almost falling. Paul and Max had yelled in surprise and the girls had screamed. Richard didn't realize he'd screamed until he felt his throat burn—he'd darted toward the door to the bedroom in an effort to be near Melody. It was from that position that Richard had seen what had attacked Sparky.

The baby must have only been six months old when it died. How a baby could have wound up in a condemned building was beyond Richard's comprehension, but they'd seen evidence of squatters here. Maybe a homeless couple with a baby had sought refuge here at some point. If so, the infant had died in this room and his parents had left it, probably in the crib—that explained the falling sound; the baby had fallen to the floor as it pulled itself out of the crib. Maybe its parents had left shortly before all hell had broken loose, too emotionally traumatized to take their child with them and whatever force powered the zombies had moved in. As Richard watched in a stunned kind of horror, he noticed how the infant's purplish-white, mottled skin was stretched thin over brittle bones. The poor thing had been malnourished. Could that have been what killed it? Could that be why it sank its infant teeth into Sparky's ankle and bit hard, holding on with thin limbs as Sparky yelled and kicked at it, trying to shake it off.

"Get it off!" Sparky had yelled. "Get this fucking thing off me!"

Everybody had been frozen, unsure of what to do. Sparky's attempt to shake the thing off made him lose his balance. He fell to the floor. The assault rifle clattered to the ground. Richard thought it would go off, but it hadn't. Sparky kicked his right leg out as if trying to shake a mean little dog that had fastened itself to his ankles. The zombie baby clung stubbornly. Its baby teeth broke off from the force of its bite. Richard had seen blood well in the bite wound as the zombie gnawed at the flesh. *It's gnawing on him with the bones of it's jaw*, Richard had thought, fascinated. *Jesus, that's sick!*

It had been Max who'd darted forward and, like a punter racing to score a goal for his team, had launched a kick that connected solidly with the zombie baby. The creature flew across the room and crashed against the wall. Paul leaped for the rifle, brought it around, aimed, and fired a volley of shots as the creature began crawling toward them. Most of the shots missed, but the last five blasted the little creature apart in a spray of dried bones and skin. The last was a headshot; it's skull exploded like old pottery being blown apart by an M80.

In the panic that ensued Robert had been quick thinking. "Quick!" he'd said. "We need to get him downstairs."

Max had stepped forward and helped Sparky stand up. Sparky was stunned; he was breathing heavy, his eyes wide with shock and surprise. "Fucking shit, man, you see that? What the fuck was that?"

"Come on," Paul said. He'd approached Sparky to help Max.

Robert sprang forward, knowing he had to act quickly. He

turned to Paul. "Hang on to that," he said, gesturing to the assault rifle. He turned to Sparky, who was more concerned with his bloody ankle than his weapons. "Let's get some of this stuff off you and get you downstairs," he said. He began pulling Sparky's coat off—it was a large, blue denim coat that was loose and baggy.

As he pulled the coat off, Sparky shrugged out of it, favoring his right leg. He handed the coat to Richard and turned his attention back to his ankle. "Fuck, man, look at that shit! What the fuck was that thing?"

Richard quickly patted the coat down. There was a handgun stuffed in the inside left pocket and several clips of ammunition in the other pockets. Hoping he'd gotten them all, he urged Sparky forward. "Come on," he said. "Let's get the hell out of here."

"Yeah," Sparky said. If Sparky noticed that he no longer carried any weapons, he didn't give any indication.

Richard, Paul, and Max herded Sparky out of the room. As they moved past the girls, who were cowering in the hallway, Richard told them, "Follow us."

Sparky had talked on the way down. "Fucking little piece of shit bit my ankle! Did you see that? Damn!" He clearly favored his ankle, and he hobbled as quickly as he could, supported on either side by Richard and Max. Paul led the way, cradling the rifle.

When they got to the first floor Paul glanced at Richard, who nodded. Paul had been on his wavelength. It was like that with them. They'd been best friends since they were eight years old. When Richard had wanted to build a fort in his backyard it had been Paul who'd agreed with him that they would not allow Carl Guran to join their club by suggesting they build their fortress in the large oak tree in Richard's backyard. Carl was afraid of trees. Wouldn't go near them for some reason. What kind of moron was afraid of trees for God's sakes? Carl annoyed both of them in other ways, though; he wiped his runny nose constantly and left smears of snot on their comic books whenever they got together; he picked his nose; he picked his butt; he also played with himself in full view of everybody, even the girls. Richard and Paul had complained to their parents about Carl, but their mothers insisted he was harmless. "He's just slow, honey," Richard's mom had told them. "He's mentally handicapped. He can't help it. Go easy on him, okay?" So they'd been forced to go easy on him for most things, but when it came to their clubhouse Richard had put his foot down. Richard didn't want Carl to have access to the clubhouse at all. Neither did Paul. Each of them knew the other didn't want to have anything to do with Carl, so Paul had casually suggested that Richard build the clubhouse in his tree. Problem solved.

That simple nod was all it took. When they reached the basement door, Paul opened it and stepped aside to cover their entrance with the assault rifle. Sparky began to head down the stairs and then Richard gave him a hard shove the moment he entered the basement's threshold. There was a startled, "What are you doing?" protest from one of the girls behind him, a startled yelp from Sparky, and then the gang-banger was crashing down the stairs and Paul shut the door and put his back to it. His eyes had been wide and panicked as they'd stared into Richard's face.

The fall didn't kill Sparky. If anything, it had only made him mad. After cursing the five of them loud and vehemently, he'd limped back upstairs and started pounding on the basement door, shoving against it, trying to force it open. In the three minutes it had taken Sparky to muster the strength to come upstairs, Paul had nodded at Max and told him to go upstairs and drag down the bureau that was in one of the bedrooms in the apartment. It looked pretty sturdy. By this point, all five of them were on the same wavelength—Sparky had been bitten. He was going to turn into a zombie. Therefore, they had to isolate him before he turned.

Except…Richard wasn't so sure, When he paused to think about it. Yes, in movies and books it was the bite of a zombie that infected a person, but was that really happening in real life? Hadn't they seen zombies outside that showed no signs of being bitten? Frowning, he decided to keep his uncertainty to himself.

"You putos," Sparky said, his voice growing weak. "I fucked myself up going down those stairs. Look at all this fucking blood. You better open the door. I need help."

Max and Mary had gone upstairs for the dresser. Melody had been too stunned by everything; she was still trying to process what had happened just a few minutes ago upstairs with the zombie baby. By the time Sparky had come around and was trying to shove the basement door open—why couldn't there have been a way to lock it from the outside as well as the inside?—they had gotten the bureau down the first set of stairs and were trying to maneuver it around the landing. That was when Dad had called.

Richard had to call out to Max and Mary to help him and Paul hold the door shut while he fumbled for his cell phone. Sparky's threats had given way to begging and pleading. Finally, his voice faltered, and he simply sobbed. Then, even that ceased.

"Think he's dead?" Paul asked.

Richard nodded.

Max frowned. "What's wrong with you, Richard?"

"What if we're wrong? What if it wasn't the bite that—"

It was at that point when Sparky's corpse began beating the door.

"*I can smell you out there, meat!*" It cackled madly. It's strength had seemed enormous, more so than any normal human's. It had taken all five of them to hold the door closed as the zombie pushed at it, inching it open a bit at a time. Richard had managed to tell his dad the building they were trapped in was the third apartment building down from where the street was fenced in, then the connection was broken. He was positive he'd heard him. It sounded like Dad was on the way.

"Dad's coming," Richard had said as he joined them in holding the door to the basement closed.

"Oh, thank God," Melody had said.

"What are we gonna do?" Max asked. His face was slick with sweet. His once cocky-attitude had deteriorated in the last sixteen hours or so. He looked absolutely lost at sea.

"We can't hold him in there forever," Mary said. She was leaned back into the door with her brother, huffing and puffing with the exertion.

"*Listen to her, meat sacks!*" the zombie cackled. Its voice was rough and gritty and not human. "*You can't hold me in here forever. Soon, you will grow weaker. And as you weaken, I will get stronger! When I get out of here, I will dine on your bone marrow and your intestines. I will make a necklace out of your spine!*"

And just like that Richard and Paul locked eyes with each other again and knew what they had to do. They nodded. Richard took a deep breath, mentally preparing himself for what was to come. The thing down there was right—they couldn't keep it shut down there forever. They were already starting to get tired. If Dad didn't get here soon, it would break free and they would all become legions of the dead.

Paul shifted his weight on the door a little to the right, closer to the hinges. Melody took up the slack and he gripped the assault rifle, keeping the barrel pointed to the floor. He motioned to Richard. "Give me another clip," he mouthed. Richard had grabbed Sparky's jacket, which he'd set on the floor near the basement door. He pulled out a black magazine that was fully loaded and handed it to Paul.

"What's happening?" Mary asked. She was starting to break down as the zombie grew stronger and began to hammer at the door with greater strength. The door was edging open more. Soon they wouldn't be able to keep it closed—it would slip a hand through, giving it a greater chance of escape.

Paul ejected the clip in the rifle and slapped in the fresh one Richard had given him. For a guy who'd never handled a gun in his life, Paul was doing okay. With the fresh clip in place, Paul nodded at Richard. "Guys, on three I want you all to stop holding the door closed and get out of the way."

The zombie cackled downstairs. "*Yes! Stop holding the door closed! Let me through!*"

Mary looked confused. "We can't let it out, are you crazy?"

"Do as he says, Mary," Richard said, his voice stern.

Mary turned to Richard and saw something in his face that

helped her get the message. She nodded, turned to her brother with a sense of resolve.

"Okay," Paul said. He stepped away from the door carefully and quickly positioned himself across from the door. The others had to work that much harder to keep the door to the basement from opening. They pushed and strained against the force applied against it, but with Paul no longer there that was becoming much harder. The door inched open further. Max yelped as the zombie's fingers waggled between the edge of the door and the jam.

Paul raised the assault rifle. He set the stock against his shoulder and placed his right eye slightly behind the scope, taking aim. "On three," he said.

Richard nodded and he knew the others had gotten the message. The zombie cackled again behind the door. *"On three I get to eat you! And more of my brothers will be let forth from the Void to occupy your miserable sacks of flesh!"*

"One..." Paul began.

The door inched open more.

"Two..."

The pressure from the basement suddenly ceased and the door was slammed shut. Richard felt a momentary sense that the creature had a trick up its sleeve, but then he realized that maybe it was just anticipating what came next.

"Three!"

Richard, Max, Mary, and Melody scrambled away from the door, darting to either side of it. For a moment nothing happened.

Then the door was shoved open quickly. It banged against the wall and Sparky was there, his eyes blazing with a presence that Richard saw for a brief moment. Despite being the eyes of the undead, there was a sense of intelligent malevolence in them. Richard saw its brief grin and that grin turned quickly to surprise as Paul opened fire.

The gunshots propelled the zombie down the basement steps, where it clattered to the bottom with a rough cry. Paul stepped toward the doorway, aiming the rifle down the stairs. Melody called out from beside him. "Did you get it?"

From the basement, a mad cackle: "*You need to learn how to aim correctly, ese!*"

"You want me to aim correctly?" Paul muttered as he sighted on the zombie downstairs. "Fine. How about this?" He let out a series of shots that clattered in the condemned building. The sound of the rifle going off was enormous— his ears were still ringing from the earlier encounter with the zombie baby upstairs. Despite the enormity of it he could still hear the zombie cackling madly downstairs. Amid the barrage of gunfire, the laughter was cut off. "Got you, motherfucker!"

Richard's ears were ringing. He took a cautious step away from the wall to get a better look at the doorway leading into the basement. Paul took a step back, giving them all a better view. For the first time since their ordeal had begun last night, Paul had a sense of victory. "Took care of that."

They crowded close to him and peered down. The zombie was lying at the foot of the stairs. One leg was splayed out at an unnatural angle from one of its falls down the stairs. A large chunk of flesh had been ripped out of the right side of its abdomen. Its head was nothing but a mass of shapeless flesh. It looked like a pumpkin that had been smashed repeatedly with a hammer.

"Holy fuck," Max said, his voice hollow.

They stood there staring down at the zombie for a moment. Richard found it hard to feel guilty about what they'd done. The man they'd met yesterday who'd once inhabited that body, Sparky, had died the moment the zombie baby bit his ankle. They didn't kill him. Maybe they'd set him free. Richard hoped so.

"Sparky knew the plank on the cellar window was loose," Mary said. "Why didn't he just go out that way and come in through another door or something?"

"Maybe there are still some of those lobster things outside," Richard said.

"What do we do now?" Max asked. His eyes were transfixed on the dead zombie.

"We can't go back down there," Melody said. She turned away, looking like she was going to be sick. "There's no way…" She looked at her brother, at Mary and Paul. "We can't hide ourselves back down there! Not now, with that thing down there."

"It's dead, Melody," Richard said.

"I know it's dead but what if there's another one in here!" She said, her voice shrill.

Richard held his hands up to quiet her down. "Take it easy, Mel."

Mary looked just as scared as Melody. She wouldn't leave her brother's side. "She's right," Mary said. "Even if it's not going to come back, it's still dead. It'll rot." Her face screwed up in disgust.

Richard nodded at Paul. "We should stay up here."

"And what?" Max asked. "What if some of them heard the gunshots?"

"Oh God," Melody said. She turned a fear-stricken face to Richard. She grabbed at his shirt, her knuckles white. "Dad's coming, right? He did say he was coming—"

"He's coming," Richard said quickly. He put his arm around her, regarding the others in the enclosed space in the first floor hallway. "He knows where we are. I told him what street we're on, what the building looks like. He's on his way."

"Should we wait here?" Max asked.

"It's the only thing we can do," Paul murmured.

For a moment all was silent. The ringing in Richard's ears made it hard to listen for what was going on outside. He didn't like the idea of being on the ground floor with the doors and windows all boarded up, unable to see outside. At least if they went upstairs, even to the second floor, they could peer out one of the windows and have a chance to see what might be going on.

"We should go back upstairs," Richard said.

"What if there's another one of those things up there?" Melody asked.

"We'll conduct a more thorough search this time," Richard said. He gestured to Paul. "Paul's got that rifle. And we also have this." He took his arm off Melody's shoulders and rooted through the jacket Sparky had left behind. When he pulled the

211

handgun out a collected gasp rose from the group. Richard held the gun with the barrel pointed up. "I don't know shit about guns, but I know enough to keep it pointing away from you all. And that all it takes to stop these things is to point and shoot."

"You have to shoot them in the head," Max said.

"Yeah," Richard agreed. He held on to the handgun, slightly apprehensive about how to handle it but knowing that he had to. There was a button on the side of it—that had to be the safety. It was probably on; it had to be, otherwise, Sparky wouldn't have just carried it so casually in his jacket pocket like that, right?

As if reading his thoughts, Max said, "Are you sure you're comfortable with that thing?"

"Fuck no, I'm not comfortable," Richard said. "But it is what it is. What other choice do we have?"

There was no answer to that.

Max crept to the front door of the building and put his ear against the door. After a moment of silence he turned to the others. "Sounds quiet," he said.

"What do we do if we have to get out of here in a hurry?" Mary asked.

"The place is boarded up from the outside," Paul said.

"The back didn't look boarded up," Richard said. "Maybe the back door…"

They turned to the back door at the very end of the hall.

"I didn't think there was a back door," Paul said.

"I didn't either," Richard said, "but there it is. We must have missed it when we first came up here. It is kind of dark back here."

"This door is along the same alleyway as that basement window we used to get in here, isn't it?" Max asked.

"Yeah, I'm pretty certain it is," Richard answered.

"I only remember seeing windows boarded up," Melody said. "Not a door. What if it's a false door and doesn't open to anything?"

"You mean like a wall?" Richard said. "I don't think so. I think we were just too rushed and panicked to notice it."

"Okay, what if it's unlocked and we manage to get it open. What if there's something out there?" Mary asked.

"The apartments in the back," Paul began, heading for the stairs, "their windows should look down on that alley. Let's take a look."

Cradling the rifle as if he'd suddenly gained military experience, Paul edged toward the stairs. "Come on," he said. "I'm positive we won't run into any other surprise. That zombie baby that got Sparky, we missed it due to its size and the fact that it was a baby. If there were others in here, we would've known by now."

Richard realized Paul was right. If there'd been even one adult zombie in this building, it would have been camped outside the door to the basement since last night. "He's right," Richard said. "We should move upstairs. We can watch all corners of the building from any of those apartments. We'll be able to see Dad when he shows up."

This seemed to boost all their spirits. Max nodded vigorously. "Yeah, let's do it!"

With Paul leading the way and Richard bringing up the rear, they headed upstairs to the second floor.

# TEN

"Jesus," Michele muttered as they drove into town.

Clark eased the car forward slowly, weaving in and around the carnage. Mount Shasta rose over fourteen-thousand feet above them, deceptive in its beauty, for nestled at its feet was absolute devastation. Michele glanced around, but everywhere she looked, she saw one horrific scene after another. A sign for the Mercy Medical Center had a bloody handprint on it. Another sign for the Mt. Shasta Ski Park had been splattered with someone's intestines. Carrion birds picked at the still-wet morsels. Michele couldn't tell if the birds were alive or dead. Burning cars and buildings spewed smoke into the sky, and bodies littered the streets and sidewalks. Some of the corpses still moved—zombies, lacking legs, suffering severed spinal cords, or having their mobility hampered by other injuries. Other corpses lay still, each one having suffered some form of head trauma.

"It's starting to stink already," Clark said, closing the dashboard vents and turning off the air conditioning. "Try to breathe through your mouth."

A severed head perched atop a mailbox glared at them as they turned onto Pine Street. Its lips moved, mouthing threats and curses. A dead cat with a broken back pulled itself along the street with its front paws. Clark swerved toward it. The cat's head crunched beneath the front tires.

"Looks like most of the mobile zombies have moved on," he said. "But we'll still need to be careful."

"What happens next?" Michele asked.

Clark parked the car in the middle of the street and turned off the ignition. Then he pocketed his keys and un-holstered

214

his weapon. "Now?" He pointed at the snow-topped mountain looming over the town. "We head up there."

"The mountain?"

He nodded. "Lonely as God, and white as the winter moon."

"Joaquin Miller," Michele said. "Right?"

"I'm impressed." Clark grinned. "It was indeed Joaquin Miller. What else do you know about this area, Michele?"

"The mountain is a volcano. It's also one of Earth's power points. Ley lines converge here, just as they do at other power points such as Stonehenge and LeHorn's Hollow. And much like those places, there are all sorts of paranormal phenomena associated with it. The Native Americans believe it's inhabited by the godlike spirit of a chief named Skell. There have been a number of UFO sightings here over the years, as well as abduction reports, and eye-witness accounts of everything from ghosts to cryptids. Oh, and there's supposed to be a hidden city deep inside the mountain itself, where a group of advanced beings who are survivors from the lost continent of Lemuria live."

"Very good," Clark said. "You're right, except for that part about the Lemurians. That's bullshit. As far as we know, the Nazis killed the last of the Lemurians shortly before the end of World War Two, when they were sending U-boats to Antarctica to set up bases there. But yes, it is a power point. Indeed, it's one of the strongest. From here, we can not only access the Labyrinth, but open a door to the Void, consign the Siqqusim back into it, and then close the door again, sealing them off from this level."

"You make it sound so easy."

"Oh, it's not. The ritual is extremely difficult. The strain... well, let's just say that it would definitely kill you, and I'm not even sure I can survive it. Banishing the Siqqusim isn't a job for novices."

"Has anybody ever successfully done it?"

"Sure. Moses. Solomon. Jesus of Nazareth. John Dee. Even one of our own agents."

"Who?"

"Director Kaine, long ago. Back when he still worked in the field and hadn't become a desk jockey."

Michele sat up straight. "Well, surely Director Kaine is still alive! Couldn't he—"

"No," Clark said. "The first thing the Siqqusim would have done was exterminate our group, along with the Seven, and anybody else they saw as a threat. And with everything else going on, we were blindsided by their invasion. We were focused on the Clickers. As a result, the breach was swift. They overwhelmed us. You saw for yourself what happened in San Francisco. I'm certain it happened everywhere else. Look how quickly they decimated this town, for instance. The bottom line is that they beat us. Black Lodge is no more."

"How can you be sure, sir?"

Clark tapped his chest. "Because I feel it in here." Then he touched his forehead. "And in here. We're it, Michele. We're all that's left. The closest thing we have to an ally are the Clickers, and they want to kill us just as bad as the Siqqusim do." He chuckled. "At least the Clickers have a good reason."

"We can't be all that's left," Michele said. "Other agents must have survived!"

"If they did, then why haven't they checked in? Granted, maybe they're in hiding, or on the move, like we are. But we can't assume that. We have to operate with the belief that you and I are all that stands between the total annihilation of all life on Earth."

Michele stared at him, unable to speak. Tears welled up in her eyes. She blinked, and the world turned blurry. When she wiped the tears away, Clark was smiling.

"Come on," he said, opening the car door. "Let's go shopping."

"Shopping?"

He pointed at a small, quaint storefront across the street. The sign above the door indicated that it was a New Age bookstore—not an uncommon sight in this region. The display window was full of books on crystal healing and love spells, and various fairy and dolphin-shaped incense burners. Michele cocked her head and frowned.

"Beggars can't be choosers," Clark explained. "We left in a hurry, and I'm going to need some things before we begin. This place looks like our best shot. Stay on guard. I don't think we'll have to worry about Clickers this far inland, but there are bound to be some Siqqusim still about."

Nodding, she followed him across the street, glancing around nervously as they approached the storefront. Both of them held their weapons at the ready, with the safeties off and a round chambered. When they reached the door, Clark bent his head and listened carefully while Michele watched the street, making sure the coast remained clear. After a moment, Clark took a deep breath and tried the handle. It was unlocked. The door swung open, jingling a tiny silver bell above it.

Clark tensed. "Shit."

*"I'll be right there,"* a voice called from the back of the store. *"Come on in."*

Clark brought his weapon up and extended his arms in front of him. Then he stepped into the doorway. Over his shoulder, Michele saw an old woman dodder out of a back room and toward the cash register. Her hair was beautiful, as white as the snow atop the nearby mountain. Her fingers were adorned with rings of blue lace agate, amazonite, and bloodstone, and her earrings were quartz crystal. She wore a simple yet elegant dress. All of these—her hair, clothes, and jewelry—were covered in blood. Someone had flayed the skin from her face, revealing the glistening musculature and pink meat beneath. Her teeth flashed garishly with no lips to cover them, and where her ears and nose had once been there were now three ragged holes. Before Clark could squeeze the trigger, the zombie spoke. Michele recognized the tongue as Sumerian.

*"Ssalmani-ia ana pagri tapqida duppira. Ssalmani-ia ana pagri taxira duppira."*

"Shoot her," Michele cried, peering over his shoulder.

"I can't," Clark said. "She's—"

*"Ssalmani-ia iti pagri tushni-illa duppira,"* the corpse continued, speaking so fast that the words ran together. *"Ssalmani-ia ina bi'sha duri tapxa-a duppira! Ssalmani-ia*

217

*ana GISHBAR tapqida duppira!"*

"Michele, I can't move. She cast a Sumerian binding spell. Shoot her!"

Michele tried to aim her weapon, but her superior was blocking the doorway. She glanced down and saw that Clark was standing in a pentacle surrounded by runes, all drawn on the floor in blood.

*"That's right,"* the old woman tittered. *"My host body was naturally adept at magic, though her idea of a binding spell would have been to take your business card and pin it to a cork board. So silly, these mortal flesh-bags. I simply opted for something much older. And now that it worked, I will take my time with you."*

The zombie reached behind the counter and pulled out a razor knife—the kind used for opening boxes. Humming, she lumbered toward them. Clark grunted, straining to move, but nothing happened. Michele saw the veins standing out in his head and neck, and the sweat bathing his forehead, yet he remained frozen like a statue, barely able to talk as the forces around him grew stronger. Michele knew from her studies that the only way to break this particular binding spell was to counter it or kill the spell-caster. Since she didn't know Sumerian, there was no way of countering the spell. That left her with one choice.

"Sorry, boss."

She shoved him hard, knocking the paralyzed man to the floor. Then, in one swift motion, she brought her gun up and fired. The first round hit the zombie just above her right breast. The creature slowed, staggered, and then charged forward, screaming obscenities.

*"I'll eat your eyes, you bitch! I'll fuck you with this knife and then I'll cut off his dick and fuck the wound with that. I'll—"*

Michele's second shot pulverized the zombie's teeth and blew out the back of her head. The dead woman flew backward, crashing into the counter. Glass shattered. Blood and brain matter splattered all over a display of Shirley MacLaine books. Michele approached cautiously, her weapon out in front of her. She stood over the body and prodded it with her toe. Satisfied that this time, the old woman was really dead, she hurried over to Clark and dragged him away from the crimson design on the floor. Coughing, he sat up and wiped his forehead with his shirttail.

"Good job," he gasped, wincing. "If there's a planet left after this, I'll have to put you in for an accommodation."

Michele grinned, helping him to his feet. "I thought you said that you and I were the only agents left?"

"Well, then it should be pretty easy to get approved." Clark dusted his pants off. "Okay. Let's search the rest of the store, and get what we need. We've got a long hike ahead of us."

Michele paled. "We don't have to go all the way to the top, do we?"

"No. Not at all. On the Western slope, just above the Buddhist monastery, there's some sacred ground that the Modoc tribe used. That should suit our purposes."

"That's a relief."

"It shouldn't be," Clark said. "Like I said before, it's still a heck of a hike, and we'll be out in the open and totally exposed. We should probably try to find a sporting goods store, too. Something tells me we're going to need more bullets."

*San Pedro, California*

"Are you sure we're safe?" Tammy whispered.

Jim nodded. "I'm positive. We just need to stay quiet. We've blocked the doors and windows. As long as they don't see any lights or don't hear us, we should be okay."

For now, he thought, but didn't say it out loud. He looked at his ex-wife and his son, and his heart broke. The three of them were cowered together inside Tammy's bedroom closet. They'd made a game out of it for Danny's sake, allowing the toddler to bring along some toys and books and a flashlight. Jim's plan was for them to wait it out inside the closet until the Clickers and the zombies moved on. After that...well, he hadn't figured that part out yet.

They hid there for the better part of an hour. Despite that

morning's trauma, Danny was in remarkably good spirits, his fears and sadness eased by the fact that he had both parents there with him. Eventually, he fell asleep with his head in Tammy's lap. She and Jim remained quiet for a while, until they were sure he wouldn't stir. Finally, Jim cleared his throat.

"So, what happened? Do you want to talk about it?"

"Not really. I mean, I guess I should, but…"

"Can you at least tell me what happened to Samhain?" Jim kept his tone gentle but persistent.

She sighed. Jim saw the lines of worry and sadness etched in her face. He longed to reach out and touch her, to stroke her cheek with his fingers and look into her eyes and tell her that everything would be okay. Instead, he folded his hands in his lap and tried to listen simply as a friend and co-parent.

"When we woke up this morning," Tammy began, "we didn't realize anything was wrong. Anthony spent the night last night. He said he heard some police sirens, but we didn't think anything of it, you know? I was making breakfast and Anthony was just getting out of the shower."

"Where was Danny?"

"In the living room, watching TV. I'd just told him to come eat breakfast. Samhain came running, too, just like he always does."

She paused, smiling. Jim smiled, too. The dog had a preternatural ability when it came to understanding the different human words for food. When they'd been married, the two of them had often had to spell words like bacon or hamburger, lest Samhain get excited.

"I opened the screen door, the one that leads out onto the deck, so Samhain could go potty. He started barking, but I didn't think anything of it. I was still waking up. Hadn't had my coffee yet. I turned around to get Danny his juice and Samhain's barks…changed. He sounded meaner. More serious. I'd never heard him sound like that before. Then Danny screamed and pointed, and when I looked out the sliding glass door, Samhain was running toward a cat. It was injured—the cat, I mean. It was missing its tail and one of its back legs was broken, and there was blood all over its fur. But that didn't stop it. Instead of running away from the dog, the cat charged him. Next thing I knew, they were fighting."

She took a deep breath and shuddered. Jim reached out one tentative hand and rested it on her calf. He gave her a reassuring squeeze. Tammy looked up at him and smiled, but her eyes were dark and haunted. She patted his hand and then continued.

"Before I could do anything, a bunch of birds came down out of the sky. One minute, it was Samhain and this cat, and the cat was really laying into him. The next minute, there must have been two dozen or so birds dive-bombing him. Samhain yelped, and started to run for the deck, but they kept tripping him up. They…they went for his eyes…"

Her voice cracked, and Tammy began to cry. Jim squeezed her leg harder, blinking back his own tears. Between them, Danny continued to sleep.

"Anthony heard me shouting. He came running out with a towel wrapped around him. When he saw what was going on, he grabbed the broom and went outside. He…he started beating at the birds. By then, they had Samhain down on the ground. He wasn't moving, Jim. I could see his tail and one of his front paws, but the rest of him was just covered in birds. And that was when I realized that the birds and the cat were dead. They had to be. Nothing alive could have moved around with the injuries some of them had. Anthony must have realized it, too, I think, because he hesitated. But then Samhain twitched, and Anthony moved toward him, beating the birds aside. The cat ran at him, scratching and biting his leg, and then one of the birds got under his towel…and… and it had his…in its beak…oh, God…he was screaming. I'd never heard him scream like that. And all I could think was that I couldn't go outside to help him because I had to be there for Danny, and I couldn't open the door because then they'd get in. And then the birds were going for his lips and nipples, and then Samhain got up and…he wasn't Samhain anymore. He wasn't our dog. And he bit into Anthony's stomach…"

She bit her knuckles, trying to muffle her sobs. Danny stirred as she trembled. He mumbled something, smacked

221

his lips together, and then went back to sleep. Jim slid closer, and put one arm around Tammy's shoulder. She leaned her forehead against his chest. His shirt grew wet from her tears.

"I'm sorry, Jim. I know this must be hard for you to hear… but I loved him. I did. I still love you. I always will. You're the father of our son, and you're a good man. But I loved him, too. And he…and Samhain…"

Jim clenched his jaw and let her cry. She wept quietly, muffling herself against his chest. He reached down and stroked Danny's hair, and felt the boy relax beneath his touch.

"Tammy," he whispered after a few minutes had passed. "Where are they now? Samhain and Anthony? What happened to them?"

Sniffling, she sat up straight again. Danny groaned, stirring once more. When she spoke again, her voice was a monotone. She sounded tired and beaten.

"Samhain…charged the doors. He kept butting his head against the glass, trying to break in. Then Anthony got back up again. I could see right away that he was dead. It was in his eyes, mostly. They looked the same, but…different somehow. He said something to Samhain. I couldn't hear what. And then they both just walked away. The birds and the cat left, too."

Jim frowned. That didn't make any sense. From what he'd seen on his way here, the dead were tenacious bastards, committed to killing and maiming as much as possible. Why would they have departed so easily when Tammy and Danny were still alive inside? He had no good answer, but he was relieved that, whatever the reason, his family had been spared.

His family…

"I'm sorry about Anthony," he said. "I really am. I know you loved him. I know he made you happy. I could see it in your eyes, and hear it when you talked about him. And that's all I ever wanted, Tammy—was for you to be happy. You may be my ex-wife, but you're also one of my best friends. Even after everything. Hell, we get along better now, and talk more now than we ever did when we were married. You're the mother of my son. If you're happy, then he's happy. That's all I wanted for you."

She reached out and touched his cheek. "Thank you, Jim."

Danny stirred again. Yawning, he sat up and stared at them in confusion. "Are we still in the closet? Have the monster people gone yet?"

"I don't know, buddy." Jim tousled his hair. "I'll go peek and see."

"Jim…" Tammy reached for him as he stood up.

"Yeah?"

"Be careful."

"I will. Don't worry. I'm not going to let anything happen to my two favorite people."

He opened the closet door and stepped into the darkened bedroom. Then he glanced back at her.

"You be careful, too."

Tammy grinned, but her expression was puzzled.

"That can be our new thing," Jim explained. "Instead of stumbling over whether or not it's appropriate to say 'I love you,' we can just say 'Be careful'."

Tammy's smile grew broader. She gave Danny a hug.

"Sounds good to me," she said. "It means the same thing."

*Palos Verdes, California*

Janice could only sit on one of the chairs in Al's cramped little office downstairs as he listened to the guy relate his story over the ham radio frequency. The guy had identified himself as Stuart, his call letters were WB3SDS and he said he was transmitting from the top floor of an apartment building in downtown Philadelphia. Center City, he called it. "It's so nice to hear from somebody on the west coast," he'd said.

"So good to hear from you, too," Al told him. "So tell me, what's the situation there?"

"It's crazy," Stuart said. "These Clicker things just swarmed out of the river yesterday afternoon and started tearing into people. It was a mad house. We had the police, military people, folks with guns trying to shoot them, but there were so many they just overwhelmed the area. I was up here in my apartment working and—"

"Working?"

"I'm a software engineer," Stuart said. "I work freelance. Spend most of my time holed up in my apartment working. I keep my radio equipment in my office."

"Oh," Al said. "Okay, gotcha."

"Yeah. So anyway, I'm up here working yesterday and… well, I don't know when shit started happening for you folks in California, but for us it happened at five o'clock during rush hour. I can see the Delaware River from my apartment and at first all I heard was screaming, then I started hearing sirens. So I look out my window and I see something happening, but it was kinda far away. Couldn't really make it out that well. So I got my telescope—"

"You have a telescope?"

"Yeah, just a little cheapie one. I use it to look at the Big Dipper mostly. And I can see across town with it. I could see things perfectly yesterday afternoon, it was such a clear day before things spiraled out of control. And let me tell you…the things I saw pouring out of the Delaware…well, it was like something out of one of those old Roger Corman movies."

"The Clickers?"

"Yeah! The Clickers. A ton of them!" Stuart sounded like he was excited to be reliving it, like this was the singular most important thing he'd ever lived through. "For at least the next hour all I could do was watch these things tear through Center City. I could hear people in the apartments next to me looking out and talking about it. And I saw some pretty awful shit, as you can imagine. People dying…the way these things could just cut you in half with their claws…and their stingers! My God, when they sting you, you fucking *explode!* You have to be careful around them things, Mr. Post. It's like—"

"I'm quite aware of the toxicity level of their venom, Stuart," Al said, remembering how the heat of the venom on his latex-gloved hand felt yesterday when he'd examined the specimen from Huntington Beach. He thought about clueing Stuart in that he was a marine biologist, that he was one of the lucky few scientists to get a good close look at the creatures in a laboratory setting, but then decided against it. He wanted to hear this man's story first.

"Well, then you know how fast it works," Stuart said. "How it just dissolves everything—bone, tissue, flesh, the works?"

"Yes." Al glanced back at Janice, who remained seated in his easy chair. She looked disturbed by what she was listening to.

"That shit was happening all over Center City," Stuart continued. "I was watching people die on the street fifteen floors below me. It was hell on earth. And there wasn't a damn thing I could do to stop it."

"There's nothing you could've done," Al said. It sounded like Stuart was beginning to become emotionally affected by the carnage he'd witnessed.

"But that isn't everything," Stuart said. "A lot of these people, especially the ones that merely got chopped up by their claws...they were killed...but then they started coming back."

"The zombie epidemic," Al murmured.

"Is that what they are?" Stuart asked. "Because they aren't like zombies in those movies like *Night of the Living Dead*. They go after other people and eat them, yeah, but they're not slow at all. Most of them are really fast. And they seem to think...like they have some sort of intelligence. They talk. Shoot guns. Drive fucking cars."

"So you've had the chance to observe them?" Aside from what Al and Janice had heard on the news, he knew nothing else about what the press had reported on the zombie epidemic.

"Oh, hell yeah! They're zombies all right. People die, they come back almost instantly. I saw people cut in half by those things' claws and they were still moving. They couldn't do much, and it was really gross watching them drag themselves down the street with their guts hanging out, and they should've been dead, but they weren't. What else could you describe them as? They're fucking zombies!"

"Of course," Al murmured.

"You seen them where you are?"

"I've been holed up in my house ever since things started

breaking down," Al answered. "All I know about the zombies is what I've seen on TV." He didn't add that he thought his neighbors, George and Ginny and their daughter, had probably turned into the undead yesterday late afternoon. Why they hadn't lumbered over to his house to try to attack he and Janice, Al didn't know. He needed more answers from Stuart, something more concrete to base his hypothesis on. "I can hear the sounds of a dying society outside my home office window," Al continued. "And from what I saw on TV and heard outside, I knew enough to stay inside."

"And we can't get through to our son," Janice said. Her voice was sudden and haunted-sounding from the corner chair.

"Who's that?" Stuart asked.

"My wife, Janice," Al answered.

"Hello, Janice," Stuart said.

"Our son's in Washington DC," Janice continued. "He'd just gotten a job with a good law firm there. Do you know if…"

"I don't know, ma'am," Stuart said, his tone cautious. "DC is facing the same problem every other major city is right now. I did hear that President Genova had been killed."

"My God…" Janice shook her head sadly. "Have you been in contact with other survivors?"

"Yes. All over."

A thought occurred to Al. "What about more inland areas? I understand the Clickers are coming ashore all over the world, that coastal cities are facing a double onslaught. I would imagine areas much further inland are only experiencing problems with the zombies."

"Yeah, that's what I'm hearing, too," Stuart said. "I've been in touch with people in Kansas City, Detroit, Chicago, Denver. I even talked to a retired doctor in Montana. He's got a large cabin off in the middle of nowhere that runs off a generator. He was telling me he shot a zombie deer that came up onto his property."

"A zombie deer?"

"Yeah. This virus, or whatever it is that reanimates the dead…it's affecting wildlife, too."

Al was overwhelmed at this information. It was one thing to be presented with a previously unknown species from the ocean floor and try to wrap your head around it; it was quite another to be presented with another scientific anomaly in the reanimation of the dead.

"You haven't seen this phenomenon, have you?" Al asked Stuart. "The animals, I mean?"

"No, I haven't." There was a short pause. "Actually, I take that back. I think I have…birds."

"Birds?"

"Yeah. Last night, around dusk. It was getting dark. Most of the fights were over by then and—"

"Fights?"

"Oh yeah. What the media calls the Clickers? They were fighting with the zombies."

Once again, Dr. Alfred Post was stunned.

Stuart pressed on. "At first they *weren't* fighting. At first it was just the Clickers streaming onshore from the Delaware river attacking and killing and eating everybody. Then I started seeing people that were dead come back to life. The zombies, they started attacking and killing live people. You know, people that were either trying to get away on foot or in cars. They were coordinated attacks, too, like they were ganging up on groups of people and it all seemed…I don't know… strategic, in a way. The Clickers were still streaming out of the river but there were so many of them, they were overpowering the people. Most of the people they killed simply dissolved into this bloody goo. The Clickers, they were eating that."

"Did people die right away after being stung?" Al asked.

"Not all of them. Some of them were screaming as their flesh bubbled off their bones, then they died of shock, I guess. Those Clickers would start eating them while these poor people were still alive, then they would come back to life. As soon as they started trying to move away, the Clickers would sting them again and the zombies would just start to dissolve again. It was the freakiest thing I ever saw!"

"I bet," Al said.

"This one guy, he got stung in the leg. His leg just started bubbling and he screamed so loud it was painful to hear. The Clicker that got him, it was small, maybe the size of a large dog. It started eating his leg and the guy died. Maybe ten seconds later, his eyes opened. The creature was still eating him, only this time it had moved up his body and was eating his stomach. It was ripping at his insides with its claws. The zombie tried to take a bite out of the creature but it stung him again in the chest. Zombie couldn't really bite the thing anyway, they have these hard shells. Anyway, the zombie started falling apart where it got stung, its flesh was just sizzling like acid. And the creature starts eating it and the zombie's trying to get away now, only it can't, it just dissolved into this pile of gunk."

"And the Clicker ate that?"

"Yeah."

"I assume this was happening all over?"

"It pretty much was," Stuart admitted. "That's when the zombies and the Clickers started fighting each other."

"So they turned on each other?" All the thoughts to the zombie birds were gone. Al was more interested in hearing about these battles between the Clickers and the zombies.

"The zombies turned on the Clickers. In fact, from what I saw it became a coordinated attack. It was almost as if they'd gotten orders from somewhere. You know, like they were all tuned into some greater power."

"A greater power," Al mused. This was the first he'd heard anybody float the idea that the zombie catastrophe was not just a random event but something calculated and deadly, designed to wipe out every living thing on earth. "That doesn't seem to fit in with your virus hypothesis."

"Maybe not," Stuart said. "I don't know how else to describe it. And you want to know something else weird?"

"What?"

"The more I watched what was going on and the more I was coming to those conclusions...that the zombies were acting on orders from some higher power...like maybe they were all possessed by some kind of demon or something...the more I got this weird feeling of déjà vu."

"Déjà vu?"

"Yeah. Like I'd seen this all before or even witnessed it." Al searched his mind for the resemblance to what was going on now to the few post apocalyptic zombie films he'd seen and could find no comparison. "Well, the mind is a funny thing, Stuart. Maybe you just saw a movie where something similar happened and—"

"I know, maybe my mind was playing tricks on me. But I gotta tell you, the entire experience of watching the zombies attack those creatures, that feeling that they were possessed by some kind of demonic or alien entity...it felt like I'd lived that before. In fact, last night I dreamed about it, only in the dream it wasn't zombies, it was.... well, it was like everybody had gone crazy or had reverted to their most feral, most primitive state and had de-evolved into wild animals and they were just attacking other people. There were no Clickers in this dream, but it was still very similar. I was in my apartment watching it through my telescope and I just *knew* that these wild people were all possessed by this demonic entity that was trying to take over the world. Isn't that weird?"

"Yeah, it is weird," Al answered. "But you've been living under a lot of stress the past twenty-four hours. The mind tends to play tricks on you like that as a way of dealing with it."

"Maybe so, but it was real detailed," Stuart said. "I even remember other details. Like who was president, and what was going on in the world, all kinds of weird stuff."

"And who was president?"

"Some black guy with a funny name. Sounded like 'Yo Momma' or something."

"Maybe whatever name it was you picked up in a book," Al suggested. "And your subconscious stored it the way it does everything else."

"Yeah, I know that's how dreams work. It just seemed... so damn vivid!"

Something about what Stuart related wouldn't leave Al's mind. "You said in your dream that the wild people were being controlled or possessed by something. Do you still feel the zombies are being controlled by something?"

"Absolutely. I know they are."

"Are they being controlled by the same thing in your dream?"

"No. The thing from my dream was completely different. Don't ask me how I know, it's just a feeling I have."

"But it's interesting that you would have a dream that would strangely parallel your current situation," Al continued. He was thinking out loud now, trying to fit pieces together. "Let me ask you something. You said you had déjà vu prior to falling asleep and having this dream, right?"

"That's correct?"

"Did that dream *strengthen* the feeling of déjà vu?"

"It did."

Al thought about this. His educational background told him that Stuart was merely experiencing stress as a result of the traumatic situation he'd been thrust in. However, due to Al's own personal studies of physics, especially string theory, what caught his interest was Stuart's description of the zombies being controlled by some unknown force. Stuart's deja-vu feeling and his dreams described a similar force, and a very similar situation: stuck on the top floor of his apartment building, watching civilization crumble around him as people either turned into wild primitives or zombies (*and let's not forget being eaten by scorpion-lobster-crab hybrid creatures that poured in from the river, most likely swimming up river from the Atlantic*, Al thought). "What was the force called?" Al asked. "In your dream?"

"The demon controlling the wild people?"

"Yes."

"I don't know. I just had this image that it was a thing from another world. Kind of like a demon, but not really."

"With horns and wings, the whole nine yards?"

"Kinda."

"What about the force controlling the zombies? Do you have any kind of sense of a name for it?"

"No, I don't. It was like the thing from the dream, but different. There are a lot them."

"A lot of them?"

"Yeah."

"What do you mean, a lot of them?"

"There's a bunch. Maybe twelve, thirteen of them. I get the sense they all come from the same place, that they have weird names. Leviathan, for example."

"The deity from the Bible?"

"I don't know. Maybe. And Ob? Does Ob mean anything to you?"

"No, it doesn't." Al didn't know what an Ob was.

"Maybe it doesn't mean anything. It's just that's the word that keeps coming to my head when I get the sense these things are controlled by some great force."

"But you know this force, whatever it is, it's different from the force controlling the wild people in your dream?"

"Yes, it's very different. I think it's more dangerous. Obviously it's more dangerous because this shit is really happening. This isn't a dream."

"This feeling of deja vu…was yesterday the first time it came to you?"

For a moment, Stuart didn't answer. Al had the sense he was thinking carefully about his answer. A moment later, the confirmation to his suspicions was answered. "No," Stuart said, his voice low. "I can't describe it but…I had a similar dream a few times over the past few years. Last night it was simply more vivid. It was like the dreams before were just little bits and pieces of the greater whole and then last night it opened a floodgate."

Al nodded. "Of course."

"Have you had dreams like that?" Stuart asked.

"No, I haven't."

"I don't think anybody else has, either. You're the first person I've mentioned them to. I hinted at them a few times, but everybody I talk to didn't know what I was talking about, so I would change the subject."

Al quickly changed gears. "How many other people are you in contact with?"

"About two dozen." Stuart's tone of voice changed, became all business again. "I've got call letters and frequencies. Got something to write with?"

231

"Yep." Al pulled a pad of paper and pen over and got ready to write. And as Stuart began reciting names, call signs, and frequencies, Al jotted them down and tried to make some kind of sense out of what he'd just heard. He was disturbed by the idea that the zombies were being controlled by some kind of outside entity. Or perhaps even multiple entities. If this being or beings could take possession of all living things, it could probably possess one of the Clickers. That would be very bad. He shook his head. For all he knew, maybe they already had possessed the Clickers.

"Let me ask you something else, Stuart," Al asked when he was finished jotting down the names and call signs. "Have you been in touch with any government official or even a staff member? Or any kind of scientist?"

"No, I haven't. I wish I was."

"Okay." Another idea came to him. "Do you have internet connectivity?"

"Internet? I don't know, I haven't even tried getting on. CNN and Fox was down last time I tried to access the internet."

"Try again." Despite the chaos and destruction that was happening, if major LAN lines were still running and power was still being supplied to Internet Service Providers, the internet might still be up, at least partially.

"It's not," Stuart reported, a moment later. "I get a network error."

"Try rebooting your router."

Stuart tried, and a few minutes later the results were the same. "Okay, it was worth a try. But I'd like you to try something else for me, Stuart."

"Sure, what's that?"

"Get back on the horn and connect with some of these other folks you're in contact with. See if any of them have any internet connection."

"Why do you want to connect with the internet so bad?"

Al couldn't explain it, but he couldn't contain his enthusiasm, either. He grinned. "I've got an idea. An idea involving string theory and alternate realities—other versions of our Earth. Maybe we—"

At that moment, the house shook. The light swung back and forth overhead, and the glasses and plates rattled in the kitchen. Al glanced at Janice. She stared at him with wide, frightened eyes. Gripping the arms of her chair tightly.

"You still there?" Stuart asked.

"Yes," Al said. "We're having an earthquake. Just wait for a moment and it should—"

CLICK-CLICK...CLICK-CLICK...CLICK-CLICK...

"Oh no..."

"I know that sound," Stuart shouted. There was a sudden electronic squeal of feedback. "You gotta hide!"

Al leapt from his chair and grabbed his wife's hand. Around them, the shaking grew more intense, and the sounds got louder, drowning out what Stuart was saying.

"The basement," he yelled, pulling Janice with him. "We've got to—"

The windows in the living room shattered, and the sounds of the Clickers grew deafening. Their briny stench seemed to fill the house. He heard wood splintering. Then the windows at the rear of the house broke.

"What do we do?" Janice's fingernails dug into his hand. "What do we do?"

"Your idea," Stuart shouted. "Tell me your idea!"

A horde of dead Clickers charged into the house. He heard them smashing furniture and slashing at the walls. More barged into the rear of the house, cutting them off from the stairs. One of the hybrids tried to squeeze through the door into the room, but got stuck in the frame. It squealed with frustration, thrashing about. Its shell scraped against the doorframe. The wood splintered. Behind it, other Clickers began tearing away chunks of wood and drywall. Apparently unsatisfied with their progress, they then ripped the stuck Clicker to shreds, slicing through it with their claws. With a final push, they shoved through the wall just as the hybrids at the front of the house gained access to the room. One of them swiped at the radio equipment, smashing it to the floor and silencing Stuart's voice forever.

"Janice?"

Her only response was a frightened sob.

"Janice," he repeated, squeezing her hand. "We'll be together in another world."

Al was still squeezing his wife's hand when a massive stinger punched through his chest. His blood sprayed like a geyser, arcing over the creature's shell and his wife's horrified face. He felt the venom surge through his veins. Al opened his mouth to tell Janice that he loved her, but vomited blood and his own rapidly liquefying insides instead. The last thing he saw before his eyes bubbled from their sockets was his wife screaming as the same thing happened to her.

*San Pedro, California*

It took Rick another two hours to reach Sunken City.

By the time he reached the San Pedro city limits, the SUV was covered with decaying flesh and blood, and there were spider web cracks in the front windshield. Rick had to fight to keep the vehicle on a straight course. At some point during his mad race through Harbor City, he'd come across a horde of zombies who had given chase through the streets. Rick had damaged the rear axle of the SUV while driving over something. Weren't SUVs supposed to be able to be driven over rough terrain? Maybe in rural areas, but not in the middle of the city in the aftermath of a post-apocalyptic showdown between zombies and Clickers.

A showdown was the only thing Rick could call it. While he saw the creatures roaming around the streets on his journey, they were mostly sitting around eating dead things. And why not? It was a smorgasbord out here. Likewise, when he came across the zombies they were usually in groups. Most times he came across them they were a safe distance away and he always drove away from them. Only occasionally would they give chase, usually by foot. These zombies weren't like the ones in the Romero films. Rather, these zombies were like the ones in the film *28 Days Later*, only smarter. They could drive cars, too, as evidenced by that zombie kid he saw in Compton trying to drive a Lincoln. So far, the ones he'd come across piloting vehicles were in cars that were pretty beat up, and he'd been pretty lucky and able to speed away from them because of it.

Princess had remained in the front passenger seat throughout the trip, ready and alert for anything. She'd sat up, ready and at attention like a canine soldier. The few times Rick was driving through unknown territory, Princess seemed to sense something up ahead and would bark in such a way that Rick came to instinctually trust. Depending on the tone of the bark, he would either stop the vehicle and head down another street or, if she were looking in a particular direction while she was barking, Rick knew not to venture down that avenue. The few times he passed such streets, Rick had chanced a glance and had seen zombies milling around.

At one point he'd passed an intersection and glanced to his left to see a full-on war. He didn't stop to watch it. The brief glimpse he got as he zoomed past was enough to burn in his memory. It also brought a sense of realization to him. *No wonder I've made it this far*, he thought.

That brief glimpse he'd caught was this:

A large mass of zombies were gathered in a park and they were facing off an opposing mass of Clickers. The moment he breasted the intersection and glanced toward them they ran toward each other like Norsemen and Saxons coming together on an ancient battlefield. Claws clicked, snapping zombies in half. Zombies ducked, flipped some of the Clickers over and then attacked their soft undersides; stingered tails jabbed into zombie-flesh and that was the extent of what Rick saw. As he drove away, putting the battle at a comfortable distance behind him, he could hear the squeals of the Clickers and the mad clicking of their claws grow faint in his ears. And with it came the realization for why he wasn't experiencing much in the way of attacks from both Clickers and zombies.

*They're fighting each other*, he thought, his heart pounding. *That's what those sounds I've been hearing are. The Clickers and zombies are fighting each other all over. If we'd only had an invasion of one of them, things would be much worse. But they arrived at the same time and now they're battling for supremacy.*

Rick didn't know why this battle was being raged, but it didn't matter. It was providing him with the perfect diversion to get to Sunken City and save his kids.

As he reached Cameo del Mar Street he thought briefly of Jeanette. He'd tucked her away in the back of his mind this morning, offering a silent prayer that she was still alive. Then he'd gone back to the task at hand. Save the kids first. Then, if possible, try to reconnect with Jeanette somehow. See if she was alive. Most likely, she wasn't. Rick knew this was the most likely scenario, and while emotionally he wasn't prepared to face this yet, he had considered the very real possibility that she was dead and he was never going to see her again. He only hoped the kids would be prepared to deal with this loss as well.

And then he was at the end of Cameo del Mar, driving past puddles of congealed goo. A zombie Clicker that had been smashed by something was trying to move—it's entire bottom half was crushed, one of its claws had been severed, and it could only move by pinioning itself on its remaining claw. It eyed the SUV as Rick pulled up to the rundown gate and threw the vehicle in park. Rick watched it as it tried to move itself forward. It couldn't move at all. It was stuck to the pavement. Rick thought briefly of putting a bullet through its brain, but decided against it. He didn't want anything to be attracted to the gunshots. Plus, he didn't know what he was going to be facing beyond that gate. He needed all the ammunition he could get right now.

On the heels of that, he had another thought as he glanced at Princess. *It's not just people coming back to life…it's every living thing.* Realizing that Princess was at risk, that if she was killed and could come back and turn on him as one of the undead, raised the risk exponentially.

Rick eyed the rundown street, noting other piles of goop and a resurrected head lying in the middle of the street. Richard had said they were hiding in the third apartment building. He could make out the structure perfectly—it was about fifty yards from where he was sitting in the SUV. He gave the fence a quick visual inspection, then turned to Princess. "So what do you think? Wanna come with me?"

Princess wagged her tail and gave an encouraging whine. "We're going in there to get Richard and Melody and their friends. I need you to have my back. If you sense any trouble, you let me know. Okay?"

Princess gave a low bark.

*Jesus, this is weird*, Rick thought. *It almost feels like she understands me.*

Princess didn't take her eyes off Rick. Her ears were alert, tail raised. She was sitting in a strong, dominant position, as if she were ready to kick some ass and take names. He'd heard about people having a strong connection with their pets, and while Princess had always been a good dog and a great family pet, the connection he felt with her today seemed different. They were connecting on a different level. It was instinctual. That was the only word Rick had for it. They each knew that they needed each other to survive. They were going through that fence to find and rescue Richard and Melody and, if possible, their friends. If there was any trouble, Princess would defend them from any threat, and he would defend her as well. They were going to work together to get out of this.

Rick ruffled Princess's fur behind her neck. "Let's go. Stay with me, okay?"

Grabbing the rifle, Rick let himself out of the vehicle and Princess bounded out after him. He debated leaving the vehicle running, but then decided against it. What if somebody else was hiding out nearby, saw the running vehicle, and decided to steal it? Rick couldn't take that chance, so he turned the SUV off and took the keys. He put them in his jeans pocket, pulled out the backpack that contained the extra clips and shells, then closed the door. Princess was already at the gate, looking down the street toward the zombie head glaring at them with mad eyes. Rick approached the gate beside her and looked down into the heart of Sunken City.

It didn't look like anything he remembered from his youth. Every time he'd come down here he'd been drunk or stoned with his goofball friends. It was always night when they'd come down here, too. From what he remembered, the area had no streetlights. Rick glanced along the side of the streets and, sure enough, no streetlights. As Rick visually inspected the immediate area, he was struck by how narrow the street actually was. He spied a small concrete path that led down to the rocky beach below. He wondered if that was the same path he and his friends used to take to get down to the beach on those nights they came down here. It probably was.

With the exception of the severed head that was looking at him with a kind of insane rage, there were no other zombies in the immediate area. He looked up at the building the kids said they were hiding in and thought of calling out to them. He decided against it. His best course of action was to get through the fence, approach the building, then maybe look up and see if anybody was watching the street from one of the upper floors. From this vantage point, he didn't think anybody watching from the second or third floor could see him.

"Come on, Princess," Rick said. He pushed at the gate and it was stopped by the padlocked chain that had been wound through it. Thank God the chain had been wrapped loosely around the bars. He squeezed through the gate, gritting his teeth as his belly brushed against the steel. *If I live through this, I'm going on a weight loss program,* he thought as he slid his bulk through the gate. He managed to get through with a little difficulty, then Princess came through effortlessly after him.

They stood at the other side of the gate for a moment, listening, observing. The coast was clear.

Rick and Princess began to move down the street toward the apartment building.

# PART THREE

# ELEVEN

*Pasadena, California*

Greg Weaver had been holed up in his suburban tract home nestled in the foothills of the San Gabriel mountains since late yesterday afternoon. The house didn't have a basement, so Greg had chosen the next best place to hide—the back bedroom that had been converted to Elizabeth's office.

The kids had gone to visit his parents a few days ago down in Orange County. He currently had no way to get in touch with them. Phone service had been down since last night, and most of the major networks had gone off the air in the early hours of this morning. The moment shit started going down, Greg had retreated to Elizabeth's office and had monitored events on the Internet until it, too, went offline.

Elizabeth had been at work in Burbank, where she was employed as a staff writer for the television show *Criminal Minds*. Greg was between jobs this summer, so he'd elected to stay home and hang out with the kids. Elizabeth's busiest time as a writer for television was between the months of June through March, when prime-time network series shows were in production. This was Elizabeth's second season as a staff writer for the show, and with six of the last two season's episodes written by her, she had accumulated enough points in the Writer's Guild to continue her health benefits until work resumed in June. In a way, it was like her old job when she was a high school teacher and had nearly three months off every summer, only this time she was usually off between April and June.

That worked well for Greg. He could stay home this summer, hang out with the kids, and read scripts his agent sent him.

Greg hadn't had a job in nine months. Not even a walk-on for a prime-time dramatic series episode. His last real gig of any importance was nine months ago when he'd taken a bit role in a feature, the sequel to a horror film called *The Fury*, which was completely unrelated to the 1978 film of the same name. *The Fury* was the title of a horror novel, published in 2006, by a novelist/screenwriter named David Spires, who Elizabeth knew. David had written the screenplay. The 2008 film adaptation had done reasonably well, so the producers had arranged for a sequel, which Greg had worked on in 2001. He'd played the Catholic priest who the hero and heroine consulted with at the top of the third act.

After that gig, there hadn't been a whole hell of a lot.

Residuals still came in for past projects, and he still had his SAG benefits. And thank God Elizabeth was gainfully employed. Greg had kept busy during the kid's school year by running an actor's workshop in Glendale. When school let out, and no serious casting calls came his way, he decided to take the summer off from the workshop circuit. Hounding his agent over the phone didn't require much effort anyway. He could do that in his sleep, from anywhere.

When society started breaking down and the zombies and crab-creatures had begun wreaking havoc, Greg had tried calling his parents down in Newport Beach and Elizabeth in Burbank, but had been unable to get through to either of them. Stunned with the realization that they could be in incredible danger, even dead, he had slumped in Elizabeth's office chair in shock, glued to the internet until it, too, went offline.

And now he was hearing a noise outside.

Greg rose from the desk, his knees popping. He winced at the flare of pain caused by the stiffness of his joints, then cocked his head listening. There was the slam of a car door in the driveway. Was that Elizabeth?

Greg raced through the house to the front door. From the living room window, which had not been shuttered with the curtains, Greg could see part of his driveway. Sure enough, he could see the rear portion of Elizabeth's Nissan Altima.

"Elizabeth!" Greg leaped for the door, fumbled for the

242

lock, got it open.

Elizabeth stood on the front stoop, grinning at Greg. Her hair was mussed up, tangled with sweat and blood. The blue jeans she'd worn to work the day before were gone, stripped off her body. Only the top portion, where the belt loops rested and strips of denim that flopped along her bruised and torn legs remained. There was a gaping hole in her neck, and Greg could see the bones of her spine through the flesh. Greg took a step back, gaping in horror.

"*Hi honey, I'm home!*" The Elizabeth thing screeched. She reached forward, grabbed him, and pulled him to her. Greg screamed.

Moments later, Greg was gone and a Siqquism occupied his brain. It searched through his memories, learned where his children were, as well as some of his friends and colleagues. Some lived close by.

"*Why don't we see how are friends are doing?*" it cackled to Elizabeth.

"*Honey*," the Elizabeth thing said, grinning. "*You are so full of great ideas.*"

*San Pedro, California*

"Hey, I think I see Dad!"

Melody's voice brought a burst of relief from Richard as he raced from the north-facing bedroom to where Melody was stationed on the other side of the building. The others rushed in from their stations along the other four corners of the apartment complex and joined her, crowding around the window to get a good look.

Melody pointed outside to the street below. She was grinning. "See? Isn't that him!"

"And it's Princess, too!" Mary squealed in excitement.

Richard suppressed the urge to quiet the girls down. It was Dad, all right. He was walking cautiously down the narrow pot-holed street carrying his hunting rifle, a backpack slung over his shoulder. The late afternoon sun bled orange across the horizon, shadowing their father's face from view, but it was clear he was focused on their building. "It's him. Let's see if we can get this window open."

Paul and Max helped him at the window. It was nailed shut, and the rust of long years had all but welded the window shut. Finally, Paul pulled a drawer out of a broken dresser in one of the second floor apartments and approached the window. "Stand back," he said.

Paul rammed the drawer through the glass, which shattered and fell into the room, some crashing to the sidewalk below. Richard saw Dad look up at the window as Melody shouted down. "Dad! We're up here!"

"Get down here!" Dad called down. "We don't have a lot of time!"

"Let's go!" Richard said. All five of them headed out of the apartment and pounded down the stairs to the first floor.

They were just reaching the front door when they heard a single gunshot from outside. Richard felt his heart lurch. "Dad?" he called out.

"I'm okay," Dad said. "Just had to shoot something. Hold on." There was a few more gunshots, then the sound of footsteps mounting the front steps to the building. A moment later Richard heard Princess sniffing around outside, whining. "This front door is completely boarded up. Let me see if I can pry these boards off." The sound of Dad trying to pull the boards off the door; grunting, straining. "Shit!"

"The back door!" Max said. His face was pale, shiny with sweat.

"Dad, we're going out the back," Richard called out. "The back door isn't boarded up!"

"I'll meet you back there," Dad said. "Be careful!"

Richard, Melody, Max, Paul, and Mary rushed down the hall to the rear of the apartment building.

*Columbia, Pennsylvania*

Tim Gaines and Mike Lombardo had been preparing to pay a visit to their Pastor when the End Times came with a bang.

Of course, they'd argued about it with Jennifer Wasco,

Mike's roommate. Jennifer was as dumb as a rock and spent most of her time on the sofa scarfing down potato chips and watching stupid reality shows; *The Jersey Shore*, *Bridezilla*, anything with Real Housewives. Mike thought such shows were sinful, and Tim agreed, but didn't do much to try to encourage Jennifer that she shouldn't poison her mind with such filth. They'd been arguing about the alleged merits of such television programming, when the news had interrupted with the first reports on the monster invasion.

It became quickly apparent the things that were invading every coastal city weren't monsters. They were demons, pure and simple. Why couldn't anybody else see that?

"If I have to listen to this scientist start yattering about evolutionary theory when talking about these crab creatures, I'm changing the channel," Mike had proclaimed at one point. The three roommates had huddled on the sofa, absorbed by what was going on. All thoughts to visiting with their Pastor was now gone. They were hopelessly addicted to watching the world crumble around them outside, which they saw through the wonders of modern technology.

This had led to several discussions as the night wore on. Were the creatures really things from hell or were they perhaps warnings from God the way He had sent a flood? That was Jennifer's theory. God had been warning mankind for decades and maybe this was how He had decided to show humanity just exactly who was in charge. Mike and Tim held differing opinions. Both thought this was some form of the End Times finally come round at last. Jennifer had dismissed that. "If it's really the End Times, why are we still here?" she'd asked. "I didn't hear any trumpet, and I sure didn't hear any cars crashing, there's been no news reports of airplanes crashing or—"

"It's not going to be like that *Left Behind* series," Mike had said.

"Of course there's been accidents," Tim had countered. He'd gestured toward the TV, then the living room window. The window was closed, and even though the rented house they shared was way off in the boonies, in the middle of acres of vast fields, with a diary farm a quarter of a mile away, they could still hear police sirens braying constantly. They could also hear other things—people screaming, shouting at each other. They could hear gunshots. The gunshots had prompted Tim to retrieve his Marlin .22 rifle and his Smith & Wesson .38 caliber pistol. There'd been a box of shells for the Marlin, but only half a box left of .38 caliber bullets. Mike had lost his temper and told Tim that he was stupid for not having enough ammunition. "We live in a small town!" Tim had yelled back. "How was I supposed to know Armageddon was coming?"

At some point they'd held a prayer circle. Mike Lombardo led it. He always led prayer, even in Bible study. Ever since being saved when he was twelve years old, Mike had felt a strong connection to the Lord. He could call on Him at any time and he usually did, several times a day, even if it was to say hello. Now he called on Him with even greater fervor, asking Him to give them strength, wisdom, and courage in the face of this oncoming battle. He also asked the Lord to forgive his sins. He suggested the others do the same, and it was then when he learned what Tim and Jennifer had been involved with when Mike wasn't at home.

"Lord, please forgive me for the sin of committing adultery," Tim had prayed.

"Adultery?" Mike had glanced at Tim. They'd been standing in their prayer circle holding hands for the past five minutes. Now Mike glanced at him curiously. "Really?"

Jennifer had interrupted his thoughts. "Please forgive me, Jesus," she said. "Please forgive me for committing adultery, too."

Mike had turned to her. "You, too?"

The two of them had looked at Mike and it suddenly became clear. "You mean the both of you have been—"

"We tried to keep it secret," Tim began. He didn't look shameful. If anything, he looked embarrassed. "We didn't want you to know because we know how you get about things like this…sex outside of marriage…adultery, gay marriage…"

"How I get about things like that? How about how God feels about it? You know that sexual activity is seen as adultery if it is outside the confines of marriage! It's a sin and it's—"

"What about you and Pastor White?" Jennifer said. "Don't tell me that the only reason you spend so much time with him in your bedroom is because he's your Bible teacher! I've seen the way he looks at you!"

"He *is* my Bible teacher!" Mike protested.

"That's not what we heard," Tim murmured.

"Listen, let's just forget about it," Mike had let go of each of their hands, ending the prayer circle. But the damage was done, and Mike Lombardo had felt conspicuously embarrassed the entire evening.

However, that embarrassment had quickly turned to concern, then fear as things got worse.

At midnight the power went out in their house.

They'd sat up all night, huddled together on the sofa, too afraid to venture forth to any other part of the house for fear something outside would hear them. They were already hearing the zombies outside—they called out to each other in strange, buzzing voices, and Jennifer had shivered at the sound of them. "If there was any doubt in my faith in Jesus, that faith is restored one hundred percent after hearing those things." She'd turned to Tim and Mike. "Those things are possessed by demons from hell. You guys realize that, right?"

Mike and Tim nodded. Mike had been praying silently, but his lips moved occasionally. Tim had remained silent, not moving from his corner of the sofa.

They'd eaten the remaining lunchmeat in the fridge. They had to before it could go bad. There was bottled water and some fruit, and after lunch they'd stood in the kitchen and made a plan. "We need to get out of here," Tim had said. "If we stay here, we're sitting ducks."

"I disagree," Mike shook his head. "God wouldn't want us to leave. There's a reason He set this up. There's a reason the three of us are here and this is happening."

"Are you out of your mind, Lombardo? Look what's happening! This isn't some kind of Biblical prophecy come true—"

"The dead are walking! What more prophecy do you need?

When Christ returns, he will raise the dead. Acts Chapter twenty-four, verse fifteen. I rest my case."

"Jesus," Tim muttered.

"Exactly!"

Tim looked at Jennifer, then turned back to Mike. "Fine. You can stay here. Jennifer and I are leaving."

"It's hell on earth out there," Mike stated, and the tone of his voice made Tim and Jennifer stop and take pause. "The dead have risen and are walking the earth. That is the sign that Christ has returned. It is also the sign that Satan has control of the dead. Can't you see that?"

He could get to Jennifer. He could tell by the way she looked at him, her expression torn between wanting to go with Tim and continue living her life of sin in this post-apocalyptic world, or stay behind and be saved. Mike pressed her on the issue. "If you go out there, Jennifer, you *might* live. You and Tim might be able to seek shelter, find more food, weapons, you might even be able to get to a place where the dead aren't roaming. But you'll still be damned. You'll still be un-reconciled with God for your sins. Do you really want that?"

"What about *your* sins, Mike?" Tim barked.

"*I've* repented! I've *asked* for forgiveness! I've—"

They were still arguing about this when Mike's Bible teacher, Bob White, burst through the door. "Quick!" He panted. "We've got to get out of here! Everything's turning. My God, *everything's* turning, even the—"

A large shadow fell over the house and a strange buzzing sound emanated from outside. To Mike Lombardo, it sounded like a hideous moo from a mutated cow.

Bob White turned back and his face went pale. "Oh God."

Mike had seen the cows far off in the distance, at the diary farm from down the road. They'd been grazing in the field since late last night, around dusk. Earlier in the day most of them had been gone, but as they'd stood there arguing with each other over the past few minutes, Mike had seen them begin slowly making their way out of the barn and across the field in that bovine gait they had. He hadn't paid much attention to them.

Maybe he should have.

It was clearly a cow…or used to be a cow. The general shape was bovine, even though it stood on its hind legs directly behind Bob White, who could only look up at it in shocked fear. The black and white markings were clearly visible. The twitching ears, horns and tail were all cow. It's fat, round udders were still intact and hanging under its belly.

The rest of it was beyond description.

At one point the cow had been bitten by a zombie. That was the only thing Mike could think of. It had been bitten, mauled somehow, had died, then come back. The thing that stood over Bob White on its hind legs (*a cow on its hind legs? Mike thought. Am I losing my mind?*) was dead but still walked. While flies buzzed around its form and it gave off a horrible stench, it was its face that was the worst. The once docile cow face was now a hardened mask of pure evil. Its teeth jutted from its mouth at odd, crooked angles, like fangs. The mouth itself was pulled back into an open crevasse of pink and red twitching flesh. Thick dark saliva dripped from its maw in stringy ropes. Its eyes burned with power and ancient evil. The left one was larger and bulged out of the cow's twisted skull at an odd angle, giving it a wall-eyed look. What made it more bizarre was the long, feminine lashes of its eyes still hung over them, making the creature even more repulsive. The oddest thing about this abomination was the cowbell around it's neck and the tag affixed to it's collar. Mike could clearly see a name engraved in the large steel tag: Imogene. *Jesus, those crazy Amish people had named one of their cows Imogene?*

The zombie cow bellowed in a hoarse roar and swiped out at Bob White with its right hoof, which had somehow become broken and now resembled a twisted claw. The force of the blow knocked Bob to the ground and the zombie cow stomped down on Bob, crushing his chest. Its cow head dipped forward, its jaws opened and sought purchase on a limb, and amid the clanging noise of the cowbell, it sank its teeth in deep.

"Yaaahhhh!" Tim and Jennifer screeched in unison. They turned and ran toward the back door. Mike took a quick glance out the front door, saw that more zombie cows were marching toward the house, and took off after Tim and Jennifer.

As he burst out the back door, the first thing he noticed were the misshapen, crab-scorpion-lobster things scuttling up through the woods toward the fields off in the distance. Tim and Jennifer were running in the opposite direction, cutting a diagonal path away from the zombie cows. The lobster creatures were heading inland, probably from the nearby Susquehanna River, and Mike hesitated for a moment, not knowing which way to go. The lobster-creatures saw Tim and Jennifer and started chasing after them. Mike backtracked, then headed catty-corner to the house and was about to head towards the woods when there was a loud thudding noise that shook the earth.

He skidded to a stop, his heart lodged in his throat. The trees ahead of him were smoking, as if they were on fire. There was a sudden crash, and suddenly the trees came down as if knocked over by a giant. A giant black lobster-scorpion creature stood before him from twenty yards away, clicking its claws together and hissing. It raised its stingered tail over its back and Mike screamed.

He turned and started running back toward the house just as a gush of liquid hit the back of his legs with great force. It felt like he'd been hit by a strong, pressured stream, as if from a fire hose.

The pain started immediately and Mike fell to the ground. He looked down at his legs and couldn't believe what he was seeing.

His legs were melting.

"Oh shit," he said, not even aware of what he said. Mike didn't curse. He had quit cursing years ago, when he got saved. But he cursed now unbidden, shock setting in his system as the flesh of his legs began to bubble and sizzle. He tried to move, to get away, but he flopped on his belly, his legs useless now as they melted into the grass below him. He couldn't feel pain, perhaps he was in too great of shock to feel pain, and the last thing in his conscious memory as he tried to escape the great, black demonic thing that had sprayed the corrosive venom on his legs, was that he was looking forward to seeing the Lord, that he couldn't believe this was fucking happening to him, and then he heard a hissed squeal, a bellowed moo, and then he knew no more.

*San Pedro, California*

Rick's heart thudded as he ran between the apartment buildings, his senses on high alert. Princess ran ahead of him, sniffing the ground and as he rounded the corner he saw the door. The windows along the back of the building were boarded up and seemed to be in worse shape than the wood used to cover up the windows and door along the front of the building. Rick gave the area a quick visual inspection, and a moment later the door burst open and Richard and Melody peeked out cautiously.

"Over here!" Rick called out.

Richard and Melody turned to him and ran out. Rick moved the barrel of the rifle down and reached out to embrace them as they came out. Paul and Mary followed, as well as a tall nervous-looking blonde kid who Rick assumed was Max.

"Thank God you're all right!" Rick said.

"We're so glad to see you, Mr. Sychek," Paul said.

Mary and Max murmured similar sentiments. Princess wagged her tail and greeted Richard and Mary in typical doggy-fashion—standing up and placing her paws on their shoulder for face licks.

"We need to get out of here," Rick urged.

"Yeah, let's do it," Richard said.

Rick got a firm grip on his rifle and took charge again. "Stay close to me." For the first time, he noticed that Paul was carrying a nasty looking military assault rifle and Richard had a handgun jammed down his waistband. "Where the hell did you get those?"

"Long story," Richard said. He pulled the handgun out. "I know I probably shouldn't carry it like that, but—"

"You're goddamn right you shouldn't carry it like that! What are you, crazy?"

"Can we just leave?" Melody said, her voice pleading as she looked up at her father.

"Yes," Rick said. "Let's do that." He was just about to herd the kids out of the alley and back onto the street when Max started screaming.

Rick whirled around and what he saw brought his heart to his throat.

A zombie had crept around the corner from the other end of the building and had launched itself at Max. It had a firm hold on Max's left arm and was pulling him toward it. In the brief time that passed—maybe a second or two, tops—Rick saw that the zombie had once been a young man in his mid-twenties who'd probably been a typical Southern California beachgoer. He was trim, with dark, stylish hair, a once handsome face, wearing baggy green shorts and a white tank top. His chest was covered with gore and his left arm was gone. Fluids leaked from his empty left eye socket, but the right eye blazed with a kind of evil intelligence. It pulled at Max again. Max, in his mad scramble to get away, had grabbed at the first thing he could find, which happened to be Melody.

"No!" Melody screamed as Max grabbed her and held on. She tried to pull away from Max, but he screamed as the zombie pulled him closer. "Let go of me!"

Princess didn't even bark. She launched herself at the zombie, grabbed its left leg in her jaws and started shaking her head, like a terrier shaking a rag. The force of her attack almost knocked the zombie backwards.

Max screamed again as the zombie pulled him toward it and buried its teeth in his neck. Blood spurted from the wound and ran down his chest. Rick could hear cartilage and bone crunch as the zombie bit down hard.

Reacting quickly, Rick brought the stock of the rifle against his shoulder, sighted the zombie's head in the cross-hairs of the weapon's scope, and pulled the trigger. The zombie dropped, pulling Max down with it and, since Max still had a hold on Melody's arm, she fell on top of them, still screaming at the top of her lungs and struggling to escape. Princess let go of the zombie and began pacing the area, a low growl in her chest as she took up patrol.

Melody was struggling to free herself from Max's grip. Rick raced over, his adrenaline coursing through his veins, barely aware of the frightened yells from the other kids, which was sure to attract the attention of more zombies if they were anywhere within earshot. He quickly noted that his shot had been perfect—there was a neat, round bullet hole in the upper left portion of the zombie's head. Fresh gore coated the ground below the zombie's head. Max was struggling to free himself from the zombie, who still had a grip on his arm.

"Get it off me!" Max was yelling. "Please, get it off me!"

"I'm so sorry, son," Richard murmured. He'd noted the horrible bite wound on Max's shoulder. It was huge. Blood jetted from the wound in large gouts. The hole was too large to apply a tourniquet. Rick peered closer and realized that he could see the inside of Max's neck. He'd be dead in minutes, without medical assistance.

And then...

Rick decided that he wasn't taking any chances. Acting quickly, before any of the kids could react, he brought the stock of the rifle down hard on Max's head. Max fell back, unconscious.

Melody was up and over to her brother instantly. Mary took her in their little huddle as she looked back at the scene, her eyes wide with fright. "Did he get me?" she asked in a shaky voice. She was looking down at her torso, running her hands over herself. "Did it get me?"

"No, it didn't get you" Richard said.

Max's eyes opened. He looked at Rick and grinned.

Rick acted quickly. He brought the rifle up, aimed the muzzle at Max's head, and pulled the trigger.

"Dad!" Richard shouted. "What are you doing?"

Rick felt an instant stab of guilt in his gut as he stood over Max's corpse. Another clean headshot. The newscasters had been right. It was just like in the movies. You had to shoot them in the head.

The kids were freaked out and Mary and Melody were crying. Rick turned to the kids, his features set. "I'm sorry, I had to. He…he came back."

"Holy shit," Paul said. "I—you killed Max!" He was staring wide-eyed at Max's corpse, then he glanced at Rick, as if he couldn't believe what had just taken place. His sister, Mary, was welded to his side, her face turned away.

"I didn't kill him. He was already dead. I'll do what I have to do to keep you kids safe." Rick turned to them, his senses now on high alert. "Come on. The faster we get out of here, the better."

Princess had investigated the side alley they'd come down last night and now she came back, looked at them, then turned back toward the side of the building. *Come on*, she seemed to say. *This way! The coast is clear!* Princess made a low woof sound, went to the mouth of the side alley, then back to the group, her message clear. They had to leave now.

Rick gripped his rifle, looking at Princess. "You're okay," he said to her. "Good girl. But be careful next time. I don't need these things killing you, okay?"

Princess headed back to the mouth of the side alley.

"Let's get going," Rick said, as he herded the kids after Princess. They reached Cameo del Mar, then began to head toward the chain link fence and the SUV.

Richard sniffed the air. "Something stinks out here."

*South Atlantic Ocean*

As far as Dave Thomas could tell, he was at least five hundred miles out to sea from the tip of South Africa, heading on a northwest projection toward the US mainland. It would take another four days to get there at his current speed, but Dave wasn't taking chances. He had to get home. The news he was receiving from satellite radio and the other frequencies were pretty much unanimous that it was global chaos. Dave could see that even from the yacht he'd managed to take-over and pilot away from South African waters on a mad rush to reach the US coast. Out here in the middle of the ocean it didn't appear that all hell was breaking loose on land. But if you looked closely you could see those crab-lobster-scorpion things—Clickers, the people on the radio had called them, before the radio went silent. Sometimes he could see schools of fish madly swimming away from them. The ocean was a large place, and Dave's position in the middle of it had put everything in perspective. He was just one small cog in the tree of life. One little drop in the ocean. But if he could make it back to North Carolina and his house in the Outer Banks, everything would be okay. And even if it wasn't okay, then at least he'd die in the place he loved more than anywhere else in the world.

Dave eased off on the throttle and checked his position. He was still on track. He had to conserve gas. He'd taken off knowing the boat had a full tank and two extra tanks of reserve fuel. That should be enough to get him to the US mainland. If he hit a storm, there was a chance he'd waste a significant amount of fuel trying to battle his way through it or have to make a wide detour off course just to avoid it. So far from what he'd been able to tell from the satellite images coming through, there was a tropical storm heading north from the Caribbean. If he continued on his course at the current speed, he'd be well ahead of it.

Looking at the vast ocean ahead of him, Dave realized if he hadn't acted quickly after Todd Perry turned greedy, he'd probably be dead. It was either act accordingly, or wind up at the bottom of the ocean like his crew or Todd and his men.

After pulling up stakes back in the location of the shoot, Todd and Peter had a talk. The result of this talk was Todd had changed his mind about fleeing back to South African shores. He'd wanted to head back to shoot footage of the carnage so they could sell it for top dollar to network news organizations. He'd even tried convincing Bob Thurman to start shooting some footage. And because Bob Thurman was as dumb as a sponge, he'd actually started doing it. Dave had told Bob to shut off the camera, and that's when things had gotten ugly.

There's been an argument. Dave wanted to head back to shore. Todd wanted to remain out at sea at least until the sun went down so they could capture more footage. "Are you crazy?" Todd shouted at Dave. "Just look at this shit! We can be rich!"

"I'm not risking my life or the life of my crew to get footage of what's happening here," Dave said. "This isn't what I signed up for, and it isn't what *they* signed up for. Now turn this boat around and get us back to shore."

"No," Todd had said, smug defiance creeping in his face. The argument had commenced immediately after Peter abruptly steered the yacht back into deeper waters. Todd gestured back to Peter, who was standing at the wheel. "Keep going! Go back to our former location!"

"Yes, sir," Peter had said.

Doug Chambers and Jack Becker had been standing at the edge of the boat, spellbound by what was happening. Doug hadn't been able to take his eyes off the carnage in the water. All Jack could do was mutter about that asshole Todd. No wonder things had been so fucked up in South Africa for so long. It was all due to assholes like Todd Perry who felt everyone was beneath them. Doug and Jack had been so absorbed by with their own little world during this argument that Dave had pretty much forgotten about them until Doug started screaming.

Bob Thurman, and Jack Becker started shouting. "Oh my God, look at that shit!"

One of the Clickers had surfaced and seized Doug by the arm in its massive claw. The thing looked as big as school bus. It was clearly big enough to sink the yacht. It must have seen Doug peering over the edge and decided to pluck him out of the boat for a snack. Doug screamed and the thing pulled him into the water.

Todd Perry yelled at Peter Oldsdale. "Full steam ahead. Get us the hell out of here!"

Peter pulled up on the throttle and headed further out to sea.

"No, we have to go back," Dave had said. "We have to get out of here." Looking around at the carnage, it was clear to him that they had to get out of this area.

"Fuck you," Todd had sneered. "We're just getting away from that creature for a bit, then we're going to start filming from another angle." He'd turned to Jack. "You—get in that skin diving gear and get ready. I'm going to give you a camera and—"

"Jack's not setting foot in these waters," Dave had said. That was about the time he'd started getting incredibly angry. And when Dave got angry, he got explosive.

"And I'm telling you to shut yer nob!" Todd shouted. He was standing almost nose-to-nose with Dave. "You sit your ass down on that bench and keep yer yap shut!"

"Fine!" Dave had fumed. He'd turned around and without another word went to his seat where his large canvas duffel bag had been stowed and sat down.

As Peter had piloted the boat out into deeper waters, Dave had seen that the carnage was intensifying. He could see large schools of fish leaping through the water as they attempted to escape the creatures. Larger fish—swordfish, sharks, even whales—were leaping through the water to try escaping them. Every so often one would leap out of the white-foamed water in a bloody spray only to splash down again amid bloody, frothy water, but for the most part they seemed to get lucky and avoid much of the carnage.

What hadn't stopped was Dave's rage.

He'd reached into his duffel bag and quickly brought out his Taser gun. Dave Thomas owned an M-26, which was the US Military version of a commercial Taser. He carried it and replacement cartridges everywhere he went. He didn't have a special license to carry it or anything. He just felt the need to have one. A Taser was a very reliable weapon. It didn't make any noise, didn't leave people dead unless you really continued to give them the juice, and for the most part, Taser guns generally couldn't be traced back to you. Dave had never used it on anyone, and it was a good thing he insisted on carrying it everywhere he went because now was the perfect time to put it to use. If this was the end of the world, then by God, it was time he did the things he'd always wanted to do.

Todd and Peter weren't even paying attention to Dave. Instead, Todd was trying to bully Jack into donning Doug's scuba diving gear to get back into the water again.

Dave wasn't having that.

He rose to his feet and turned the Taser on. Six thousand volts of electricity hummed at the push of a trigger. Dave marched over to the forward position of the yacht where Todd and Jack were arguing.

"Hey, asshole," Dave said.

Todd had looked up, momentary confusion giving way to grim realization. "Hey….no, you don't know what you're—"

Dave pulled the trigger, firing two small dart-like electrodes that hit Todd's face. Their barbed ends stuck firmly in Todd's face and he was immediately incapacitated as thousands of volts of electricity flowed through the conductive wires, causing him to lose immediate control of the muscles of his body. Todd yelled once and fell to the deck with a thud. His jaws clattered together with such force he bit his tongue. Dave pressed the trigger, delivering jolts of electricity into Todd.

Jack stood near the edge of the boat, stunned. "Dave?"

But Dave wasn't letting go. He was determined that Todd Perry receive his full wrath.

"Todd?" That was Peter, calling down to his boss.

Bob Thurman stepped forward. He cast an angry glare at Dave. "The guy was an asshole, but you didn't have to Taser him! Jesus Christ, Dave!"

Dave didn't say a word. He replaced the cartridge casually. Todd Perry moaned in pain on the deck.

"When this is all over, the Discovery Channel is going to hear about this," Bob continued.

"Oh, are they?" Dave asked.

"You bet they are," Bob sneered.

"Do you know what's going on? Do you even think there'll be a Discovery Channel left when all is said and done?"

"You're insane," Bob said. "Just you wait until—"

Dave raised the Taser at Bob and pulled the trigger, sending the electrodes into his bare chest and stomach. Bob became completely incapacitated as he began convulsing as electricity surged through his body. Bob fell forward. Jack, who had been standing near the edge of the yacht watching in stunned shock, stepped back to get out of the way and slipped. He fell overboard.

"Shit," Dave said, releasing the trigger on the Taser gun. "Look what you made me do! I just lost Jack!"

There was a dim splash from below. Then, Jack started yelling. "Help! Oh, God help, get me out of here!"

"You piece of shit bastard!" Dave said, advancing on Bob's motionless body. The electrodes were still fastened to Bob's chest and the cartridge still had juice. Dave pulled the trigger again and Bob's body shuddered and jittered, smoke rising from the burn marks that were starting to appear. There was a whiff of flame and then Bob's shirt caught on fire.

"Fuck," Dave said. He stepped back. It looked like Bob was dead.

The sound of footsteps behind him. "You crazy sonofabitch, what did you just do?"

Dave whirled around, ejecting the spent cartridge and slapping in a fresh one with all the skill of a master Taser gunslinger. Peter Oldsdale stopped up short and Dave grimaced madly, pointing the weapon at him. "Fuck off and die," he said, squeezing the trigger again. The electrodes hit Peter's bare chest. Peter yelled, leaped up, and tried to run away.

"Motherfucker." Dave tried to give chase. The electrodes were still embedded in Peter's chest and Dave pulled the trigger again, sending another series of electrical charges through to Peter, who screamed and fell to his knees. He curled up into a fetal position as Dave pulled the trigger again. This time Peter started convulsing. His feet beat a steady staccato on the yacht's deck. His eyes rolled up, showing the whites.

Out in the ocean, Jack's screams became more high pitched, then suddenly cut off. Dave stopped torturing Peter, stepped toward the edge of the yacht and cast a look down.

Jack was gone. All that remained was a rapidly spreading pool of blood.

Dave turned to Todd, Bob, and Peter. Todd was beginning to recover, but he was dazed. Bob was unconscious or dead and Peter looked completely incapacitated. Dave ejected the spent cartridge and slapped in another one. "Let's see if these things like their meals cooked."

Todd looked up at Dave and his eyes grew wide. He raised his hands up. "No! No, not again, not—*aaauugghhh!*"

"Take that!" Dave muttered, shooting Todd again with the Taser. He kept his finger on the trigger as electricity jolted Todd's body, making him quiver and quake. A moment later he fell to the deck unconscious.

Dave dragged their limp, unconscious forms to the edge of the yacht and managed to get them over the side and down. They fell like sacks of meat. Then he watched as they floated in the water only to be devoured by the Clickers.

That had been almost twenty-four hours ago. Since then, Dave had caught the cliff-notes version of what was now a global event—that his fears had been confirmed. The world was ending, not just by the invasion of the Clickers, but by the simultaneous rising of the dead. To head back to shore would be suicide, especially if there were really zombies on land. The mayhem on land was undoubtedly worse there than it was here—according to the reports he heard, the crab-scorpion-lobster things were beaching themselves, scuttling onto shore and attacking people. Once dead, the people were coming back as zombies and turning even *more* people into zombies. It sounded like one of those Sy Fy Channel movies Dave liked to watch, only this was the real thing. Therefore, Dave opted to head out to deeper waters. With the yacht's navigation equipment, he hoped he'd be able to spot any unnatural activity in the waters, allowing him to steer far away from it. The first few hours had been touch and go, and his stomach had been in knots as he navigated the vessel into deeper waters. But the further out he got, the less he saw of the creatures. Finally, at around eleven-thirty last night, he'd retired below deck, satisfied that he'd been able to steer himself as far away from the creature's migratory pattern as possible. Once in the yacht's cabin downstairs, he'd fallen into one of the beds and fell asleep.

Upon waking up he did a quick survey of his location and found he'd drifted about ten miles slightly off course. He'd turned off the engine last night and had let the yacht drift in open waters. After raiding the downstairs kitchen galley for food—a banana and some graham crackers—Dave had headed back up to the steering wheel and resumed his journey. Four days was his estimate on being back in North Carolina. He'd tried radioing in to his Discovery Channel contacts, his agent in New York, he'd even tried calling his friend Jeff back in the Outer Banks. He was unable to reach anybody. This worried him, because what news was coming out of the scanners had completely ceased. Everything was dead. No information was forthcoming.

For most of the day, Dave wondered if the lack of news meant that civilization had collapsed entirely.

*How can it go down so fast?* He thought.

Dave pondered this and other things on his journey west. He thought about his life, his career as a producer for the Discovery Channel's programs he loved so much. What had happened off the coast of South Africa was tragic and horrifying, but Dave also knew that if he were on the other side of the fence—that is, a normal citizen at home who had an interest in watching the kind of material he produced for television—he would have killed for a chance to watch a special on what had happened. Those creatures, whatever they were, had been the ultimate killing machines. They'd killed one of his staff members. They were ferocious in their appetite for pretty much anything in the ocean. And they'd completely destroyed a Great White shark, a large one too, judging by the size of that dorsal fin Dave had seen.

*So long as those things stay out there*, Dave thought. He wasn't going to take the chance and get too close to the edge of the yacht the way Doug did yesterday. He was staying right in the middle of the boat. Of course, if a big one decided to smash its way in he was toast, but for now Dave really felt that the safest place was on the yacht. While the overwhelming desire to make sure his house was okay was strong, Dave already had a plan for that. He would cruise by slowly along the Outer Banks where his house was located. He would be able to see it from the ocean. And if things looked hairy, he was staying put.

*No way I'm going to shore when there's zombies around.*

A series of splashes in the water caught Dave's attention. Frowning, he peered over the steering wheel. Once again, it looked like the same patterns from yesterday. Schools of fish appeared to be fleeing from a large predator. *Probably another mass of those Clickers*, Dave thought. He turned around and looked back at the water behind him, trying to see what was going on. All he saw was a mad migratory pattern of large fish, including dolphins and porpoises, swimming like mad in a north west direction as if they were trying to escape something.

And then Dave saw something else. He stared at it, squinting in the sunlight. "What the fuck?"

Dave grabbed a pair of binoculars that were resting near the steering wheel. He brought them to his face, made an adjustment. It took him a moment to realize what he was seeing, but when he finally realized what it was, he saw that it was heading toward him at a fast speed. "Holy fucking shit!"

Dave raced down to the deck, still clutching the binoculars. He stopped, sighted in on the object again, his breath held. It was amazing.

A giant dorsal fin was plowing through the water heading in his direction. It was clearly the dorsal fin of a Great White. Judging from the size of the fin, it was a monster specimen, one of the rumored behemoths he'd heard of but had never personally seen. Great White Sharks were rumored to grow as large as thirty feet in length with a total weight of four tons. One had allegedly been caught off the coast of Rhode Island in the late eighties, but that catch wasn't verifiable by scientists. The biggest one Dave had seen during his career was a twenty-one footer off the coast of Australia. Dave was a very accurate judge of dimensions and weight, and judging from the size of that dorsal fin sticking out of the water, the shark it was attached to was close to thirty feet long.

"Where's my cameraman when I really need him?" Dave said to himself. "Oh, that's right. I killed you yesterday, Bob. You were being an asshole."

That explained why the fish were racing to swim away. It was a phenomena Dave had witnessed before. Dave picked the binoculars up and watched again, mesmerized as the monster shark drew closer.

A moment later it was close enough to observe with the naked eye. Dave watched, spellbound as it swam past the boat. Its huge dorsal fin was easily five feet high. As the monster shark swam by the yacht, Dave followed its movement, at once awed and frightened by how close it was. He also realized his initial estimate of its size was way off. As the shark swam by the boat, Dave realized it was closer to forty-feet in length. *Oh my fucking God,* Dave thought. *I never thought I would see a shark this big, but this has to beat the cake!*

Dave continued to watch the shark swim away, spellbound. It was clear to him that this was a Great White and not its extinct cousin Megalodon, which was believed to have surpassed the Whale shark in size. Whale sharks grew to about fifty feet in length; Megalodon's were thought to exceed lengths of sixty-five. The specimen Dave had just seen swimming past his boat was in no way bigger than this fifty-foot yacht, but it was clearly forty feet. Definitely big enough to take the yacht down if it wanted to.

His awe was short lived, however, because the beast was clearly not a perfect specimen.

It was missing a large chunk of its mid-section. He could see it clearly as it swam past the boat, about fifty yards out. The wound was wide and gaping red. Even this far out, flies were buzzing over it, speeding along the surface of the water as the great beast swam at the top surface of the ocean.

*What the fuck?* Dave watched, gap jawed as the beast swam out past the boat, away from the direction the fish were swimming in. *How can it be alive? How can it—*

And then the realization of what he'd just seen hit him.

The zombie shark turned around and began heading back toward the boat.

Dave's face went ashen. "Oh shit."

The beast was picking up speed. Dave dropped the binoculars and turned to run.

There was a splash and then a terrific *whump!* as something heavy with great strength behind it fell onto the side of the yacht with a terrific amount of force. The yacht tipped over. Dave yelped and fell, landing on his left arm. He felt his fibula snap with a resounding crack. There was no pain. What Dave was witnessing eclipsed all pain.

The monster shark had launched itself out of the ocean and landed on the side of the yacht. It had heaved itself out of the ocean and through the air at the yacht just like the shark in the movie *Jaws*. Things slid down the deck and bounced off the shark, falling in the ocean. Dave grabbed onto the deck chair that was bolted into the floor and kicked his legs, screaming. The monster shark gnashed its teeth together, chomping those things that slid into its massive jaws—it ate a pillow, several toolkits, a fishing pole, Doug's wetsuit. Dave tried to scramble up as the yacht tipped into a dangerous angle.

"Oh fuck!" Dave screamed. His fingers were slipping. Looking into its eyes, Dave saw that this wasn't just a gigantic Great White shark. This shark was clearly dead. It was often said that sharks have dead eyes—large, black, with an empty look to them. This shark had those eyes, too, only there seemed to be something else about this specimen that was different. Something lived in this great beast, this behemoth that had lived for decades in the deepest ocean, allowing it to grow to such a massive size in order to become the most feared predator of the ocean. Something lived in this shark that was clearly dead judging by the decay that was already beginning to set in to its skin, which was turning white and mottled and had a sheen of slime on it from rot. And whatever it was that lived in the shark, it was evil, and intelligent, and it wanted Dave.

*"Holy fucking shit, I'm about to be eaten by a zombie shark!"* Dave screamed. His legs kicked as he fought to maintain his grip.

The zombie shark continued whipping itself around, trying to secure better leverage on the sinking yacht. Its jaws clashed together—its mouth was a good four feet across in diameter.

Dave felt his grip loosening even more. The pain in his left arm started to radiate outward now from the fracture and then...

His sweat-slicked fingers lost their grip and Dave plunged down the deck right into the zombie shark's massive jaws.

"*Aaaaughhh!*" Dave screamed once before being killed immediately as the zombie shark's teeth cut Dave in two at the torso. Dave's legs and hips disappeared down the zombie shark's throat and then the rest of him slid down into its waiting jaws.

And then once Dave Thomas was completely swallowed by the massive zombie shark, it scuttled back and slammed its bulk into the waters of the South Atlantic and continued on in search of prey. Two hours later, it was sliced in half by a monstrous Clicker three times its size. The reanimated corpse of Dave Thomas spilled from the wound in a cloud of blood and innards.

*Mount Shasta, California*

"This is insane," Michele grumbled as she squeezed off another shot. "This is like every bad B-movie, cheesy 80's horror paperback, and old pulp magazine all rolled into one."

If Clark responded, she didn't hear him over the thunder erupting from his 16 gauge shotgun. She turned in time to see another zombie—a small child—fly backward. It slammed into a tree and slumped to the ground, minus most of it's head.

"Eyes front," Clark snapped. "Don't let them flank us. Keep moving."

They struggled onward up the steep, winding trail, slipping on the rocky terrain, stumbling as the thick vegetation deepened the gloom around them, hounded by an army of the dead. The creatures laughed at them, cursing and jeering in a multitude of languages, screeching foul promises of the crude, evil things they'd do to them once they'd been caught.

The zombies had set upon them just a few hundred yards north of the Buddhist monastery. Until that point, their progress had been relatively easy. After Clark had procured the things he needed for the spell from the New Age bookstore, they'd found a hardware store and a sporting good store on the same block. They'd encountered a few zombies in each building, as well as out on the street, but nothing they couldn't handle. Clark had wondered aloud to Michele if perhaps the rest of the dead had wandered off, maybe heading to the next town to slaughter the citizens there. In the sporting goods store, they'd armed themselves with an assortment of rifles, shotguns, handguns, and knives. Each had taken a backpack, as well. Michele's was full of extra ammunition. Clark's held more ammunition, as well as the stuff from the New Age shop. He had cautioned her not to weigh herself down too heavily, but to have plenty of extra weapons on hand. Before packing everything, Clark said some charms and blessing over the ammunition. Then, armed and equipped, they began the long hike up the dormant volcano.

At first, the mountainside had seemed deserted, but just after creeping past the monastery, they'd been attacked by a group of undead birds—everything from large, fat crows to tiny starlings. They'd managed to destroy the attackers with their shotguns, but the noise of the battle had attracted the attention of a group of dead Buddhist monks. The zombies had streamed out of the monastery, screeching and howling, armed with clubs and knives. Soon, the pursuit was joined by an array of other dead creatures—deer, squirrels, skunks, raccoons, and even a pack of coyotes.

Michele's .45 clicked empty. In one fluid movement, she tossed the weapon aside and drew a second .45 from one of the many holsters around her hips. Sweat stung her eyes, and her face bled from a number of scratches and cut the birds had inflicted.

"How much further?" she gasped.

Clark didn't answer. Not wanting to risk taking her eyes off their rear, she shuffled backward, and uttered a surprised cry when she bumped into him. Her supervisor had come to an abrupt stop in the middle of the trail.

"About five hundred yards," he panted. "But I don't think we're going to make it. They're all around us now. Keep your back to me. I'll take twelve o'clock to seven. You cover six o'clock to one. Don't stop shooting until we run out of bullets or run out of zombies."

"Oh fuck…"

"Michele," Clark said, keeping his gaze fixed ahead of them, "you're a damn good agent. It has been an honor to serve with you."

"Thank you, sir. The honor has been mine."

The dead emerged from the forest, encircling them. The stench of decay and putrefaction was overwhelming, and it grew stronger as the creatures drew nearer. Michele's eyes watered. Her stomach roiled.

"You fucks need a bath," Clark muttered. "Or maybe a couple gallons of Old Spice."

The creatures didn't respond to the taunt. They crept forward in silence, leering, teeth bared, knives and claws flashing in the shadows. Then, as one, they surged forward with a horrible cry. Michele and Clark stood back to back and reigned bullets down upon them. The guns grew hot in their hands. The air filled with smoke. Empty brass casings littered the ground at their feet. And still the dead kept coming.

# TWELVE

*San Pedro, California*

"But I don't want you to go outside, Daddy."

Jim glanced up at Tammy as Danny clung tighter to his leg, pulling at his hand. She didn't have to speak. He'd been married to her long enough that he knew the expression on her face all too well. Sighing, he pried Danny loose and knelt beside him, looking the boy in the eye. When he spoke, he kept his attention fixed on Danny, but talked to them both.

"Listen, squirt. We're going to be safe here in the house. Mommy and I barricaded all the windows and doors—that means we blocked them off. The monster people can't see us. They don't know we're in here, so they'll leave us alone, as long as we're quiet. We can stay in here a long, long time. But to do that, we need some things—food, water, medicine—stuff like that. I'm just going out to get some. I promise you I'll come back."

"Like Anthony did?"

"No, Danny…" Jim struggled to speak around the lump in his throat. "Not like Anthony or Samhain. It will be me. I promise. And besides, I bet you'd like a few new comic books, right?"

Danny's eyes widened. "Yeah!"

"Well, I'll bring back some of those, too. And Butterfinger ice cream for Mommy." He glanced up at Tammy. "If that's still your favorite?"

Despite her misgivings, she smiled. "I'm surprised you remember."

Jim shrugged, grinning slyly. "I bet I remember more than you think."

Tammy blushed as her smile grew broader. Danny stood

between them, staring up at them both. Then he grinned.

Jim reloaded his handgun, and grabbed a butcher knife from the block on Tammy's kitchen counter. He stuck the knife through his belt, letting the blade rest against the back of his thigh.

"You're going to cut yourself," Tammy cautioned. "Hang on a second."

She disappeared into the hall closet, rummaged around inside, and came out holding a small hatchet.

"Where'd that come from?" Jim asked.

"Anthony picked it up at a yard sale a few weeks ago, but he keeps...I mean he kept forgetting to take it home. I put it in there so Danny wouldn't play with it."

Jim removed the knife and hung the hatchet in its place instead. "Much better."

"Be careful," Tammy said.

"You, too." He gave Danny a hug. "You be brave, and take care of Mommy until I get back, okay?"

"Okay, Daddy. You promise you'll come back?"

"I promise. I love you."

"Love you, too."

Jim moved the furniture away from the front door, sliding it slowly so it wouldn't squeak. When the door was free, he peeked outside. Verifying that the street was clear, he opened the door and hurried outside. After a moment, he heard Tammy locking it behind him. Too late, he realized that he'd forgotten to bring anything to carry supplies in. Glancing around in frustration, he scanned the street and nearby homes, and spotted a wheelbarrow several houses away, laying on its side in someone's yard. A dead Clicker lay close by. Even from this distance, Jim could see the dark cloud of flies hovering over it. A pick-axe jutted from the creature's head.

*That's why it isn't up and moving around,* Jim thought. *Destroy the brain, destroy the zombie.*

Stepping onto the driveway, he wondered if the head was a particular weak spot for the Clickers. Obviously, destroying the brain was the only way to stop the zombies, but what about the Clickers? Their shells seemed so tough—virtually impenetrable.

Was there less of a carapace around their heads? Was the shell thinner there, perhaps? He hoped he wouldn't encounter any more of them, but if he did, he intended to find out.

Cautiously, he stepped out into the street and headed for the wheelbarrow. The neighborhood was quiet. Gone were the screams and gunshots, the sirens and shouts, and the incessant sound the Clickers' claws made as they clacked together. The wind shifted, and Jim became aware of the smell—a putrid, road kill stench, like spoiled meat left sitting out too long in the sun. Beneath it was a briny, pungent odor that reminded him of dead fish rotting on the beach. Jim assumed that must be what it was. Tammy's home was very close to the cliffs—what the locals referred to as Sunken City. The Clickers had undoubtedly come ashore there, and the beach was almost certainly covered in the carcasses of whatever sea creatures or sunbathers they'd slaughtered as they came ashore.

Unless of course those victims had reanimated as zombies...

Jim stopped in the middle of the street, listening. Just where were the zombies? It seemed strange that the entire neighborhood was vacant of them now.

As he edged closer to the wheelbarrow, his tension mounted. Tightening his grip on the pistol, Jim reached for the hatchet with his free hand. He could hear the flies and other insects now, buzzing madly as they busied themselves with the Clicker's corpse. The smell wafting off the dead sea creature was intense, but not strong enough to account for the more overpowering stench that seemed to hover over the neighborhood like a cloud.

"What the hell is that?" he whispered.

A loud, electronic chirp answered him. Shouting in surprise, Jim swept the pistol up and turned in a frantic circle. Further down the street, he saw several figures standing next to an SUV. One of them was a man about his age. The rest were kids. A dog was inside the vehicle, and one of the teenaged boys had just shut the door. The dog barked, the sound muffled inside the closed vehicle. The group stared at him, seemingly just as surprised as he was. Slowly, almost as an afterthought, the man pointed a rifle at him.

"Drop it," Jim yelled.

"You drop it first!"

"Dad!" A tall teenaged boy ran over to the man with the rifle. "If he was one of them, wouldn't he have shot us already?"

*Shit,* Jim thought. *They think I'm a zombie.*

"I'm not dead," he called, pointing the gun up into the air. "I'm not one of them."

The man motioned with the rifle. "Come closer. Slowly. I want to make sure. And put that pistol on the ground."

"I can't do that," Jim said. "How about I holster it and keep my hands in the air?"

The man frowned, considering the request. Then he shrugged. "Fair enough. But so help me God, if you try anything, I'll drop you quicker than a sack of wet cement."

Jim shuffled toward them, making an exaggerated effort to show that he meant no harm. When he reached the side of the street directly across from the SUV, he stopped and slowly turned in a full circle. Then he looked at the man and smiled.

"Can I take my hands down now?"

Nodding, the man lowered the rifle.

"Thanks. Name's Jim Thurmond."

"Rick Sycheck. These are my kids, Richard and Melody, and their friends, Paul and Mary. And that's Princess inside the SUV there."

The kids nodded. Jim waved in return.

"I take it you've been hiding out?" he asked Rick.

"The kids were. Down in the ruins on the shoreline. I came here to rescue them. You?"

"The same. My ex-wife and my son live nearby. I came here to rescue them. Instead, it looks like the best I can offer is for us to hunker down inside. I came out here to find some supplies quick."

"Yeah, I guess we shouldn't stand out here talking too long," Rick agreed. "No telling when those things will show up again."

"Plus, it stinks," Richard said. "No offense, Mr. Thurmond."

"None taken. I noticed the smell, too. Not sure what it is."

Then, two thing happened simultaneously.

Behind them, they heard a voice say, *"It's me and my friends. That's what you're smelling, Jim."*

And down the street, Tammy screamed.

To Jim, it seemed as if time suddenly slowed to a crawl. He noticed the shocked expressions on Rick and the kids' faces as they stared at something behind him. The rotten stench grew more powerful. He turned toward his house and saw a group of zombies coming toward them, carrying Tammy and Danny in their clutches. And behind him stood Anthony, Samhain, several other dead neighbors, a few dead animals—and a horde of zombie Clickers. Then time snapped back to normal, and Jim screamed. Hands on his hips, Anthony threw back his head and laughed.

Rick's aim swayed as he glanced around in panic. More zombies came out of hiding, quickly surrounding them. Melody whimpered in fear. Richard tensed, fists clenched at his sides. Mary closed her eyes.

"Fuck this," Paul said, and ran.

"Paul," Richard yelled. "Don't…"

The dead fell on the fleeing teen before he'd taken a dozen steps. A zombie yanked a canister of pepper spray from its pocket and sprayed him in the eyes as he ran by. Paul fell to the ground, shrieking, eyes clenched shut. Then Samhain darted forward, going for his throat. At the last minute, the stunned boy managed to blindly throw his hand up to ward off the attack. His hand slid into the dog's mouth and the slavering jaws snapped shut, severing his fingers at the knuckles. Paul yanked his ruined hand free. Blood spurted from the stumps, squirting all over his attackers.

Rick swiveled the rifle toward them, and fired a shot at the dog. Instead of hitting its target, the round slammed into the thigh of the zombie with the pepper spray. The creature simply laughed.

*"Lower your weapons, Jim."* Anthony grinned. *"And tell your friend to do the same or we'll tear Tammy and Danny apart right here in the street."*

Jim knelt, laying the .45 and the hatchet on the asphalt. Then he glanced back at Rick.

"The hell are you doing?" Rick's eyes were wide.

"Do it," Jim gasped, glancing back at Rick. "Please? He's got my family."

Scowling, Rick did as Jim requested.

Anthony smirked. *"They're not your family anymore, Jim. You're divorced. They're my family now. Well, my host form's, at least."*

"Anthony," Jim pleaded. "Why are you doing this?"

*"Because I'm not Anthony. My name is Ob. Now I want all of you to watch this, because if you don't obey me, this is what will happen to Jim's family—and to all of you."*

Writhing in the street, Paul screamed as the dead encircled him. He kicked and thrashed as they held him down and tore into him with their bare hands, clawing open his stomach and reaching inside.

"No," Mary cried.

Rick reached for her as she ran to help Paul, but she slipped past him.

*"Humans,"* Ob muttered. *"They never listen."*

A zombie Clicker charged into the street, blocking Mary from reaching Paul. As she skidded to a stop, it jabbed forward with its tail, plunging the stinger into her abdomen. Gasping, Mary reached down and grabbed the appendage. Her hands came away slick with her own blood. The tail pulsed and throbbed as the zombie pumped venom into her. Then, with a wet sucking sound, the creature withdrew the stinger. It glistened in the sun, and parts of Mary's insides clung to it. She fell to the ground, the gaping hole in her stomach bubbling and steaming as her flesh began to melt.

"Oh God," Richard moaned. "Do something, Dad. We've got to do something!"

"I…" Rick shut his eyes, unable to watch.

The horde continued shredding Paul. His intestines, kidneys, and lungs were yanked from his body and pulped in the zombies' fists. One of the creatures stuck its head inside his open chest and made motorboat sounds. The others cackled gleefully.

"He's still alive," Melody wailed. "Paul's still alive, Dad!"

Rick opened his eyes again, and stared. Paul was indeed moving, but the smile on his face told him all he needed to know. He hugged his daughter tight, turning her head away from the carnage.

"He's not alive, baby. That's not him anymore. It's one of those things."

Ob nodded. *"Very good, Mister...?"*

"Rick Sycheck. And go fuck yourself."

*"I like him,"* Ob said, turning his attention back to Jim. *"He reminds me of you."*

Tammy and Danny's captors reached the rest of the group. They shoved the two forward. Both of them rushed to Jim's side. He picked Danny up and hugged them both tightly.

"Daddy," Danny sobbed. "I'm scared. You said they wouldn't get us."

"Ssshh." Jim kissed his head, breathing in his son's scent. "It will be okay, Squirt."

*"Awww, how touching."*

"Anthony, if there's any of you left alive in there, then let them go. It's me you have a problem with. You loved Tammy, right? So why do this?"

*"I told you once before, I am not Anthony. My name is Ob. Do you not know me?"*

Jim shook his head. "Should I have?"

*"We've met before, on other worlds than this. You blew me up once, in the sewers beneath New York City. And you dropped me off a mountain in West Virginia. And out of an airplane, once. Oh, and you cut my head off in Japan. Those are the times I remember, at least. I'm sure there were more. When you are as old as me, you sometimes forget the little details. But I certainly haven't forgotten you, Jim Thurmond, or your brat there, or your friends Frankie and Martin."*

"I don't know anyone named Frankie or Martin. And I don't care who you are—don't talk about my son that way again."

*"Always defiant to the end,"* Ob replied. *"Well, you got one thing right, Jim. I do indeed have a problem with you."*

"Fair enough. Let my family go then. And these folks, too.

They've done nothing to you."

"*Yes, they have. They were born. That is affront enough. They are beloved by the Creator, as are you all. That alone is cause to hate them.*"

"What are you going to do with us?" Rick asked.

"*With you?*" Ob asked. "*I'm sure I'll think of something creative. There are so many different ways to kill. But you'll have it easy compared to the Thurmonds. I want Jim to suffer.*"

Tammy moaned. Jim squeezed her tight, keeping Danny protected between them.

"*But in general,*" Ob continued, "*we will continue with the corruption of all flesh. Normally, that takes some time, but the Clickers, as you call them, unwittingly helped us speed up the process. Remarkable creatures. I wish I could be one all the time. When the last of the meat on this planet has been conquered, my brother Ab will then arrive with his fellow Elilum, whom he leads just as I do the Siqqusim. They will decimate the plant and insect life. Then, when all life had been extinguished, our brother Api and his Teraphim will burn this planet to cinders. Pity we won't be here to see it, but we will have already moved on to the next version of Earth.*"

"I don't understand half of what you've said," Rick replied, "but do you honestly think we're just going to let you destroy our planet without doing something about it?"

"*And what would you do, little man? Look around you. Behold the small army I have amassed against you right here on this suburban street.*"

He made a sweeping gesture with his hand. The zombies leered and grinned. The human corpses raised a cheer. *Engastrimathos du aba paren tares! Hail, Ob!*" The dead Clickers raised their claws and clacked them together. The noise was nearly deafening. *CLICK-CLICK...CLICK-CLICK... CLICK-CLICK...CLICK-CLICK...CLICK-CLICK...*

Inside the SUV, Princess howled.

"Stop it," Melody screamed, slipping loose from Rick and clapping her hands over her ears. "Just make it stop!"

"*As you wish,*" Ob said. "*We'll kill you quickly, let one of my minions inhabit you, and then Daddy can watch while you choke him with his own intestines."*

Melody collapsed to the street, skinning her knees on the bloody pavement. Rick glanced at the rifle, but two zombie Clickers edged toward him, tails hovering menacingly in the air above him.

*"Oh, don't take it so hard,"* Ob said, turning back to Jim, Tammy, and Danny. *"That's nothing compared to what I'm going to do to Jim's little brat. Here, I'll show you."*

Danny screamed.

## Mount Shasta, California

"Keep them off me," Clark said. He sat cross-legged in the dirt. "And whatever you do, don't break the circle."

Michele glanced down at her feet, insuring that her toes were indeed inside the line that Clark had etched into the soil with a sharp stick. She was dizzy and out of breath. The two had left a mound of twice-killed corpses on the trail behind them, just above the monastery, and both had numb hands and a persistent ringing in their ears from all the shooting. When there had been an apparent lull in the pursuit, they had plunged ahead, reaching a small clearing a few hundred yards up the mountain. Despite their exhaustion, Clark had wasted no time in unpacking and preparing for the ritual.

Beyond the tree line, something growled, low and menacing. Michele shivered. She studied the array around her, but it was beyond her understanding. As a remote viewer, she only knew the basic tenants of magical theory and practice. What Clark was attempting was something beyond a mere adept. He had drawn a series of concentric circles in the dirt, and had bid her stand inside the one farthest from the center, which he filled with salt. Then, closer to the center, he'd etched both a pentagram and a hexagram, along with a series of runes and symbols. He'd then placed black, white, and red candles at various points, as well as several copper bowls filled with sage, bay leaf, coriander, garlic, jasmine, and more salt. He lit the dried bundles of sage, letting the smoke fill the air around them, and then lit the candles, as well. Finally, he'd sat down, cross-legged, and concentrated on his breathing.

The trees rustled. Michele spotted a flock of zombie birds nestled in the branches. She heard the growl again, and caught a glimpse of a large, furry form pacing in the shadows.

"They can't cross the circle," Clark told her. "Remember that. As long as you stay inside of it, they can't touch you."

"Then why do you need me to cover you? Why bother shooting them?"

"Because they might have guns."

"But a bullet won't penetrate a circle of protection, sir."

"No, it won't. But if they fire it at the ground, and break the circle. That would be very bad. Also, don't step into the circles closer to me. The energy will be very high in here, and I don't want you getting caught in the backlash. I don't think you'd survive it. Just stay in that outer ring, and keep the Siqqusim from breaching it. Okay?"

"Got it. Anything else I need to remember?"

"Yes," Clark said. "Just one last thing. There is one ingredient I forgot to tell you about. One thing we couldn't find at the store in town, and that we didn't bring along from San Francisco."

"What's that?"

"A sacrifice."

Michele paused. "What?"

"To conduct a working of this magnitude, to exile the Siqqusim back to the Void and seal them off from our world, a sacrifice is required—at least for someone of my skill level. That's the only way it will work."

Michele had a sinking feeling in her gut. She took her eyes off the perimeter and slowly turned to face him.

"Are you saying—?"

Clark stared at her with half-lidded eyes. When he saw her expression, he smiled.

"No, Michele. For God's sake, I'm not talking about you. What kind of monster do you think I am?"

"Then who?"

His smile grew sad.

"You? But sir, you can't just…"

"I can and I will. It's our only chance, Michele."

"So you knew all along? What about all that talk on the way here?"

"I wanted to keep your spirits up. Also, I didn't know how familiar you were with the greater rituals. But I meant what I said about the accommodation. Were I to survive, I would have most certainly recommended you for one. Now, eyes front. No more arguing. They're creeping up on us, and it's time to begin. Don't let me down."

"But—"

Clark pulled a pocket knife from his pocket and faced East. Then he closed his eyes and took a deep breath. When he spoke again, his voice was clear and strong—free of the fatigue and fear they'd both felt only moments before.

"I present these herbs and other offerings to the four Elements—Air, Earth, Water, and Fire. I have placed them in the acceptable manner and ask that you find them pleasing. I have made the signs to the four corners of the Earth—East, West, North, and South, and to all that is contained within. Yod, Nun, Resh. Virgo, Isis, Scorpio, Apophis, Destroyer. Osiris, who was slain and then rose again."

Upon hearing his words, the dead emerged from the forest and rushed toward them. Michele took her time, reminding herself that they couldn't breach the circle, and lined up her shot. Steadying herself, she took a deep breath, held it, and then fired. A dead Buddhist monk collapsed. She exhaled, took another breath, and brought down the corpse of a deer.

"Vegevura," Clark continued. "Vegedul, leom…"

Michele felt the air begin to vibrate. A persistent low drone that seemed to come from the ground itself filled her ears. Her arms prickled and her hair crackled with static electricity. The zombies halted, obviously surprised by the incantation. Then, they crept forward again. One of them searched the ground, found a softball-sized rock, and picked it up. Before the creature could throw it, Michele gunned it down.

"Before me is Raphael." Clark's voice grew louder. "Behind me is Gabriel. My right hand is the hand of Michael. My left hand is the hand of Uriel. About me are the flames of the Pentagram, and I am covered in the light of the six-rayed star. I call upon the Gatekeeper, who gave to us the Nomos, which is the Law. I call upon the Doorman, who is the Burning Bush and the Hand That Writes and the Watchman and the Sleepwalker. I call upon the voice of the Tetragrammaton. I call upon he who is called Huitzilopochtli and Ahtu. He who is called Nephrit-ansa and Sopdu. He who is called Hathor and Nyarlathotep. I call upon he who's real name is Amun. I call upon you and humbly request a closing. The woman with me in the circle is under my protection. By following the Law, and by naming you, I humbly ask for your aid. I humbly ask that you help me to banish this blight from our world, and consign them to the Void. I humbly ask that you protect us, and that we not be harmed or molested by the denizens of Hell, or the realms between, or the Thirteen, or the things that live in the wastes beyond the levels. I beg of thee, and hope that so shall it be."

With a roar, a zombie bear lumbered out of the forest. Lowering its head, the beast charged, brushing past the other zombies. The humming noise grew louder. Around them, outside the circle, dust motes began to form, swirling like miniature tornados. As the bear barreled toward her, Michele sighted on it, biting her lip. When it was only a few feet away, she squeezed the trigger. The shot caught the dead animal in its shoulder. It reached the line and then crashed, as if slamming into an invisible wall. Blood splattered from its snout. Bared fangs snapped off and fell to the ground. The creature rocked backward and howled.

"You're doing good," Clark murmured. "Now comes the hard part."

*San Pedro, California*

"Danny," Jim whispered, "go to Mommy."

*"Kill them all,"* Ob ordered, *"but keep the Thurmond's alive. I want to take our time with them."*

"Take him," Jim said, thrusting Danny into Tammy's arms.

Tammy staggered backward, clutching their son tight, and then ducked as the zombies came for them.

"Jim," she hollered, "be careful!"

"You, too." He ducked as a zombie fired a shot at him. The bullet pinged off a nearby stop sign. "Rick, go!"

Rolling across the pavement, Jim felt Mary's still sizzling remains seep into his clothes. Only her skeleton and her head had escaped dissolving. The head lolled toward him. The entity inside of her tried to speak, but then her skull melted. Jim snatched the .45 from the ground and sprang into a crouch, aiming for his ex-wife's dead boyfriend. He was aware of a presence standing next to him. From the corner of his eye, he saw Rick. The man had his rifle leveled at Anthony, as well.

*"I'm going to strip the flesh from your brat,"* Ob warned. *"And feed it to you before you die."*

"Ob. Anthony. Whatever the hell you call yourself," Jim growled. "I told you not to talk about my son that way."

He and Rick fired at the same time. The volley of rounds erased Anthony's head from the jaw up. His decapitated corpse stood there for a moment, jittering, and then dropped to the pavement in a shower of gore. Dimly, Jim and Rick became aware of their loved ones screaming.

A dead Clicker snatched the rifle from Rick's grasp and snapped it in half. Enraged, the zombies charged.

*Mount Shasta, California*

"All-powerful Amun," Clark shouted, "who walks between the levels and who is beyond the comprehension of all save the Creator, hear me in my plight! In the name of the Igigi and the Annunaki, I beg of you. Banish the Siqqusim from our level and close the gate. Ia Namrasit! Ia Kia Kanpa! Mashrita Zia Ashtag! Ia Uddu-ya!"

The soil churned faster, lifting into the air outside the circle and forming a whirlpool pattern. Sticks, rocks and other debris zipped past, spinning in mid-air. The zombies clutched their heads, wailing in fear and gnashing their teeth. They ripped at their hair and tore their skin open with their fingers.

"Ia verminus Ob…" Clark's voice faltered.

Michele turned to him, and gasped in horror. Blood ran

from his mouth, nose, ears and the corners of his eyes. His fingers, lips, and other extremities had swollen, bulging and pulsating from an incredible pressure within him. The humming noise increased, and her teeth began to ache. Dropping her pistol, Michele clamped her hands over her ears and stumbled toward Clark.

"Stay…back." His hands flailed, warning her away. "Ia destrato Ob!"

Clark exploded in a cloud of wet, red pulp. Screaming, Michele shielded her eyes with her hands as bits of him rained down upon her, blotting out the circle. The hum ceased, and the dust cloud dissipated. Snatching up her weapon, which was now slick with Clark's blood, she turned toward the zombies, only to find them all laying motionless on the ground.

Pensive, she approached the bear and nudged it with her toe. It didn't move. When she placed the barrel of the gun between its eyes and pulled the trigger, it was still dead.

They all were.

Dead again.

Collapsing to her knees in the bloodstained remnants of the circle of protection, Michele McKenzie, the last Black Lodge agent left on Earth, raised her face to the sky and wept.

*San Pedro, California*

Rick, Jim, and their loved ones stood in the middle of the street, gaping as all around them, the dead died once more. The zombies collapsed in mid-charge, slumping to the pavement, unmoving. One of the monstrous Clickers toppled over onto a car, crushing the vehicle's hood and setting off the car alarm, which blared in the sudden silence.

For a long time, they just stood there, blinking in confusion, bodies still tensed in anticipation of a fight. But as the minutes passed and their foes didn't rise to confront them, they began to relax. Slightly nauseous from the leftover adrenalin coursing through their veins, both men trembled as they held their children close. Richard let a very upset Princess out of the SUV. She jumped and barked and licked their faces, tail wagging happily.

They retreated back to Tammy's home, where they convalesced for several hours. Occasionally, they peeked outside, waiting to see if a new horde of zombies or a marauding band of Clickers would emerge, but the streets remained empty. Eventually, Richard was able to get a signal with his phone. Soon, he verified that the same thing was happening all over the world. The zombies had all been rendered mysteriously and suddenly inactive. Now, various military units were dealing with the remainder of the Clickers.

"Try to call your Mom," Rick urged his son. When they couldn't reach her, Rick assured the kids that maybe her cell phone service was still down.

But deep down inside, he felt the truth. Maybe the world hadn't ended, but he and his children had suffered a personal apocalypse all their own.

Hours later, the ragtag remnants of a National Guard unit passed through. Their halftracks clanked on the pavement, and the diesel engines belched plumes of blue smoke into the sky. As they advanced through the neighborhood, survivors began emerging from their homes. Jim, Tammy, Rick, and the kids did the same. The guardsmen assured them that the threat of the Clickers had passed, for the moment, but that units were still engaging them on other parts of the coast.

After they had passed on, Rick stuck out his hand. Jim clasped it firmly. The two men shook.

"You're welcome to stay for a bit," Tammy told them. "I've got room, and Jim just lives a few blocks away."

"No," Rick said. "I appreciate the offer. I really do. But I think the best thing for us to do is go home and start picking up the pieces of our lives."

"You going to be okay?" Jim asked. "I'm betting parts of the city are impassable. And you heard what he said. There might still be a few Clickers about, not to mention people who might be taking advantage of the chaos."

"We'll manage," Rick said. "It's not like we don't have firepower."

Jim nodded. "True enough."

"Thanks again for your help. We really appreciate it. Stay safe."

"You, too. Are you sure you'll be okay?"

"Maybe one day," Rick replied, as Richard, Melody, and Princess got into the SUV. "Until then, I'm just happy we're still alive."

Jim, Tammy, and Danny stood on the sidewalk and watched them drive away. After the SUV had turned the corner, they surveyed the damage to the neighborhood. Dead bodies lay everywhere, along with the carcasses of dozens of Clickers. Most of the homes had broken windows or doors. Wrecked cars lined the street. Telephone and electrical poles lay like fallen trees. The air smelled of smoke.

Tammy reached out and gave Jim's hand a squeeze. "Looks like you were wrong."

"About what?"

"It's not the end of the world after all."

"Isn't it?" He grinned. "It sure looks like it from here."

She nodded, staring at the devastation. "Yeah, I guess it does. Danny, I want you to stay inside. Don't go wandering off."

The boy, who'd been inching close to a dead Clicker on the neighbor's lawn, drooped his shoulder in resignation. "Okay, Mommy."

"Do you really think we can rebuild?" Tammy asked.

"We'll have to wait and see," Jim said. "I think, in time, anything can be rebuilt. Like Louis L'Amour said, there will come a time when you believe everything is finished. That will be the beginning."

They each took one of Danny's hands, and together, they walked back inside the house.

## ABOUT THE AUTHORS

**J. F. GONZALEZ** is the author of over a dozen novels of terror and suspense, including *Back From the Dead, Primitive, Survivor, The Beloved*, and *Bully*. His short story collections include *The Summoning and Other Eldritch Tales* and *When the Darkness Falls*. He also works as a technical writer and screenwriter. A Los Angeles native, he resides with his family in Pennsylvania. Visit him on Twitter @jfgonzalez or online at www.jfgonzalez.com

**BRIAN KEENE** is the author of over twenty-five books, including *Take The Long Way Home, Urban Gothic, Dead Sea, Dark Hollow*, and *The Rising*. He also writes comic books such as *The Last Zombie*. Several of his novels and stories have been developed for film, including *Ghoul, The Ties That Bind, Castaways*, and *Darkness on the Edge of Town*. Keene lives in Pennsylvania. You can communicate with him online at www.briankeene.com or on Twitter at @BrianKeene

# deadite press

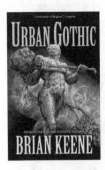

**"Urban Gothic" Brian Keene** - When their car broke down in a dangerous inner-city neighborhood, Kerri and her friends thought they would find shelter inside an old, dark row home. They thought they would be safe there until help arrived. They were wrong. The residents who live down in the cellar and the tunnels beneath the city are far more dangerous than the streets outside, and they have a very special way of dealing with trespassers. Trapped in a world of darkness, populated by obscene abominations, they will have to fight back if they ever want to see the sun again.

**"Ghoul" Brian Keene** - There is something in the local cemetery that comes out at night. Something that is unearthing corpses and killing people. It's the summer of 1984 and Timmy and his friends are looking forward to no school, comic books, and adventure. But instead they will be fighting for their lives. The ghoul has smelled their blood and it is after them. But that's not the only monster they will face this summer . . . From award-winning horror master Brian Keene comes a novel of monsters, murder, and the loss of innocence.

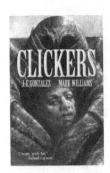

**"Clickers" J. F. Gonzalez and Mark Williams-** They are the Clickers, giant venomous blood-thirsty crabs from the depths of the sea. The only warning to their rampage of dismemberment and death is the terrible clicking of their claws. But these monsters aren't merely here to ravage and pillage. They are being driven onto land by fear. Something is hunting the Clickers. Something ancient and without mercy. *Clickers* is J. F. Gonzalez and Mark Williams' gore-soaked cult classic tribute to the giant monster B-movies of yesteryear.

**"Clickers II" J. F. Gonzalez and Brian Keene-** Thousands of Clickers swarm across the entire nation and march inland, slaughtering anyone and anything they come across. But this time the Clickers aren't blindly rushing onto land - they are being led by an intelligence older than civilization itself. A force that wants to take dry land away from the mammals. Those left alive soon realize that they must do everything and anything they can to protect humanity – no matter the cost. *This isn't war; this is extermination.*

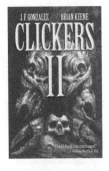

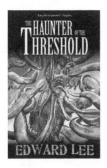

**"The Haunter of the Threshold" Edward Lee -** There is something very wrong with this backwater town. Suicide notes, magic gems, and haunted cabins await her. Plus the woods are filled with monsters, both human and otherworldly. And then there are the horrible tentacles . . . Soon Hazel is thrown into a battle for her life that will test her sanity and sex drive. The sequel to H.P. Lovecraft's The Haunter of the Dark is Edward Lee's most pornographic novel to date!

**"The Innswich Horror" Edward Lee -** In July, 1939, antiquarian and H.P. Lovecraft aficionado, Foster Morley, takes a scenic bus tour through northern Massachusetts and finds Innswich Point. There far too many similarities between this fishing village and the fictional town of Lovecraft's masterpiece, The Shadow Over Innsmouth. Join splatter king Edward Lee for a private tour of Innswich Point - a town founded on perversion, torture, and abominations from the sea.

**"The Dark Ones" Bryan Smith -** They are The Dark Ones. The name began as a self-deprecating joke, but it stuck and now it's a source of pride. They're the one who don't fit in. The misfits who drink and smoke too much and stay out all hours of the night. Everyone knows they're trouble. On the outskirts of Ransom, TN is an abandoned, boarded-up house. Something evil happened there long ago. The evil has been contained there ever since, locked down tight in the basement—until the night The Dark Ones set it free . . .

**"Genital Grinder" Ryan Harding -** *"Think you're hardcore? Think again. If you've handled everything Edward Lee, Wrath James White, and Bryan Smith have thrown at you, then put on your rubber parka, spread some plastic across the floor, and get ready for Ryan Harding, the unsung master of hardcore horror. Abandon all hope, ye who enter here. Harding's work is like an acid bath, and pain has never been so sweet."*
- Brian Keene

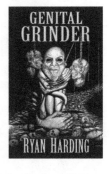

**AVAILABLE FROM AMAZON.COM**

CPSIA information can be obtained
at www.ICGtesting.com
Printed in the USA
BVHW040802310322
632882BV00006B/508